IT'S HARD TO FLY STRAIGHT
WHEN YOUR HEART'S OFF COURSE

TAUNTING GRAVITY

JESSICA KAYE

Stag
Beetle
Books

PROLOGUE

Trevor Lee's scuffed boots clanked hard against the ramp as he descended from his ship, the dull gray of the hull smoking as it cooled from re-entry. A gust of exhaust hit him full in the face and he coughed twice.

Another day, another planet.

He reached asphalt, his steps heavy in the increased gravity, the ramp retracting behind him. The navigator waved at him from the clear polycarbonate bubble of the bridge at the top of the ship. Trevor gave a half-hearted gesture. Although the new guy, Dak, annoyed him a little, he'd navigated Trevor's ship adequately so far. It wouldn't hurt to indulge his enthusiasm.

Dak had raved about this planet, "a tropical paradise with sandy beaches caressed by turquoise waves." So far, Trevor had seen exactly three beaches from the air. He didn't mind keeping it that way, but a few of the crew muttered their disappointment about the tight deadline of this job.

The blue-green foliage lining the paved path softly fluttered in the steady, warm breeze. They had landed deep inland on one of the sparsely populated islands, with little sign of man—except for the ship dock and the unmarked road leading into the dense jungle.

Their destination—an out-of-the-way junk shop hidden among the towering trees—built the best racing ships in the galaxy. Few people had ever seen the hermit that owned it. Still, Trevor hoped with this job he'd get a chance to order a few custom parts for his own ship.

He glanced up as the sky growled. The heavy air and dark clouds promised a storm. *Let's make this quick.*

"All ready here, Captain."

Chase, his security officer, held up a remote. He and Jakob had already unloaded and strapped the cargo to a large metal cart.

"Let's move then." Trevor scratched the back of his neck. This was one of the smoothest deliveries they'd had in a while.

After their recent high-risk jobs for Omni Authority, he figured the crew deserved a nice, easy payday in the private sector, and if Trevor could procure his custom parts, everyone would walk away a winner.

He led the way, the servos on the cart humming behind them. The mystery liquid they'd been hired to deliver sloshed in its plastic container.

It was a quiet walk. Trevor wasn't much of a talker, Chase was downright stoic, and Jakob had been piloting with them long enough to know both.

Something rustled in the tall grasses, and a bird with bright-green wings took flight, cawing a warning.

The back of Trevor's neck itched. He scratched it again, but it wouldn't go away. Like something wasn't quite right. Like …

He jolted. *Like they were being watched.*

"Chase," he snapped, pulling his stunner from his belt.

With the simple command, Chase drew his rattler gun and dropped to one knee, scanning the tree line.

Trevor's heightened senses isolated the breathing of seven people, their camouflaged helmets peeking over the bushes, shiny weapons glinting between the leaves. *Stripped screws.* His wandering mind had blindly stumbled past the obvious threat.

"Three to the right, four to the left, roughly thirty feet ahead," Trevor whispered so only his crewmates could hear him. "Each with a rattler. At least one knife. Two incendiary launchers, four—"

Before he could finish, a weapon rattled as it warmed up, then a blast *zinged* past them. Trevor grabbed his shipmates' shoulders and shoved them down. The next hit found their cargo, knocking them flat as the liquid exploded, heat washing over them.

Trevor yelled as burning liquid splashed his arm, his ears ringing. He rolled until the flames went out. Through the smoke, Chase pulled himself toward Trevor as more shots sizzled overhead. Jakob lay on the ground, unmoving.

Coughing, Trevor slapped at the dog-tag communicator hanging from his neck.

"Charlie!" he rasped, choked by the acrid smoke. "We're down! Repeat, *we are down and need medical attention!*"

"Cap'n ... I'll be there," the doctor's voice slurred. "Very quickly ..."

No, no! Not now! Charlie had been hitting the bottle again. He wouldn't be able to help them.

Trevor staggered to his feet, his bad arm pressed against his side. He grabbed Jakob's collar, and together, Trevor and Chase dragged him behind the black, smoking husk of the delivery cart. Chase hissed through his teeth and slapped at his arms, the sleeves of his uniform scorched, the exposed skin red and black as the burning liquid continued to eat away at him.

The shockwave of another explosion knocked them to the ground.

"We have to move," Chase shouted in his ear.

Trevor nodded, his grip tightening on Jakob again.

Chase shook his head. "We can't!" he said. "Captain, he's … he's dead! There isn't time."

Unacceptable.

Trevor strained as he hauled Jakob over his shoulder. Gravity here was double that of Earth's, and even Trevor struggled to carry Jakob's dead weight.

Don't say dead. You don't know if he's dead.

"Captain! *Leave him!*" Chase shouted, grabbing Trevor's shoulder in a white-knuckled grip.

"Get back to the ship," Trevor ordered. "Go!"

Chase's eyes narrowed. "Not happening."

Trevor squinted ahead, eyes burning in the cover of the thick smoke. It gave them a measure of protection as explosions and laser fire rained down all around them, the rattle of the guns competing with the ringing in his ears.

He almost didn't hear the whir of the ship's ramp extending. Charlie's silhouette stumbled toward them, less than twenty feet away. Trevor mustered all his strength and took another step.

Almost there.

Charlie collapsed next to them, coughing. "I'm here … Cap'n …"

Trevor dropped to his knees as Charlie fumbled against Jakob's neck, feeling for a pulse.

"Is he alive?" Trevor asked.

"I think …" Charlie slurred, a pained look crossing his face. "I think I need to lie down." He passed out in a heap, knocking Trevor over and dropping Jakob's body to the ground.

"Charlie! Wake up!"

Trevor shook him. Hard. Charlie's head flopped around, but his eyes didn't open.

No, no, no, no. There was no way he could carry two of them, not in this gravity. Chase was little help with his injuries. It was all on him.

"Charlie!"

"Captain, we have to go, *now!*" Chase urged, his voice rasping.

Trevor hoisted Charlie over his shoulder and grabbed Jakob's arm, dragging him behind. He took a belabored step, then a second.

The gun rattles grew louder as the attackers approached.

Trevor's gut lurched. Chase was right. They would never make it carrying two.

For the second time in his life, Trevor froze. He trembled, not from the shots zinging past his head, not from the choking smoke, not from the burn on his arm, or from the spray of asphalt against his legs as explosions tore through it.

One.

He could only save one.

1

Trevor took the elevator down and down, well below street level. Omni Authority had buried the director's office deep within their Earth headquarters, far from snipers, rocket launchers and a dozen other security risks.

Gone were the peaceful days when Omni Authority first emerged as a uniting force for all people across the galaxy. It saved mankind from the brink of universal war by destroying the taboo super-soldier program. After the dust settled and the unifying, common enemy of fear was removed, the galactic territory protected by Omni Authority quickly splintered into factions.

For the most part, the organization closely regulated all space travel in their territory. They trained and supported crewmen, licensed and registered ships, and logged flight information,

As one of Omni Authority's captains, Trevor and his cargo ship supported them with pick-ups and deliveries—of anything. Animal, vegetable, mineral, weapons, information; they did it all.

The secretary behind the desk looked up as the elevator doors slid open, a smile lighting up her face. Trevor guessed her curly hair was supposed to be dyed blue, but it had faded over time enough that now this poor woman in her early twenties had a head full of what looked like gray hair.

She batted her unusually long eyelashes at him. "Captain Lee! It's always nice to see you. How are you today?"

Trevor inclined his head. She always smiled at him, but ever since she'd asked him for his personal number, things had turned somewhat awkward. At the time, he'd replied he didn't have one, as phones didn't work in space. He couldn't think of a reason why she'd need to call him anyway.

Only later did Charlie explain to him that asking for someone's number often indicated a romantic interest.

Silence stretched between them when he didn't engage her in conversation. They had nothing meaningful to discuss. He didn't even know her name.

The smile on her face grew tighter, her lips stiffening into a thin line. Trevor shifted his weight. *So, so awkward.*

She *tsked* and depressed a button on a communicator. "Captain Lee is here to see you." Her words were short and clipped, devoid of emotion.

Pressing another button, she watched as the biometric security door to the director's office slid slowly open. It looked like any other expensive, wooden door, except for two extraordinary features: first, it didn't have a handle, and secondly, it could only be opened by a handful of people, herself included.

Director Hart grimaced from behind a massive mahogany desk as Trevor entered. Over the years he had earned a few more wrinkles around his face—definitely not from smiling—and had shortened his thinning hair since Trevor's last visit.

The door slid shut again behind him. Away from the secretary, the knot between Trevor's shoulders eased. "Director," he said, inclining his head.

The director jutted his chin out, indicating for Trevor to sit.

Trevor helped himself to a chair. "What's the job, Director Hart?"

Hart nodded. "Always to the point." He paused, squinting at Trevor. "You look like you've crawled out from under a ship's engine."

Trevor smiled. "Well, you know—"

"Where's the officer's uniform I sent you?"

Trevor shrugged. "In my quarters, somewhere. Probably." He fought to keep the smile off his face; it always irked them. "This is more practical."

The lines in Hart's face deepened as he gestured with a meaty hand. "Does it *have* to be a mechanic's get-up? Even a ... a *navigator's* shirt would be better than this."

Although Trevor usually followed Omni Authority's guidelines to the letter, he made it a point to wear whatever he wanted, a minor defiance he indulged in. He hadn't worked as a mechanic with his dad in years, and had long out-grown his navigator's shirt. First week as captain, he'd special ordered the mechanic's uniform to accommodate his height.

"Is there someone I'm supposed to impress?" A corner of Trevor's mouth ticked upward against his will. The uniform issue *really* irked them.

Hart's gaze flicked up to the ceiling, accompanied with an extended sigh, but then back to Trevor. "Captain Lee," he continued, "I have a vital mission for you and your crew. A very ... sensitive ... mission."

Now Trevor allowed himself to smile. "Absolutely," he said, nodding. "Transporting? Information or goods? Is it dangerous?"

"Yes. Both. And extremely dangerous," Hart said. "It's to the planet Cerise in the Ruby District."

Trevor leaned back, eyebrows raised. The Ruby District was already in the midst of a trade war, with a civil war brewing internally. A mission to a place like that *was* serious.

Hart held out a pen—an old-fashioned ink pen. "This contains a flash drive with schematics for a very specialized bomb. Our people there have been caught in the crossfire of the conflict, and we can't send this information through the usual methods. An intercept is always a risk, and in the wrong hands, this data could lead to the production of bio-weapons. I want you to take these schematics to Dr. Greg Penn."

The director smiled. Sort of. "Hence the unique carrying case. Can you do this?"

Trevor rubbed his stubbled chin. "Bio-weapons, huh?"

Hart's lips tightened, but the director didn't need to worry. It didn't matter *what* he transported; this was Trevor's job. He always took it seriously.

"I think I can handle it," Trevor said as he nodded.

"Good." Hart set the pen on his desk and leaned back again. "If anyone but Dr. Penn unscrews the casing, the information it contains will be wiped."

Trevor nodded. A small, innocuous object he could carry on his person was brilliant.

"It's his design, so he'll know how to operate it. The sick and wounded on Cerise need supplies, so your crew will also be transporting food and medical items. Think of it as your cover."

It was a good plan—with a small hole. "Will that cover be enough to get us safely through?"

Hart hesitated.

"Uh-huh," Trevor said, unsurprised by the reaction. "What about the blockade?"

"That's the good news." Hart picked up a small tablet pen off his desk and flicked across one of the screens in front of him until he found what he wanted. "As of this week, the fighting has settled down. The blockade has been dissolved, and the civil unrest has called for a cease-fire. This open window of peace is our chance."

Trevor mulled this over. *Windows can close, too.* He and his crew were Omni Authority's best chance to get there and back alive. Lives depended on this.

He leaned forward, elbows on his knees. "When do we leave, and where do we pick up our cargo?"

"Immediately, if possible," Hart said. "When you're ready, call my secretary. She'll tell you where to pick up."

Trevor nodded and stood. He'd ask Charlie to call her.

"One last thing, Captain."

Hart took a deep breath, bracing himself.

"I believe that your crew is short a member."

Trevor tensed. No amount of assurance that Jakob's death six months ago was not his fault would ever be acceptable to him.

He should have seen the ambush coming that day. Recognized it sooner. The loud breathing of the men, the click of a safety thumbed off. A flash of sunlight glinting off a gun barrel. He should have caught the acrid aftertaste of a recently fired weapon. He always saw everything; he'd been complacent, hadn't been paying attention, hadn't put the pieces together.

He'd left Jakob, not even knowing if he was dead or alive.

Trevor looked down, tightening his shaking fists. The physical scars on his arms could never compare to breaking the news to Jakob's family. Watching Jakob's father wilt, his face crumpling as Jakob's mother raised a hand to her mouth to hide her quivering lips—it was like a punch to the gut.

If the director launched into another—

"You need a new pilot."

Trevor's head snapped up. Not what he'd expected.

His fists relaxed, but he immediately shook his head. Introducing a new, unknown member to the crew for such a sensitive mission could be disastrous. "We're fine."

"No, Captain, you are not."

Hart leaned forward, pointing the tablet pen at Trevor. "You're going into dangerous territory. You need a new pilot."

"I can fly the ship."

Hart shook his head. "No, you *can't*. Omni Authority revoked your license. Again. Look, you're a decent fly, but you lack the finesse it takes to survive a mission like this. You need a good pilot."

Trevor scoffed. "You know they took my license because—"

"No!" Director Hart thundered, the air vibrating with the word.

Trevor fell silent, his lowered eyebrows and crossed arms speaking volumes. The director rarely lost his patience. The situation on Cerise must be dire.

"I know you're wary of new people," Hart continued in a quieter, more conversational tone. "As you should be. But this mission takes priority over your personal comfort. I'm sorry, but you *will* accept the pilot we have assigned you."

Trevor took a deep breath, held it, and then nodded. Not like he had a choice. "Who?"

Hart slid an info tablet across his desk. "The best pilot we have. Graduated top of the class in flight school last year. The information's all there, also sent electronically to your account. Contact me before you leave."

Trevor read over the tablet. Gemma Stone, age nineteen. Impressive scores, plenty of space flight logged time ...

What kind of name was Gemma? It sounded like a girl's name. He snorted and then froze.

Wait.

"This—this pilot is a girl," Trevor stuttered.

The director raised an eyebrow. "Is that a problem?"

Trevor gaped at him. Of course it was a problem! The dangers of space left no place for women. It would create more headaches for him, at the very least. How could he do his job well while simultaneously taking care of her? She'd need and want all kinds of things, things that would distract the crew. How would a captain even act around a girl? Could he really add her to the duty roster? What if she cried?

"Well, she ... I ..."

A pale face flashed across Trevor's mind. The sickening mechanical whirring of a breathing machine drowned out every thought—

"You'll contact the pilot who's been selected for you," said the director, bringing Trevor back to the present.

"But ..."

"You need the best for this mission." He pointed at the tablet. "And that's her. Understood?" His tone left no room for argument.

Trevor's fingers tightened, the info tablet shaking in his grip. "Yes, Director," he said, voice stiff. He grabbed the pen, turned, and walked out of the room.

The secretary jumped as he marched past her desk toward the elevators. "Have a nice—"

Her words cut off as the elevator doors closed.

Trevor shook his head, the info tablet in his hand finally buckling under the pressure and cracking in his grip.

A girl on board was a bad idea.

This would not go well.

Sitting alone on a padded chair outside the dressing room of the bridal shop, Gemma groaned softly and dropped her head into her hands, her blonde ponytail flopping over her head.

Racks of white dresses hugged the walls, lace and frills and sequins and shiny fabric spilling out the sides. People weaved between mannequins modeling various gowns: bridal, bridesmaid, prom, flower girl; it went on and on. Thousands and thousands of dollars' worth of glittery junk. Jewelry and veils and tulle and sparkly tiaras and all sorts of torturous pastels she knew she'd have to squeeze into.

The curtain parted and Gemma looked up, pasting a smile on her face.

Sandy strode out, glowing in a princess-y wedding dress. Her golden hair flared out as she twirled. "What do you think?"

Gemma's fake smile faltered. That was a *lot* of dress. Sure, the sparkly top hugged Sandy's curves, but the layers and layers of fabric in the skirt poofed out to make her appear four times as wide. Could she even *sit* in that thing?

Gemma deflected the question. "What do *you* think?" she asked, leaning in.

"Well ..." Sandy plucked at the shoulder straps, a slight dent forming between her brows. "It is cutting into me a little bit, and I'm not sure if I want it backless."

"Oh, we do alterations!"

Gemma jolted and whipped her head around. *Sneaky ninja saleslady.*

"We're fine," Gemma insisted, her voice a little louder than it had been the last three times.

The saleslady's red-lipped smile twitched, and she turned on her heel and click-clacked back to the sales counter. She continued to watch them from across the room, tape measure at the ready,

Gemma returned her attention to her older sister. "No. If you don't love every bit of it, it's a no from me. Next."

Dress number seven: Eliminated.

Let this end soon.

Sandy had always been the girly-girl in the family. She and Mom had enjoyed dress-up and tea parties together. She'd stopped inviting Gemma to the tea parties because Gemma always flew the cup and saucers around in a space battle, her little gun-shooting sounds and explosions making Sandy cry because Gemma "wasn't doing it right!"

Sandy sighed. "I'm getting a little tired. Maybe we should pick this up again tomorrow."

"Yes!" Gemma jumped to her feet. The new space flight simulator game at home called her name.

Sandy turned back to the trifold mirror, running her hands over the smooth fabric with a sigh, eyes downcast.

Too late, Gemma realized her mistake.

"You really hate this, don't you?" Sandy said in a small voice.

Gemma plucked at her jeans, not looking Sandy in the eye. "No! It's ... fun."

Sandy had only recently let her long-time boyfriend, David, propose to her. She wanted to wait to get married until she turned twenty-one, like their mother had been when she walked down the aisle. Sandy had no greater cheerleader than Gemma, but their sensibilities had never quite been aligned.

"Come on. Go get changed and I'll take you out for ice cream," Gemma said, taking advantage of Sandy's weakness.

"With what money?" Sandy called, disappearing behind the curtain again.

Gemma scowled at her reflection in the mirror. Sandy was right. She barely had ten dollars in her checking, and had to close her savings account the week before because she couldn't keep the required minimum balance. All her inheritance had gone to flight school.

Fat lot of good *that* had done her. A whole year later, and her feet were still planted firmly on terra firma.

Her chin dropped to her chest.

Not one job. *Not one.*

Surely ten dollars was more than enough for a single scoop. Maybe she should see how much a kiddie cone cost.

Her pocket vibrated, and Gemma reached down for her phone. Her first instinct was to not answer the unknown number, but with a few applications for pilot work still pending, she finally swiped to green.

"This is Gemma," she said.

"Charlie Jenkins," a deep voice on the other end said. "Ship's doctor. I'm calling you about a job."

2

Gemma watched through the little oval window in the side of the plane as they approached the massive, glass-faced building. The words *Jefferson Memorial Intergalactic Spaceport* glowed bright out front, despite the sunny morning.

She'd hopped on a plane a few hours after she'd received the call and hadn't slept a wink on the flight. Her bouncing leg drove her seatmate to find a new spot farther back on the plane, so she'd had two seats to herself for the whole ride. She'd gazed out over the wing, the dark night dimming before blazing into a fiery sunrise.

Her first job. *Finally*.

Her fingers flexed, opening and closing. It had to be better than flight school. It had to be. This time, they needed her. Actually wanted her. No one planned to gang up on her, hoping she'd quit.

No. No, this was a crew of *professionals*. They would treat her with respect, at the least. At the most ... maybe she would even make a friend.

But now, walking down the gangway to the busy spaceport entrance in an ill-fitting pilot's uniform, her hair pulled back, a single duffle slung over her shoulder, Gemma tensed, trying not to tremble. Other passengers bumped and jostled her, hurrying to make their connections.

This is going to go well. It has to.

She took a last deep breath and stepped onto an elevator in the concourse.

When the doors opened, she approached a security station queue for cargo flights and the docks for the space-faring vessels.

A uniformed security agent squinted at the orders Gemma handed him, then looked at her, then back at the orders, then to her presented ID. She looked him in the eye, her gaze unwavering. Apparently, they didn't often get women dressed as pilots coming through here. She'd been one of only three girls in the flight program, and she had fought for every inch of the road to reach graduation.

She resisted the urge to fidget with Omni Authority's symbol stitched in gold on the shoulders of her blue pilot's jumpsuit. They didn't typically make pilot uniforms in women's sizes—and there hadn't been time to order a custom-fit one—so she had to make due with one that had at least had enough room for her hips. The rest of the uniform settled over her like a tent. She'd rolled up the pant-legs and sleeves, tightened a belt around her waist, and had to wear an undershirt to prevent any wardrobe malfunctions from the wide neck.

The guard finally waved her through the security checkpoint. Gemma ignored the stares around her, repeating the berth number over and over in her head. She had to keep hiking up her uniform neckline back to her shoulder, fighting against gravity and the rubbing of her bag strap.

I am supposed to be here.

The carpet gave way to metal floorplate with a raised diamond pattern. The terminal's air system filtered out the oil, exhaust, and fuel choking the spaceport, but it couldn't keep out the metallic tinge. Butterflies rising in her stomach, Gemma slowed her pace and stared through the huge windows, extending from the floor to the high ceiling, supported by the steel frames of the spaceport walls. Outside, landing pads of various sizes, some docked with ships and some without, had maintenance crews in orange uniforms working on them.

All around her, the spaceport corridor buzzed with activity —the beeping and grinding of working machines, most carrying cargo crates; luggage being hauled; and people all yelling to be heard over the racket that bounced against the metal floor, the echo adding its own voice. Even if someone had made an announcement over a loudspeaker, no one would ever hear them.

Stop gaping like a tourist. You belong here. She hiked up her neckline again and recited the berth number.

Gemma walked right by the berth and had to backtrack. She had expected at least a shuttle and a long walk. Either this Captain Lee had gotten lucky, or he had friends in high places.

She took the stairs two at a time.

Traditional airplanes needed a runway, but could roll up next to the building below for passengers. Spaceships didn't need runways, but didn't have wheels, and so landed on the open-air circular platforms jutting out from the roof of the building.

She glanced at her orders again, triple-checking the number. Showing up at the wrong platform would not be a great start to her career. A cargo ship was not where she ultimately wanted to be, but if she could make this work, it would be another step in the right direction to a high-class Omni Authority vessel.

The heavy metal door slammed shut behind her and she stopped, blinking in the stark sunlight, the mixed smells of jet fuel and exhaust washing over her.

The ship was on the small side as cargo ships go, and it certainly wasn't state-of-the-art. Maybe ten years old. The dull, gray hull protected a bulky body, patches of lighter metal covering old scars. Someone moved in the clear polycarbonate bubble of the bridge that curved upward over the blunt nose.

Oversized engines jutted out on either side, with smaller thrusters dotting the entire ship to make it agile, ready to move in any direction at a touch. The laser weapon system tucked under the stubby wings would be controlled by the security console on the bridge.

A man walked the roof conducting pre-flight inspections of the hull and the fully extended, glimmering solar sails. *Michal* was painted on the hull in red.

The ship was beautiful.

Gemma bounced on her tiptoes and flexed her fingers. She couldn't wait to fly it.

"Um, excuse me? Uh, Miss?"

Snapping out of her trance, Gemma glanced over her shoulder at the orange-clad dockworker, then turned and continued walking toward the ship. Maybe if she ignored him …

"Er— can I help you?" he asked, following her. "Are you lost?"

Go away. She'd had a late night, her uniform squeezed her hips, and it was too early in the morning to deal with this stupidity. He wasn't even on the crew.

"No, I'm good, but thanks." Gemma's voice rose as she sped up, but the hoses and wires snaking across the concrete slowed her as she picked her way over them. *Don't raise your voice, don't even bother talking to him. You're a professional, you don't get mad.*

He stepped directly in front of her and stopped, holding his hands up. "You're not really, uh, supposed to be here."

Gemma's jaw clenched, her neckline slipping off her shoulder again. *That's it.* This man now blocked her way, and had no authority over her.

Fist on her jutted hip, she opened her mouth to say so, when a hand clapped onto the man's shoulder.

"Hello."

She looked over as a dark-skinned, white-haired man smiled at her. "You must be the new pilot, Gemma Stone." He offered her his other hand. "Charlie Jenkins, ship's doctor. We spoke on the phone?"

"Oh. Yes," Gemma said, nodding as she took his hand in hers. "Nice to meet you." He wore the white shirt and khaki pants of a doctor, the caduceus medical symbol stitched in red over his heart.

"You as well." The doctor nodded to her, then used his other hand to steer the dockworker away from Gemma, giving him a light push. "Thank you for your concern," he said, his voice deep and overly-serious.

The dockworker slunk away, glancing back at her. She didn't hide her smirk when he tripped over a hose.

"Follow me." Dr. Jenkins led the way to the ship. Despite his age—maybe twenty years older than Dad would have been?—he kept a brisk pace, his back straight.

"Welcome to our crew," he said. "I'll give you a quick check-up, then the grand tour."

"A check-up?" she repeated. *Ugh.* "But I had one just last month."

"And I'm sure that doctor did an excellent job." The unmistakable sarcasm in his voice raised her eyebrows. "I prefer to see all crewmembers at least once before they get sick, so I have a baseline to compare their health to. Everyone is different, and I've seen all kinds in my time." Jenkins smiled again.

He stopped outside the ship's airlock and handed her a set of dog tags on a chain. "This is your key to the ship," he explained. "The basic drill; bio code, locator chip, emergency close-range communications. Take good care of it and keep it on you at all times." He tapped it twice and locked eyes with her. "*At all times.*"

"Understood."

"We usually keep on the more talented crew, and from what I hear, they don't get much more talented than you."

Gemma fidgeted with the ship keys, fighting the urge to smile. His words were true, but you didn't make friends going around bragging about it. "Oh, I don't know about that." She slipped the chain over her head and tucked the keys under her shirt.

He wagged a finger. "Don't shortchange yourself, kid. I saw your flight school records. We're lucky to have you." He hesitated, as if he debated saying something else, then shook his head. "Come on. First stop on the tour: the sickbay."

They walked up the gangway and onto deck two.

She knew what he hadn't said. Despite her talent, this was the first mission she'd been offered in the year since she'd been out of flight school. An entire year of no work—some days spent on long, wandering hikes through the mountains, other days sitting at home playing video games—while all the idiots she'd gone to flight school with zipped around space.

No one had wanted a "young woman," two simple words that amounted to two massive strikes against her.

Until now.

The white-walled, squeaky-clean sickbay had one exam table, padded and covered with a sheet. The sharp, antiseptic smell improved the air quality compared to outside the ship—but not by much.

Dr. Jenkins—*Charlie*, he insisted she call him Charlie—gave her the basic checkup: eyes, ears, nose, mouth, pulse, temperature, weight, height, reflexes, medical history. Though, unlike her regular doctor, he checked her muscle mass and did an EKG.

"Ouch." She rubbed the inside of her elbow where he'd stuck her with the needle.

"We're all done here." Charlie put aside his info tablet. "Your blood test results will be processed in a few minutes if you care to see them. But I suppose you're ready to tour the ship?"

Gemma jumped off the exam table. "Am I ever!"

He led the way out, sliding the door closed behind them. "If you ever need anything, feel free to stop by sickbay, anytime. I'm always here."

"What, you sleep here?" she joked.

Charlie chuckled. "Yes, I do. I sleep over in the life pod attached to the infirmary. I have everything I need in there."

Gemma balked. "Are you serious?" The life pods were even narrower than the crew quarters. She verbally backpedaled. "I mean, it must be ... nice?"

"It is," he said. "Plus, I've programmed it to jettison if we ever get in enough trouble."

"Have you ever been launched accidentally?"

Charlie smiled and nodded. "I have, actually," he admitted. "When I first set it up, I set the parameters too low. We had an all-systems check while we were out, including an alarm sound. They had to come back and get me."

They both laughed, then Charlie's face sobered. "But, once I got the settings right, it has saved my life." His tone didn't invite her to ask.

Charlie took the lead down the corridor, the passageway so narrow they couldn't even walk side-by-side comfortably. "The fitness center is the next door down this hall; be sure to follow the exercise schedule I gave you, or you'll answer to me. We can't let your muscles get weak in the lower gravity."

"Sure thing." She gave the room a cursory glance. Stationary bike, resistance devices, treadmill, weightlifting machines, a mirrored back wall. The gravity was stronger here than in the rest of the ship, at least as strong as Earth's. The usual. The ship must have recently been cleaned; even the fitness center didn't reek of BO. Yet.

They climbed a ladder to deck three. Charlie slid open another door and swept his arm around the largest room on the ship, with a long, fake-wood table bolted to the floor on one side, surrounded by chairs. Some cushy furniture and a thick throw rug, along with the ship's entertainment system, took up the other half of the room. A large window looked out onto the platform, the surrounding walls a soothing blue, probably the only color on the ship.

"This is the community living area," he said. "Here is where we relax when we aren't on duty, and where we eat. We share all our dinners together—though someone is always on the bridge keeping watch. We bring them a plate."

She inhaled the scent of fresh coffee. Though she despised the taste, the rich aroma brought back good memories.

Charlie led her through the only other door in the room, at the far wall near the table. "The galley. We're on a rotating schedule, so we take turns cooking, cleaning up after dinner, dust-mopping, laundry, and watch-duty. A couple of things you'll want to—"

"Cooking?" Gemma interrupted. Her stomach clenched. Sandy had always done the cooking.

"Yes, cooking," he repeated. "We all have to take a turn.

Don't worry too much, we'll help you out. You can always ask someone to trade jobs with you. Now, pay attention to this."

He opened the cooling unit set into the wall. "We use only these top four shelves to make our meals. This bottom shelf is for personal food, so if you want to bring a snack, put it here. Leave a note on it; otherwise it's fair game."

Large, clear plastic boxes—stuffed with meats, cheese, and bread—took up most of the bottom shelf, each clearly labeled CL.

"Got it," Gemma noted.

Charlie gave a brief overview of the rest of the kitchen—including a terrifying stove and friendlier instant-rehydrater—and then led her past the communal washroom and cleaning station to the sleeping quarters on the same deck.

"Yours is the last one in the hall."

She swiped her bio-card and gasped as she walked in. "It's huge!"

Although a massive bed took up half the space, it still left enough room to pace in. It even had shelves and a small desk. Most ship bunks consisted of a twin bed and a little storage space. "And it has its own bathroom! I thought cargo ships were concerned with saving space."

That's why all the doors on a ship were analog sliding doors. Ship designers made use of every square inch of room they could on the space vessels to keep them efficient—and taking out the bulky machinery of automatic sliding doors saved quite a bit of room. The only automatic doors on the whole ship were the airlocks.

Charlie cleared his throat. "Actually, this is usually Captain Lee's quarters."

Gemma froze. "What?"

"He decided to switch to avoid any ... awkwardness in the communal showers."

Whoa. The captain gave up his room for her? "Wow. He sounds like a really nice guy." She couldn't wait to meet him.

Charlie hesitated, not looking at her for a moment. "He is," he finally said. "You just have to get to know him."

Another pause, before he pasted on a smile. "Don't be late for your duties, and you'll get along fine." Before she could ask more, he clapped his hands together. "Anyway. Stow your gear, and we'll see the engine room and the bridge."

"I'll do it later," she said, tossing her bag onto the bed. Every crewman wore their issued uniforms at all times, except for when using the fitness center and sleeping. She had four uniforms that wouldn't take long to stow along with her other clothing. Later, though. "Let's see the rest of the ship!"

Charlie explained that Joe, the engineer who oversaw the ship's engines, worked in the engine room on the lowest deck of the ship. They slid down a particularly slick ladder, undoubtedly coated in engine oil.

"Joe!" Charlie called over the clamor of pre-flight engine checks. "This is Gemma, the new pilot."

The large man, clad in the gray jumper of a mechanic and red badge of an engineer, turned and raised his eyebrows. He lifted his cap and scratched his bald head.

"Welcome to the crew," he said in a gravelly voice. He offered her a greasy hand, visibly pleased when she took it.

"I like a girl who's not afraid to get her hands dirty," he said, his chubby cheeks lifting in a smile. By the grip of his hand, she'd say he had plenty of muscle hidden beneath his soft exterior.

"Girl?"

A tousled, sandy-haired head popped out of an open compartment in the floor. The boy lifted his goggles onto his forehead and blinked at her, mouth hanging open. "You *are* a girl!"

"The observant wire-rat is Zane," Joe said. "Zaney, this is our new pilot."

Zane's eyes widened. "No way!" He was all knees and elbows as he pulled himself up, his green uniform baggy around his thin frame. He extended a hand. "Zane, ship's electrician," he said. "It's a pleasure to meet you."

"Gemma." She smiled as she shook his hand, surprised by the grip of his thin fingers. "You don't look old enough to be an electrician." He couldn't be older than thirteen.

Zane winked. "Maybe not legally, but talent knows no age, and in the dead of space, you definitely want talent on your side." He shrugged and lowered his voice. "Though, if you wouldn't mind keeping that to yourself while we're in port?"

"Of course," Gemma said, lowering her voice to match his.

The two of them gave her a tour of the cramped engine room—made more so by Joe's large size—running down the numbers she would need to know. She read the dials and gauges on the walls, ducking to not hit her head on exposed pipes. The small space intensified the smells of metal, grease, and sweat.

She turned suddenly to ask Joe about thruster stability, and smacked right into Zane— holding her music player in his hands.

He froze.

She stared for a second, unsure what she was seeing, and then slapped the back pocket her music player had been in.

Empty.

"What are you doing!" she shrieked, her voice too loud for the small engine room. "Are you ... stealing my stuff?"

Zane cringed. "Um, you dropped it?"

Out of a zipped pocket? Unlikely.

She snatched the player back from him and fixed her eyes

on him, seething. "Don't you *ever* touch my stuff. What is wrong with you?"

"I'm sorry! I'm sorry." Zane shrank away, as if afraid she would hit him.

Gemma glared at him and shook her head in disgust. "That is not okay."

"Zane!" Joe reached over and cuffed him on the back of the head. Not hard, but Zane flinched. "You know better, now!"

"I know, I know! I just ... I wanted to know more about her," Zane said, his voice quiet, eyes downcast as he scuffed his shoe against the metal floor. "You can tell a lot about a person by their music." He looked back up at her. "I'm really sorry. I'm not great about remembering to ask first. It won't happen again."

Gemma took a deep breath and uncrossed her arms. She let out the breath and shoved her music player back into her pocket, zipping it shut. "You know," she said, "you can also find out a lot about a person by just talking to them. *In real-life conversations.*"

The boy nodded and shrank into himself even more.

Calm down. Be professional.

She let out a long, exasperated sigh. "It's fine," she said finally. "I accept your apology." She tried not to glare at him.

"Thank you. I mean it, I swear it'll never happen again," Zane said, the words spilling out of him as he relaxed. "An' I was going to give it back, I promise! It just would have been ... later."

Gemma said nothing. She'd have to keep an eye on him.

"He didn't mean any harm," Joe said.

Charlie crossed his arms, his eyebrows raised, though she wasn't sure if he judged Zane's actions or her mini rant. "It's a bad habit of his."

Heat flushed her cheeks. *Way to overreact.*

"Come on," Joe said, leading Zane away. "You finish pre-check while I talk to Gemma about thruster control."

Joe would have kept her all day, talking about engine top-speed and the modifications he'd made, but Charlie reminded them of the approaching launch time.

As they left the engine room, she smiled. Besides the little pickpocket incident, this was already going so much better than she had dared to hope.

Charlie had her take a glance at the cargo hold. A big, empty space with two exits: one a standard airlock at the very back, and the other one spanning the entire floor. To pick up large cargo, the floor would open as the ship settled around the cargo. A robotic, magnetic claw would then lift the cargo to the ceiling before the floor closed again under it.

On the way to the bridge she met Chase, the security and weapons officer. Clean, straight-backed, high collar, thinning hair parted on the side. His uniform shirt was a similar blue as hers, with gold piping around the edges, but he wore black pants. He gave her a polite nod, but didn't seem interested in talking, muttering something about pre-flight inspections.

"And now the moment you've been waiting for: the bridge." Charlie gestured toward the metal ladder. "I'm going to let you go up by yourself. Again, it's been a pleasure to meet you, Gemma, and if you need anything, you know where to find me."

She thanked him and waited until he'd disappeared through another door before she took a deep breath, releasing the grin she'd been holding in.

This was real. This was finally, really happening.

When she'd gotten the call, she hadn't hesitated to accept, even though they hadn't told her the destination. When they wouldn't tell you the destination until after launch, that meant it was dangerous. But, like she'd told her sister, it would be even more dangerous for the crew without her. They needed a good pilot.

They needed *her*.

Of course, Sandy had argued that she needed her Maid of Honor, so she'd better come back safe.

Gemma inhaled deeply and pushed Sandy's teary farewell out of her head. Of course she'd come back safe. She wouldn't let her sister get married without her.

But right now she had a bridge to see. A destination to discover.

Accepting her role as the ship's new pilot, Gemma gripped the ladder rungs and began to climb.

3

The two men on the bridge stopped their conversation at her arrival. The really tall one—who must have been not much older than she—frowned, his dark hair short with a buzz cut, and his jaw tight. Gemma tried not to stare. He was *really* tall. She had never considered herself short until now.

Besides the shock of his height, his narrowed eyes struck her as the prettiest shade of blue she'd ever seen.

The second one gave her a warm smile—his teeth so white that he probably bleached—his light-brown hair styled in such a way that his bangs just brushed the top of one eyebrow. She'd guess his age somewhere in the late twenties.

"Gemma Stone, pilot, reporting in," she said with a smile, but as she looked back and forth between the two, the smile froze. "Um ... is one of you the captain?"

Neither wore a captain's uniform. In fact, the taller wore mechanic grays, and the other sported a red navigator's shirt. Did they have an engineer and a mechanic? This ship didn't seem large enough for the engineer to need an assistant.

"That would be me, Captain Lee," said the mechanic, his voice cool and matter-of-fact. He scrutinized her, his brows lowered over those remarkable eyes. "Let me make this clear, Pilot: I think having a woman onboard is a bad idea. You'd better be as good as they say you are."

Gemma's mouth hung open, her words dried up. Everyone had been so welcoming. The last person she'd expected this from was the captain. He'd even given her his room.

Oh. Her fists tightened, the familiar annoyance flaring. He'd given her his room, not for her sake, but to keep her from distracting the rest of the crew. *Because I'm a girl.*

She opened her mouth to say something that was probably stupid when the navigator stepped between them and gave her a megawatt smile. "Don't mind the captain. He's a little old-fashioned. I'm Dakota, ship's navigator, though you can call me Dak." He took her hand from where it hung at her side and shook it. "It's a pleasure to have you on board."

"Oh ... Nice to meet you." Gemma forced her mouth into a smile.

She took a deep breath. Dak's intervention had given her the moment she needed to get her mouth under control.

The captain gave a snort. "This is what I was talking about. Don't get any ideas, Dak."

He handed her an info tablet. "Get familiar with the controls. System checks start in thirty minutes, then we'll take off as soon as we're cleared. Coordinates for cargo pickup are on there. Once we're out of the atmosphere and on course, crew meeting in the dining area."

His hand on Dak's arm, the captain steered him back to the readouts they had been discussing, leaving Gemma standing there, staring at the info tablet.

She chewed her lip. *Focus.* She had work to do before the launch. She'd show him she was *better* than they said she was.

The flight deck consisted of the pilot's seat in the middle, flanked on either side by consoles, one for security, the other for navigation. The captain sat at the back, higher than the others due to the subtle incline of the floor, where he could see everyone's screen at once. The clear polycarbonate above gave them a panoramic view of their surroundings, with additional monitors displaying what was below and behind them.

Chase, the straight-backed security officer, joined them.

Gemma snuck a glance over at the captain. How did he get away with wearing a different uniform? Maybe captains had the authority to do that. But why would he want to? No one would know that he was in charge.

Well, maybe on a small ship like this, everyone knew one another, so it wasn't needed. But what about on large ships? Or on-planet?

Though he'd be hard to miss with his ridiculous tallness.

The captain didn't say two words to her during the system checks. At least he wasn't leaning over her shoulder double-checking everything she did, like some of her flight instructors had. The tension between her shoulders eased as she went through the familiar motions of a pre-flight check. She'd flown all types of spacecraft in flight school, so the layout of the console didn't hold any surprises.

"All systems ready, Captain. We are go for launch," she said.

Captain Lee nodded. "Take her up."

The ten-minute flight to the cargo pickup point struck her as a little strange. They could have loaded their cargo at the spaceport, couldn't they? Why pick up at a seemingly random landing pad in the middle of nowhere?

With steady hands, she executed a smooth turn-around and settled the ship over the crate. The screen in front of her guided her down, mere inches to spare on either side.

She felt the captain's eyes on her, but her attention didn't waver.

Touchdown. The ship hissed as locks engaged and the cargo secured.

Chase did a visual inspection from the outside. While she waited, Gemma tweaked the pilot settings. She felt Captain Lee still watching her. *I will not be intimidated by a giraffe in a mechanic's uniform.*

"All secure," Chase reported, climbing back onto the bridge. "Clear for liftoff."

The launch was typical—except that it was the official take-off of her *first-ever mission!* She worked the control column and the pedals on the floor. She tried to look as unim-pressed as the rest of the crew, but couldn't smother her grin. The engines roared, fighting against Earth's gravity, the ship shaking and jostling her against the five-point safety harness, the control column vibrating in her grip. The ride smoothed out as they shot out of the atmosphere. With the flip of a switch, she engaged the artificial gravity before anyone got disoriented.

She had gone through these procedures a thousand times, lifted off hundreds of aircraft, flown for more hours than she could count. But this time—for the first time—she flew to a destination as the pilot. *The* pilot. Not a backup, not a student, not an observer. They *needed* her to get them there.

Gemma smothered a laugh, but let herself smile. Finally, she could spread her wings.

Speaking of wings—

She pressed the button to extend the solar sails, glancing through a rear engine camera as the silky-looking sail unfolded behind the ship, tinting the stars behind it in a translucent shade of gold. The sails absorbed all solar light within sight—even a bit from the stars—and fed that energy back into the engines, supplementing the power they generated so less fuel was needed.

The entire blue jewel of Earth hung in space behind them by the time the captain unclipped his harness.

"Come on, Pilot, crew meeting." He slipped out of sight down the ladder before she'd even punched the autopilot, Chase following.

"You coming?" she asked Dak, who hadn't moved from his seat.

"Nah, I've already been briefed." He gave a wink. "Can't take off if the navigator doesn't know where we're going. I've got watch duty."

Gemma let herself slide down the ladder, moving in the lower gravity with practiced ease. Most ships generated a weak gravity field, just enough to keep things from floating.

The window of the common room showed stars and the now far-off dot of Earth, as everyone took a seat at the large table, the entertainment half of the common room still and quiet.

"Sit here, Gemma!" Zane pushed out a chair for her, the loose sleeve of his uniform around his skinny arm catching on the armrest of the chair before he shook it off. His voice dropped. "I'm really sorry—"

She gave him a smile, resisting the urge to ruffle his messy hair. "Don't mention it."

"This mission is classified," Captain Lee said to the group as soon as she sat, his voice stern. "You may not disclose any of the details, including our destination, in outside communications. Doing so will earn you jail time when we return to Earth."

Hmm. Classified cargo explained the alternate pickup point.

Charlie raised a hand.

"Yes, Charlie?"

"Aren't you going to introduce our new pilot?"

Gemma's cheeks flushed, and it took everything she had not to look down at the table. Charlie was trying to be nice, but she really didn't want the attention. Especially after the captain's condescending reception.

The captain glanced at her. "Hasn't everyone met her already?"

Charlie arched an eyebrow.

"Please welcome our new pilot." Captain Lee gestured to her. Gemma crossed her arms and met his eyes with a steady gaze, determined not to be intimidated.

Before anyone else could say anything, he looked away and continued. "We are hauling emergency relief supplies to the planet Cerise inside the Ruby District. We will stop for refueling before crossing the Terminus. Any questions?"

Gemma uncrossed her arms and gripped her knees under the table. A war zone surrounded the Ruby District, and they didn't have an armed escort. Wasn't it illegal to go beyond the Terminus?

She kept her mouth shut. No one else asked any questions, and she knew she would look dumb asking things probably obvious to everyone else. Especially in front of the captain. She could ask Charlie later. At least *he* wouldn't make her feel stupid.

"Dismissed," Captain Lee said. "Duty roster will be posted within the hour."

Chairs scraped against the metal floor as everyone stood. "Pilot."

Gemma turned from following Zane. "Yes, Captain?"

He paused while everyone else filed out until they were alone. Gemma glanced after the rest of the crew, shifting her weight. She didn't have a good feeling about this.

The captain stood straight, his hands clasped behind him as he towered over her. "I wanted to make sure your room is in order."

She opened her mouth for a snarky remark, but bit it back. Even if he didn't like having her on board, he was still her captain. Copping an attitude on the first day would not bode well for the rest of the mission. Besides, he did give her the best room on the ship.

So, she smiled. "Yes, it's great. Thank you for your consideration."

He gave a nod. "Good. Now, for the rules—"

"Rules?" she repeated, a heavy feeling in her stomach.

"No one is allowed in your room," he continued. "You don't share the fitness center, and no loitering in the hallways. Is that clear?"

Her mouth worked for a moment before she found her voice. "Are these ship rules, or *my* rules?"

Captain Lee had the nerve to look her dead in the eye as he said, "Yours."

Her face reddened as she raised a finger. "Now look here, *Captain*. You can take your idiotic rules and shove them out an airlock because I am not going to take this. I've worked too hard to be treated like some second-class citizen when I am an essential member of the crew. You will give me some respect."

So much for getting along.

His icy gaze and hard expression didn't flicker at her tirade. With a steady, even voice, he said, "This is my ship, and you will do as you're ordered. Or would you like to request a reassignment?"

Gemma's mouth snapped shut, her hand dropping to her side. Reassignment to what? This was her one shot. She had to stick it out for this one mission, then she could leave. She'd have experience then, and could surely find another, more reasonable captain.

"I—" She swallowed hard. Her jaw clenched, but she managed to grind out, "Aye-aye, *Captain.*"

Without another word, he turned on his heel and strode out of the living area.

Gemma crossed her arms. She was going to make sure she broke every one of his stupid rules.

4

She found Dr. Charlie in sickbay, a cup of coffee in his hand.

Yes, there was a war going on. No, it wasn't illegal to go beyond the Terminus, it was just dangerous to be out of Omni Authority's territory. An armored escort would have been nice, but was unlikely. The only question Charlie refused to answer was one that she had asked in passing, but his refusal intrigued her.

"If he wanted you to know his first name, he would have told you," Charlie said, leaning back with a tablet on his lap, a pair of glasses on the counter next to him. "But he prefers to be called Captain or Captain Lee. Don't even bother asking him because he won't tell you."

Gemma gave her sweetest smile. "I bet you don't even know his first name."

The doctor chuckled. "My own grandkids can't get reverse psychology to work on me, young lady. You don't have a chance."

She frowned. Why would the Captain want to be known by only a title and his last name? She wouldn't care for someone calling her 'Pilot' all the time.

"It's not just you," Charlie assured her. "The only people who know it are me and Joe, and that's only because we've known him since ... well, Chase might know it, being a security man, but he's pretty tight-lipped."

Hmm. Very mysterious. So far, the captain was tall, mean, and quite frankly—odd. "It seems weird to not even use your own name ..." she ventured.

"Drop it, Gemma. Digging into the captain's personal life will only irritate him." Charlie took a sip of his coffee.

"How about you?" She took in the meticulous labels on every drawer and cabinet in sickbay. "You seem ... organized."

Charlie barked a laugh. "Thanks for putting it so nicely. The guys say I'm anal. I just have a system. Drove my wife crazy." He pointed a finger at Gemma. "I'm telling you right now, don't try to help yourself to any of my drugs. I know exactly where everything is and how much of it we've got. And I don't respond well to self-diagnosis. So, let's agree: you don't tell me how to do my job, and I won't tell you how to fly the ship."

"Sounds good to me," she said with a nod. She doubted she would have any trouble getting along with Charlie.

"Now, you need anything? Something to help you sleep? I know you're probably jet-lagged from your flight. And without sunlight, the days can run together a bit."

She waved a hand. "I'll let you know if I have any trouble."

Gemma wandered down to the engine room to find Joe again. She had an idea for customizing the thruster control. She also wanted to know more about the cranky, yet infuriatingly fascinating, captain.

The large engineer squinted at a screen, raising his cap and scratching his head as he turned knobs and adjusted levels. Zane sat on the narrow worktable, eating an apple. The kid needed a haircut and a crash-course in using a comb.

"Well, if it isn't the girl!" Joe said with a grin, tipping his hat.

Zane's head whipped around so fast he dropped his apple.

"Gemma!" He smiled a goofy grin.

"Pick that up, would ya?" Joe said, wiping his greasy hands on his equally-greasy pants. "Gotta keep things clean, you know."

Gemma glanced around. Clean was not how she would describe the engine room.

Zane picked up the apple off the floor, brushed it off, and took another bite.

"Oh, gross!" Gemma laughed.

"I've eaten worse," Zane said around a mouthful. "What're you doing down here?"

"I wanted to ask Joe about the captain's first name," she said.

Joe laughed at her. "If I told you that, he would give me clean-up duty for a week."

This was becoming a bigger deal than she'd expected. The question originally rose from the swirl of casual thought, but now it piqued her curiosity.

A smile tugged at a corner of her mouth. She bet finding out his name would irritate him. Not enough for her to get in trouble—but just enough to get under his skin.

"I can't get him to tell me either," Zane whispered to her. A loud whisper, as the rumbling and grinding—punctuated by the occasional clank—of the engine room made it difficult to hear anything. "And you definitely don't want to ask the captain himself. He had me washing dishes for *three weeks*."

So, if she kept prying, there might be consequences. But Gemma wasn't afraid of dishes.

What really knotted her stomach was the prospect of cooking.

TREVOR LAY ON HIS BED IN THE TINY SLEEPING QUARTERS, HAVING finished the duty roster. He couldn't even stretch out completely in the room, much less fit on the bed.

He still thought giving her his room was a good idea, but he hadn't expected to feel quite so miserable himself. He'd slept in quarters like this his whole life, ever since his dad found him. But apparently, he'd gone through a growth spurt since he'd been made captain.

He shifted again, but couldn't get comfortable.

She definitely doesn't belong on my crew. She lacked respect and discipline. Her little tantrum gave evidence of that. Not surprising. This was her first mission, and test scores never told the whole story. They don't test initiates on following orders, and when he'd looked into her record, he found only one letter of recommendation, regaling her natural talent. Nothing about her character.

He gritted his teeth. He'd had a navigator once who made it clear he thought Trevor was too young to be a captain. He copped an attitude and questioned every one of Trevor's decision. Reassigning him and replacing him had been easy.

Trevor tried to stretch out a leg, but ended up bumping his elbow. This was going to be a long trip. He'd have to wait until they returned to Earth to fire her.

Chairs scraped as everyone took their seats at the large dinner table in the common room, except for the captain, who was on watch duty. Chase hadn't brought out dinner yet from the galley.

"Fifty bucks it's spaghetti," Zane said to Gemma. He grinned, with all the confidence of a thirteen-year-old hustler.

"I think I know better than to take that bet," she said. She could smell the garlic and meatballs.

Zane chuckled. "You're right. Chase *always* makes spaghetti. Except that one time, when someone accidentally bought linguine. He still served it with meatball sauce."

Straight-backed security officer Chase entered the dining room and set the pot of spaghetti and meatballs on the table. He didn't say anything as he served everyone, and gave a tight smile when Gemma thanked him. Zane already held out his plate for seconds by the time Gemma picked up her fork.

She had thought about asking Chase about the captain's name, but she could hardly get a hello out of him, much less crew secrets.

Then Joe lifted his hat. "A launch calls for something special!" He disappeared into the kitchen and came back with a six-pack of beer. "I managed to smuggle a couple of these aboard."

Zane's hand shot up. "I'll take one."

Joe held it out of his reach. "You're too young."

Zane rolled his eyes. "Aw, c'mon, Joe!"

After a moment, Joe's serious face broke into a grin. "I'm just messin' with you, kid."

Charlie gave a thin smile and held up a hand when Joe offered him one. "None for me, thanks."

Gemma took a sip. The icy cold beer complemented the spicy spaghetti sauce.

"How long have you been a pilot?" Joe asked. Even at dinner, the engineer had greasy fingerprints on his shirt.

Gemma glanced around the table. "Um ... I graduated from flight school last year."

"Top of the class," Charlie put in. "Some of the best scores I've ever seen."

"Impressive," Joe said, nodding.

"That's a high compliment," Zane whispered to her loudly. "Charlie is *really* old, so he's seen a *lot* of test scores. I think he helped test the Ford Model T car."

Gemma coughed to hide a laugh, beer shooting up into her sinuses, but thankfully not out her nose. Oh, did that burn.

Charlie laughed with her. "You're not wrong, kid."

"What made you want to become a pilot?" Dak asked, smiling with a suave tip of his head, his hair just right. He ate slowly, likely so he didn't splash tomato sauce on his pristine navigator shirt. He probably wouldn't give Joe a handshake.

She lifted the corners of her mouth and steeled herself. "I guess I've always liked—"

"Put that thing away." Joe snatched a gaming device out of Zane's hands under the table, unknowingly saving Gemma. "Talk to people."

"Hey! I was almost through that level!" Zane reached for the game, but Joe dropped it into his pocket, buttoning the top shut.

"Not at dinner," Joe said.

"C'mon Joe! That's not fair," Zane whined. "At least let me finish the boss fight."

Joe pushed Zane's grabby fingers away. "Eat your dinner."

"Do they always bicker like this?" Gemma asked. She loved it. It felt like family.

"Always," Chase said, sipping his beer. He didn't seem to love it as much.

Somehow, the conversation migrated from Gemma's flight school—which she was *not* inclined to talk about—to Charlie's days at med school.

Joe laughed at something Charlie said, leaning over and elbowing Chase—who didn't seem as amused—when Gemma caught sight of Zane's quick fingers pulling the gaming device out of Joe's pocket.

Zane met Gemma's gaze and froze. She raised her eyebrows at him, then pointedly looked away. Out of the corner of her eye, he grinned.

Just like that, she'd made a new friend.

A full plate in hand, Charlie stood. "I'd better get this to the captain."

"Pass this along to him, would you?" Joe held out a beer to him.

Charlie's shoulders tightened, and he took a small step back. "I don't think he should drink on watch duty."

Joe shrugged. "Then give it to him for after. Take it, the can's not gonna bite you."

Charlie hesitated, then shook his head. "You take it to him later." He left the room.

"Hey Sandy. It's me. Gem. Your sister." Gemma waved at the camera recording her. Leaving a message for Sandy felt strange. This was the first time she hadn't been able to have an actual conversation with her sister.

Setting up the message on the standard computer console set into her room's wall only took a few seconds. The emergency clean-up of her stuff out of the background took a few minutes more. Sandy hated when Gemma left her stuff everywhere.

"It's only day three, and I miss you already," Gemma continued. "I don't know when you'll get this message with the lag-time, and we'll be gone for—uh, longer. Sorry, I can't tell you where we're going." She hesitated. She couldn't tell Sandy how dangerous this mission really was. "I'll be home safe with you in no time.

"Everyone here has been so nice to me. Well, almost everyone. The only one who seems not to want me here is Captain Lee, whose first name I don't even know. After being given the captain's quarters, I hadn't expected him to be such a jerk."

Gemma looked down at her hands. "I shouldn't have gotten my hopes up. After meeting everyone else, I let my guard down. I know you're going to say, 'five nice guys out of six is great!' And you're right. If he wasn't the *captain*, I'd count it as a win. But ... he's the decision-maker. The last word. His opinion matters, and he doesn't like me, and that's what's scary." She forced herself to give a brave smile. "But he's *not* going to push me around. I'm not going to let him.

"I'm not used to the close spaces here yet, but I'll get there. It must be worse for the captain, being so tall. He's probably one of the tallest people I've ever seen. He ducks to get through the doorways. It explains why his bed is so long. I mean ... I guess it's my bed." She cringed at her own awkwardness.

Her watch beeped, reminding her of the time. "Duty calls. Love you."

Send.

Gemma climbed the ladder to the bridge, metallic taps echoing in the passageway as her rubber-soled shoes connected with each rung. "I'm here to relieve you, Captain."

He nodded, not looking up from his tablet. He had a pencil in his other hand as he jotted something in a pocket notebook.

"What are you reading?" she asked, leaning forward. It wasn't an info tablet he wrote on. His old-school pencil and paper reminded her of how Dad made diagrams and models for his projects.

"Nothing," he said, too quickly, blanking the screen and tossing it aside. The notebook went into his shirt pocket as he unfolded himself from his chair. He didn't look at her. "I leave the bridge to you."

"Okay." She bit her lip, twisting her fingers together. Was she supposed to say something?

Then the 360-degree view of the stars drew her eyes upwards. Her hands relaxed, her voice taking on an awed tone. "Aren't they beautiful?"

The captain paused at the top of the ladder with an unreadable expression. "What's beautiful?"

"Uh, the stars." She gestured upward. "Don't they take your breath away?"

He looked around, as if just noticing them. "Not really."

Gemma blinked. "How long have you been in space?"

Captain Lee hesitated. "All my life." He swung down the ladder before she could ask anything else.

Gemma slumped into her pilot's seat with a sigh, looking up. It really was pretty.

She reached forward to scroll through her screen's readings when something shiny caught her eye. The captain's tablet lay in his chair. A smile pulled at the corner of her mouth. Maybe she could find out what interested him so much. He had been quick to hide it.

She picked it up and woke the screen. Darn it, it had a passcode. She tried a couple of combinations, but gasped and held it away from her when the screen locked up. It wouldn't unlock for sixty minutes. If he came back and saw it, he'd know she'd been fooling with it.

She glanced around in desperation. There was no way he wouldn't come back for this. *Bye-bye, Gemma.* Fired in under a week. And it wasn't even for breaking a rule—stupid or otherwise—but just being *nosey*—

Finding out his name would irritate him. But this—this was an invasion of privacy. She didn't know if she could come back after this bad decision.

If he caught her.

She shoved the tablet under her seat, then waited. Even the stars couldn't stop the bouncing of her leg, and she chewed her thumbnail, wincing when she bit it too low. Thirty minutes passed. As long as he didn't come back until—

At that moment, footsteps echoed from the lower deck.

Captain Lee appeared at the ladder, stopping before he reached the top, his head and shoulders visible. He looked around. "Pilot, have you seen my tablet?"

"Tablet? Uh, no. Nope." She forced a smile. "Haven't seen it."

His eyes narrowed momentarily. "I haven't been anywhere else since yesterday. I thought I left it in here. My mistake." He turned to leave.

"Since yesterday? Wait." She held up a hand. "You had watch duty last night, too? Am I the first to relieve you?" Gemma tilted her head and stared at him. "Were you up here *all night?*"

He avoided her eyes. "I don't sleep much," he mumbled before climbing back down.

She let out a breath. Crisis averted. *Note to self, leave the captain's stuff alone.* She'd stick the tablet in the common room after her shift.

Hmm ... the captain didn't sleep much? *Maybe the lack of sleep makes him cranky.*

At first, watch duty was exciting. She had hundreds of hours logged flying in the local solar system, and hundreds more on a simulator, but she had only been in deep space a handful of times. And she'd never had watch-duty; the instructors had never trusted her with it.

She repeatedly checked every screen, making sure all readings fell within normal parameters. She tried fooling around with the sensors, but the security station was completely locked. She guessed Chase didn't play around when it came to his part of the job.

After the first hour, she lay back in her chair, feet propped up on the console as she stared at nothing.

Weeks of babysitting the bridge? She brought up a screen at her station and scrolled through the media library. At least the ship had a decent assortment of music. She'd once spent an entire summer working at a car wash, perfectly happy as long as she had her music on. Now that she knew constant vigilance wasn't necessary, she could rock out.

After Dak relieved her from watch duty—his hair was *always* so perfect. Who was he trying to impress in space?—Gemma dropped the tablet off at the common room. Zane worked at the dinner table. His goggles up on his forehead, he had his toolbelt spread out across the tabletop.

"What are you working on?" she asked, leaning over the back of the chair next to him.

He grinned. "Disassembling an old communicator. I'm trying to boost the signal with a chip I designed. What are you up to?"

"Just got off watch duty." She leaned over his shoulder. Some of the components were familiar—Sandy's fiancé did computer work—but other than a resistor or a screw, it just looked like ... electronic stuff.

Zane took a deep breath. "You smell good."

Gemma bit her lip and straightened quickly. "Um, thanks?"

His ears reddened, and he looked down at his project. "Uh —I meant, you smell better than Joe. *Everything* smells better than Joe."

The tension released, they both laughed.

The door slid open and Captain Lee strode into the room. He paused, his voice low and controlled. "Zane. What have I told you about leaving your junk on the table?"

"I'm gonna clean it up before dinner!"

"I—" Something across the room caught the captain's eye. He picked up his tablet from the couch. "I know I looked here. Zane, did you take my tablet?"

Gemma squirmed.

Zane raised his hands in defense. "Never, Captain. I swear it wasn't me. Never again, I promised."

"Good man." The captain clapped him on the shoulder, gave Gemma a suspicious look, and went into the galley.

She let out a slow sigh, leaning her hip against the table. "What happened before?"

Zane shook his head, waving his hand in an emphatic

gesture. "Nope, not talking about it. I value my ship privileges, thank you very much."

She didn't want to chuckle at the adorably serious look on his face, so she changed the subject. "Those are some interesting gloves you're wearing."

"Thanks, aren't they cool?" He held up his hands to show off his black fingerless gloves. "The LEDs in them light up when I'm working in the dark, and the wrists are magnetic to stick screws and stuff to."

Gemma raised her eyebrows. "That is actually pretty cool. I meant they were weird."

"Thanks." Zane nodded, admiring his own work.

She walked over to the posted duty roster, almost colliding with the captain when he exited the galley, sandwich in hand. His eyes narrowed again, but he said nothing as he left the common room.

She let out a breath, and looked over the duty roster. The tightness in her shoulders eased. The captain hadn't given her more cooking or cleaning or laundry duty than the others. The jobs looked evenly distributed. At least she didn't have to deal with that particular stereotype.

What was with him anyway? Clearly, he didn't want her there, but he treated her like anyone else.

... *Except* for the stupid rules he had given her. She had to take care of that right away.

Tread lightly. Enjoy irritating him, but don't get him mad. I need this job.

"Zane, I'll take watch if you want to cook tonight," Gemma said.

"Again?" He didn't look up, focused on the communicator again. "Didn't you just get off watch duty? Like, five minutes ago?"

"Maybe I like it." It wasn't so bad with music.

"It's fine with me. I like cooking; I get to sample everything."

She had seen Zane eat and categorized him as a black hole to food. Gemma had maybe six inches on him in height, but she bet he'd shoot up another foot.

"Where are you going?" Zane asked when she turned away.

A mischievous smile spread across her face. "I'm going to loiter in the hallway."

5

"Zane?" Trevor's eyebrows raised as he entered the galley. Trevor had his perpetual hunger under wraps that afternoon, but the smell of garlic, onion, and meat made his stomach rumble. "What are you doing here? I thought it was the pilot's turn to cook."

"You're looking for Gemma?" Zane asked, licking his fingers.

"No." *Why would I look for her? I have nothing to say to her. I really should be* avoiding *her.*

Trevor opened the cooler and grabbed a soda he hadn't planned on taking. "Wash your hands."

Zane wiped his hands on his shirt. "Then why are you here?"

Trevor pointed to the sink. "Wash. With soap."

"Okay, okay." Zane dutifully washed his hands, splashing more water than necessary, and then flinging water droplets at Trevor's face as he shook them dry.

Trevor smiled. "I guess I don't need a shower now."

"Oh no," Zane said. "Believe me. You need a shower." He

turned back to the stove where he had two pots and a pan simmering.

After Trevor picked the kid up off the street and brought him onboard, Zane had absorbed the knowledge of his two favorite subjects as if he'd breathed them in: food and electronics.

Trevor watched him work, leaning against the counter as he sipped his drink. "What do you think of the new pilot?"

"She's nice. And pretty," Zane said. "And she smells good."

A pause. "She smells good," Trevor repeated, taking a sip of his soda to give him time to process that. "Why are you smelling her?"

"Stand close to her," Zane said, not looking up from his work, but smiling despite himself. "You'll see."

"Don't let her distract you, Zane," Trevor warned. He knew this could happen. A girl was such a bad idea.

Zane rolled his eyes. "She's not going to distract me. *You're* distracting me right now."

"Right." Trevor cleared his throat. "Carry on, then."

"Captain?" Zane said as Trevor turned to leave. "What do *you* think of the new pilot?"

Trevor's brain stuttered. "She's adequate at her job." He desperately tried to keep a straight face and his mind blank. *Do not think about her.*

"No." Zane shook his head. "What do you think of *her*?"

"I don't know her," Trevor snapped, turning and walking out. He never intended to get to know her, either.

A few weeks. That's all he had to do, get by for a few weeks and she'd be off his ship. She wasn't cute, she wasn't nice, she didn't smell good, and she was just the pilot. Keep it professional.

After a few days, Gemma still hadn't encountered the captain in the hallway, but she understood him better in regards to watch duty. The view of nothing but stars got old. Even though the ship screamed along at an astounding speed, the glowing pinpricks of light seemed to drift by. She read a little of the books in the ship's media library, but spent most of her time on watch duty with the volume cranked, dancing around the bridge.

Chase relieved her that evening—she'd only been able to get a handful of words out of him so far—and she went to stand in the hallway outside the common room, as she had done every spare minute of the past few days, after doing morning chores and whenever she wasn't on watch duty. She sat in her usual spot, back against the wall, and woke the screen on her tablet.

"What are you doing?"

She looked up from a match-three game, a little disappointed to see Dr. Charlie instead of Captain Lee.

"Loitering in the hall," she said casually, silently begging him to ask why.

He glanced around. "Uh, why?"

Before she could answer, sweet success rounded the corner. The captain stopped, the way to the common room effectively blocked by Gemma and Charlie.

"What's going on?" he asked.

Charlie cleared his throat. "She's 'loitering' in the hall?"

Gemma worked to keep her smile innocent as she stood, clasping her hands behind her back. This was all the more satisfying with Charlie as audience. "Is there a problem, Captain?"

The captain's eyebrows lowered. "I specifically told you *not* to loiter in the hallways."

"Oh, it must have slipped my mind." With her sweet smile in place, she tilted her head as if confused, her voice dripping with sugar, spice, and everything nice.

"So, this is your doing?" Charlie said to the captain, pointing at her.

"No! I told her *not*—"

"Uh-huh." With a slight shake of his head, Charlie dropped a hand onto the captain's shoulder and steered him away. "Let's talk, Captain. Gemma, get out of the hallway and into the common room."

She saluted, unable to stop her smile from widening. "Yes, sir!"

Gemma skipped into the common room, coughing to hide a giggle. *One rule down, two to go.* Not enough to get in trouble, just get under his skin a little. The way his ears turned pink had been cu—

Let's stop that thought right there.

The common room's couch in the middle of the entertainment area faced a large screen mounted on the wall, flanked by two recliners. Gemma dropped onto one end of the couch, Joe already at the other end, his hands clasped over his wide belly, eyes closed. Zane tinkered with some gadget on the rug.

"What's so funny?" Zane asked.

"Nothing." She tried to straighten out her smile. Charlie knowing about the captain's stupid rule satisfied her enough. It wouldn't be right to badmouth the captain to his crew.

She booted up the common room's entertainment system and scrolled through the catalog.

"OMG, you have *The Blue*! This is my favorite game!" She

selected it, and the main menu came up. She hadn't played *The Blue* since she'd been accepted to flight school. After a grueling year at flight school and another year of hopeless unemployment, she needed a reset. "I see you unlocked all the worlds."

"Yeah, it's Captain's favorite," Zane said. He nudged Joe's foot. "Don't go to sleep. You snore."

Joe shifted. "I'm just resting my eyes."

The captain's favorite, huh? Let's see how he likes this.

"Do you like to play?" she asked Zane.

"Yeah. I like the level with the asteroids," he said without looking up from his tinkering. "And the helicopter one, too."

"Those are some good ones." Of course, *The Blue* didn't have any bad ones. Dad made sure of that. Down to the smallest detail.

Gemma chose an earth-bound level, starting with a tiny, thumb-sized girl. She navigated her character around the screen, eating and collecting supplies until she could build wings.

Within a few minutes she'd customized her wooden wings and hopped into the air. She upgraded her materials as she collected items throughout the level, while avoiding hungry birds and bats.

"Whoa, you're good!" Zane leaned toward the screen, the gadget forgotten on the floor.

Higher and higher she flew, until she'd collected enough clouds to create the final form of her wings. Next level: messenger of cloud city.

Zane watched her play for a solid hour. She smoked the level, then saved her game to her new profile.

"Wow, this brings back so many memories." She smiled, staring out into nothing as she sunk into them. Hours spent with her dad on the computer and those elaborate diagrams he used in planning. Sandy sitting in the same room as them, drawing pictures of flowers. Mom bringing in brownies for everyone, and always a cup of coffee for Dad.

Zane jumped to his feet, snapping her back. "Joe! She didn't even die once, Joe! Did ya see?"

Joe chuckled, lifting his hat. "I saw, I saw."

"And in record time too. And that hidden level in the caves? I've never seen that one before!"

His hands clapped to the sides of his head. "Holy cow! You beat the captain's score! He's gonna be mad at you." Zane chuckled. "I beat his score last year, and he did almost nothing but play until he topped it."

Did he, now? "He won't be able to beat this one." Gemma crossed her arms with a smug smile. "I just played a perfect game."

"What?" said a voice behind them.

The three of them turned to see Captain Lee standing behind the couch, his mouth open. "How did you do that?"

"Oh. Uh, hi, Captain." Zane winced.

Captain Lee's arms hung limp by his sides, his shoulders hunched, those blue eyes so wide and defeated as he stared at the screen.

She dropped her smile. *I didn't mean to …* "Don't feel too bad. I've been playing this game since I was six."

"Wait." Zane did some silent counting on his fingers. "But it hasn't been out that long."

"My dad designed it," she said.

"What?!" Now Zane stared at her. "Your dad made *The Blue*? Holy cow! It's, like, the most popular game ever!"

Gemma chuckled. "'Ever' is a bit of an exaggeration. It had a good run when it came out." She switched off the controller. "He tested all the prototypes on me. It was his last project before he …" Her throat constricted, and she had a hard time swallowing.

"What's he making now?" Zane asked, bouncing from foot to foot.

"He's … retired." Gemma forced a smile. Even though a few years had dulled the pain, it never really stopped.

"That's too bad," Zane said. "I wanted to volunteer to test drive the next one."

The captain cleared his throat. "Good game, Pilot. I guess I'll have to find something else to play."

Gemma smiled for real this time. She thought blasting those levels would irritate him, so this was a pleasant surprise; he was a good sport about it. "You can call me Gemma, you know."

He gave her a tight smile, one corner a little higher than the other, his blue eyes flashing. "I know."

Gemma's eyes narrowed. *Challenge accepted, Captain. Challenge accepted.*

A chime signaled lights-out in ten, and the group dispersed.

TREVOR HAD ORIGINALLY GONE TO FIND THE PILOT TO LIFT THE OTHER rules he had given her, after Charlie had pointed out how petty they were.

They weren't really petty, as Trevor had designed them to protect the rest of the crew. Charlie hadn't seen it that way.

When Trevor saw her score on *The Blue*, all other thoughts evaporated. *Dang.* He had competition. Zane played a good game, but nowhere near Trevor's level.

The Blue was his favorite game of all time. And, it seemed like … he actually looked forward to competing with the girl.

"Gemma!" Sandy's voice squealed in the video message. Gemma couldn't help but smile at her sister's dimples. *"I was so happy to get your message!"*

Sandy's face changed into an appropriately indignant expression as she continued, *"Your captain sounds like a jerk! I'm so sorry you're stuck in that tin can with him. At least the rest of the crew sounds reasonable. Hang in there, Gem, you'll show him."*

Gemma smiled. Sandy always knew what to say.

"So, tell me more about everyone! Anyone cute?" Sandy winked.

Gemma rolled her eyes. *Almost* always knew what to say.

Someone found a deck of cards, so the next night after dinner the five of them, minus the captain and Chase, played spades around the table in the common room

"How long have you known the captain?" Gemma asked Charlie.

"Let's see." The old doctor stroked his chin. "Maybe seventeen years? He was just a tyke when I met him, his dad the mechanic on our ship. Where he went, the captain went."

"You've been with him this whole time?" Gemma played a card. "Is it weird to take orders from someone you knew as a baby?"

Charlie threw his head back in a long, deep laugh. "He's

grown up since then, so I don't have a problem with it. But, no, I haven't been with him the whole time. After a couple of years, my marriage hit the rocks. I took time off from space work to reconnect with my family. After my children moved out of the house and my wife passed, I came back to work for him. Joe's been working under him longer."

"Only by a year," Joe said. The engineer took a sip of his beer. He seemed to have smuggled more than 'just a couple' aboard. "I knew the captain when he was a navigator. Stayed on with him when he was promoted to captain and given this ship."

"How long ago was that?"

"Almost three years."

"I've been here two years," Zane said, playing a spade. He took the trick and led with another ace.

Dak snorted. "What were you, eight when you joined?"

Zane crossed his arms and raised his chin. "Eleven." He jerked his thumb at Dak and said to Gemma, "Dak has been here only a few months. Our last mission was his first with us."

"Almost as new as you," Dak said, giving her a nudge and a charming smile. "Though, to be honest, my skills are highly sought after. I have some pretty impressive scores myself when it comes to navigating. No offense, but I also have quite a bit of experience."

She made an effort not to roll her eyes.

"Zane, are you cheating again?" Joe said, eyes narrowed.

Zane's face blanked. "No."

Joe reached out tand slapped him in the back of the head. "Stop cheating. Re-deal."

"Where's the captain from?" Gemma asked.

Joe shrugged. "No idea."

Charlie was very interested in the cards in his hand, not meeting her eyes.

"He said he's been in space all his life," she persisted. "But that must be an exaggeration, right? He must be from somewhere. Charlie?"

He shook his head. "I'm not talking about this."

Gemma arched an eyebrow, but let him be. "What about Chase?" Tight-lipped security officer Chase didn't spend much time in the common room with them, even during his off-duty time.

"Maybe three years? Right after the captain became captain." Zane shrugged as Joe shuffled and dealt.

"What happened to the last pilot?" she asked, studying her cards.

Gemma looked up at the sudden silence. Now everyone was very interested in their cards.

"Gee, you're full of questions," Dak muttered, his smile gone.

Gemma's eyebrows rose. "Did something happen?"

"It was a heart attack," Charlie said, but he didn't meet her eyes. "Never saw it coming."

Zane's head snapped up, but he looked down at his cards again, not saying anything. Maybe she could worm some information out of Zane, if she could get him alone.

"Ooookay then. What kinds of other missions do you guys go on?" she asked.

She could feel the general sigh of relief. Zane leaned toward her. "Last year, I'm pretty sure we transported a spy."

Gemma tilted her cards away so he wouldn't be tempted to look at them. "Really?"

"You don't know that," Joe said.

"Mostly cargo for Omni Authority," Charlie said. "Sometimes we're hired for a private job."

Gemma's brow wrinkled. "But isn't this an Omni Authority ship? How can you do private jobs?"

"Well, yes, Omni Authority made him a captain and gave him a ship," Joe explained. "But some captains outright buy the ship they've been given, so it's really theirs. And that's what Captain Lee did."

Gemma gaped. "How could he afford that? Is a captain really paid that much?"

"Think about it," Charlie said, "Captain Lee has been working his whole life in space, and not spending any of his paycheck. So, he had quite a bit saved up."

She whistled. "So, he can do whatever he wants with it?"

"Pretty much." Joe played a card. "But he's a cargo captain all the way. You'll never see him in charge of a luxury cruiser." He chuckled, readjusting his cap. "He wants to deal with as few people as possible."

That sounded about right. Captain Lee seemed pretty stern, and not terribly interested in being buddy-buddy with anyone. The only one he really talked to was Charlie.

"What kind of cargo?" Gemma asked.

Zane shrugged. "Usually we don't know."

Gemma stared. "You don't? Aren't you tempted to look?"

Joe shook his head. "Never look in the box. That's rule number ... er ... three. Maybe four. It's mostly classified. What the cargo is, is Chase's area. And the captain's. Knowing more than we need to can get us into trouble. We're just here to keep the ship running."

"And the crew," added Charlie.

Gemma considered her cards, then laid one down. "What's Chase's deal?"

"Oh, he always wanted to be an explorer," Zane said. "So, he signed on with Omni Authority right out of school."

"Really?" said Joe. "He told me he's doing it to support his daughter."

"I wasn't aware he had children," Charlie said slowly. "He

told me he went to space to escape the guilt of his best friend's death."

Everyone looked at Dak.

He shrugged. "He said it was his duty to protect Earth."

Gemma laughed hard as she took the trick. "He's quite the mystery."

"Apparently so," Charlie said, chuckling.

"What about you, Dak?" Gemma asked. "What brought you to space navigation?"

Dak groaned, pressing a hand to his forehead. "An ex-wife and two kids. I'm good with math and mapping, and had to make money to pay that alimony every month."

Joe smacked the back of Zane's head. "Zane! I saw that! Re-deal."

Zane's communicator chirped, the captain's voice come across. "Zane to bridge. It seems we have an electrical short in a sensor. I need you to check it out."

Zane slapped the communicator against his chest. "On my way, Captain." His chair scraped as he stood and threw his cards on the table.

"You *were* cheating!" Gemma laughed.

Zane's face pinked. "I cannot confirm nor deny." He left the room.

"He must have to keep busy," Gemma said. "This ship is pretty old."

"Watch your mouth," Joe said. "It's not nice to speak so about a lovely lady. We gave the girl a complete makeover when the captain got her. Overhauled the whole system. She doesn't keep us any busier than a ship half her age."

Gemma bit her lip to stop her smile. "I take it back. I didn't mean to offend such a reliable ship."

"Don't you forget it," Joe said, stroking the bolted table as if soothing the *Michal*. "Don't listen to her, girl," Joe murmured. "You're a beauty."

Charlie chuckled, Joe shooting him a glare.

"Uh huh ..." Dak laid down his cards. "On that note, I'm going to head out." He winced. "I forgot to finish my cleaning assignment today."

The game broke up, each going their own way as Gemma settled on the couch and booted up the entertainment system.

6

Trevor walked along the hall, hardly looking up from his tablet as he knew the way to the bridge by heart. The coordinates on the map looked right, but the numbers were off, for some reason …

The sound of another set of footsteps gave him warning of the pilot approaching as well.

He and the pilot arrived at the bottom of the bridge's ladder at the same time and stopped. They stood there, neither making a move to climb.

Trevor forced himself to meet her hard gaze. *What is she waiting for?* Why wasn't she going up? Was this supposed to be some battle of wills, who would blink first?

"Pilot," he said stiffly.

"Captain." She crossed her arms, her chin out. "What are you doing here?"

Um, it's my ship? "Dak called me with a navigation question." Trevor had forgotten he'd scheduled her for watch duty. He gestured up the ladder. "You can go first."

"No, you go first," she snapped, her eyes hard.

Trevor's eyebrows lowered. After the talking-to Charlie gave him about his rules for Gemma, Trevor was trying to be nice. *Why does she keep making things more difficult?*

"Just get up there," he said through gritted teeth.

She opened her mouth, then closed it and climbed the ladder.

DAK AND THE CAPTAIN HAD LEFT HER ALONE ON THE BRIDGE AFTER only a fifteen-minute discussion; now it was time to rock out. No one would check on her for another few hours.

The bridge didn't have a lot of space, but Gemma still managed to dance in it, singing along to her favorite songs at the top of her lungs. The only time she used her music player instead of the ship's library was at the fitness center or in her room, and only then because she liked it so loud that people in the adjacent rooms would hear it. Up here on the bridge was perfectly safe.

A tap on her shoulder.

She screamed and lost her balance, tripping over a chair. A large hand caught her arm and righted her, before reaching past her and tapping the pause button.

She spun around, her heart hammering in her chest. "Captain! I'm sorry, I didn't hear you." The guy had lightning reflexes.

"Clearly." The corner of the captain's mouth twitched upwards. Had that almost been a smile?

She refused to be embarrassed, and met his eyes, even as her cheeks warmed. "Can I help you with something?"

"Forgot my tablet." He pointed behind her.

"You forget that thing a lot, don't you?" she said, clasping her hands behind her back. Her face grew hotter despite her attempts at casualness.

His eyebrows rose. "It's harder to find when someone takes it."

Gemma struggled not to bite her lip. The heat got worse. "Someone took your tablet? Shame on them."

"It's just a suspicion." He pointed behind her again. "May I?"

"Right. Tablet." Gemma spun and grabbed the tablet and handed it to him. "There you go."

"Thanks. Might I suggest lowering the volume? You need to be able to hear any alarms or intercom messages. Not to mention the damage to your hearing." Both corners of his mouth lifted. "And mine. Charlie will have a fit."

Gemma stared at him. Was that a joke? He smiled when he said it. Did the captain just say something almost funny?

She lowered her gaze to her shoes, not sure how to take it. "Heh. Right."

He waved the tablet at her. "Carry on." He slid back down the ladder.

She slumped in the chair, hand covering her face. *I looked like a total idiot.*

TREVOR LEANED HIS FOREHEAD AGAINST THE COLD METAL WALL OF THE hallway. The girl was completely tone-deaf, but that didn't stop the scene that greeted him on the bridge from being ... mesmerizing.

The deafening music reached his ears from three decks away. He stomped up there to shut her down.

He'd frozen at the top of the ladder to the bridge. The way she danced, fast and smooth, her face alight with joy, made him smile.

He groaned. An ace pilot, a gamer, a dancer ...

Also, spitefully disregards orders.

That's right. She might be an interesting and talented person, but clearly, she did not belong on his crew. She cranked up her music to reckless levels. She had stolen his tablet. She had yelled at him—her captain, and ...

And Zane was right. She did smell good.

"Hᵢ Sᴀɴᴅʏ. Mʏ ᴄʀᴇᴡ ɪs sᴏ ɢʀᴇᴀᴛ."

"I think Zane is my favorite. He's a brilliant electrician, despite being just thirteen. He's so enthusiastic about every-thing. But you've got to watch your stuff with Zane around. He's got sticky fingers for electronics. My music player went missing, and when I found it again, he'd tweaked the volume. The walls shook when I played it. Which, I admit, I kind of loved.

"Joe is the engineer. He reminds me a lot of Dad. Well, maybe a messier version of Dad. Dad didn't even change his own oil in the car, and Joe definitely has years of grease caked under his fingernails. He's always jerking Zane's chain, picking arguments with him. I don't think Joe believes half the stuff he says, he just takes whatever position is opposite of Zane's.

"Chase does security, and is a pretty mysterious guy, keeps to himself. No one seems to really know much about him.

"If anyone is cute, it'd be Dak. He always looks like he stepped out of a magazine, but he's got a lot of baggage I'm *really* not interested in—including an ex and kids.

"Charlie, our doctor, is another favorite. He loves to laugh. And read. Whenever I'm near sickbay, I stop in, and he's always reading. He wears glasses when he reads. When I asked him about it, he said he'd never trust another doctor to do surgery on his eyes. Despite being a doctor himself, he's pretty critical of the medical profession.

"The captain ... There's not much to say about him. I know him about as well as Chase. The man won't even use my name, just calls me 'Pilot.'" Gemma winced. She would take the dancing-on-the-bridge episode to her grave.

"I miss you. I look forward to hearing back from you! Any wedding planning going on? How's David? How's work?"

Gemma stopped her recording, a wave of homesickness choking her. She didn't want to be alone. She'd already finished laundry duty that day.

She sent her message and went to the common room, hoping someone else would be there, although it was between meals.

Captain Lee leaned back in a recliner with his tablet and that little notebook again, his feet propped up. The plate beside him held a half-eaten sandwich. He looked up when she entered.

"Pilot," he acknowledged.

"Captain." Gemma hesitated. He was the last person she wanted to see, much less spend time with him, with his stupid rules and his disrespect of her gender. In that moment, though, his eyes didn't feel quite so stern, his shoulders and jaw relaxed.

She glanced around the room and even craned her neck to look through the open galley door. He was the only one here.

This might be a chance to get to know him. Maybe even change his mind about me.

So, she plopped down on the end of the couch nearest him.

He jumped to his feet like she was contagious. "I'll get out of your way."

"No, no, you don't need to do that," she said, unable to say what she really wanted to. *I'm sorry for being so irritating. Please don't leave me alone.*

Maybe he could read it in her eyes, because he didn't leave. He stood there, glancing between her and the door, running his hands around the edges of the tablet.

David had looked like that when she had first met him, unsure and ... nervous. Sandy had been so excited to introduce her new boyfriend to Gemma, but introvert David froze.

Gemma smiled. She had given him *such* a hard time. But, hey, someone had to make sure Sandy didn't date an idiot.

Sandy. Another wave of homesickness crashed over her, dousing her smile. She hadn't cried yet, and she didn't intend to now, but she needed a distraction.

The captain stared at her openly, head cocked to one side. "Are you okay?"

"I'm fine." Gemma forced a smile and gestured to the entertainment system. "Want to play a game?"

A slow smile spread across the captain's face. "I don't know. Are you a sore loser?"

She blinked. His smile lit up his face, his blue eyes full of humor. She hadn't seen that before.

"I can take it." She responded with her own genuine smile. "Can you?" He didn't stand a chance.

"What do you want to play?" Captain Lee powered up the system and took the couch seat next to her.

"How about a racing level in *The Blue*?"

The captain gave her a suspicious look, his eyes narrowing

and his smile lifting more on one side. "Why do I get the feeling you'd have the advantage there?"

He was absolutely right. She raised her eyebrows. "What, are you afraid of a challenge?"

"Racing it is. What level do you want?"

"How about cloud sailing?"

"Fine with me."

The captain already had his ship's design saved in the system, but Gemma took a few minutes to build her own.

He snorted. "There's no way you can win with that. You wasted all your money on speed."

He thought he knew it all, didn't he? "Increased handling would slow me down."

The captain shook his head. "It's too touchy, you're going to be bouncing all over the place. And you don't have enough firepower."

Gemma smirked. "As fast as I'll be going, I won't need firepower."

"But your shield is minimal."

"Watch and learn, Captain."

He smirked, elbows on his knees as he hunched forward, gaze locked on the screen.

The flag dropped, and Gemma took off like a rocket. The captain couldn't keep up. As predicted, he never got close enough to fire off a shot.

She looked over and gave him a smile as she crossed the finish line. "You were saying?"

Without a word, he went back and tweaked his design, muttering to himself. Just then, he looked ... so normal. Not like a scary ship's captain with a stern voice and hard eyes, jaw tight. But like a—how old was he? Twenty? Twenty-one? Like twenty-one-year-old guy playing video games.

Gemma smiled to herself. She liked this version of him better.

She beat him the second round, but the third went to Captain Lee.

"Go faster!" he yelled at the screen on their eighth round.

"Not this time!" She rammed her ship into his, knocking him off the track. Again.

He threw up his hands. "Will you stop that?"

"All's fair in love and racing." She laughed as she won again.

The captain held up a finger, his face serious. "One more." He'd said that the last three races.

A laugh behind them. "I'd bet on her."

They both jumped and turned. Charlie leaned against the door frame, nursing a cup of coffee.

"Uh." Captain Lee stood, the controller clattering to the floor. His face hardened again as he slipped back into captain mode. "I should go."

"You don't want a rematch?" Gemma asked, her face falling. She'd never had anyone come close to beating her before. It had been fun.

"Maybe later." He picked up his tablet and the rest of his sandwich, then strode from the room.

Gemma frowned, wishing he would stay. "Is he okay?"

Charlie shrugged. "Probably embarrassed he's getting beaten by a woman." He paused. "Or that he's getting along with one. He threw quite a fit when you were assigned to us."

She winced, then held up the controller. "Want to play a game?"

Charlie shook his head. "Oh, no. I don't play those silly games."

"Right." She tossed the controller aside. Playing didn't seem so appealing now that she was alone.

TREVOR COULDN'T PACE HIS TINY ROOM. HE COULDN'T THINK. HE could hardly move in there, but with Gemma still in the common area, he couldn't think in there either.

He stalked the hallways, hands shoved in his pockets, looking at the floor as he tried to sort through his thoughts.

When they'd first left Earth, he couldn't stand her. But now, for some reason, she looked so ... cute.

She didn't wear makeup, and had her long, blonde hair pulled back in a simple ponytail. He cringed for her. That uniform fit was really awkward. Yet, he'd found himself fighting the urge to stare at her during their races.

Trevor clapped a hand to his forehead. This was so, so bad.

It had just been a game. No big deal.

Charlie's appearance had reminded him: don't get attached. Don't get too close. Not to *anyone*, much less a girl.

He swallowed hard. Not to anyone. It had always been this way, especially since Dad died. Why was this any different?

Why did it feel different?

"DEAR GEM,"

"Your crew sounds fantastic! I was worried you'd get stuck with ... well, I was worried."

"Maybe you should give Dak a chance. No one has ever been good enough since Alex left. You're always looking for flaws. But

that was three years ago. You were so young to be so serious. You were children. It's time to move on, don't you think?

"Anyways, wedding planning is going so great. I know we were supposed to go dress shopping together, but I found the perfect dress!" Sandy held up a white gown against her body. *"Ta da! What do you think? Do you like it? You hate it, don't you? Say the word and I'll return it. And, I promise, no bridesmaid dress shopping without you."*

Gemma chuckled, surprised at the ache in her chest. Although she hadn't had much to do yet, she loved being in space, and looked forward to doing some interesting flying.

They'd never been so far apart before. She never thought she'd ever want to go dress shopping—but right now she'd do anything, so long as she was doing it with her sister.

And the dress really was gorgeous.

"David's good. Never runs out of business. Mine has been a little slow, but handmade cards and paintings aren't so popular these days. People want the cheap printed ones.

"Don't let Captain Jerk get you down.

"Love you!"

Gemma cued up the video immediately to send a reply.

"Sandy!

"I love that dress! Put it on, I want to see."

Gemma pointed at the screen; her face serious. "I don't care how slow business might be, *never* stop doing what you love. You should be happy. I want you to be happy. Mom and Dad would have wanted it, too. I know you're not a quitter, but I wanted to remind you of that."

She smiled. "I had to wait a year after flight school to get my dream job. And it happened. Even—" She glanced away from the screen, her cheeks warm. "Okay, maybe I was a little bit critical of the captain. We played a video game together. It was Dad's game. I guess the captain's not the stick-in-the-mud I thought he was. It's nice to know he can act like a normal person. It was really fun.

"You know, most girls would say Dak's better looking than the captain ... but, so far, I like the captain better."

Gemma choked, her face flaming.

"Not *like* him. I meant—I don't even know him."

"WE'VE REACHED THE FIRST JUMP-POINT," CAPTAIN LEE'S VOICE SAID over the ship's intercom. "Everyone to their stations."

Dak and the captain waited for Gemma as she climbed the ladder onto the bridge. She looked out the bubbled window. Although invisible to the eye, the sensors showed the blue field directly in front of them, the depression of exotic matter that allowed passage between two points in space.

Gemma slid into her seat and retracted the solar sails. The captain turned on the ship's intercom to keep everyone apprised of their status.

"Preparing to enter jump-space," he said.

Years ago, scientists discovered how to establish wormholes using depressions of exotic matter. This significantly cut down distances in space travel, and they called the throat, or interior of the wormholes, jump-space.

Out of the corner of her eye, she watched Captain Lee, but he didn't seem to be paying any attention to her.

"Calculating our route," Dak said. The shifting nature of the depression made timing critical. Once the wormhole was established, they could safely travel jump-space between the two ends of it. Getting *into* the wormhole was the tricky part.

"Everyone, strap down," Captain Lee ordered through the ship's com.

Dak counted down from ten.

Gemma gripped the control column with one hand, the other snapping up a small cover and resting her thumb on the switch. Her first jump on her first mission.

"Three, two, one—"

Gemma propelled the ship into the field, flipping the switch at the same time.

The ship shuddered. Gemma squinted against the sudden white surrounding the ship. They'd be traveling through the whiteout for the next few days.

In jump-space, a ship could only travel a few days to a week. Any longer would deplete their fuel too much. With no solar to power their sails in the wormhole, even their ultra-efficient engines would be hard-pressed to continue beyond that.

"We've entered jump-space," Dak said. "We'll be in here for three days." The longer they flew in jump-space, the farther they went. He gave her a thumbs up. "Good job, Gemma. I hardly felt that."

"Good work, everyone," the captain said, then flipped off the intercom. "Especially you, Pilot. That was one of the smoothest transitions I've ever been through."

Gemma gasped, her hand going to her heart, and said in a high voice, "Me? A female? Could I possibly be as good as they say I am?"

To her satisfaction, the corner of the captain's mouth twitched. "Don't push it. You're dismissed. See you at dinner."

"I switched with Joe," she said, her voice back to normal but a proud smile still on her face. "I'll be on watch duty."

His eyebrows went up. "You really don't want to cook, do you?"

"Not really." She bit her lip, her face warming. Never in her life had she been embarrassed not to be able to cook—until now.

"I'll have Chase bring you up a plate." The captain disappeared down the ladder.

CHASE RELIEVED GEMMA OF WATCH DUTY LATER THAT EVENING.

She could hear the raised voices as she passed the common room, the shouted words unintelligible until she leaned inside.

"Just because you've never seen one, doesn't mean they don't exist!" On his feet in front of the screen mounted on the wall, Zane's hands balled into fists as the lights on the screen flashed and moved behind him. Gemma had never seen him so worked up, his teeth bared and his thin limbs shaking.

Joe lounged on a recliner, feet propped up. Dak sat on the couch, leaning far to the side to see around Zane as his thumbs mashed buttons on the controller. The captain sat writing at the table.

"All I'm sayin,'" Joe said, lifting his cap and scratching his head, "is we've been all over this galaxy and never once—not once—have we found any evidence of aliens."

"The galaxy is a big place. We haven't been all over it. Look at all the M-class planets we've found," Zane said. "Don't you think there's bound to be intelligent life on one of them? Gemma, what do you think?"

"What?" She still stood in the doorway. "What am I walking into the middle of?"

Zane pointed at Joe. "He doesn't think aliens exist."

"Because they don't," Joe said with a smug smile and a glint in his eye she hadn't seen before.

"They argue about it all the time," Dak said, not looking away from the sliver of screen he could see. "Best to stay out of it."

She glanced at Zane and could see the appeal to getting him riled up—his red face and serious expression was kind of hilarious. But it also wasn't very nice.

"What do you think?" Zane asked again, his eyes pleading.

Gemma bit her lip. "I would love to meet an alien. Always wanted to. Although, so far, the only intelligent life in the galaxy is from Earth, but I think they *could* be out there. Somewhere."

Joe snorted. "Next you'll be telling me you believe in Tubies."

Gemma frowned, leaning against the doorframe, arms crossed. "Aren't Tubies kind of fact?" She remembered when the first news reports about them came in during a math test at school. She hadn't done well on the test, after that.

"Yeah," Zane said. "They even teach about them in school."

"You've never been to school," Joe said.

"I went to the first couple of grades."

"I bet they didn't talk about Tubies though," Joe muttered.

"But the live TV coverage," Gemma persisted. "The labs, the arrests, the 'We interrupt this program with breaking news.' Don't you remember that?"

The news labeled it a major catastrophe, and it had turned into a generational-defining event. Countries and colonies demanded information and hurled threats, trying to discover the power responsible for creating the perfect army. It wasn't until Omni Authority swooped in to save the day that life got back to normal. With the project dismantled, the whole galaxy sighed in relief.

"All a hoax," Joe said. "Genetically engineered super soldiers grown in tubes? Give me a break."

"I'm not sure about that—" Gemma started.

"But it was Director Hart who spearheaded Operation Purification, when Omni Authority wiped out the illegal super soldier program," Zane said. "That's how he got his position as head of the space program."

Joe raised an eyebrow. "*Spearheaded?* You sound like a news report."

Zane crossed his arms. "I like to be well-informed. What do you think, Dak?"

"I think the experiments were a twisted crime against nature," Dak spat, surprising Gemma with his vehemence. His eyes never left the partially-blocked screen, but his button-mashing came faster and harder. Gemma worried about the controller.

"If you ask me," he continued, "destroying all those monsters was the best choice a government has ever made. The thought of them makes me sick."

Gemma didn't get a chance to ask why he assumed that a clone was automatically a monster.

"I believe Omni Authority was covering up something big," Joe unknowingly interrupted. "Something more likely and more incriminating than a handful of scientists making Tubies."

"There were more than a handful—" Zane started.

"What do you think they were covering up?" Gemma asked, taking a seat next to Dak on the couch. Having said his piece, Mr. Perfect Hair tried his very hardest to ignore them and play his game, although Zane still stood in front of the screen.

Joe's eyes flashed, and he levered himself upright, dropping his feet to the floor. "Prison camps."

Gemma shook her head. "Those camps are illegal now." And not nearly as newsworthy. Why cover up something practically mundane with something that threatened to turn into a galaxy-wide war? "Omni Authority would never—"

"Omni Authority is not all peaches and cream," Joe said. "It has a dark side. Eventually, the truth will come out."

Zane rolled his eyes. "I can't believe you."

"Captain, what do you—" But when Gemma turned to look, no one sat at the table.

7

Three days passed and they left jump-space, once again surrounded by black space and stars. Gemma smiled. She preferred the stars to the white-out.

After the jump, the captain unbuckled his harness. "Good work, everyone. We'll arrive at the refueling port late tomorrow morning."

He turned off the intercom and looked at her. "Pilot, I expect you on the bridge by nine in the morning."

"Aye-aye, Captain."

The captain always gave her a weird look when she said that, but that's what made it so funny.

Dak left the bridge, and Gemma fiddled with the controls for a minute after extending the sails. She'd have to talk to Joe, there had been the slightest delay when she'd pushed the left thruster—

She sensed the captain standing beside her and looked up. Way, way up.

He didn't look at her or say anything for a moment.

"How are you adjusting?" he asked. "To space travel?"

Gemma smiled. "It's going great, I love it."

He nodded. "Good." He turned to the navigation console.

Frowning, Gemma sat there for another minute. That's all he wanted to say? He very purposely walked over and stood by her chair to ask how she was doing?

Her face warmed for some reason. *Why?*

She refused to look back at him when she flipped on the autopilot and went to her room. A message from Sandy waited for her.

Sandy spun in the dress. Gemma gasped at how it hugged and flared in all the right places. And how happy it made Sandy.

"I've got the flowers all picked out! David and I clashed on the cake and frosting a little, but I think we worked it out: funfetti cake with vanilla buttercream. I know, pretty basic." She grinned. *"But the frosting is going to be all the colors. You know how much I love color."*

Gemma smiled, her chin resting on her hand as she watched Sandy spin. Sandy didn't fool around when it came to color. She had painted the bedroom in her background in patterns of vibrant colors. Instead of clashing, somehow the patterns worked.

Gemma looked around her gray room with a sigh. Years ago, Sandy had painted Gemma's room at home with a dazzling, colorful galaxy pattern.

The current gray walls definitely dampened her mood. What if *she* painted her walls?

She chuckled. The captain probably wouldn't appreciate it.

Sandy sat close to the camera again, her glowing face filling the screen. *"Okay, so the captain is nice now? That's a good thing. Is he cute?"*

Gemma rolled her eyes.

Someone knocked at the door.

"Who is it?" Gemma called, hurrying to close the message. *What kind of question was that, Sandy? Cute?*

"It's Zane. I've got something to show you!"

Zane came into her room carrying a bag with at least a dozen pockets.

Gemma smiled to herself. *Rule no-one-allowed-in-my-room, check.*

He set it on the bed and beamed at her. "I made you a present."

Out of the front pocket he pulled a softball-sized sphere. "Watch this."

He pressed a button, and the sphere blossomed like a flower, the face of a clock glowing above the open bloom.

She gasped. "Zane! It's beautiful!"

"Voice activated, too. Clock off."

The sphere closed.

"Does it have to be open to hear the time?" she asked.

"Nope! What time is it?"

"The time is ten-seventeen," Zane's voice chirped from the sphere.

Gemma pushed the open button again, admiring it. She resisted the urge to ruffle his hair. She'd figured out early on how much it annoyed him. "That's fantastic."

"Want to see what else I'm working on?" He dug through his bag. "This is an oxygenator I rebuilt." He handed her a heavy box.

"This one scrambles signals," a small tube with a clicker on the end came out, "and this is a voice changer."

He held the voice changer up to his mouth. A deep voice said, "How do ya like me now?"

A sudden, high-pitched squeal made him wince. "Still working on that one." It and the scrambler went on top of the heavy box in her arms.

Gemma laughed. She couldn't get enough of this kid.

He talked faster as he loaded more devices onto her. "This is a leak finder ... a camera ... I made my own battery; lasts a *lot* longer than anything on the market ... careful, this one is a custom stunner. I knocked myself out making that one." He wedged the stunner at the top of the pile under her chin. *Please don't let me get knocked out.*

"You built all of these?" Gemma said.

"Yup." Zane's green eyes sparkled like stars. "Most of them aren't very innovative, but they're fun to make. Oh, oh! Check out my lifeform scanner." He added another one to the stack.

"Can I put these down?" she asked, afraid she would drop the heavy pile.

"Oh! Sorry, yeah. Here, I'll take them." He dumped everything onto the bed and opened the scanner. "See this extra chip right here? It's a signal booster I designed. It triples the signal of whatever it's connected to. You can scan for lifeforms for fifty miles with this baby."

"That is amazing." Gemma poured all her enthusiasm into her smile, causing Zane's smile to widen into a grin. She held up the spherical clock. "Thank you for the gift."

He grinned at her. "Holy cow, it's great to make you smile."

His smile slipped and his eyes bugged after realizing what had come out of his mouth. Gemma bit her lip to keep from cringing, her own face heating up. Not the direction she wanted the conversation to go. Zane was just a kid.

"Zane, do you even know what a cow is?" she asked, trying to divert his attention.

He shrugged, not meeting her eyes. "I've seen pictures. But I heard someone say it once, and thought it was hilarious." He repacked his bag, his face still red. "If you ever want to borrow anything, let me know. You can use my camera for shore leave tomorrow."

"That would be great," she said. "Thank you. You're the best."

She held up the camera and snapped a picture of Zane's grinning face. "Here, let's get one together. Say cheese."

"Cows!" Zane said.

Gemma looked at the picture. "That turned out really good. This is good quality. And it's compatible with other devices?"

"Completely. You can upload your pictures over the wireless." He dug in his pockets until he came up with a cable. "Use this to charge it with."

Despite all her time spent in space, Gemma had never been off the ship anywhere that wasn't Earth.

She couldn't suppress her smile. *It's going to be amazing.*

Zane slid open the door and gave a wave before disappearing through it.

She couldn't bring herself to look directly at the computer camera, her face red. The thought had been rattling around in her head the entire day. "Sandy! He's my captain! I can't think of him as 'cute.'"

She let out a breath. No matter how Sandy badgered her, this closed the discussion for Gemma. Don't talk about it. Or even think about it. Ever.

"Look what Zane gave me." Gemma held up the clock and demonstrated how it worked. "Isn't it beautiful?

"Tomorrow is port. I can't wait. I'll message afterwards and tell you all about it."

AFTER RECEIVING CLEARANCE, THEY ENTERED THE ATMOSPHERE OF THE port planet. Gemma guided the ship to circle the platform, then pulled up and engaged the thrusters for a soft landing.

"Crew meeting in the common room," Captain Lee said into the intercom.

The fast slide down the ladder startled her. The planet's gravity tugged on her heavier than the ship's had.

Gemma took the seat at the table between Zane and Joe.

"We'll be here for eighteen hours," the captain said. "Be back on board well before then. You know the rules: no fights, no getting into trouble. No sticky fingers, Zane."

Zane raised his hands in defense. "Why are you picking on me?"

Joe chuckled.

"If anyone is arrested, you'll be left behind," the captain warned, looking at each face in turn.

"He always says that," Zane whispered to Gemma. "Hasn't left anyone behind yet."

Captain Lee gave Zane a glare. "Don't tempt me. If you *do* get into trouble, contact me immediately. Chase oversees refueling and resupplies. Any questions? ... Dismissed."

He stopped Gemma on the way out. "Pilot, you stay near the ship with Chase."

She blinked, her thoughts stuttering. "Wha ... why am I

staying with the ship?" she asked. "I can't help with refueling. I want to see the port."

"Just do as I say," Captain Lee said, and walked away before she could object more.

Her stomach bottomed out, leaving her hollow. Completely numb, Gemma slowly walked back to her room. When she opened the door, the camera Zane gave her gleamed on the bed.

That snapped her out of it. She clenched her teeth, slammed the door shut behind her, and flopped onto the bed. This wasn't fair! Her first time on an alien planet, and he'd confined her to the ship.

She snatched her pillow and screamed into it until she ran out of breath.

What did I do wrong? She hadn't yelled at him once since the first day, he didn't even know she'd broken the room rule, and she'd been doing her job well. Extremely well. Why was she being punished with staying on the ship?

No ... She sat up. He said stay *near* the ship. It would probably be okay to look around a little near the berth.

Gemma ignored the little voice whispering in the back of her mind and nodded to herself as her plan developed. She wouldn't wander far, and she wouldn't go alone.

Her smile restored, she snatched up the camera and ran out the door. Hopefully Zane hadn't left yet.

Her footsteps clanked on the ramp leading down to the landing pad. Ground crews lugged fuel lines to the ship while Chase supervised.

Gemma found Zane still standing outside the ship as he checked the wiring under an outside panel. She hesitated. Did Zane know about her orders to stay on—er—*near* the ship?

"Zane, where do you go at a port like this?" she asked, her

voice as sweet as she could make it without sounding like a baby.

He shrugged. "I dunno. I'm usually in the shops looking for parts. I've been here lots of times, but there's nowhere special."

She frowned. She had zero interest in shops. Shops she could find anywhere. Besides, the signing bonus they'd paid her for this mission she'd already vowed to give to Sandy for the wedding. Not that Sandy knew that, yet.

"Where do you think a tourist would want to go?" Gemma persisted. "Without going too far from the ship."

Zane tapped his chin, then snapped his fingers. "I know a place to eat."

"Great! Will you take me?"

He grinned. "Sure!" He replaced the panel, ratcheting it tight with a pneumatic drill.

The landing platform stood on pylons over a dense jungle. They shared a wide, concrete staircase with five other platforms. She followed Zane down to solid ground, hoping to see new plants and interesting creatures.

The stairs let them out onto a sidewalk, vehicles speeding by on the adjacent street. Gemma took a picture of the street full of honking taxis and buses whooshing by, which looked like any other city street on Earth. All asphalt ground, glass store fronts, concrete buildings with graffiti on them. They had cleared out the alien jungle to make way for the colony city and spaceport. The only real difference between here and an Earth city street was the stench of ship exhaust and the massive shadows cast by the raised platforms where vessels docked, blocking out the twin suns.

Gemma's lower lip stuck out in a pout. Humans came in and ruined everything. Major disappointment.

Ah ha! An exotic flower grew in a pot in front of a store. She zoomed in to take a picture. The purple, twisty stem had long, curved petals tilted towards the sunlight. Sandy would love that. Flowers were her favorite subject to watercolor.

"Stay close," Zane said. "This port can be a tough place. There's a lot of traffic going through here."

Other people bumped and jostled them, rushing to a nearby bus stop as a vehicle pulled up to it, its brakes squeaking. Gemma grabbed Zane's shoulder to stay with him. Most people around here wore space travel uniforms, but a fair number of black suits and briefcases hurried by.

She caught more than a few looks her way. Gemma swallowed hard, smoothing her hair into place in her ponytail. She hadn't checked it after her therapy session with the pillow.

No, that couldn't be it. People *really* looked at her. There were apparently a lot more men than women in this part of the spaceport.

"Why are people staring at me?" she whispered.

Zane shrugged. "Your uniform. They don't see many lady pilots. At least, I've never seen one. Except you, of course."

She should have guessed. It had been that way since she graduated. She'd even been accused of wearing a costume once.

Ignore them. "Have you really been arrested before?" It sounded like something Zane would do.

He grinned. "Once or twice. Captain bailed me out though."

They waited at a traffic light, then weaved through the crowd to a bar with a neon sign above it saying *The Watering Hole.* She looked back to see the nose of the ship jutting out over the edge of the landing platform. Near *the ship, check.*

Zane held the door as she stepped into the dingy interior.

The crowd made the small space feel crushing. Gemma coughed in the smoky air. Signed photos and scrawled messages covered the walls. On a stage, a scantily-clad girl framed by fraying curtains sang, her music lost in the clamor of the bar. The waitresses all wore the bare minimum, carrying loaded trays high above their heads. Gemma was the most-dressed girl in the room.

"Hey, I see an open table." Zane pointed, almost yelling over the scraping of stools and a loud sports game playing on the screen in the corner. When a ball went in the net, the patrons nearest the screen leapt to their feet cheering, spilling their drinks on the table.

The white wall of noise from conversations, laughter, and arguments surrounded her, making her feel more claustrophobic than the press of bodies did as she followed Zane. She breathed through her mouth to try to avoid the smell of beer, sweat, and smoke. It wasn't working. Her grip on Zane's shoulder tightened.

He glanced back at her. "Are you okay?"

She nodded. *Nope. Not okay. Maybe we should leave.*

They passed close to the bar when a man caught her around the waist and spun her toward him. She gasped, inhaling not just the bar smells but the man's strong body odor. An eagle tattooed on his bald head reflected in the mirror behind the bar.

"Zane!" she cried.

"Gemma!" Zane's thin fingers grabbed her shoulders and tried to pull her back as she pushed against the arms around her, but she didn't budge an inch. The man holding her ignored Zane, his greasy gaze sliding down her from head to toe.

"Hey sweet thing. How much?"

Gemma's heart stuttered—and not in a good way. He couldn't be serious. "Excuse me?" She tried to push away, but he held on tight.

"How much are you? I gotta tell ya, I'm diggin' the uniform."

She shoved him off, her lip curled. "I am *not* for sale."

He grinned, showing off yellow teeth. "Everyone is for sale."

"Not her." Zane grabbed his arm, but the man brushed him aside hard, knocking him to the floor.

"Zane!"

Before she could help him, the man's arms had slithered around her again, his hands firmly gripping her rump.

Gemma's eyes flashed and she drew back her fist.

A hand caught her wrist before she could punch. A large hand. The man's paws fell away as Captain Lee pulled her toward him, until she was pressed against his chest.

"She's taken," he growled.

A little gasp of relief escaped her as she looked up. Gemma felt small next to him, his broad shoulders tight, his eyes hard.

The man's jaw dropped as he looked up at the captain, and he raised his hands. "No problem here. I didn't know."

Wait, *taken?* "I certainly am no—!"

The captain nearly yanked her off her feet, pulling her farther away from the bar with an unbreakable grip.

She slapped and scratched at his hand. "Let me go!"

"Shut up," Captain Lee said, as if he was commenting on the weather.

She blinked. "Say what?"

"You alright, Zane?" he said.

Zane stood and dusted himself off. "I'm fine." He didn't sound fine and couldn't meet Gemma's eyes.

"Let's go then." Captain Lee led the way, dragging Gemma by her wrist. Zane followed them, head down, his hands in his pockets.

"I could have dealt with him if I'd brought my stunner," he mumbled.

The captain shoved his way through the crowd, and they left *The Watering Hole*, no one giving them a second glance.

Gemma tried to pull on the captain's fingers, shove him off, punch his arm—nothing fazed or slowed him. "Let me go!" She thought about biting him, which would serve him right for treating her this way. He dragged her all the way across the street.

"Go about your business, Zane," Captain Lee said over his shoulder.

Zane hesitated. "Where are you taking her?"

"Back to the ship."

Zane let out a breath, his face relaxing. "See you at dinner, Gemma."

He disappeared into the crowd, leaving her with the captain standing at the bottom of the stairs to the raised platform.

"I'm letting go now," he said, his voice as warm as the vacuum of space. "Don't pull or you might fall over."

She stopped struggling, and he released her.

Gemma rubbed her wrist. It hadn't hurt—he hadn't squeezed—but it was red from all her tugging.

"What do you have to say for yourself?" His cold voice was low, but just loud enough to be heard over the background sounds of machinery.

The spicy words she had for him faltered. With a tone like that, she knew she was in trouble. "Captain, I'm sorry I left the ship, but I was going to go crazy, and I didn't go far—"

"That's enough." He still didn't raise his voice as he gestured for her to go ahead of him to the ship.

People walking by still stared at her. She had so much attention on her now that she hung her head as she climbed the steps, hiding her molten-lava face, her hands shoved in her pockets to conceal their trembling.

She'd made a mistake. A big one. She'd not only been grabbed at, but Zane could have gotten hurt. How could she come back from this?

They crossed the yellow safety line in silence and approached the ship, stepping over the fuel lines. He followed her up the ramp. After the bright sunlight, she couldn't see anything in the dim interior.

"What you did—" the captain started.

"Captain, let me explain," Gemma said.

Her eyes hadn't adjusted enough yet to see his face, but his voice rose a little louder. "Don't interrupt me—"

"Please, I needed to get off the ship." Gemma had her hands clasped under her chin.

"Pilot, stop."

"I didn't mean to make trouble!" she insisted.

"Not another wor—"

"And it was my first time on an alien planet—"

"I told you to stay on the ship!" Captain Lee exploded, his voice a roar. "I *ordered* you."

Gemma blinked but refused to take a step back. She could see him now. He towered over her, his jaw and fists tight, his brow furrowed, and those blue eyes flashing; definitely in Scary Captain Mode.

Trying to hide her shaking, she planted her hands on her hips. "Listen. I already apologized. Obviously, I regret my decision. Besides, you said to stay *near* the ship."

"While we're off Earth, you're my responsibility," he said, his voice lower but nowhere near calm. "Do you realize what that guy was going to do to you? Do you have any idea?"

Gemma tried not to squirm. She had a pretty good idea. "It was never going to get that far. Really, what's the worst that could have happened? I'd have punched him, maybe caused a fight, and we might have gotten arrested. Zane didn't think jail was that big a deal."

"What if you broke your hands?" the captain snapped at her. "How would you fly then?"

Gemma inhaled sharp breath. She didn't have a quick answer for that.

Captain Lee shook his head. "And what were you doing at *The Watering Hole*, of all places?"

She crossed her arms, not ready to admit she'd wanted to leave anyway. "Zane suggested it. He said it was a good place to eat."

The captain gave her a look. The look that made her feel like an idiot. She hated that look. It was the look they gave her in flight school every time she got something wrong. It hadn't happened often, but when it did, all she could hear was, *A girl? In space? You'll never make the cut.*

"So, you think the suggestion of a teenage boy is a good idea?" the captain demanded, bringing her back to the present. "He wasn't thinking with his brain on that one. Didn't you notice—"

"If it's such a bad place, then what were you doing there?" Gemma shot back.

"Following you!" Captain Lee ran a hand through his short hair. "Why would you go off alone?"

"Zane was with me."

"Zane can't protect you."

She bristled. *Excuse me?* "I don't need protecting."

He pointed back the way they had come, his voice rising again. "Clearly, you do."

"What, you're my knight in shining armor now?" she shouted. "The little girl can't get along without some big, strong man to save her?"

"No, I— You— I—Argh!" His fists tightened. Now they were both shouting. "Why can't you follow orders?"

Gemma stuck out her chin. "Stop treating me like I'm an idiot just because I'm a woman."

He pointed back toward the bar again. "If you stopped *acting* like an idiot—"

She gasped. "Excuse me?"

His hands dropped, his mouth working for a second as he realized his mistake. "No, I meant ... "

Gemma's shrill voice echoed in the metal interior of the ship. "You think I'm an idiot?"

"What? No!" The captain backed up a step.

She planted her fists on her hips. "So, it really is because I'm a woman."

"Will you stop it! You're—you're—" He threw up his hands. "You're impossible."

She folded her arms. "Get used to it."

He sputtered for a moment, before turning and stomping off.

"Idiot," Gemma muttered. "Who's really the idiot here?" But even though he'd left, her face wouldn't cool down, and she bit her lip. She couldn't really call that argument a win.

"You should listen to him," said a voice behind her.

Gemma jumped and spun around, hand on her heart. "Chase! You scared me." A beat went by. "Um ... How long have you been standing there?"

"The captain has only your best interests at heart," Chase said, coming up next to her. "He's not your enemy."

"Oh yeah?" She couldn't look Chase in the eye. This was her first real conversation with him. An embarrassing one at that. "What do you know about it?"

"Honest, the man is on your side."

"I can take care of myself," she insisted.

Chase raised an eyebrow.

She closed her eyes and took a few deep breaths. "Does he blow up like that all the time?"

Chase looked off at nothing, tapping his chin. "No. Usually he's the quiet and dangerous type. It's just with you."

She sighed and touched her forehead. "What a privilege."

Chase reached out as if to pat her shoulder but let his hand drop.

"It wasn't fair of him to order me to stay with the ship," she muttered.

Now both Chase's eyebrows rose. "Fair? Since when does fair matter? Your captain gave you a direct order. He's not obligated to explain why to you. Frankly, I'm surprised you're not on cooking duty for the next three weeks." He paused. "Though the duty roster hasn't been posted yet."

Gemma smothered a moan. She'd really messed up. "What can I do?"

Chase shrugged. "There's nothing you can do. You made your decision, now you'll have to deal with the consequences." He gave her a tight smile. "That's the way life is."

He was right. The captain was right.

Well, not right about ordering her to stay on the ship, but he was right that she should have listened.

Gemma sighed, deflated. Maybe an apology would be in order.

"You'll be fine," Chase said, turning away.

"Hey, Chase." She stopped him. "I've been meaning to ask you. What brought you to space? Really?"

He smiled a real smile this time. "The money."

TREVOR STOMPED DOWN THE HALL. *SHE WAS SO ... THIS SITUATION is so ...*

He'd been right all along. Instead of doing all the things he should have been doing right now, he had to waste his time protecting her. Why were girls so—what was it called?—high maintenance? Even Anne hadn't been any trouble, that he remembered. Except when—

When was the last time he'd completely lost his temper like that? She brought out the worst in him, and that was unacceptable. He wasn't a good captain if he couldn't compartmentalize.

But she's just so ... so ...

Trevor slammed the door open to his bunk and knelt on the floor, breathing deeply through his nose. Now, of course, he could think of all the things he should have said. Had she noticed the man had a weapon? Or that he was drinking with at least two other guys? If a fight had broken out, they would have been outnumbered. She probably would have been killed and taken Zane with her. Did she realize how irresponsible it was to be overconfident?

He would have said them calmly, too. Like he always did. He wouldn't have blown up.

But that girl ... His hands tightened into fists. Why was this happening? What was he going to do with her?

"Captain to the bridge."

Trevor took in a long breath and stood, outwardly perfectly calm. "On my way."

8

"Status reports," Captain Lee snapped.

"Refueling complete and everyone accounted for," Chase said.

"Ready for takeoff, Captain," Gemma said.

"Take her up."

Gemma sighed at her last glimpse of the planet. Admittedly, she hadn't been able to explore the jungle like she'd wanted, but even the tiny bit of freedom in port, outside the small ship, had been a breath of fresh air.

Well, a breath of ship exhaust. At least she could stretch without hitting a wall.

She resisted a look back at the captain. He'd had her cooped up in the ship for the entire rest of the stay. Chase was right. She should have followed her captain's orders. Even stupid ones.

Once the autopilot was engaged and the sails extended, she walked off the bridge without a word to anyone.

"What's eating her?" she heard Dak ask.

She paused on the ladder out of sight.

"I don't know," the captain said.

At least he wouldn't embarrass her by telling the story to the rest of the crew. She had to get to Zane before he told Joe, Charlie, and Dak about her being dragged back to the ship.

Zane waited for her back at her room, shifting from one foot to the other. "Are you alright?"

She smiled the best she could. "I'm fine."

"I'm really sorry I took you—"

"Don't worry about it," Gemma said. "At least I got out a little. Thanks for checking on me."

"Yeah. Glad you're fine." He still looked at the floor, shifting his weight, his hands deep in his pockets.

She placed a hand on his shoulder. "Zane. Really, I'm okay. Cheer up. I don't like to see you like this. I'm not mad at you."

"I'm sorry I got you in trouble, but ... " He grinned. "I kinda wish I could have seen you punch that guy in the face."

Gemma laughed. "I would have liked to see that too. Would you mind not telling the rest of the crew about what happened today?"

He saluted. "My lips are sealed."

"Now go to bed, it's late."

Gemma lay down, exhausted from feeling both guilty and angry all day, but her eyes wouldn't stay shut. She stared out at the dark.

Listening to the captain was the smart thing to do. She admitted it. It was just the *way* he said it ...

Gemma rolled over. She would usually use the word condescending, but he trusted her to fly his ship. So professionally, she felt respected. But personally, he insulted her.

Ugh. She flopped onto her back again. The man drove her crazy. She wanted nothing to do with him.

The realization hit her like an engine misfire, and she

covered her face with her hands. *She's been acting like a child.* This whole trip, she'd considered herself a professional, when really her immaturity had soured almost every interaction she'd had with the captain. No wonder he blew up at her.

Gemma cringed. She needed to stop this. She *would* stop this.

She knew she could, because not *everything* had been bad. Playing video games with him had been ... fun. And the way his face lit up when he smiled—

Shut up.

GEMMA PADDED BAREFOOT TO THE COMMON ROOM THIRTY MINUTES later, the metal floor freezing her toes, the only illumination the safety lights lining the floor after lights-out.

When she arrived at the common room, the lights were on, but low. Charlie sat at the table, reading on his tablet with his glasses perched on his nose. He looked up as she entered. "Gemma, what are you doing up?"

"Can't sleep," she said. "I'm going to watch a movie."

"Mmm." Charlie nodded. "Too jazzed up from the day's excitement, hmm?"

"Something like that." She hesitated. "How much do you know?"

"Hmm?" He cocked his head to the side. "About what?"

The captain hadn't even told Charlie. She'd have to thank him for that.

"Nothing." Gemma flopped onto the couch and pulled a blanket around herself, including her icy feet. "Want to watch with me?"

"No, thanks, I was just going. I need to stay on schedule." He folded his glasses and stood. But as he headed for the door, he stopped and reached into his pocket. "Here, take this."

"What's this for?" She looked down at the small pill he gave her.

"Something to help you sleep," he said. "We can't afford to have you get off-schedule either."

"Thanks." She couldn't afford to be tired tomorrow. She needed to perform well in front of the captain if she hoped to stay employed.

She got a water from the galley before throwing back the pill.

She spent a few minutes flipping through the movie catalog, before coming across a movie she hadn't expected to see there. It would be perfect. Nostalgic, at the very least.

Just then, Captain Lee strode in.

Gemma sat up from her position stretched out on the couch. Guilt nipped at her at the sight of him. She winced. Yes, she felt more guilty than angry. "Evening, Captain."

He stopped. "What are you doing up?"

"Couldn't sleep. Thought I'd fit in a movie." She wrapped her arms around her knees. "What are *you* doing up?"

He shrugged. "I don't sleep much."

Silence followed. Gemma tapped her toes under the blanket, afraid to look at him. After a deep breath, Gemma said, "Tha—"

At the same time, the captain said, "I hope—"

They both stopped. It would have been funny if not for the tense mood.

He gestured to her. "You go first."

"Thanks for not telling anyone," she said, her voice soft and cheeks warm. She worked hard not to break eye contact. "About today, I mean."

He inclined his head. "I don't think it's anyone else's business."

Now she did break eye contact. *Wow.* Her respect for him went up a notch.

Gemma looked back at him again. "Anyway. Thanks." She hesitated. "Want to join me for the movie?"

He looked away, shifting his weight. "Aren't you still angry with me?"

She bit her lip. The invitation to watch the movie had been a peace offering, but he didn't seem to get that. "Not really. No. I'm ... I'm actually sorry for my actions today. I shouldn't have disobeyed a direct order, even if I didn't agree with it—Are you mad at *me*?"

The captain met her eyes. "Thank you for your apology. I'm sorry I overreacted; I guess we all make mistakes. No, I'm not mad."

She cringed. "Are you giving me cooking duty for the next three weeks?"

The corner of his mouth quirked. "It had crossed my mind. But no, no more than the usual rotation."

"Then take a seat." She swung her legs off the couch to make room for him.

He glanced between her and the door. "What movie?"

"*Seven Brides for Seven Brothers.*"

"Never heard of it."

Not surprising. "It's *really* old. I used to watch it with my great-grandma, who had watched it with her grandma. It's a musical."

His eyebrows raised. "A musical?"

"You know, where the cast spontaneously bursts into song and dance?" She had assumed he wouldn't like a musical, not that he'd never heard of one. That needed to be remedied. "Sit down and watch with me."

He pointed toward the galley. "I'm going to grab myself a cup of coffee and a sandwich."

Gemma chewed her lip while he disappeared into the galley. Was this a mistake? Was it weird to ask the captain to watch with her? What if he hated the movie?

She took a deep breath. *His attitude toward me has mellowed. That's really what matters. Now, if I just*—she cringed—*behave, things will go smoothly.*

Captain Lee came back out a moment later with his coffee and sandwich, taking the seat next to her. She started the movie.

As the first song played, he chuckled. "People really enjoy this stuff?"

"Shh!"

As they watched, the captain gradually leaned forward, elbows on his knees, his gaze intent. Alex would never have been caught dead watching a musical, but Captain Lee seemed to enjoy it.

He had inhaled his sandwich, and now glanced down at his empty mug. "I need another coffee. Pause it for me?"

She grinned. He was totally into it.

A yawn came unbidden. *What time is it?*

He came back and she resumed the movie, but she had to squint to get the picture in focus. She blinked, her eyelids heavy. That pill Charlie gave her must be kicking in. She should probably get to bed.

She couldn't seem to move. *So, so tired.* Her head nodded, her vision swimming. What in space had he given her? A horse tranquilizer?

Her eyes slid closed and she leaned to the side, unable to support herself—right into the captain, her head on his shoulder.

He looked down at her in alarm. "Don't go to sleep!"

"I'm not," she murmured as her consciousness slipped into a dream.

TREVOR FROZE, STARING DOWN AT THE PILOT AS SHE LEANED AGAINST him. What should he do? He glanced around, not sure if he was looking for help or making sure no one else would see.

Gently, he pressed his index finger against the side of her head and pushed to get her off him.

She made a small noise and he pulled his hand back as she snuggled against him again.

Trevor swallowed hard. This was bad.

He slowly scooted away, easing her down until her head rested on the couch. He turned off the movie and tucked the blanket in around her.

Wisps of hair curled around her serene face. She looked...

He looked away. What was going on with him?

Trevor couldn't leave her here. He kept the common room cooler than the sleeping quarters, and how embarrassing would it be to be found asleep in here in the morning? The corner of his mouth twitched. He'd love to be here for it, though. Her face would turn so pink, her eyes so wide—

He stamped down a smile and the rest of that thought, as if putting out a fire. *No, Trevor.*

Trevor shook her shoulder. No response.

"Pilot?" he ventured. "Pilot. You need to get up."

She made that little noise again and shivered. Definitely couldn't leave her here.

He looked out into the hallway. No one around. He knew

from experience that no one usually roamed the halls during lights-out. No one would see them. It wasn't far.

He sighed, scrubbing his face. *Fine.*

Very carefully, he lifted the pilot off the couch, her head lolling to the side. He held her close so her cheek rested against his shoulder.

Trevor didn't know why his heart hammered, as if he'd just sprinted a mile. He hoped it didn't wake her up.

He carried her down the hall to her sleeping quarters. She was so light ... and soft.

Trevor shook his head. *Focus.* He swiped her bio card to open the door to her room.

Laying her on the bed, he pulled the blanket up to her chin. She mumbled something, and he caught himself staring at her. Most of her ponytail had come undone, her hair wild, her mouth slightly open as she slept.

He quietly fled the room, closing the door behind him.

Now he would never get to sleep. *Might as well finish that movie.*

WHEN GEMMA SLOWLY AWOKE IN HER OWN BED, SHE COULDN'T remember any of the strange dream, except that the captain had been there.

She opened her eyes, the lights on full. *Wait, what time is it?* She looked at her clock. 1100? She was supposed to be on the bridge at 0800!

Oh, she was in so much trouble. Again.

She changed her clothes, fixed her ponytail, and flew out

the door, not even bothering to shower. In the hallway, she ran straight into Dak.

"Whoa, whoa, where's the fire?" he asked her.

"I'm late!" she said, scrambling up the ladder.

Captain Lee sat in his chair on the bridge when she arrived, his feet propped up as he played with his tablet. He looked up at her.

"Good morning," he said. "How did you sleep?"

"I'm so, so, so sorry I'm late," she said, her hands fluttering as she tried to explain. "I didn't set my alarm, and I think that pill Charlie gave me really knocked me out, and I didn't mean—"

"You looked like you needed the sleep," the captain said, standing. He opened his mouth as if to say more, but then he shook his head. "Don't worry about it. Finish your shift. I expect you to be on time next time."

She blinked. "Yes, sir."

When he turned away, she blurted, "You're not mad at me?"

He paused, rubbing the back of his neck. "I guess not." He climbed down the ladder.

"Sandy,"

Gemma fidgeted under the table, out of sight of the camera.

"Well, port was a total wash. Captain Lee ordered me to stay on the ship and ... it's kind of a long, embarrassing story. Basically, what happened is ... "

She hung her head. Gemma couldn't leave that in a

message. She needed her sister face-to-face. "Yeah, I don't want to talk about it."

"But remember the really old movie *Seven Brides for Seven Brothers*? I watched it with the captain last night. I think he really liked it. And then—"

She winced. "Never mind. I don't want to talk about that either."

9

Gemma blinked awake when the morning lights came on. *A new day, let's make a new start. A less ... embarrassing start. A more mature start.*

Quick shower, then she looked at herself in the mirror. She touched her hair. Hmm. She had worn her ponytail every day since they left Earth. Maybe she should do something different. Something fun.

She spent a few minutes doing her hair before she skipped through the hall to the common room, her French braids bouncing against her shoulders in the low gravity.

Gemma moved along so fast she almost slammed into the captain. She stumbled back, but his quick reflexes seemed to kick in as he grabbed her hand, stopping her fall.

He frowned. "What's the hurry?"

"Sorry, I was just ... uh, skipping." She pressed her cold hand against her hot face. So much for a less embarrassing day. Forget mature. How did she keep doing stupid stuff in front of him?

When she looked up, the frown had disappeared, but he

stared at her. She'd never seen that expression on his face before, wide-eyed and slack-jawed.

Gemma shifted her weight, fidgeting with one of her rolled-up sleeves. "What? Something wrong?"

He snapped out of it with a sharp shake of his head. "Oh, sorry. No, it's just, your hair. You look so … uh …"

Her fingers twisted together, now self-conscious of her braids. Maybe it had been a childish choice. "Does it look bad?"

"What? No! No. Just the opposite. You look—" He cleared his throat, then he turned and walked back the way he'd come without another word.

She stood there a moment, her forehead wrinkled. *So, so weird.*

Still thinking, Gemma entered the common room. Trying to understand this new expression was going to bug her.

Chase threw darts at a dartboard in the back of the otherwise empty room, two already buried in the center bullseye.

She could use a distraction.

"Hi," she said, acting more cheerful than she felt. "May I join you?"

"Sure." He handed her a few darts. "Cute braids. Ever played darts in low gravity before?"

"No, but I was pretty good back on Earth—" She threw her first dart, and it pinged off the metal wall a foot above the target.

Chase gave a tight smile. "It's a little different up here. Try again."

She adjusted her aim, and after a few tries her dart hit the board.

"Nice one," he said, throwing one of his. Bullseye. Again.

She crossed her arms, eyes narrowed. "I get the feeling you're no fun to play with."

He chuckled. "Not if you like to win." He threw another, his sleeve inching up his arm at the movement.

Gemma stepped closer with a gasp. "What happened to your arm?"

Chase jerked his sleeve cuff down to cover the angry, red scar encircling his forearm. "A plan gone wrong," he said smoothly.

"What happened?"

He gave her his patented tight smile. "Classified. Your throw."

She missed, but the dart after that hit.

"So," she said, "what brought you to space?"

"I served in the military on a moon outpost. When I got out, I didn't feel like I belonged on Earth anymore, and so found a job that would keep me moving."

She arched an eyebrow. "I thought you said it was for the money."

Yet another tight smile. "Did I?"

Her hands went to her hips. "You did. Tell me the truth."

He raised his eyebrows. "Tell me about your parents."

She resisted the urge to step back, biting her lip.

"That's what I thought." He smiled, a genuine one this time. "Want to see something cool?"

In one fluid motion, he drew a knife from his belt and threw it at the target, his eyes not moving from hers. It hit the center, sending all the darts pinging to the floor.

"Wow." She watched wide-eyed as he retrieved his knife. "Why would you do that?"

He winked. "Anything to impress a lady."

Gemma tried not to smile. "But why do you need a knife in space? Is it really good for anything?"

"We'll have to see," he said. With a wave, he left the room.

She gave a huff, bending over to retrieve the darts. He didn't even stay to help clean up.

After standing behind the line on the floor, Gemma narrowed her eyes and threw dart after dart. She considered the board with a smug smile. Not bad. Definite improvement. Not Chase-level throws, but certainly respectable.

As she pulled the darts from the board, she almost dropped them when the captain strode into the room.

She smiled. "Hey, Captain! How about a round of darts?"

He paused, hand on the galley door. "I have to—uh ..." His eyes flicked around the empty room.

"Please?" she said, her hands clasped together under her chin.

He hesitated. "I have a few minutes. Hit in the center, right?"

She handed him the darts Chase had been using. The captain's brow furrowed in concentration, and he threw the first one. It went wide—really wide. It pinged off the metal wall so hard, it bounced back, landing at their feet.

Gemma laughed. "You're terrible!" She picked up the dart, the point slightly bent. "Wow, not so hard! Here, don't stand with your feet together, put one foot forward." She nudged his foot with the toe of her shoe into the right position. "Hasn't anyone shown you how to play before?"

He smirked. "It would be one more game for them to lose at."

"You should try playing with Chase," she said. "He's a darts shark."

He stared. "You and Chase played darts? You sure it was Chase?"

"Yeah, and I lost. Badly. Okay, hold up the dart. Relax your hand. No, relax it, not fist up your pinkie. Here." She grabbed his hand and pulled his fingers away from his palm. "Relax."

When she looked up, his intense gaze studied her. His large hand warmed her chilly fingers.

Her thoughts stuttered to a stop. *Too close. Too close!*

She dropped his hand, clearing her throat as she looked away. "Now try it."

"Right." He looked away too, for a moment his grip on the dart a little tighter than it needed to be.

"Relax," she reminded him.

He took a deep breath, relaxing his hand. Without looking at her, he threw, and hit the outer edge of the target.

"Much better!" she said with a grin.

He smiled too, that smile that changed his whole face from stern captain to—to something else.

Her heart gave a thud.

"Right." She forced herself to meet his gaze, working to keep her face neutral. "Do it again."

Charlie grabbed Trevor's arm as they passed in the hall.

"Watch it," Charlie said in a low voice. "Don't get too cozy with the pilot."

Trevor swallowed hard. He had done nothing wrong.

Then why do I feel guilty about it?

Crossing his arms, he met Charlie's gaze. "I don't know what you mean."

"I'm glad you're accepting her and becoming comfortable around her," Charlie said, "but it has to stop there. I saw you two playing darts."

Trevor worked to keep a straight face. How much had Charlie seen? Once Trevor got the hang of it, it had been easy to beat her at the game. But there was that moment at the beginning ... even thinking about it sped up his pulse, though he wasn't sure why. "It was completely professional."

"Be. Careful." Charlie looked around. "You know you can't—"

"And I don't plan to," Trevor interrupted, shaking his head. "It was nothing. I was treating her like anyone on the crew. It was a game."

He could still feel her cool fingers against his hand.

Charlie sighed. "Trevor, I don't think you understand. You have zero experience with women. I don't want you to get hurt—"

"Her?" Trevor scoffed. "How could she possibly hurt me?"

The doctor gave him a steady look. "You'd be surprised." He let go of Trevor's arm. "Be careful."

"You said that. And I will be."

But Trevor wasn't exactly sure what he was being careful of.

Laughter came from the common room. Gemma stopped in the doorway, having finished her morning chore. Zane and the captain sat on the couch, each tapping away at a controller with their thumbs.

"There is no way that's true," Zane said.

"I swear it," Captain Lee said, a grin on his face. "It was the only time he ever got them mixed up, but it completely killed the engine. We had to stop and flush out the system. Lost two days."

Gemma smiled. "What's so funny?"

The smile slipped from the captain's face when he caught sight of her, but Zane still laughed.

"He's telling me about Joe's first mission," he said, shaking his head. "He is never going to live this down."

The captain stood and held out the controller. "Did you want to play?"

"Yeah, come play with us, Gemma," Zane said, scooting to one side on the couch. "We're playing one of the cooperative levels."

She smiled. "I'd love to."

The captain sat back down, his expression tight. Gemma grabbed a third controller, then sat between them. She tried to take up as little space as possible, but her leg touched the captain's. She could feel him tense up, and her face warmed.

It's no big deal, she told herself.

Captain Lee no longer laughed—in fact, he looked a little ill—but Zane didn't seem to notice.

"Want some coffee?" Zane asked. "I'm going to grab some."

"Oh, no thanks," Gemma said. "I hate coffee."

When Zane got up, Gemma resisted the urge to scoot away from the captain. It would make things even weirder. She looked around the room—anywhere but at him—hyper-aware of the hot spot where their legs still touched.

Silence stretched between them. Gemma glanced at him out of the corner of her eye, but he also didn't look at her. His fingers tapped against the edges of the controller in a staccato rhythm.

"Any secrets in this level?" Zane asked, plopping back down beside her.

"I mostly played by myself," she said, grateful to see him. "My sister hates video games. I'm not as great at the co-op levels."

After a few minutes of playing, the captain's posture

relaxed. Gemma breathed a sigh of relief. How did he make her so nervous?

"No, Pilot, don't go up there alone—yeah, you died." Captain Lee shook his head, a small smile on his face. "I thought you were supposed to be good."

Gemma laughed. "Let's see you do better."

"It's all about timing," he said. "Come on, Zane, up top. We can bring the pilot back at the next checkpoint."

"Unless you die," Gemma said with a gentle nudge to his side.

He flinched. "I'm not going to—" The captain's character went up in flames. "Stri—forget it. I'm dead."

"Don't worry, I've got you, Captain," Zane said.

"Be careful! If you die too, we'll lose all our progress," Gemma said.

"I've got this." Zane's tongue stuck out as he concentrated. He missed a jump, and his character fell off the edge. "I don't got this."

"Oh, Zane!" The captain slapped a hand to his forehead. Zane laughed.

Gemma pushed the captain's shoulder. "Like you can talk. You died before him."

Captain Lee's face reddened, and for a second Gemma thought she'd made him mad. But she grinned as the realization hit.

"Oh my gosh, Zane!" Gemma pointed. "The captain's blushing. He's embarrassed."

"I am not," he grumbled.

Zane laughed. "First time I've ever seen that!"

"Maybe I should leave you guys … " The captain stood.

Gemma grabbed his arm. "No, stay. We're just teasing you. Come on, don't leave."

He slowly sat down again. "Alright."

She realized she still held onto his arm and quickly let go.

"Again?" Zane asked.

Gemma shivered. "Is it me, or is it getting a little cold in here?"

Zane frowned. "Yeah, me too, now that you mention it. Captain?"

"I hadn't noticed." The captain slapped his communicator. "Joe to the common room."

Chase's voice came out over the intercom. "Captain and Gemma to the bridge."

They looked at each other, eyebrows raised, then stood. Zane followed them, the game forgotten.

THEY MET JOE ON THE WAY TO THE BRIDGE. "WHAT'S UP, CAPTAIN?"

"Does it feel a little chilly in here to you?" Trevor asked.

Joe hesitated. "Now that you mention it ... "

The familiar vibration of the engine stopped. Never a good sign.

Trevor reached the bridge first. "Status report."

But the problem was obvious: a swirling mass of violet, glowing clouds filled the view. "Some nearby solar flare activity triggered a storm." Chase rubbed his hands together and blew into them. "Also, it's cold."

Dak leaned over his station, muttering to himself. Zane had followed them up. The small space got crowded, especially when Joe arrived and took up an unfair amount of room.

"We're going to have to detour around," Dak said. "I've already mapped out a tentative route."

"Tentative?" Trevor repeated.

Dak shrugged. "You know these storms are unpredictable. It might take three days, it might take a week."

Trevor's fists tightened, eyes narrowing at the readouts. They didn't have time for this. The longer they took, the more likely their window of peace would close, and the more danger his crew would be in. "How long to go through?"

Joe dropped his toolbox on the floor with a metallic thud and pried up the floor panel with a screwdriver, revealing a crawl space. "I'll get to work on the environmental controls. Hang around, Zane, I might need you."

"Through? Maybe an hour, maybe less," Dak said, frowning. "But it would be suicide. There's no way we could—"

"I can do it," Gemma spoke up behind them.

Trevor, Dak, Chase, and Zane all turned to her. Joe clunked around in the crawl space.

"I can get us through," she repeated, her voice confident.

Trevor considered her. Going around the storm was obviously the safer route—the smart choice—but if they could get through it in a few hours as opposed to a few days ...

"Captain," said Dak, "you're not seriously considering—"

Trevor raised a hand, and Dak's mouth shut. Even Gemma quietly clasped her hands together under her chin.

Hmm. Trevor leaned over the readout on the navigation computer. It would take some fancy flying and quick reflexes—

He glanced up at Gemma. Her eyes sparkled with what could only be excitement.

Trevor looked away quickly, his heart thudding hard.

"Take us in, Pilot," he said.

She whispered, "Yes!" under her breath as she slid into her seat.

"Captain." Dak grabbed his arm. "What are you thinking? This is a bad idea. It's reckless. Listen to me. We have to go around."

"I've made my decision. Everyone, strap in," Trevor ordered over the ship's communicator although most of the crew had already jammed themselves onto the bridge.

"Captain!" Dak shook his head so hard his picture-perfect hairstyle flopped against his forehead. "I can't go along with this."

"You don't have a choice," Trevor said. "Strap in."

"You're going to get us killed!" Dak marched over to the ladder and slid down. His voice carried from the deck below. "I don't know how she convinced you, but now we're all going to die."

Trevor tightened his jaw. There was no point in saying *his* decision had nothing to do with her. He didn't answer to Dak, and responding to him would sound childish.

Nobody else spoke. Zane's mouth hung open, his eyes large.

"The magnetic field could have shorted out the temperature control," Joe mumbled, his voice echoing up from the hole in the floor where he worked.

"Need me down there?" Zane asked.

"You two need to strap in," Trevor ordered.

Zane ran to comply, but Joe waved a hand. "I will, I will, this'll only take a second."

"Joe—"

A bolt of lightning shot across the nose of the ship, making everyone jump. The lights flickered, but didn't go out.

Trevor took his chair, tightening his own harness. "Take us in, slow and steady."

A wicked grin crossed Gemma's face.

"I mean it," Trevor warned. "*Slow and steady.* Or we're going around."

She gave a dramatic sigh, but restarted the engines, the ship rumbling as she retracted the solar sails.

GEMMA'S JAW SET, SHE POWERED THE SHIP FORWARD TOWARD THE storm.

She weaved between the clouds to avoid the worst of it. The masses of solar wind plasma churned, sparks of lightning flashing between them.

Tense silence permeated the flight deck, broken only by the occasional clunk of Joe working below.

The first half hour passed with a smooth ride. Gemma's firm grip on the controls, her composed posture, and her eyes focused on the screens kept them steady. She couldn't let her guard down for even a second.

Then a cloud bubbled out from the side, moving fast, purple with lightning.

Gemma heaved on the control column, the steep ascent pushing everyone back into their seats.

A loud squeal of metal scraping metal set her teeth on edge, followed by a crash, then what sounded like metal rain behind her. She kept her eyes glued to the view, even when a belt unclipped and Zane cried out, "Joe!"

The ship shook as the thrusters strained, her teeth rattling with the deep vibration. She found herself in a narrow tunnel between the clouds, lightning sparking against the hull. But at the end of the tunnel, stars glittered in the distance.

The walls of the violet tunnel closed in, the lights on the bridge flickering. Slow and steady wouldn't get them out in time. She accelerated, weaving through the purple tendrils that threatened the ship from all sides. The ship jerked as she engaged full speed—

As if shot from a cannon, they burst out of the storm, wisps of the swirling mass trailing behind them.

Gemma blew out a breath, her hands relaxing as she eased up on the ship's speed.

At Zane's gasp, she whipped around. The captain pulled Joe out of the floor, blood gushing from the engineer's head. The hard acceleration had scattered the toolbox's contents across the floor and flung the heavy toolbox into the hole where Joe had been working.

"Joe!" Zane unbuckled and knelt by him. "He's unconscious. Is he alive?"

"Charlie to the bridge, ASAP." Captain Lee felt Joe's neck. "He's alive. Zane, press against the cut to slow the bleeding." He produced gauze pads from the first aid kit on the wall.

Oh no.

With the ship back to normal speed again, Gemma hit the autopilot, and had levered herself out of her seat when Charlie arrived.

Charlie checked Joe with the medical scanner. "We've got to get him to sickbay."

Gemma stared as the captain slung Joe—who was not a small man—over his shoulder and slid down the ladder. Zane and Charlie followed.

What have I done?

Chase laid a hand on Gemma's shoulder when she stepped toward the ladder. "Hey, are you alright?"

"No." She twisted her hands together, her eyes wet. "Poor Joe. I could have killed him!"

"You didn't kill him," Chase said, his voice surprisingly sympathetic. "He'll be fine."

She swallowed hard. "Do you need me here, or can I go check on him?"

Chase stepped aside. "Go ahead."

Gemma slid down two decks and almost ran into the captain as he closed the sickbay door.

"Pilot—" he said.

"I'm so sorry, it's all my fault." Gemma bit her lip, close to tears. The words poured out of her. "I was too cocky. I never should have asked you to let me fly through the storm. Everything seemed to be going fine, but then that cloud—"

Captain Lee rested a gentle hand on her shoulder, stopping the flow of her words. "It's not your fault. It's my responsibility. I should have made him strap down."

"But if I hadn't turned the ship so hard—"

"Then we *all* wouldn't be here." His grip on her shoulder tightened a little. "You did good work today."

She sniffled, wiping her eyes on her sleeve. "Really?"

"Yes. Joe will be fine."

Gemma let out a deep sigh, then frowned. "Did you see that?" She exhaled again.

His eyes narrowed. "I can see your breath. I've got to get that temperature control working."

With one last pat on the shoulder, he walked past her.

"Captain," she said.

He stopped and looked back.

She hesitated. "You do good work, too," she blurted.

He gave a nod, but when he turned away again she saw the back of his neck redden. *Embarrassed twice in one day.*

Gemma slid open the door to sickbay.

Leaning over Joe, Charlie shook his head at her. "Can't be here right now."

"I was checking if—"

"Not now, Gemma. And take Zane with you."

Zane shook his head, his eyes red-rimmed. "I'm not going anywhere."

"Fine," Charlie said. "Zane, hold this ... "

Gemma closed the door, keeping her hand on the latch. *Please, please let him be okay.*

She climbed back to the top deck, slower than when she had come down. Reaching the top of the ladder, she looked around the empty bridge. Someone muttered from the open floor panel.

She poked her head in. "Where's Chase?"

"Gave him a break," the captain grunted, his tall frame folded into the square tunnel that ran under the bridge. Gemma bit back a smile, seeing him wedged into a space that even Joe had fit in. The captain had a hard time maneuvering his long limbs in it. "There's a set of wrenches somewhere up there. Hand me an eight-millimeter?"

Gemma dug through the toolbox. "Do you always keep your tools this disorganized?"

"No. I threw them back in 'til Joe can sort them how he wants."

She handed him the wrench and he disappeared further down the crawlspace, his voice echoing up to her. "You alright?"

"I'm fine." She chewed her lip. "I hope Joe's okay."

"He will be. Charlie's the best. Needle-nosed pliers and wire-strippers."

His hand appeared. She handed over the pliers and what she thought might be wire-strippers.

He handed it back. "Try again."

She sifted through the box. "I don't know," she admitted.

The captain scooted out and stood up, rummaging through the tools. "Huh. It's not here." He held up a knife. "This will do." He disappeared again.

"How do you know so much about the ship's systems?" she asked.

"A good captain should know his ship inside and out." He popped up with a grin. "That, and my dad was a mechanic."

Her heart sped up a little at his smile, and she looked away. "I, uh ... I think I knew that. Guess I forgot."

"Can you find a roll of wire anywhere?" He crawled out again, making a racket as he upended the toolbox. "It's not here either. It's unlike Joe to not have all his, and some of Zane's, tools."

She hunted around until she came up with a spool behind the captain's chair. "Found it!"

"Found the wire strippers." He took the wire and disappeared again.

Gemma had a sharp intake of breath. Her hands trembled as she picked up Joe's cap from behind Chase's station.

She hugged it to her chest and sat brooding on the floor, her chin on her knees. Everyone said Joe wouldn't die, but what if he sustained a serious injury? Would he be able to work in the engine room? It had been a blow to the head, what if he got amnesia and couldn't work on the engine anymore? Had one change of direction doomed their entire mission?

"Done." The captain threw everything back into the toolbox. Halfway out of the floor, he paused, his brow wrinkled as he considered her. "Are you sure you're fine?"

"What if he *does* die?" she blurted.

The captain climbed all the way out and replaced the floor panel. Then he offered her a hand up. "Pilot, he is *not* going to die. Everything is going to be fine. You did good work. Don't worry."

"Thanks," she said, looking up at him as he pulled her to her feet. They stood close together, her hand still in his.

He arched an eyebrow. "I can tell you're still worrying."

She blinked to try to stop her eyes from tearing up. "No, I'm not."

"It's going to be okay," he said, his voice a soft rumble. He squeezed her hand.

She inhaled, eyes closed, comforted by his touch. Her own grip tightened. "Thank you," she whispered, meeting his gaze again.

He gave a start, snatching his hand from hers. "Right." He cleared his throat, not looking at her. "You should probably ... get some rest."

Gemma blinked, lowering her hand. She thought she felt a connection, but he'd quickly severed it.

Her hand curled against her chest and she slumped in on herself. It was like when Alex gave her the silent treatment when he was mad at her.

"Right," she echoed. "Um." She shifted her weight. "I guess I'll go to my room."

After a moment of silence, she turned to leave. Climbing down the ladder, she glanced back and caught him looking at her. His eyes snapped upward to the stars. She wanted to say something—*but what?*—and instead shut her mouth and continued down.

Gemma's spirits lifted when she entered her room and saw the blinking notification of a message waiting for her.

"*Hey Gem!*

"*Okay, the captain is back to being a jerk. But then ... you watched a movie together? So ... not a jerk? You need to make up your mind.*

"*Also, you haven't told me if he's cute.*"

Sandy's grin widened. "*We're making honeymoon plans!*

David really wants to go off-world, but I told him he'd have to do it without me. So, somewhere more local, within driving distance. Then, I had an inspired moment: a cruise! One of those week-long ones. Sounds fun, right?"

GEMMA MUSTERED UP A SMILE AS THE VIDEO RECORDED. "A CRUISE sounds like a great idea. I'm sure you'll have fun."

Her façade crumbled. "Sandy, I feel so horrible. I almost killed Joe with my flying. The captain says it's not my fault, but I think it is."

Gemma related the whole story but hesitated toward the end. When the captain had squeezed her hand and assured her it wasn't her fault, it felt … special. Was she imagining things?

There was no way she could tell Sandy about that. Not yet. Sandy would make a huge deal about it, and then it would probably be nothing. This needed to be a face-to-face conversation.

Gemma's heart ached, missing her sister terribly.

" … then he fixed the environmental controls and told me not to worry. But how can I not worry? I won't feel better until I can talk to Joe myself."

10

Early the next day, Trevor rapped a knuckle on the open sickbay door. "Anyone home?"

"Come in, Captain," Joe said, propped up in the bed with pillows, his head bandaged. He gave him a chubby-cheeked smile. "Charlie's out getting me a bite to eat. Though he's refused this poor man a decent drink."

Trevor steeled himself and entered. He swallowed hard and tried not to look at the needles and the vials and the cold, white walls …

He cleared his throat, focusing on Joe as he took a seat in Charlie's chair. "How are you feeling?"

"A little woozy," Joe said. "The doc's keeping me over another night for observation. But doing pretty good, all things considered."

Gemma would be glad to hear that. "That's great. How's Zane holding up?"

"Eh. A little shook up. He's tough stuff, he'll be all right. I sent him to bed."

"Good, good." Trevor nodded, looking down at his hands

gripping his knees. It was right to visit Joe in sickbay. He was being a good captain. It wasn't Joe's fault that sickbays made him nauseated.

Joe tapped Trevor's arm to get his attention. "You just missed Gemma. She was checking on me, too." He held up his cap. "She even found this for me. Lucky there's not a drop of blood on it! She said she felt guilty for what happened." He eyed Trevor. "You didn't make her feel that way, did you?"

Trevor's face grew hot. "No! I told her it *wasn't* her fault, that it was *my* responsibility."

Joe waved a hand. "There you go again, trying to take all the blame for yourself. I'm a grown man; it's my own fault for not listening to you. Anyway." He raised his eyebrows, his head tilted, a sly smile on his face. Trevor had never seen this expression on Joe before.

"She's quite pretty, isn't she?"

Trevor stopped breathing. "Who?" He looked away and wouldn't make eye contact. She was adorable.

"I've seen you look at her."

Trevor risked a glance up, and Joe grinned. "Eh? Am I right? I know Zane's in love with her, but I'm pretty sure she's got her eye on you."

Trevor stood so fast he knocked the chair backward, a zap racing through his limbs, his heart pounding. *No.* No, that would be a bad thing. Joe couldn't be right.

"I—I'm glad you're feeling better," he stammered, heat rising in his neck. "I've got to ... " He gestured toward the door. "Go." He slammed the sickbay door open, barely avoiding a collision with Charlie by sidestepping around him.

"Captain? You alright?"

Trevor mumbled something about watch duty and stepped into the hallway, walking away with his hands stuffed into his pockets, his heart hammering in his throat.

"What did you do to spook the captain?" Charlie asked Joe as he slid the sickbay door shut again.

Joe's laughter chased him even through the closed door. Trevor walked faster, his face burning.

This was a disaster. If Joe was right—which he wasn't—it was a disaster. Joe was wrong, but even Trevor thinking about it would lead to disaster.

But if Joe was right, that would be even more of a—

Stop saying disaster.

Still, the thought of it caught his breath. He rubbed a hand against his chest. Why did it make him feel so—what was this feeling even called?

He had to think. He needed to work this out in his head.

Trevor reached the door of his room and swiped his card. Nothing happened. He tried again.

Oh. This is Gemma's room. Right.

He resisted the urge to punch the wall, and instead rested his forehead against the doorframe, taking a deep, shaky breath.

What am I going to do?

Out of breath from her workout, Gemma wiped the sweat from her forehead with a towel. The higher gravity in the fitness center really pushed her. Joe and Charlie assured her he'd recovered and would return to work in the morning. Still antsy, she worked out her frustration in the fitness center. She chugged her water bottle, ready for a long, hot shower.

"Hey, Gem."

She turned toward the doorway. Dak leaned against the

frame, his arm out, blocking the way. Something about him looked off. Maybe the way his hair lay limp against his forehead, as if he didn't care about it. Or the way his eyes squinted, as if he had trouble focusing on her.

"Hi. Gym's free." She pointed past him. "Do you mind?"

Dak stepped inside the fitness center, still in the way. She could smell a couple of Joe's beers on his breath. He slid the door shut behind him and clicked the lock.

"You." Dak jabbed a finger into her shoulder, and didn't seem to notice when she slapped it away. "It's your fault."

Her breath caught. She kept her back straight and met his eyes, but she trembled. It was flight school all over again.

Gemma's hand went to her dog tag keys and tapped them, her voice hardly above a hoarse whisper. "Captain to the fitness center." And she left the line open. The captain would hear everything they said.

"You embarrassed me," Dak snarled.

"You do that just fine on your own," Gemma said, struggling to keep her voice even.

"Captain's Pet," he slurred, poking her shoulder again. Maybe he'd had more than a couple of drinks. "Gender experiment."

"Don't touch me," she warned him.

"I said go around, but *nooooo*, Ms. Hotshot wanted to go on through."

She crossed her arms. "We got through safely."

"Oh yeah? How's Joe doing?" He wobbled, his balance shot, his face red, his breathing heavy. "You think you're invincible. Well, I'm telling you now, *Sweetheart*, you're not."

He took a step forward. She leaned away, the backs of her legs hitting the weight rack. She had nowhere to go.

"I have more experience!" he shouted, his arm sweeping wide. "He should have listened to *me*."

She swallowed, but her anger gave her strength. "So, what? You're here to teach me a lesson?"

He shook his head, lowering his arm. "Naw. Life is gonna do that."

Gemma's fists relaxed a little and she almost gasped in relief. He hadn't come to hurt her, just yell at her. Well, she could dish it out, too.

Before she could take a breath, a deafening bang shot through the room as the door flew open, the remains of the lock pinging off the metal walls.

At the sound, Dak spun around, lost his balance, and fell against Gemma.

Captain Lee stormed in, face red, a vein throbbing in his forehead. "Get away from her!"

The captain grabbed Dak by the collar and hauled him into the air with one hand. The other hand a fist, he pulled it back. Dak cried out and tried to shield his face.

"Captain, don't!" Gemma screamed.

He froze and looked at her, then at Dak's wide eyes as he hung by his shirt.

The captain let go, dropping the shaking Dak to the floor in a heap.

"Stay away from the pilot," the captain said through gritted teeth, then strode from the room without looking back.

Gemma gaped after him. What just happened?

A groan from the floor snapped her out of it.

"Are you okay?" she asked Dak, giving him a hand up.

"I'm fine." Dak shook his head, hand clutched at his heart as he sank down on a bench. "I thought I was dead meat for a moment there. Never sobered up so fast in my life."

"Do you need any help?" she asked him.

He waved her off. "I think we're done here." He staggered out of the room.

Gemma's hands trembled. She thought she'd seen his scary-captain look before, but even that hadn't terrified her the way this one had. He had truly lost his temper. His eyes had never looked so ... murderous.

Gemma had broken the captain's rule about being alone in the fitness center, but she didn't feel good about it.

THE DAY AFTER THE FITNESS CENTER ... INCIDENT ... TREVOR STOOD outside sickbay, nausea clenching his stomach. Joe had been sent back to his normal duties, leaving the bed empty.

He ran a hand through his hair. He'd made a serious mistake. He knew that much, but he didn't know what to do next. Charlie would lecture him as if he was still a child. Trevor deserved it.

Charlie was also the only one he could talk to.

Trevor knocked tentatively. "Charlie?"

The door flew open. "What happened in the fitness center?" Charlie demanded, stepping out into the hallway with him, a dangerous thundercloud in a small space. "Dak said you almost knocked his head off."

Trevor shifted his weight and stuffed his hands in his pockets, his face burning. "Maybe the situation got a little out of hand—"

"A little? You could have killed him."

"Keep your voice down." Trevor glanced around the empty hallway.

Charlie was never one to keep his voice down. "Just because he was making advances on Gemma?"

"He wasn't making advances—"

"Whatever he was doing—"

"She called for help." He wouldn't meet Charlie's eyes. Trevor had overreacted. Again. This time, he'd lost it *completely*, for the first time in his life.

"That," said Charlie, poking Trevor in the chest, "is exactly what I tried to warn you about. That's what happens when you get emotional. You can't afford to be emotional. You're the captain. Not to mention—"

"Then let's not mention it," Trevor cut him off, voice low. He didn't need a reminder. He knew it, every second of every day. He would never be free of it.

Charlie sighed, rubbing the bridge of his nose. "Captain—"

"I understand what you're saying. But Gemma was—"

"I knew it!" Charlie pointed at him. "You're calling her Gemma? And you're thinking it too, aren't you?"

"I meant, the pilot." Trevor's fists tightened. Charlie was right. "The pilot."

He'd known having a girl would cause problems, but he'd had no idea how she would affect *him*.

DAK STAGGERED, BLEARY-EYED TO BREAKFAST AND SAT DOWN, HEAD on the table. He arrived only moments after Gemma, but before anyone else.

"Um." Gemma hesitated. "Are you okay?"

He groaned. "I think I'll live. Barely."

She breathed a sigh of relief. "I was worried."

He shrugged, still not lifting his face off the table.

"You may want to lay off the beer," she suggested. "It's affecting your judgment."

"Maybe you're right." Dak looked up and smirked. "Captain's Pet."

Her hands went to her hips. "I am not!"

Dak's eyebrows went up. "You see him doing that for anyone else on the crew?"

Gemma sat there, frozen. "Well, I ... I mean—" She had asked for help, not ordered an airstrike.

She shouldn't have asked for it in the first place. Once she realized Dak didn't intend to hurt her, she'd had no reason to.

Zane flung himself into the chair beside Gemma, breaking the tension. "What's for breakfast?"

Only minutes before lights out, a knock at the door made Gemma pause from brushing her hair.

She chuckled. "Go to bed, Zane." His *Good night, Gemma* routine was getting out of hand.

"It's Captain Lee."

She whipped around in her chair, mouth open and eyes wide. "Um—Just a minute!"

Gemma hurried to pull on some pajama pants and threw her scattered clothing onto the bed. With only one leg in, she tripped and went down with a thud.

"Uh, is everything alright in there?"

"Fine! I'm fine. Just a minute more!" With all her clothes off the floor, she threw a blanket over the pile on her bed and ran back to the mirror. She jerked her hair into the fastest ponytail of her life, then checked her teeth.

Out of breath, she wrapped a jacket around herself and

stood near the head of the bed, so there would be an appropriate amount of distance between them. "Come in."

The captain stepped in, ducking his head through the doorframe, and cleared his throat as he slid the door shut behind him. "I came by to see how you were doing."

"I'm fine," she said, a little too fast. *Get a grip!* "Um, thanks for asking. It's more Dak that I'm worried about."

"I checked on him, too. He's fine." The captain shifted his weight. "I'm ... sorry. I got carried away. I didn't want him to— I felt like I needed to—"

"Don't you dare say 'protect' me," she warned, cringing inwardly. But she *had* wanted him to protect her. Of course he'd jumped in. Hadn't she practically cried out for help like a little girl? "I don't think he was going to hurt me."

The captain frowned. "He was yelling at you."

"You think I can't take a little yelling?" Her eyebrows rose. "It was fine."

He was quiet a moment. "I don't think he was going to hurt you, either. It was still harassment. It's necessary to keep order among the crew, and make sure everyone is safe so they can do their job." He looked away and cleared his throat. "I am sorry. I may have overreacted."

She crossed her arms. "*May* have?"

He still didn't look at her. "I will endeavor to react in a calm and appropriate manner in the future."

The automatic lights-out routine engaged. As if things couldn't get any more awkward. She fumbled with her bedside light before it flickered on.

The captain still stood there; his hands stuffed in his pockets. He blinked in the sudden light. "Well. I guess I'll—"

Another knock at the door. "Good night, Gemma!" Zane called.

The captain's brow furrowed, and he opened his mouth.

Her adrenaline kicked into overdrive, and she jumped at him, jerking him down by his collar and slapping a hand over his mouth to keep him from saying anything. He leaned away, his eyes wide, but she held him in place, her hand firmly over his mouth. She did *not* need Zane to know about this.

"Good night, Zane!" she called, her voice a little higher than she'd intended.

"Want to play a late-night game?" Zane asked through the door.

"Uh, no. Thanks. Not tonight."

The captain had pulled her hand away from his mouth. A cleft formed between his brows, as if he didn't understand. Her eyes pleaded with him to stay quiet.

"You sure?" Zane sounded heartbroken. He loved to play games after lights out for some reason.

"Go to bed, Zane. See you in the morning," she said.

She could hear him sigh outside the door.

After several moments of silence, she released a breath, her grip on the captain's collar easing.

Her body tightened again with a jerk. Mere inches separated them. *I'm hanging on to the captain!*

She jumped away from him. "I am so sorry!"

Gemma backpedaled right into her chair and only stayed upright because the captain grabbed her wrist.

"I'm so sorry!" she whispered again.

The captain righted her and stepped back. He cleared his throat. "What was that about?"

"I ... Zane asks me to go a round of *The Blue* most nights. I thought it might be ..." *weird?* " ... awkward, for you to be in here. After dark." She winced. "Alone."

His eyes widened, as if he had only now made the connection. "I see. I apologize. You're right, I should go." He took a step toward the door.

"Wait!"

He looked back at her, eyebrows raised.

Wait, what? What am I doing?

"How did you like *Seven Brides for Seven Brothers?*" she blurted. Despite everything, she wanted him to stay.

A few seconds of silence. "Uh, yeah. Yeah. I liked it." He nodded. He cleared his throat and looked away from her.

"Did you get to finish it?" It had been stupid of her to fall asleep on him. Literally.

"Yeah, I did. After I, uh ... after you went to bed." He glanced up at her.

The image of him carrying her through the narrow hallways made her wince. She hoped no one else had seen.

He shifted his weight as another awkward moment passed. He seemed as reluctant to leave as she was to let him go.

"Want to watch another movie?" she asked, her voice tentative.

He hesitated. "Don't you need some sleep?"

"I'm kind of wired," she said. That hadn't been a no, so she pressed on. "I don't feel like sleeping."

"I don't know." He rubbed the back of his neck. "I have watch-duty in an hour. And I don't want you falling asleep on —in the common room again."

Still not a no.

"Aw, come on," she said, her voice a little brighter. "I'll pick out another musical for you. And no sleeping pills this time."

He glanced at the door. "I should go to the bridge."

"Please?" she asked, taking a step toward him, her hands clasped under her chin.

His blue gaze flicked back and forth as he searched her eyes. After a moment, he said, "Alright."

They didn't talk on the way down the hall.

In the common room, she curled up on the couch under a

blanket, flicking through the movie titles. The captain disappeared into the galley.

She'd found a movie by the time he came back, a steaming mug in each hand, two bowls of popcorn balanced between them, and a sandwich.

He must *really* like sandwiches.

The captain offered her a mug. "This is for you, Pilot."

"No thanks, I don't drink coffee," she said.

He smiled. "I know."

"Oh." She blinked, then took the proffered hot chocolate. He remembered. That—that had to mean something.

Or maybe it meant he had a good memory. *Stop grasping at straws.*

But there were too many signs for her to be imagining it.

"Thanks." She took a long sip, the hot drink soothing in the chilly ship. "Why don't you call me Gemma?"

"Uh." He sat at the far end of the couch, setting the popcorn bowls between them. "I just ... want to keep it professional."

She narrowed her eyes. "But you call everyone else by their names."

He wouldn't look at her. "So, what movie are we watching?"

"What's your name?" she asked.

He shook his head. "That's not going to happen. Hurry up and pick a movie, Chase needs to get some sleep soon."

"Here's another oldie but a goodie," Gemma said, giving up.

Captain Lee kept checking the time through the first half of *Singin' in the Rain*. After an hour, the popcorn and sandwich eaten, and their cups empty, he stood. "I have to go."

"Right." She got off the couch too and folded the blanket.

He held up his hands. "You can finish watching. You don't need to wait for me."

"Nah, I'm tired." She switched off the screen. She didn't feel like watching alone.

Was that really it? Or was it something about the captain? Because if it had been Dak or Joe leaving, she wouldn't have even paused.

"Well, I—can walk you to your room?" the captain said.

Gemma smiled. "Sure."

After another short, silent walk through the ship, they reached her door.

He gave her a deep nod. "Good night, Pilot." He turned away.

"Thanks," she said. "For yesterday, I mean."

He paused and looked over his shoulder at her. "What do you mean?"

"I mean ... sure, you were a little overzealous when you came charging in," she said. "But your heart was in the right place."

The captain turned back to her, his gaze intense. His mouth worked. "Pilot, I—"

With a step, she closed the distance between them and stood on her tiptoes. Her lips grazed his cheek above the edge of his jaw.

He jerked away, stumbling back, his eyes wide and mouth open.

Wrong call, Gemma.

"I'm sorry," she gasped, her face heating up. "I didn't mean —I thought ... "

"It's... it's okay." His wide eyes belied his words. He cleared his throat, his face red. "I don't think—it's not appropriate—"

She nodded, biting her lip. *What an idiot.* She had read the situation all wrong. "I understand. It won't happen again."

"Right ..." He stood there a moment, staring at her, then turned and walked away without looking back.

Gemma entered her room, quietly closing the door behind her. She could have smacked herself. Had she really tried to kiss her *captain*? Was there really a worse mistake she could make?

She bit her lip. She could have sworn all the signs had been there. Gemma had convinced herself that he liked her back, but clearly, she was delusional.

With a groan, she dropped her chin to her chest. She had created a new problem. How could they work together after that? Especially on a small ship with a significant amount of time left in their mission?

She flopped onto her bed, wishing she could sink into the mattress and never come out.

THE CLOCK ON TREVOR'S WATCH DUTY THAT NIGHT CREPT BY DURING the longest shift he had ever done—or so it felt like. By morning, Trevor stood fidgeting outside sickbay when Charlie got back from his shower, fully dressed, his towel draped around his shoulders.

"Captain. To what do I owe the pleasure?"

Trevor followed him in and closed the door. He took a deep breath. "The pilot ... tried to kiss me." His cheek burned at the memory, and he resisted the urge to touch it.

Charlie's eyebrows went up, his expression unreadable. "What did you do?"

"I left." Trevor couldn't figure out if he felt proud of that, or just miserable.

"Good man." Charlie nodded with a smile, turned away to hang his towel and check his reflection in a mirror.

"I don't know what to do," Trevor blurted. She ... she was everywhere. On his ship. In his mind.

He'd even dreamed about her—

Charlie glanced back. "Yes, you do."

"I know. I just ... " He took a deep breath. Trevor trusted Charlie, the only person he could speak candidly with. "I think about her."

Charlie brought up a warning finger. "Captain, you can't do that."

"I know." How could he escape thinking about her?

Charlie laid a hand on his shoulder, his voice softening. "Trevor," he said, "you can't pursue this. You know you can't."

Trevor hung his head. "I know. And I didn't. It's—really ... I never expected this."

How could this happen? It had been drilled into him as a child and through his entire life: no close relationships. With anyone.

She had cracked his shields, bursting his dam of ... *wanting*.

He had no idea if he wanted her to leave, or to stay.

GEMMA LAY ON HER BED THE WHOLE NIGHT AFTER HER DISASTER, staring up into the darkness. This took the prize as the *most* embarrassing thing she'd ever done. Of all the stupid things she'd done since coming onboard the ship, this was the worst. The worst in her *life*. And it played over and over in her head.

She curled up under the covers, her chest tight. She was never, ever going to live this down.

The horror on his face when she tried to kiss him ...

She jumped out of bed when the computer beeped with a message.

"Oh Gem, I'm so sorry about Joe," Sandy said. "I think the captain is right; it's not your fault. Is he okay?

"But you're okay, right? How's your health? You look fine and sound fine. How are you feeling? I feel like you haven't been talking about yourself very much. I miss you."

GEMMA IMMEDIATELY STARTED THE VIDEO REPLY, NOT CARING WHAT her hair or her room looked like.

"Dear Sandy. Joe's fine. And I'm fine."

She shifted in her chair, looking away from the camera. Her face flushed with shame again at the memory.

"I ... I think I like Captain Lee. Like, really like him." Gemma fidgeted. "I thought we had a moment there. We've had a lot of —*moments*—lately. But last night I realized it was just me. I looked like such an *idiot*. How can I ever face him again?" All the feelings Gemma had bottled up poured out of her as she looked at the screen again.

"There's ... there's something about him I can't put my finger on. I mean, I know I said he's uptight, but he has this smile that—like I'm looking past the rank at the person he really is. But I can't reach that guy, I just see glimpses of him. Like, when he's embarrassed, it's so cute the way he blushes..." Ugh, no matter how hard she'd tried to fight it, she finally faced the fact: he was cute.

"And last night? I, um, I made a move. It was a huge, huge mistake and ruined it all."

Gemma slumped back in her chair and looked at the ceiling.

"I've got to get him out of my head. But it's a small ship, there isn't really room to get away from him. I hope things aren't awkward between us now."

She knew they would be.

She hit the *Send* button.

Now she just had to wait for Sandy's reply. Gemma groaned. It was going to be a loooong wait.

11

After a morning chore of dust mopping the third deck, Gemma spent most of the next day in her room. Zane had checked on her, and even brought her lunch, but she begged off hanging out.

A few hours later her communicator beeped; time to enter jump-space again. She groaned. *He* would be there.

Be calm. *You're a professional.*

Still, she paused at the base of the ladder that would take her to the bridge.

"You going up?"

She startled. "Dak! How are you feeling?"

He rubbed the back of his neck. "A little ashamed, a little humiliated. But I'm okay."

That makes two of us.

He raised his eyebrows. "How about you? You're just standing there."

"Right! I'm going up." She paused. "We're good, right?"

"I have no problem with you." The corner of his mouth quirked. "Captain's Pet."

Lemon juice on the burn, Dak. Lemon juice on the burn.

She peeked onto the bridge. Captain Lee conversed with Chase, turned away from her.

As quietly as she could, Gemma passed behind them, almost diving into the safety of her station.

She buckled in and took stock of the numbers and gauges, resting her hand on the control column as she turned off the autopilot and retracted the sails.

She winced when she felt a presence standing beside her and glanced up.

The captain looked down at her, but without the frown she'd expected. More like—confusion?

"How are you, Pilot?" he asked.

"Good. Good." She nodded. "Good."

They stayed that way a moment, neither looking directly at the other. The numbers she tried to read jumbled in her head.

Finally, the captain took a breath and opened his mouth.

"What's that?" Dak asked.

They both jerked to look in the direction of the viewscreen.

The captain strode away to lean over Chase's console. Gemma checked the screen to see a blip on their sensors.

Awkward moment or not, now they each knew what to do.

"Status," said Captain Lee.

"It looks like a ship," Chase said. He magnified the image. "A very big ship."

"We're in the middle of nowhere," Dak said. "What could they be doing out here?"

"Maybe they're going to the Terminus too," Gemma said.

The captain rubbed his chin. "They're coming from the wrong direction."

Gemma looked from Dak's grim face to Chase's, and finally at the captain's, his eyes narrowed as he considered the screen. Something about the situation had everyone on edge.

"I don't like it," Captain Lee said. "Chase, see if you can establish a communication link with them."

A tense moment passed.

"No reply," Chase said.

The captain's brow furrowed as he scratched the back of his neck. "Something's not right. How long until they intercept?"

"They're headed straight for us." Chase tapped a few times at his console. "We'll be within firing range before we reach the jump-point."

"We'll just have to get there first." The captain nodded to Gemma, and she accelerated. "What can you tell me about them, Chase?"

"I don't know who they are." Chase tapped buttons, flicking images across his screen. "Their origin is unknown, not registered in our databanks. By their scan patterns, I'd say they're looking for something." He turned to the captain. "That ship is armed to the teeth. We're faster, but we can't outrun getting shot."

"But we can outmaneuver the ship," the captain said. "How long until we reach the jump-point?" Although invisible to the naked eye, their sensors clearly showed the depression of exotic matter straight ahead that would take them into the wormhole.

"At current speed, we'll reach it in five minutes," Dak said. "But you can't enter jump-space going this fast, we'll have to slow down first."

"I don't have to do anything of the sort," Gemma said, her voice confident, her gaze not moving from her screens.

The captain leaned toward her, dropping his voice. "Pilot, don't do anything reckless."

She flashed a smile. "Relax, Captain. I've got this."

Inside, though, Gemma shook. Had she ever done this

before? No. Had she ever *heard* of it being done before? No. But she wasn't about to let some law of physics keep her from doing her job: flying the crew safely to Cerise. Because if she didn't do this, she had a feeling she would fail at her job.

"Everyone, strap in," the captain ordered.

"Four minutes," Dak said. "Adjusted angle instructions sent to your screen."

"I've got 'em." Gemma altered their course slightly. The jump-point hovered directly between them and the threatening ship. Her timing had to be perfect.

"Slow down, Pilot."

"Trust me, Captain."

His voice dropped even lower. "If this doesn't work, we'll be torn to shreds."

She couldn't spare even a second to look away from her screen. "And if that ship is really as bad as you all appear to think, what will happen if we don't try?"

A beat passed. "Point taken."

Gemma could hear the tension in Dak's voice as he said, "Two and a half minutes."

"The other ship is on approach," Chase said. "I read heat signatures. Possibly warming up their weapons system."

"Thirty seconds," Dak said.

"You can do this," Gemma said under her breath.

The captain gave her a sharp look.

"Ten, nine, eight … "

A flash of light on the other ship.

"Shots fired!"

If she dodged, she'd miss the jump-point. Gemma accelerated toward the oncoming fire and flipped the switch to enter jump-space.

She gasped as the super-heated gas around the laser fire splashed against their shields. An alarm went off, but they had crossed into the jump-point before the actual charge hit. The firing ship disappeared from view.

The ship shuddered, knocking them from side to side. Gemma gritted her teeth as she held the course steady.

"Steady, Pilot. You're almost there," the captain said. The confidence in his voice tightened her grip on the control column. *This. This is what she wanted.* To push the boundaries of possibility, to have a supporting crew, and ... a captain that believed in her, the way her teachers never had.

They burst into jump-space, the white blinding them. *Take that, flight school.*

"Yeah!" Dak pumped a fist in the air. "How do you like that?"

Chase grinned, too.

Captain Lee let out a long sigh, slumping back into his chair, his hand over his eyes. "Dak, how long will we be in jump-space?"

"Twenty hours, Captain."

"Then I'll see you all back here then. Chase, you have the bridge."

"Yes, sir."

"Aye-aye, Captain," Gemma said.

The captain gave her an unreadable look as he swung onto the ladder. "Good work, Pilot." He slid out of sight.

Those three words swelled her heart. He valued her.

Professionally, of course. Her cheeks burned as she made her own way to the ladder. He didn't feel like *that.*

Gemma woke early. She looked over at the glowing clock. Too early. The morning lights hadn't turned on yet.

She rubbed her eyes, then her face flushed as the memory of her attempt to kiss the captain rushed in. She groaned and covered her face. She was a moron. Why? Why did she do that? She'd never be able to face him again outside of the bridge.

The memory burned as hot as ever. An entire day had passed, and she didn't feel the least bit better.

What was she going to do? They wouldn't be able to work together anymore. Unease from the captain would trickle down to the rest of the crew, and morale would drop, and they'll fail their mission, and she'll be fired, and if the captain tells others about her, she'll be blacklisted and *never* leave Earth again.

She couldn't think of a worse future.

Her stomach growled and she kicked off the covers. Time for an early breakfast.

When she entered the common room, she almost turned around and walked back out.

The captain sat on the couch, reading.

He jumped to his feet at the sight of her. "Pilot!"

Oh great.

Rooted to the spot, she tried not to bite her lip and instead nodded. "Captain. I, uh ... " She gestured vaguely to the galley. "I came in for breakfast."

"I just got off watch duty," he said. He looked everywhere but at her. Oh man, the awkwardness level shot higher than she'd feared. "I'll ... leave you to it."

Gemma stepped aside, not meeting his eyes as she fidgeted with her sleeve. He walked past her and straight into the door frame.

She winced for him as he rubbed his head, mumbled something, then slipped out.

Gemma breathed a sigh, the tightness in her shoulders easing. At that moment, the ship's morning lights came on. Two hours until they left jump-space. She just had to avoid him until then.

GEMMA EASED THE SHIP OUT OF JUMP-SPACE, THEN RELEASED HER buckle. Her stomach knotted as the captain said, "See you at dinner."

It finally happened, what Gemma had been dreading since they left Earth. It was inevitable, really, but she had still hoped to avoid it.

It was her turn to cook. No matter how much she begged, nobody would trade jobs with her. Chase had watch duty, and he actually liked it.

She groaned. With dinner still hours away, she needed to get her mind off it.

A video game might do the trick. Gemma headed to the common room but paused by the ladder. The captain might be there.

No common room, then. Maybe she'd visit Joe in the engine room. She probably wouldn't run into him there.

Joe reclined in his chair, his feet propped up on the console when Gemma entered the engine room, ducking below a low pipe. "Hey Joe!"

"Gemma-girl!" Joe smiled, lifting his hat. "What are you doing down here?"

"I'm bored," she said. Not a lie. "How's your head?"

"Oh, it's fine." He waved a hand. "Nothing to put me out of action."

"What are you up to?"

He held up his tablet. "Sprucing up on my book knowings for a recertification test coming up. They make us take it every couple years."

She leaned back against a wall of gauges. "Tell me about it."

After only five minutes there, her plan shattered when the captain walked in.

Gemma twitched. She couldn't get over her stupid kiss-attempt, and, apparently, neither could he. His face reddened at the sight of her, and he knocked his chin against the low pipe.

She winced. "Sorry!"

"Not your fault," he mumbled, rubbing the spot on his jaw. He promptly turned and walked out.

Joe shook his head. "He's been acting weird all day."

She stifled a groan. Even the others noticed.

Not long after, Gemma left. She didn't want to be there when the captain returned to talk to Joe about whatever had brought him down to engineering in the first place.

Ugh. She pressed the heels of her hands into her eyes. She couldn't stay cooped up in her room all day.

She checked on Charlie, but he napped in the life pod. Maybe a workout session would calm her nerves.

When the door to the fitness center slid open, Captain Lee looked up from the free weights station.

Darn it. It was so much worse because he looked so good in a sleeveless shirt, his muscled arm tensed mid-lift.

"Pilot." He put down the dumbbell and stood. His mouth worked for a second, but no sound came out, his face reddening again.

This couldn't go on. "Captain." One hand went to her hip. "Look, we're professionals. I'm sorry I messed things up—"

"No, it's fine—"

She raised her voice to be heard over him. "We're on a small ship and trying to avoid each other isn't working."

He rubbed his chin. "I agree. We need a more coordinated approach. How about one of us takes the fitness center, and the other the common room. Then switch."

Gemma nodded, her face cooling at the logical reasoning. "Sounds like a plan. Which do you want first?"

"I'll take the fitness center." He shrugged, his face also returning to a normal color. "I've already started anyway."

Another flash of heat to her cheeks. She had noticed. "Okay, I'll be in the common room."

Finally, a plan. She could handle a plan.

Gemma sighed as she slid the fitness center door closed. She winced again, feeling its loose connection to the track, after the captain had smashed through it the other day.

Safe in the common room, she and Zane played a few video games together. It almost took her mind off her impending doom. *Almost.*

Gemma looked up at a knock on the common room doorframe. The captain leaned in, dressed, his hair still wet from a shower. "Fitness center's free."

"Thanks." She let out a breath when he left. The plan worked. She'd better move it before he got back.

"What am I missing?" Zane asked.

She gave him a tired smile and tousled his hair. "Nothing. I'm going to the fitness center."

Zane waved her hands away. "Okay. Go already."

Gemma took her time during her humiliation-fueled workout, then returned to her room and showered. She glanced at the clock.

She had time, so she checked her messages. The blinking notification of Sandy's message raised her hopes.

"Gemma! You think you like the Captain? You talk about him all the time. It's obvious you like the guy." Sandy rolled her eyes.

"Really, how embarrassing could it be? After all, it's not like you kissed him." Sandy laughed.

Gemma's cheeks burned.

Almost as if Sandy could see her, she stopped mid-laugh, her mouth open, eyes wide. *"Oh my gosh, you kissed him, didn't you? Gemma! He's your captain!"*

Gemma winced, then flicked on the camera.

"I did *not* kiss him," Gemma said. She looked away from the screen and bit her lip. "I *tried* to. It was a misunderstanding! Afterwards, he really didn't say much, just that it wasn't appropriate.

"I wish you were here so we could talk about this. I need you, and I don't know what to do."

Her watch beeped. Dinnertime.

And Send.

Gemma looked around the empty common room. She braced herself as she reached for the galley door.

"It's going to be okay," she told herself, tiptoeing into the galley. "Noooo problem. Just follow the directions." She swallowed hard. *You can do this. You've flaunted the laws of physics. You can heat up something edible.*

She should have asked Zane to help her but hadn't wanted to interrupt him installing the upgrades the captain had asked him for.

Gemma woke the screen strapped to the corner of the prep table and scrolled through the list.

"Let's see ... chicken, no... stew, eww ... there's got to be something easy." She tapped on 'stir fry' to call up the recipe. It looked simple enough: rehydrate some vegetables and meat, add some sauce, heat it up on the stove and voila, dinner is served.

"I can totally do that." Gemma nodded to herself. She pulled a few bags of mixed vegetables from the cooler. About to tear them open, she noticed the labels: 'stir fry medley,' and 'Italian mix.' She put the Italian one back and emptied the 'stir fry medley' into a bowl.

"Meat, have to have meat to make it a meal," she muttered, scouring the cooler. Her father always used to say that after her mother became a vegetarian.

Gemma found only one bag of chicken already cut into chunks. It would have to do; she and knives did not have a good working relationship.

She grinned as the food sizzled in the pan, seasoning it with rehydrated soy sauce. It smelled edible. "Not bad, Gemma. Not bad at all."

Returning the extra, unused soy sauce to the cooler, she spied something on the bottom free-for-all shelf. A bag of peanuts, unopened and not labeled with a name. A peanut sauce would totally make this stir fry.

She didn't know how to make peanut sauce. She flicked through the recipes again, but didn't see it listed. In fact, when she did a word search, peanuts didn't appear in any recipe. Oh well, she'd just throw them in.

When she did a taste test, she knew she had made the right

choice. The nuts really gave it that extra something. She boiled some ramen and mixed it into the stir fry.

"Dinner's ready!" she told Charlie when he came to check on her, her grin and fist pump making him smile.

"Smells good," he said with a wink. "Table's set and everyone's here. Bring it on out."

TREVOR DRUMMED HIS FINGERS AGAINST THE TABLE. GEMMA WAS running a few minutes late with dinner. What would he be forced to eat?

Why had he given her cooking duty? She'd made it clear she didn't know how to cook. Trevor hated skipping meals. Hunger always gnawed at him, his too-high metabolism making it impossible to stay full.

Gemma beamed as she presented dinner. "The first meal I've cooked since I was a little girl."

Trevor's chest tightened at her smile. She was so ... He looked away. *don't go there.*

"Really?" Zane asked, having already served himself and shoveling food into his mouth before she got to her seat. He spoke around a mouthful. "I'd never have known, this is great!"

"You'll eat anything," Joe said. When he put his fork in his mouth, he didn't disagree.

It must not be too bad.

Trevor's eyebrows went up with the first bite. "I have to admit, Pilot, for as much as you wanted out of kitchen duty, it's not—" A cough interrupted him. He cleared his throat and swallowed. His mouth tingled.

"Come on, you can say it," Gemma teased.

"Captain?" Charlie's forehead furrowed as he narrowed his eyes. Trevor swallowed again, then began to wheeze. Charlie grabbed his arm. "Captain, what's the matter?"

Trevor clawed at his throat. He couldn't—he had no air—he couldn't breathe—

He lurched out of his chair, knocking his dish off the table. It bounced against the floor, food flying everywhere.

Chairs scraped as everyone leapt to their feet, then a loud *thwack* as a chair fell over.

Charlie took charge. "Hold him still!" He opened a cabinet in the wall and took out a tube.

Joe and Zane grabbed Trevor's right arm, Gemma and Dak latching onto his left.

He couldn't breathe. *He needed to breathe.*

Trevor tried to scream past his swollen tongue, knocking everyone aside as if shaking off the ramen noodles of the stir fry.

"Calm down, Captain!" Charlie shouted. Trevor spun toward him, but he slipped in soy sauce and crashed to the floor. At that moment, Charlie darted forward and plunged an EpiPen into Trevor's leg.

With a gasp, Trevor's muscles unclenched, leaving him lying on the floor, on top of his smushed dinner, gulping down sweet oxygen.

"What happened?" Gemma asked, teary-eyed and on her knees beside him.

"I told you to only use the food we provided," Charlie said, sounding far calmer than Trevor felt. "Did it ever occur to you that some people might have allergies?"

"I'm so sorry! I didn't know! Captain, please, I'm so sorry, I didn't think—"

"Stop," Trevor wheezed, his hands shaking as he grabbed

the edge of the table and hauled himself to his feet, strings of ramen hanging off his soy sauce-soaked shirt.

Zane still sat on the floor beside the table, rubbing his shoulder with a wince after having been thrown into it. Joe gave him a hand up.

Trevor's face burned, his arms itchy, his tongue still tingling. Allergies. He hated his own weakness, his body betraying him. "Pilot." His shoulders heaved and he glared at her, baring his teeth. "Get out."

"What? But I—"

"I said get out! You are confined to your quarters." His fist slammed against the table. "Now!"

Gemma was crying now. "It was an accident!"

He didn't care. Accident or on purpose, he could still be dead. "Now, Pilot!"

Gemma ran from the room. Joe and Dak stared at the floor. Zane still rubbed his arm, his face pale. *Did I hurt Zane?*

Charlie frowned.

"Don't look at me like that, Charlie." Trevor coughed. "She almost killed me."

"Don't be so dramatic," Charlie said, slapping him on the back. "That's why I keep the EpiPen in here. You weren't even close to dying."

Trevor groaned as he sat back in his chair, tugging at his collar. He hated that feeling, his own throat not letting him breathe. He'd faced the vacuum of space, but this was worse. "She should have followed the rules."

"It was a mistake," Charlie said. Far, far calmer than Trevor. "It could have happened to anyone. Don't be so hard on her."

"I'm not hard on her," Trevor said, with more feeling than he intended. "I treat her like I treat everyone else."

"When's the last time you yelled at Zane or Joe like that?"

Charlie asked, his voice rising to match. "And in front of everyone?"

"They never tried to kill me!"

Charlie jabbed him in the chest with a finger. "Have they ever endangered your life with a mistake? Huh?"

Yes. Yes, they had. Everyone makes dangerous mistakes in space, but a good crew pulls through together.

Trevor didn't look at him, or Zane, or Joe, or Dak. *Charlie is right.* He let emotion get in the way again. *How does she keep doing that to me?* "Maybe ... maybe I..."

"Let's finish this conversation in the sickbay." Charlie gave a nod to the other three before leaving the room, Trevor following, hands shoved in his pockets. Some captain he was. Charlie was treating him like a child, and Trevor was letting him. The truth slammed into him, and he winced. No wonder he was acting like a child.

"You have to control yourself," Charlie said as soon as the sickbay door closed.

"I know, I know—"

"No, you don't know." Despite his heated tone, Charlie pulled a vial from a cabinet and loaded an injection with rock-steady hands. "You can't lash out at people because you're embarrassed about your allergies. This situation with her is affecting your judgment."

Trevor didn't look at him. "As soon as we get back, I'll have the director assign us a new pilot."

"But what about until then, hmm?" Charlie's voice rose again. "I can't believe I thought this was a good idea. She is the worst thing to ever happen to you—"

Trevor stepped closer, towering over Charlie, his voice low and dangerous. "Don't talk about her like that."

Not intimidated, Charlie pointed at him. "See what I mean?"

Trevor was silent for a long moment. As much as he wanted to fight it, Trevor had allowed her to cloud his judgment. She just—she made it so hard to think! "I'll do better —Ow!"

Charlie pulled the needle from Trevor's arm and discarded it. "I should hope so."

"Captain to the bridge," his comm chirped. "We have a problem."

Trevor pushed the ship's intercom, striving to keep his voice even. "Everyone to their stations." He clicked off.

"Wait, I haven't examined you yet," Charlie said.

Trevor grimaced. "Isn't the shot enough?"

"No, it's not."

Trevor held up a shaking hand to the doctor, the adrenaline still coursing through his system. "I know what you're going to say. I promise to come see you after I check what's happening on the bridge."

He climbed the ladder to the bridge, entering a thick, foreboding silence. A large ship hung in space on the view screen.

"Cloak up," he snapped. "Status report."

That set everyone into motion. Calm, controlled, professional. He couldn't have asked for a better crew in this situation.

Dak's hands moved over his console. "Cloak on."

"It's the same ship we encountered the other day," Chase said. "We don't know what kind of scanning capabilities they may have. I'm not sure cloaking will be effective. It might be better to divert the power to the shields."

"We have the latest in cloaking technology. They shouldn't be able to see us," Trevor said. "How did they find us?"

"They could only have followed us here if they knew where we were going," Dak said. "They must be going to the Terminus too."

"Where are we?" Trevor took his seat.

"We're near a planet," Dak told him. "3X-527. The data's a little vague, but there's a mining colony there. It's a relatively new colony. But, unless someone needs a battlecruiser to haul ore, there's nothing here to look for—but us."

"Try to get us around to the other side of the planet," Trevor ordered, calling up the information on his own screen. "The planet's pretty dense, with no satellites to bounce scanner signals off of."

"Our change of course may attract their attention," Dak said, sweat beading on his brow.

"They're scanning our sector," Chase said, his jaw tight.

They waited in tense silence.

Trevor looked around, his gaze settling on the empty pilot's chair for the first time, the autopilot light still lit. "Wait, where's the pilot?"

A tiny flash of light from the unknown ship.

"Shots fired! Shots fired!"

"Drop cloak, shields on full!" Trevor said. "Someone get the pilot up here!" He hit the comm button to her room. "Pilot!"

A blast of angry music drowned out his voice and stabbed at his ears. That girl had her music up as loud as it could go.

He glanced up at the tactical screens. Without her, they'd never make it.

"Dak, take her seat and try to lose them around the side of that planet," he said. "I'll get the pilot."

He swung onto the ladder and slid down, hitting the hall deck with a thud and taking off at a run. What idiot designed the sleeping quarters so far away from the bridge? He had no time, if he couldn't get her behind the controls before—

The first hit rocked the ship, slamming him against the wall. What the heck kind of weapon did *that*?

He had less time than he thought.

He slapped his communicator. "Bridge, report."

"We're ejecting cargo now," Chase said, a standard move in a desperate situation. "I don't think we can survive many more of those hits."

The walls rumbled around Trevor. That would be their cargo being ejecting.

"Captain, we're heading—" But an alarm sounded on the bridge, drowning Chase's voice out.

Trevor slid down the next ladder. Almost there. He rounded the corner and could see her door.

The second hit was immediately followed by a third, then fourth.

Trevor's next step hit empty air, and he floated off the ground. He twisted, trying to get some leverage. The gravity was off. The gravity-generator was housed with the rest of the critical systems on the bridge. If that was out, then there was no way they'd survive for long.

His throat tightened. That also meant the bridge was gone.

A cry made him turn. Gemma clung to the frame of her door. He pushed off toward her. He had to get her to a life pod.

Another hit slammed him into the ceiling, and he saw stars for a moment. Everything shook, the air around them heating up to an unbearable level. A long, loud scream of metal drowned out Gemma's shouts. He struggled to breathe …

He had to save her.

With every bit of strength he had, he shoved away from the ceiling and grabbed Gemma, curling himself around her.

12

Gemma groaned. She opened her eyes, squinting to bring the captain's worried face into focus above her. She struggled to make sense of it.

"Are you alright?" he asked, his voice gentle.

She took a couple of deep breaths—she couldn't seem to get enough air—and groaned again as she sat up, a headache at her temples pulsing in time to her heartbeat.

"A little dizzy, give me a minute." Gemma squeezed her eyes shut. She gasped when she opened them. Light seeped between the cracks in the hull, illuminating floating dust particles and the twisted hallway partially collapsed around them. She could smell nothing but hot metal and smoke. Silence pressed her on all sides. "What happened?"

"We were attacked. Do you remember anything?"

"A little." She rubbed her forehead. She winced as the dinner disaster flickered through her memory. The fury on his face, and the fear and worry that overflowed in her tears.

That wasn't what he was talking about.

"I remember the ship being hit," she said, as she mentally

drew closer to the fuzzier memories. "But I couldn't get to the bridge. And then the gravity went out ... "

"Well, we crashed on the nearby planet." The wild sweep of his arm to indicate the ruined ship around them belied his calm voice. He grimaced and clutched his side. "The only reason we're alive is because we were at the heart of the ship. The heat shield held, and the parachutes deployed. As soon as you can walk, we need to get out of here. Whoever attacked us could be here in an hour, give or take a few minutes."

She stared at him, the blunt statements taking a few minutes to sink in.

"But what about everyone else?" Gemma said, grabbing his arm and dragging him back down as he tried to stand. "Aren't we going to look for them?"

"I already did," he said, his voice quiet, not looking at her. "I couldn't find them. They didn't survive the crash. I've gotten all the supplies I could find, so whenever you're ready—"

"They ... didn't ... " Tears sprang to her eyes as she hugged herself. "Why? What went wrong? How did this happen?" Her voice scraped in her throat. *This can't be happening.*

"It was my fault." He still wouldn't look at her, his voice rough and heavy. "I shouldn't have ordered you to your quarters. You didn't know I was allergic, and I was stupid for not telling you. I let my emotions get in the way of being a captain. I should have known—"

"You couldn't have known." Gemma touched his arm. "It's not your fault."

His intense gaze locked onto hers. "I was in charge. It was my call that led to the crash, it's my responsibility. If you were on the bridge, none of this would have happened."

Her lip quivered. "You don't know that."

"I do."

She finally broke away from his gaze, gasping with the

effort. That meant she was guilty, too. "Are you sure no one else is left? That they're all … "

"I'm sure." His voice was so cold, she couldn't stand to look at him. How could he be so cold? "The only reason you're alive is because the hallway is at the center of the ship, making it the most protected when we crashed. Dak and Chase were on the bridge when it was hit. They were probably vaporized. With the bridge gone, I don't think anyone could have survived outside the shrinking heat shield as it gave out. Joe was in the engine room, so he died when the floor collapsed and burned. Zane was likely with him—"

"Don't you care?" she whispered, squeezing her eyes shut. Her hands tightened into fists. How could she have ever liked him? He was so cold. She looked at him, her gaze so flinty he flinched away.

Her screams scraped her throat. "Your whole crew is dead! They're gone! You can't ever see them again, and all you talk about is *how* they died? The mechanics of it? You're not the slightest bit bothered by it. They were your best friends—"

"They were my *only* friends," he said in a low voice, such heaviness in it, as if he carried everything on his shoulders. "But I can't change it."

She looked away, trembling.

He stood, his shadow long and contorted across the buckled floor. "The only thing I can do is try to save what's left, and that's you. I don't have time to whine and cry. I have more important things to worry about."

Gemma turned her back to him, her hand over her mouth. She squeezed her eyes shut, but tears forced their way out and slid down her cheeks. Everything hurt, inside and out. The smell of hot metal choked her. This couldn't be happening.

"Pilot." He knelt so she was forced to look into his eyes, his voice gentle again, but heavy. So heavy. "It hurts, it really does, alright? You happy? But we need to leave here. Now. You can cry later; you can be sad later. We need to get away, find some shelter and water to clean out that scrape on your head. We must move."

For the first time, Gemma touched the stinging area above her ear, dried blood and matted hair on the side of her face. She nodded and he helped her stand. He steadied her as she wavered, the dizziness a sharp stab through her brain, making the world tilt. It didn't help that the ship lay on its side.

Because of the crazy angle, the doorways created holes in the floor and ceiling. Many of the crushed openings of the living quarters made them inaccessible.

"Come on," the captain said, but she shook her head.

"Let me check my room. Maybe there are some helpful things we can bring."

With the doorway only partially collapsed, she could just fit through the opening.

He lowered her down until her feet touched the frame at the foot of the bed. Climbing carefully, she searched her room for anything that could be helpful. She stuffed a blanket in her duffle bag. Her music player went in, and Zane's camera. She picked up the clock he gave her and gently pressed the button, letting out a teary sigh. It still worked. She stowed it in the bag. The clock gave her an idea.

The captain pulled her back out. "Let's go." He shouldered his own bag.

"One more place."

"Pilot, we have to—"

Gemma gently touched his arm. "One more. Please."

She barely fit in the crumpled doorway of Zane's room, the ragged edges of the doorway catching on her oversized uniform sleeves as the captain lowered her again. Scraps and parts littered the floor, digging into her hands and knees as she squeezed under the creaking, collapsed ceiling. Sifting through the mess, she picked up the signal scrambler, the voice changer, the leak finder, and the life form detector. The oxygenator split in two at her touch, and the battery leaked some kind of acrid-smelling fluid. She couldn't find the stunner and left behind the rest of the mystery devices.

The rest of the rooms' doorways had been crushed or collapsed.

"We have to go." Captain Lee kept her hand in his after he lifted her out of Zane's room.

His strong grip led her down the hallway as she wobbled on the uneven surface of the buckled walls. The ship groaned around them at their shift in weight.

Captain Lee gave her a leg-up to climb into the common room.

Her uniform's oversized neckline snagged on a metal burr, tearing her sleeve from her shoulder to her elbow. Thank goodness for her undershirt.

"Are you okay?" he demanded, the anxiety in his voice choking her. She was all he had left.

"I'm fine," she panted, climbing the rest of the way into the common room. "My uniform just ripped." She looked down at him. "I can't pull you up." The whistle of wind coming in through the shattered window above her almost drowned her out. How was he going to get up here? She needed him.

Gemma covered her face. *Don't make me do this alone. I can't do this.*

"Back up," he said.

She crawled away from the opening.

With a grunt, his fingers grabbed the edge of the doorway, and he pulled himself up and through. He crouched there for a moment, breathing heavily and clutching his side.

Splinters and stuffing littered the room where furniture

had smashed against the wall, now the floor. The couch had crushed the entertainment system, the stink of fried electronics making her wrinkle her nose. One of the lights in the galley flickered, clinging to life as it blinked in an irregular pattern, casting shadows off the table bolted to the previous floor—now the wall.

The brighter light flooded in above them, the twisted walls angling the broken window, almost close enough to touch.

The captain stood. It *was* close enough for him to touch. He gave her a hand up and another boost.

"Ow!" A sliver of metal jabbed her hand.

He lowered her again, grabbing her bleeding hand. "Are you okay? What happened?"

She squinted up at the window. "The edge is all jagged metal and broken glass." She winced as he pulled the sliver out, then inspected her hand to make sure he got it all.

They both stared up at it for a moment, specks floating down through it, the wind still whistling.

The captain turned away and searched through the furniture. He pulled the rug out from under the mess. He shook it to get stray wood and glass shards off. "Throw this over the edge and grab onto it. Hopefully it's thick enough to protect our hands."

Lifting her again, she threw the rug over the edge. It worked as he'd predicted.

Outside the window, she squinted in the bright light, the wind whipping her hair around her face, the metal of the side of the ship hot.

With a little hop, Captain Lee grabbed the edge and pulled himself up. She blinked. It hadn't taken him any effort at all.

He grimaced, pressing a hand against his side. Well, maybe some effort.

From atop the ship, wide desert land stretched out before them, with high cliffs boxing them in on either side.

They slid and climbed down the side of the ship, sharp edges leaving bloody lines on their exposed skin. The captain caught her at the bottom.

They stepped out into the sand, the air dry and dusty. Gemma squinted against the blinding light and hot, blowing wind, but saw no other life. She still couldn't get enough air for a deep breath. "Where are we?"

"Planet 3X-527. The computer indicated there's a mining operation somewhere. I don't know where it is, but maybe we'll stumble onto it," the captain said. He shrugged. "That's all I know. Come on, we need to move."

She held onto his arm, and together they stumbled away from the wreckage.

Gemma turned her head, but he touched her arm. "Don't look back. It'll make you ... it'll make it harder."

Thorny vines clung to the faces of the cliffs on either side of them. Without a way to climb them, Captain Lee and Gemma followed the valley, their footsteps crunching on the loose sand and shale. Soon her calves tightened from walking on shifty ground.

The clouds parted, and the sun beat down, heat shimmering above the dusty ground. As if opening an oven, the hot wind blew her hair back, scorching her throat and whipping at their clothes. The stunted, yellowed vegetation offered no shade, so they had no choice but to keep going. Sweat dripped down her sides, and they both gasped for air in the thin atmosphere. Her bare shoulder, where her uniform had torn reddened in the sun. The planet's gravity—though only a fraction of Earth's, but more than the ship's—dragged at her.

Gemma wanted to call it quits after the first half hour, but the captain dragged her on for two.

A dark shape appeared on the horizon. As they drew closer, the wavy image solidified into an old all-terrain vehicle, flipped onto its side.

They sank down in its shadow, the captain propping her up against the warm, rusting roof. The truck had been here a long time, judging by the blown-out windows and no glass on the ground around it.

"Captain." She tried to swallow, her voice raspy. "What are we going to do? We can't go on like this."

"Here, drink." He produced a bottle of water from his bag, and she gulped it down. He took it away too soon for her liking. "Save some for later."

They lay panting in the shade for a while. The captain looked over and touched the edge of her slashed uniform sleeve. "That could have been a nasty gash."

She shrugged. "It was just the uniform. It didn't fit me anyway."

He gave an exhausted chuckle, closing his eyes and leaning back against the roof.

We're going to die. The bleary, unwelcome thought broke through her stupor. *Sandy will be so mad at me.*

The light dimmed around them, and she looked up. Dark, billowing clouds moved in, a churning wall in the sky. Her heart lifted. "Oh, thank goodness. It looks like rain."

A fat, hot drop splattered against her hand, and another on her cheek. She tilted her face to the sky. Then her fingers tingled. She wiped them on her shirt, then the drip on her cheek burned.

Drops fell all around them now. She turned to the captain as he swiped at his own face.

"Ow," he said. "There's something wrong with this rain."

"It's not water," she said, eyes wide. "It's acid rain!"

He grabbed her hand and pulled her to her feet. "Run!"

They ran toward a cliff face under a downpour. Everything burned. The longer it stayed on her skin, the worse it got. It dripped down her back, it got in her eyes. Gemma screamed.

Then cool darkness. The captain had steered them toward a cave.

"Get it off!" she yelled, her voice echoing. "Get it off!"

The captain fumbled with a flashlight. They ran deeper into the cave, dodging stalagmites and bumping off the hard, stone walls.

She wanted to scratch off her skin. It hurt everywhere. "Captain! I can't—"

They stumbled into a pool, and they both plunged in.

Gemma came up with a gasp. The pool was only waist deep, but it was water, not acid. Cold, cold water.

The captain's skin glowed red in the beam of the flashlight, and he clutched at his side. She must not look much better. They both panted.

He coughed and winced. "Let's go back to the entrance, so we don't get lost."

Gemma let out a long breath, reluctant to leave the soothing water. "Aye-aye, Captain."

"Will you stop doing that?"

"Sorry."

FIRELIGHT LIT THE MOUTH OF THE CAVE, CASTING LONG, FLICKERING shadows on the walls. Trevor ignored them, blinded as he stared into the heart of the fire, trying to think and keep from thinking at the same time.

Gemma slept nearby, the scrape on her head cleaned and

bandaged. The water from the pool they had washed in tasted funny, even after boiling it, but it quenched their thirst.

He had checked Gemma out thoroughly with the medical scanner. She had been so exhausted that she couldn't keep upright on her own. Once he confirmed she didn't have a concussion, he covered her with the blanket, and within moments she was out. He hadn't wanted to make a fire—what if someone from the killer ship saw it?—but the temperature dropped to a dangerous level.

Trevor had a few cracked ribs that hurt when he breathed, the pain constant as he panted to take in enough oxygen. Otherwise, he was unharmed. He'd be fine in a few days.

The only medical supplies he'd recovered had been from first aid kits, with no sign of sickbay's equipment. There was a good chance ...

Don't think of Charlie. Not yet. They still had a mission. They still had to survive. They still had to get home.

Correction: *She* had to get home. He'd left his home crumpled on the surface of this planet.

Squeezing his eyes shut, he clamped down on the rising emotion, but the hurt still leaked through. None of this would have happened if he hadn't sent her to her quarters. The peanuts had been an innocent mistake.

Trevor had compromised his ability to lead and make decisions when he developed—feelings—for her. He hadn't been thinking straight for the entire mission. She'd left him completely unable to function acceptably as a captain.

He never should have let her on the crew. The director hadn't given him a choice, but there was *always* a choice. Maybe a choice he didn't like, but he could have passed on the job.

Then *that* crew could have died instead ...

No, he was the best for the job. It wasn't her fault. It was his.

The rain stopped at least an hour ago, so his head snapped around at a noise outside the cave. A footfall. He *knew* a fire was a bad idea.

Trevor touched Gemma's shoulder, covering her mouth with his other hand. She blinked awake, then frowned at him. He gestured to stay still and quiet, then crept toward the cave entrance.

He jumped about a foot when she grabbed his shoulder, tugging him back. He waved her away. She shook her head. His jaw tightening, he pointed at her, then jabbed his finger deeper into the cave. Her face hardened and she lifted her chin, arms crossed. He sighed. In one last attempt at authority, he held an insistent finger to his lips. She opened her mouth—

Another footstep outside.

Her mouth closed and she nodded, finally looking properly concerned.

He assessed the situation; the hiss of personal oxygen masks let him count at least four people, possibly more. Stunners gave off the slightest hum when warmed up, and he could count a couple of those.

On the other hand, there was only one of him, unarmed, and he had to protect Gemma at all costs. Unable to see through the darkness outside the cave, he was at a severe disadvantage.

He tipped the pot of boiled water onto the flames, which went out with a hiss and lots of steam.

The hum grew louder outside, and he saw a flash, then an explosion against his chest, searing heat everywhere. Gemma screamed, then nothing.

Trevor came to slowly, his mouth dry, head throbbing. His entire body felt like he'd gotten too close to an engine that exploded—which he had, at one point in his life, but not recently. He opened his eyes to a ceiling spotted with florescent lights and emergency sprinklers.

"Captain?" Gemma leaned over him. "Are you okay?" She held a cup to his lips, and he slurped the water, then dropped his head back with a sigh, closing his eyes. He could finally breathe. It still hurt, but it had a higher concentration of oxygen than the planet's atmosphere. Tinged with the smell of bleach.

"They hit you with a stunner, full power," she said. "Don't move yet. I'm surprised you're even awake."

He gritted his teeth, forced his elbows under him, and sat up. The white room around them had two beds, two cupboards, two doors, and not much else.

His head spun. "More water?" he croaked. She held out the cup again.

"Wow. I don't know how you're even moving after a hit like that," she said. "They threatened to zap me too, unless—"

"Do you know who has us?" He squeezed his eyes shut, trying to shake off the aftereffects.

She shook her head. "They brought us here on a land shuttle, but I'm not sure where 'here' is. I think it's the mining colony."

Mining colony? His thoughts swirled for a moment before he clamped them down. Focus. *What do we do next? What are the options?*

He had no idea.

She leaned against the wall, arms crossed. "So, what now, Captain?"

He took a deep breath, wincing and clutching his side. "I'm not sure." He cleared his throat and gulped more water. "We could see what they want. Maybe we can reason with them."

But Trevor didn't feel reasonable. His ship's destruction had trapped them on this stupid planet. Someone had stunned him and brought them to this place against their will. And his entire crew was ... his friends were ...

Trevor's face set, his pulse speeding up as his brows lowered. It was time to take control of the situation. "I, personally, am all for attacking the next person who opens that door."

"Attack? Are you kidding?" She uncrossed her arms. "That's a terrible idea. And I don't think you're in any condition to—"

"Obviously, they don't want to kill us," he said. He forced himself to stand and pace on shaky legs, talking faster. "They want to question us, which offers us a measure of protection."

He wobbled, and Gemma grabbed his arm.

"Let go of me," he ordered. He wanted to wrench away, but he might end up hurting them both.

"But if we got out of here, where would we go?" Gemma asked, her grip on his arm tightening. "Back out into that wasteland? Captain, you really should sit down."

He shook his head. "No. They'll have ships here. We have to find a hangar, steal a ship, and leave."

A deafening *click* startled them both, followed by gears turning as one of the walls rose.

Gemma let out a yelp, accidentally jerking him off balance. They teetered for a moment, and as they fell, he twisted—gritting his teeth, against the stab of his broken ribs—so he wouldn't land on her as they crashed to the floor.

He groaned and waved away her attempts to help him up. "I need a minute."

"Um, Captain?" She pointed in the direction of the moved wall. "I think you should see this."

Hissing through his teeth, Trevor forced himself upright to see a glassed room behind the raised wall.

A frail man in oversized glasses and a lab coat grinned at them from the other side. He flicked a switch and spoke too loudly into the microphone.

"Hello there!"

Trevor winced.

"Um, hello." Gemma offered a little wave.

"We're sorry to be keeping you like this, but we have a very strict quarantine policy," the little old man explained. "Anyone who has been on the planet's surface must be quarantined for twenty-four hours. I know it's a bother. But it's for everyone's safety."

"Uh ... " Trevor staggered to his feet, Gemma hovering next to him. "Where—?"

"I am Dr. Stratson," the man went on. "There are some blankets and extra clothes in those cupboards there. Should you need anything else, there's a call button beside your door. Food and water will be sent in soon. Did you eat anything while you were on the surface?"

"Um, no," Gemma said.

"I recommend you take a shower right away, in case you came in contact with any of the local flora," Dr. Stratson said. "And we have some balm for the minor burns from the rain. The rain has a rather mild acidic makeup, but I know it still hurts. You can throw your clothes down the chute in the corner. Do you have any questions?"

"Yes." Trevor's eyes narrowed. "Where are we, and who are you people?"

"I don't know much about diplomacy," Gemma whispered to him, "but I'm sure there's a better way to say that."

Diplomacy? He suppressed a laugh. He wasn't a diplomat. He was a transport ship captain, not some high-brow military operation.

Dr. Stratson smiled again. "We are a mining colony on the planet 3X-527. We like to call it Thalo. And who might you be?"

Gemma and Trevor shared a look. "We're what's left of a crew attacked by pirates and crash-landed here," Trevor said. "We were transporting food and supplies to Cerise."

He hoped pirates had attacked them. Any other reason would be so much worse.

Dr. Stratson nodded, still smiling, while making a note on an electronic pad. "We detected your crash, which is why we sent someone to pick you up."

"Did they really have to stun me?" Trevor asked. He shook himself, the effects wearing off, but his whole body ached.

Dr. Stratson waved his hand. "One of the recruits is new, and a little trigger-happy."

"What are you planning on doing with us?" Trevor asked.

"Well, once your quarantine is up ... " The doctor paused to concentrate on what he was writing. Another man came into the glass room and handed him something. Dr. Stratson's lips moved while he read, then he turned his attention back to them. "After your quarantine, you will be given a medical examination, then you may meet with our supervisor to negotiate."

"Negotiate?" Gemma asked at the same time Trevor yelled, "Medical examination?!"

Trevor's chest tightened. No, no, no. He couldn't let them examine him.

"Yes," the doctor said absently, once again engrossed in the memo he had been handed. "We would like very much to help you get home, but we have limited resources, so you will be given the opportunity to negotiate a loan or choose to stay here. I'm sorry, there is something I must attend to."

With that, he flicked off the switch, and the wall once again slid into place.

"Wait, wait! What do you mean medical examination?" Trevor yelled after him, banging on the window, but the doctor either didn't hear or ignored him. Gemma shot him a curious look.

"What's wrong?" she asked.

Trevor's hand went to his forehead, and he groaned, sweat rolling down his back. *No.* He couldn't do this. He needed Charlie.

His knees buckled, but when Gemma reached out to steady him, he flinched.

"Whoa, take it easy." Gemma eased him to sit on one of the beds. "You're still recovering from that stunner. You need to calm down."

His breathing came too fast, but he couldn't stop it, his chest even tighter. "I can't ... I can't—"

"Captain! You have to stop it!" She took hold of both sides of his face and turned it toward her. "Look at me!" He did, blinking to bring her face into focus. "You must calm down. Relax, *please*. You didn't lose it when faced with pirates and desert and acid rain. I refuse to sit back and watch you crumble now. So, stop it, okay?"

Trevor nodded. She grabbed his twitching hands between hers and held them still, his breathing still too quick.

"I'm here," she said in a soft voice. "We're alive, and we're going to get through this. Breathe. Listen to the sound of your breathing."

Too fast. His breathing came too fast.

"Close your eyes," she said.

He did, his face tight as he concentrated. *Concentrate! Concentrate* on what?

Beneath his own gasping, he did find something calming: *her* breathing.

Trevor focused on hers—listening, *feeling* it. Her soft, cool hands comforted him. He resisted the urge to press them against his hot face.

He finally pulled in a deep, painful sigh, his breathing slower.

Trevor opened his eyes, his gaze focused on his hands in Gemma's before gently pulling them back.

"Feel better?" she asked.

He shook his head. He couldn't be examined. They'd find out, and that would be the end of it. His mission would be dead. *He'd* be dead.

"It's okay," Gemma said. Her hand pressed against his forehead. "Your face is hot. Maybe you're overheating."

Even as he gently pushed her away, he missed her touch. "It's nothing." He took a trembling breath, shaking his head to clear it. *Focus.* He couldn't lose it now. *Don't be emotional.*

"I'm fine," he said. "I'm fine. Sorry."

"Are you sure?" She reached for his shoulder, but he shook her off.

"I said I'm fine," he snapped.

Gemma rolled her eyes. "Oookay then."

"What time is it?" he asked.

She shook her head. "I don't know what ship's time it is, but here it's—"

"The time is oh-nine-twenty-three," said Zane.

Trevor whipped around, his eyes searching, but didn't see anyone else. Zane?

"Oh my gosh." Gemma covered her mouth, tears squeezing

out of her eyes. "Oh my gosh, Zane—no, Captain! No, sit back down, he's not here!"

If Zane was alive— "No, I heard him!"

"It's a clock, Captain!" Her voice cracked. "Zane gave me a clock. It's just his voice. It's a recording."

Trevor sat down hard, hands shaking. For a moment, he had hoped …

Focus.

He squeezed his eyes shut and took a deep breath. Morning. The clock said it was morning. He didn't want to sleep anyway.

They took stock of the supplies in the room with them. Not much beyond his original assessment. A rattling heater warmed one corner of the room. The squeaky wheels of a cart stopped outside their door, before a panel in the wall opened and two trays were pushed in.

They took turns using the shower and changed into the gray clothing and soft-soled shoes provided. The pants stopped several inches short of his ankles, but the shirt wasn't a bad fit.

He glanced over at Gemma. It was the first time he had ever seen her in clothing that fit. It made a huge difference. She—

He turned away, face red. *Shut up.*

Trevor dropped his notebook into his pocket, and made sure to slip in the pen the director had given him. They both kept their ship keys. They could still be useful, especially the communicator.

"Captain!" Gemma gasped.

He whipped around, hissing at the pain in his ribs. "What? What's wrong?"

"Your arm." She pointed at his scarred forearm, visible under his too-short sleeve. "What happened? Chase had a burn just like that, except his was redder."

Trevor's mouth tightened. "We both got caught in the same explosion."

"What happened?"

He struggled to keep his voice even and gentle. "It's not your business."

Gemma huffed, then spotted a deck of cards in the cupboard.

"Want to play?" she asked.

Trevor's forehead creased. "I'm not sure now is the right time."

"Oh, come on." She gestured around the room. "What else are you going to do for the next twenty-four hours?"

He smiled a tight smile. At least he could distract her and keep her spirits up. "Prepare to lose."

They played slap jack, speed, and gin rummy until Gemma yawned.

"Tired of losing?" he joked.

She shook her head. "One more round." But dark smudges had formed under her eyes.

"Why don't you get some rest?" he suggested. It was the middle of the afternoon planet-time, but the exhaustion of the ordeal had caught up with them.

"What about you?" she asked.

He looked around and shrugged. "I'll keep watch."

"And watch me while I'm sleeping? No way!"

Trevor rolled his eyes. "Fine. Then I'll lie down too."

They lay down on the beds across from each other, the plastic mattresses crinkling every time they shifted. Trevor didn't intend to fall asleep, but soon they both drifted off.

Two men in uniforms carrying stunners roused Gemma out of bed. Their quarantine had ended. They'd slept longer than planned.

The men led her and the captain down a long hallway. The captain couldn't hide his anxiety, his hands constantly on the move, his face frozen in a grimace. Otherwise, he kept it together.

"It's going be okay," Gemma told him. He nodded, but didn't look like he believed her. She took a risk and slipped her hand into his. He let her. His sweaty palm gripped her tightly.

"Please, come in," a cheerful woman in a lab coat welcomed them. Maybe in her twenties, bleach-blonde, cute. Gemma glanced at Captain Lee, who paid the nurse no attention.

The guards waited outside. A paper-covered examination table stood behind her, and she waved toward the chairs against the wall. "Take a seat and we'll get started."

She told them her name while pulling on a pair of latex gloves, but Gemma could see the captain didn't hear a word she said, his jaw clenched so tight Gemma thought his teeth would crack.

The nurse took their temperatures, blood pressure, recorded their height and weight—Gemma had known the captain was tall, but *seven feet?*—and asked them a few typical questions. The nurse had concerns about the captain's high blood pressure.

Gemma shook her head. *Obviously* it was high. His high

stress level even reddened his face, although she still didn't know what his problem was.

"Alright," the nurse said, "now we're going to do a blood panel, give you a few shots, do a couple of scans, the doctor will come out and talk with you for a bit, and then we'll send you on your way."

"Where are we going next?" Gemma asked.

"Is the blood test optional?" Captain Lee interrupted. Gemma and the nurse looked at him.

"No, it's not optional," the nurse said, eyebrows raised. "I promise, it won't hurt."

"No, I know," the captain said, his hands clasped in his lap, his fingers twitching. Gemma could see him striving to be calm. "I really would rather not. Maybe I could stay in quarantine until we leave."

Gemma stared at him, open-mouthed. "Are you crazy?" she hissed. "No one wants to stay in quarantine. If you do, I promise I'm not staying with you."

"That's not an option," the nurse told him. "We need to do a blood test. Standard operating procedure for all medical exams, no exceptions."

The captain's jaw clenched. "I don't think you understand—"

"This isn't a discussion—" the nurse interrupted.

"I am not submitting to a blood test," Captain Lee insisted, standing to his full height and looking down at her.

The nurse took a step back. Gemma blinked. His height was impressive, of course, but his breathing came too fast, his voice rougher. The panic in his tone somehow frightened her more than she'd been at *The Watering Hole*—or as much as the fitness center.

In the fitness center, he'd been angry and out of control.

And now—even though it wasn't anger that widened his eyes —he seemed on the fraying edge of control again.

"Sir, please calm down." The nurse had been joined by Dr. Stratson, who now did the talking. "How about this: we'll give you the injections and do the scans first, then we'll talk about the blood test afterward." He spread his empty hands, palms up, as if to pacify the captain. "We're just trying to do our job, so let's get as much done as we can for now."

Captain Lee hesitated, then nodded, sitting on the examination table. The nurse was already finishing up taking Gemma's blood and put the vial into a machine that whirred before flashing words up onto a screen. The doctor read through the results while the nurse prepared an injection for the captain.

"Lay back," she told him. She cleaned a spot on his arm and stuck him with the needle. It took only a few seconds. She turned to dispose of the needle. The captain started to sit up but slumped back against the table.

TREVOR COULDN'T SIT UP.

"Hey—" He blinked as his vision swam. "Hey ... what ... what was that ... you ..." He couldn't move his arms. He tried to shake his head to clear it.

"Captain?" Gemma leaned over him. "Are you okay? Doctor, what happened?"

"We gave him a relaxer," he said, tying off Trevor's arm and proceeding to draw blood. Trevor could only watch in horror, his eyes wide, his mouth twitching. Even with the relaxer he trembled.

"You can't do that!" Gemma yelled. "You said—"

"We told him it wasn't optional," the doctor interrupted, inserting the tube of blood into the machine. Trevor gritted his teeth and struggled against the relaxer. His body tensed. The table he lay on rattled. The machine whirred.

"What's happening?" Gemma demanded. Trevor's eyes squeezed shut and his arms and legs jerked. He had to *move. Now!* "What did you do to him?"

"We didn't do this! Grab him!" Dr. Stratson said, trying to keep him on the table. Trevor groaned. He had to get out of here.

A soft alarm and a light flashed on the machine. The doctor turned back.

That's the moment Trevor broke through the relaxer, reached up, and grabbed the nurse, throwing her into Dr. Stratson. They both went down as Gemma screamed.

"Pilot, shut up!" Trevor said, sliding off the table to his feet. He staggered, hand gripping the edge of the table.

He had knocked the doctor unconscious, but the nurse crawled toward the comm on the wall. She screamed as Trevor hauled her over to the table.

The door slid open, and two guards rushed in, stunners raised.

"Stop right—"

Without even thinking, Trevor spun, punching the first guard in the face and elbowing the other in the gut. He threw the screaming nurse at them, and they all collapsed. Then he grabbed a chair and flung it into the beeping blood machine, smashing it.

He pressed an arm against the wall for balance as he panted, sweat dripping into his eyes. He still fought against the relaxer, the exertion shaking his body. Nausea rose in his throat. *Get out now, throw up later.*

"Captain!" Gemma gasped.

He grabbed her hand and dragged her to the door. His head throbbed in time with his pulse and his hands shook.

"How—what—why's the—" Gemma sputtered.

"Not now," he said, pulling her through the door. "We have to get out of here."

13

Alarms blared and flashed as they ran through the corridors. Trevor staggered through room after hallway after room of plastic sheets and drywall, dragging Gemma with him. He saw no sign of people in this section of the colony as they fled through the maze, currently under construction. No sign of a hangar. The rise of panic made his heart pound even more than the search did. If they didn't find a hangar soon—

Around the next corner they ran headlong into a troop of security guards responding to the alarm, still strapping on their helmets. Before the troop had time to react, Trevor flung open the nearest door and shoved Gemma into it, locking themselves inside.

Another room under construction, with half-assembled furniture and a toolbox—and only one door, the one they'd come through, trapping them. The nausea rose again.

"Captain, what's going on?" Gemma demanded. He ignored her, looking through the toolbox to find something—anything—to use as a weapon. He found a hammer and swung it, testing its weight.

Gemma snatched it out of his hands. "You can't use that, you'll kill someone!"

"What do you think they're going to do to me?" he demanded, reaching for it.

She planted a hand against his chest and held the hammer away from him. He could still reach it, but didn't try. "Why would they want to kill you?"

"I ... Because I—" He shook his head. He couldn't tell her. He couldn't face her and say it.

Maybe he could break through the wall. They seemed thin enough, but his energy waned. They wouldn't get very far that way.

"Captain!"

Banging outside. "They're overriding the lock," Trevor said, recognizing the clicking even as his head swam. "Stay back." He grabbed her shoulders and turned her to face him. "As soon as you see an opening, run for it and find a hangar. Fire up a ship, and I'll be right behind you."

Gemma frowned. "I can't help you if you don't tell me what's going on!"

With a click, the door slid open. "Get down!" He shoved her to the floor behind a desk.

Trevor darted into the hallway elbow-first, catching the closest security officer in the face.

An entire squad had assembled outside the door, more than he'd expected. Too late to turn back, he kept going. He'd faced worse odds. Maybe? He couldn't think straight, his head still woozy from the drug they'd given him. He knew if he stopped, he'd be dead.

He knocked over a second man and aimed a kick at a third. One of them grabbed him from behind, pinning his arms to his sides. He pushed back hard, then threw his weight forward. His captor's grip loosened as he was knocked off his feet. Someone took a shot at Trevor with a stunner, grazing his leg. He cried out as it burned, then went numb, his body sagging to one side as his leg refused to hold his weight anymore.

They were trying to *stun* him. They didn't know. He and Gemma had to get out of there before they figured it out.

A guard grabbed at his arm, but Trevor flung him off his feet into the one behind him.

Then the nurse came running down the hall, her lab coat flapping behind her as she shouted to the guards.

Game over.

One of the guards heard the nurse and yelled to the others, pointing at Captain Lee. Trevor saw him tuck his stunner into his belt as he pulled out another weapon that warmed up with a familiar rattle.

Someone opened fire, but Trevor ducked and rolled back into the room he'd leapt from. Cracked ribs, woozy, useless leg...

His eyes darted around the room. Nowhere to hide. Nothing to fight with. *Do something!*

His gaze settled on Gemma. She stood in the middle of the room instead of behind the desk where he'd put her, still holding the hammer.

Trevor swallowed hard. He had only one hope of living. A slim hope at that.

Limping on his numb leg, he grabbed her shoulders. "I need a hostage," he explained, spinning her around and holding her back against him, between him and the door. He dragged her backwards until the desk pressed against the back of his legs.

"Captain! What are you doing!" she screeched, hurting his ears. She dropped the hammer and struggled, but he held her tight, one arm across her neck and shoulders and the other around her waist, pinning her arms.

"Trust me," he whispered in her ear. "Do you trust me?"

"I do, but—"

The guards burst into the room.

Everyone froze. Even Gemma stopped struggling. All weapons pointed at them. Not stunners, but rattlers—killing weapons. The color drained from her face.

Trevor went cold. What if this didn't work? Then he'd put *her* in danger, too.

"Let her go," one of the guards commanded.

"I want to talk to the man in charge," Trevor said, trying to keep his voice level against the adrenaline, the sedative, and the hit from the stunner.

"Now you want to talk? Captain, what's going on?" Gemma whispered, her voice higher than normal. "What are you doing? Let me go."

"Don't worry, they won't shoot you," he whispered.

"Let the woman go first."

"No. I have no guarantee that you won't shoot me," Trevor snapped back, his jaw beginning to clench with the effort of standing.

"What makes you think you deserve to live?" shouted one of the guards. His commander silenced him with a glare.

"Let the woman go," the commander ordered.

"Test tube experiment!" interrupted the same guard. He spat on the floor. "You should have been wiped out with all the others!"

Gemma spoke slowly, a tremor in her voice. "What are they talking about?"

"In there!" The nurse shouted from the hallway. "The Tubie is in there!"

"Captain?" Gemma tensed under his arms. "No. You can't

be. Right?" He didn't say anything, and he felt her swallow. "You're a ... a ..."

"Get me the man in charge!" Trevor demanded again, his voice rough. He didn't want to hear her say it. He couldn't bear her disgust.

Grown in a cloning tank for the purpose of conquest and destruction ... He squeezed his eyes shut. He would never be free of his greatest shame.

His ears rang, and the weakness in his leg crept upwards, his body slowly falling asleep. He clung to Gemma, but she had a hard time staying upright as more and more of his weight pressed on her shoulders.

Sweat dripped down his forehead. He was going to die here, and his mission with him.

Maybe Gemma could finish it.

"I am the man in charge," said a calm voice. The guards stepped aside to allow a man through, his hands held out in front of him. Instead of a guard's protective vest and helmet, his cream-colored clothes marked him as a civilian. A high-ranking one, according to the pins on his lapel. He couldn't be much older than Trevor. "You wanted to see me?"

"The—the pen." Trevor whispered in her ear; his voice urgent but fading. He shook his head to clear it. It didn't help. "Pilot, you have to deliver the pen—"

As if she hadn't heard him, her voice strangled as she said, " ... Alex?"

The man did a double-take, his jaw dropping. "Gemma?"

"Alex, it's me," she said.

A smile spread across his face. "Gemma! What are you—"

She tried to take a step forward, but Trevor held her tight. He wobbled, his vision blurred. The smile across the man's face plunged into a frown.

"Let me go, it's okay." Gemma's soft voice reached Trevor

through the wall of cotton closing around his senses, her cool hand on his arm. "Trust me."

He unclenched his shaking limbs, his muscles spasming as he lost his grip, sagging against the desk behind him. He couldn't move. He was done, his life in her hands.

Through sheer willpower Gemma stayed standing as the captain's grip loosened, his weight sliding off her shoulders, threatening to take her with him. She glanced back. Captain Lee slumped onto the floor against the desk, his breathing shallow, his eyes glazed.

Her gaze snapped back to Alex. Her brain spun with a million questions for both him and the captain. But with Captain Lee out of commission, she focused on Alex's, which stabbed her heart. Why had he left? Where had he been? And of all the places in the galaxy, how was he *here?*

The most important question of all drowned out all the others: *What will happen now?*

Careful to keep herself between the guns and her captain, Gemma slowly held up her hands. "Alex. Stop."

"Move out of the way, Gemma," he ordered.

"It's okay, he's with me!" she said.

"*With* you?" Alex repeated, his brown eyes narrowed.

"Well, I mean—" she stuttered. She knew that tone. Alex had definitely taken it the wrong way. He had always been quick to do that. "Not—I mean—we're traveling together. Just let us go."

Alex's expression didn't soften. "So, you're knowingly traveling with a—"

"No, I didn't know." She straightened her spine and looked Alex in the eye. "But that doesn't matter. He's ... he's a good person."

Alex barked a laugh. "A good person? The blood test came back positive with genetic markers. He's genetically engineered."

Gemma swallowed hard and nodded, the implications sinking in. Tubies were seen as monsters ... but she couldn't see Captain Lee as a monster. "I understand."

Alex looked at her as if she'd grown another head. "And you still want us to let him go?"

About a dozen people crammed into the hallway behind Alex, all of them staring straight at her. Her face heated, but she tightened her fists and kept her voice from shaking. "Yes. I do."

Alex shook his head. "But why—?"

"Alex," she pleaded, "I'm telling you; he's not going to hurt anyone."

"Right." Alex's eyebrows rose. "What about the security men he's already injured?"

"Self-defense," Gemma snapped. "If you'd let me, I can explain everything." She clasped her hands under her chin. "Please, Alex. Just you and me."

He hesitated, the gears turning in his head. He could never say no to her. Except once ...

No, he hadn't said no. He'd left without saying goodbye.

"He's dangerous," Alex insisted.

"Does he look dangerous to you right now?" she demanded. She took a calming breath. "He can't even move."

Alex conferred with the commander in a low voice. The commander threw two pairs of restraints onto the floor between them.

"He'll need to be restrained," Alex said. "Wrists and ankles."

Gemma hurried to comply, as Alex said, "You may go now, Commander."

"Mr. Steele, we can't leave you—"

"It's all right, Commander." Alex's voice seemed calm, but she could read his eyes. They burned through her, a mixture of anger and a demand for answers—and he knew he would never find those answers in front of an audience. "If it makes you feel any better, I'm armed."

The door closed as the last restraint clicked into place.

"What's going on here?" Alex demanded, taking a step towards her.

"Stop!" She raised her hands, careful to keep herself between Alex and the captain. "Let me explain."

He crossed his arms and waited.

She told him about their mission, and how they'd been shot down and crash-landed here.

He only interrupted once; his eyes wide. "He's a captain? For Omni Authority? But he's—"

"Yes," Gemma said. "And he needs help. *I* need help. I'm asking for sanctuary for Captain Lee and myself."

Alex considered them for a long moment. Gemma fought not to fidget under his gaze. She knew better than to interrupt, but this time, she had no idea what he was thinking.

"I can grant sanctuary for you, but for the Tubie—"

"No. *Both* of us," she insisted. "He's a *captain*. That must count for something."

Alex hesitated, then gave a nod. "Sanctuary granted." He opened the door and leaned out into the hall. "I've granted this man sanctuary," he said. "Did everyone hear that?"

"He's not a man! He's a Tubie! He—" The voice silenced. A tense moment passed.

"Do you understand?" Alex said, a hard edge to his voice.

"Yes, sir."

"Good." He glanced over at the captain. "Get this man back to the medical station."

"Thank y—" Gemma started.

Alex held up a hand. "You stay with him to make sure he gets to the medical station alive. I have a few fires to put out."

GEMMA SAT IN A CHAIR, HER ELBOWS ON THE BED, WAITING. CAPTAIN Lee's chest rose and fell in the slow, steady rhythm of sleep.

The staff had done little to help him besides depositing him on a bed and wheeling him back to the quarantine room. Gemma had to demand a first aid kit and treat his cuts and scrapes herself. At least they'd removed his restraints before locking them in.

And now she waited.

She hid her face in her hands. Her first mission had taken a catastrophic turn she could never have foreseen. She'd been putting the pieces together while he'd slept. Captain Lee was a Tubie? And she had *liked* him?

Gemma couldn't decide if she should shudder or not. Tubies topped the list of disgusting things. But ... she couldn't put Captain Lee on that list.

It felt like forever until the captain stirred and opened his eyes.

"What happened?" His hand went to his forehead, and he winced.

"Oh, nothing," she said, her voice casual. "I just saved your life."

He blinked at her. "Huh?"

"You don't remember?" Gemma's jaw tightened. "The blood test? Alarms? Fighting? How I stood between you and a gun—multiple guns—set to *kill?*"

His eyes widened. Ah, he did remember.

"I never meant to put you in danger," he said. "Thank yo—"

Gemma pulled back a fist and punched his arm as hard as she could. "Why didn't you tell me you were a genetically engineered super soldier?" She punched his arm again.

He groaned. "That hurt!"

"I mean, it explains a lot," she said. "How you're so strong, how you recover so quickly from being stunned on full power, why you hardly sleep, your reflexes. Is this why you're so tall? Why you don't even have a first name."

He groaned again as he sat up. "I have a—"

"Did everyone know but me?" She knew they had been keeping something from her. "Does Omni Authority know?"

He looked away. "No one knows, just Charlie."

"How come he never turned you in?" She stood and began to pace, more and more questions bubbling to the surface. "How are you even alive? If you're really a killing machine, then how am *I* still alive? Is that why you're not upset about losing your entire crew? Do you even have feelings? Or just survival instincts? How strong are you?" She stopped. "Why aren't you answering me?"

He wouldn't look at her. "I have feelings."

Her heart gave a pang. *Not now.* There was so much more to know. "Why didn't you tell me?"

"What was I supposed to say?" He met her gaze, his voice as tired as his eyes. "Hi, I'm an illegal experiment designed to wipe out entire civilizations, please trust me to be your captain?"

"Okay, I can see that." She sank down in the chair next to the bed, arms folded.

She should have known that her first mission would go so awry. "This is causing a lot of problems."

"The problems are just starting," he said, rubbing his head with a wince. "I can't believe they didn't kill me. How did you do it?"

"The supervisor and I are childhood friends," she said. She swallowed. More than friends. Much, much more—

She looked up to see the captain staring at her. "What?"

His eyebrows rose. "Is that all? He believes you because you were children together?"

She chewed her lip. Maybe he should know a little more. "Alex and I dated for a while, before I entered flight school." *Before he left me.*

A long pause.

"Ah."

Gemma sighed, scrubbing at her face. "Can I trust you?"

The captain rolled his eyes. "You're still alive, aren't you?"

"Okay, you have a point." She hesitated. "Is that why you—"

The door slid open, and Alex walked in. Her heart tightened. Alex may have saved the captain's life, but he had left her. The day after her acceptance to flight school, he boarded a ship to the colonies, leaving only a short note behind.

"How's the patient?" he asked.

"Alive," the captain said. He held out a hand to shake. "Thanks to you, Alex."

"You mean thanks to her," Alex corrected, ignoring the hand. Captain Lee lowered it, his lips pressed together. "And you can call me Mr. Steele." He crossed his arms. "You've put me in a tough position, Gemma."

"I'm sorry," she said, lowering her eyes. *Sorry, not sorry.*

"Don't blame her, she didn't know," the captain said, his voice urgent. "I'm the one who's sorry."

Alex pointed at her. "But she knows now, and she's still defending you."

You bet I am. "Hey, he's earned my trust," Gemma said. "I'll do anything to protect him."

The captain raised an eyebrow. "Now who's protecting who?"

Gemma couldn't suppress a smirk.

Alex sighed. "What are you doing all the way out here?"

She schooled her face into an impassive expression. Alex wouldn't take kindly to inside jokes, but he seemed to have missed that one.

"I told you; we were transporting relief supplies to Cerise in the Ruby District," Gemma explained. "We were shot down by … " She glanced at the captain.

"An unknown ship," he finished.

Alex sighed and rubbed at his face. He'd always done that when stressed. "I can put you up for a few days, but you have to get out of here quick."

"Absolutely," Gemma said. She couldn't wait to get out of this dinky hole and back to the stars.

And *away* from Alex. Did he have any idea how much he'd hurt her?

The captain rolled off the bed and slowly straightened. "Where to?"

"You stay here," Alex said.

Captain Lee stiffened.

Gemma looked around. "This is one of the quarantine rooms."

"Yes. No one can get in or out without authorization, so it's for your protection."

Gemma's fists went to her hips. "Alex, that's not very nice—"

"Understood," the captain said. He stood ramrod straight, his hands behind his back, his jaw tight. What was he thinking? Was he okay?

Alex took Gemma's hand. Captain Lee looked away.

"Come on," Alex said. "I'll show you to your room."

She hesitated. "Shouldn't I stay with—"

"Go," the captain said. "I'll be fine."

But will I be? She glanced at Alex. Being away from Captain Lee meant being alone with Alex.

They didn't talk much on the way to her temporary quarters, Gemma clutching her duffle bag for comfort. After arriving at her door, Alex had only taken a breath before he was called away.

The sparse room he gave Gemma looked brand new. The linoleum was still shiny, the appliance manual still in the bare fridge, and she had to take the plastic off the mattress.

She explored every inch—linens and a couple of hangers in the closet, the kitchenette cupboards empty, the walls still smelling of fresh paint.

Gemma logged into her account on the workstation in her room and found a message from Sandy waiting for her.

"A MISUNDERSTANDING? HOW CAN YOUR LIPS ON HIS BE A *misunderstanding?*"

Sandy laughed, then looked thoughtful. "*Hmm ... 'not appropriate' isn't exactly a rejection ... I wish I was there to help you, too.*

"Listen, Gem." Sandy chewed her lip. *"I have something serious to talk to you about. I was wondering ... what do you think if David and I lived here in the house after we're married? I mean, if you're going to be working in space, you won't really be using it, and it's all paid off, so it would be a lot cheaper than renting ... we'd keep your room, of course."* Sandy winced. *"I have no idea what you're going to say. Please don't be mad. It's just a thought."*

GEMMA STARED AT THE SCREEN. SO MUCH HAD HAPPENED IN SUCH A short amount of time. The silly problems she had wanted to talk to Sandy about before didn't matter now.

She didn't know where to start. *Where to start?*

Gemma dropped her head into her hands. It was too much. Just too much. She needed ... she needed time. Once she figured it out herself, then she would tell Sandy.

Except for Alex. Gemma straightened up. She had to tell Sandy about Alex.

She pasted on a smile and pressed record.

"Sandy! Of course you guys can live there. I'm thrilled at the idea."

Gemma took a deep breath. "I have something big, you're not going to believe this. I found Alex. I found Alex! Can you believe it? He's been missing all this time. What a small galaxy. Just think, if we hadn't crashed here ... "

Someone knocked at the door, making her jump. It could be Alex. Or the captain. She had to wrap this letter up.

Only now did she notice her battered and scraped appearance in the small corner of the screen.

Another knock.

"I'm fine, everything is fine. Love you and miss you."

She sent it, but when she opened the door, it was neither Alex (relief), nor the captain (why did she feel disappointed about that?). A lady wheeled in a cart with a plate of food, then left.

The food was pretty good. Did they give Captain Lee anything to eat? Maybe she should save him some.

She hesitated before the next bite. Knowing who he is —*what* he is—how would they treat him?

Long after she'd finished eating, nothing happened. She considered sending a more reassuring message to Sandy, but what if someone showed up then?

She paced. Everyone now knew his biggest secret. *Is he okay?* He must be so overwhelmed. Charlie wasn't there to help him, either.

That explained why he never got close to anyone. He had been afraid they'd find out.

After three hours with no word from anyone, she decided to take the initiative and see the captain. She couldn't imagine how he felt. She needed to talk to him, and needed answers for more of her questions. Plus, she'd saved him some food.

The banging of a hammer echoed from behind a plastic sheet over an empty doorway. The strong smell of wet paint wrinkled her nose. She remembered the way through the maze of white halls back to the quarantine rooms.

The few people she saw in the halls stared, but didn't stop her.

She rounded the corner and saw the captain's room, when a voice called her name.

"Gemma!"

She turned to see Alex jogging down the hall. She forced a smile and reminded herself to breathe.

"There you are!" he said, catching up to her. His blond hair always gave the illusion of casualness, but she knew how much time he spent each morning getting every strand in *exactly* the right place.

"Alex," she said. His arms were open, so she gave him an awkward one-armed hug, her other arm holding the tray. He never did grow taller than her, like he'd hoped he would.

He held onto the hug a little longer after she had let go.

"Where have you been? Keeping busy?" she said into his shoulder.

He released her. "There was the usual business that comes with running a colony. I also had to calm some people down. Your friend caused quite an uproar."

"I meant where have you been *all this time*?" She hoped he noticed the annoyance in her voice. After two years together, he should be able to pick up on it.

"Here, mostly," he said, shrugging. He ignored her icy tone. "I go where the need is, and they needed me here. I take it that you blasted your way through flight school?"

She couldn't contain a grin. "You'd better believe it."

He hugged her again, even tighter this time, lifting her a few inches off the ground and threatening to knock over the tray she held. "I knew you would! I'm so proud of you."

"Uh huh." She patted his back. He didn't seem to under-stand how awkward this was.

He paused, setting her down. "You travel with some unusual ... company."

"But he can be trusted," she assured him quickly. *I trust him.*

"If you say so," he said. His hand still gently gripped her shoulder. "Gem—"

"We thought you were dead." The sentence burst out of her without permission, her hurt exploding in a spray of words. "You just ... *left*. You left us all behind. You left *me* behind. Did you ever stop to think about how I'd feel? It was selfish of you. You left a gaping hole in my heart." She looked away. "I … I missed you."

"Yeah, I know." Alex looked down and sighed. "I've missed you, too."

"Yeah?" Her face hardened. "Did all your messages get lost in space?"

"Gemma—" He reached for her hand.

She jerked away. "If you missed me so much, why didn't you contact me?"

"I wanted to." He sighed. "I must have recorded a hundred messages for you. I can show you them. I just could never send them."

Gemma hesitated. He had always hated being on camera. *Not an acceptable excuse.*

He took her hand, and this time she let him, but that little flutter in her stomach she'd expected didn't happen. It used to happen all the time, every time.

Gemma sucked in her breath. She had finally gotten over him and hadn't even realized it.

"I always wished you could be here with me." He took a deep breath. "And now you are." He smiled, the hope in it even more heartbreaking with her new revelation.

"But I can't stay," she said, her voice firm. "I have to get home." She had to be there for Sandy's wedding. She had to make sure the captain arrived safely on Earth.

Oh, and she didn't want to stay. Especially not with Alex.

"But we could be together again. We need good pilots—"

"I'm sorry," she said, not meeting his eyes. "I can't stay."

He smiled sadly at her. "I love you."

She smiled her own sad smile. *Too little, too late.* "I love you, too."

"I love you more."

It was an old joke. They'd argue over who loved the other more. But now ...

At first, her gaze dropped to the floor when he said it. Then she looked up at him, their eyes meeting.

"No, Alex," she said. "Not more. Just ... differently. I've moved on."

"Moved on? You don't mean—" He grabbed her arm. She flinched at his tight grip. "You're not with that ... *thing*, are you?"

"What? No!" Gemma stuttered. The anger in Alex's eyes left her mouth dry. He'd always been jealous. Apparently, he'd never grown out of it. If she gave even a hint of liking the captain, would Alex keep protecting him?

Probably not. Absolutely not.

Gemma fumbled her words. "He's ... I mean ... it's not even human. I would never—"

She looked past Alex's shoulder and saw the captain stop a few feet away from them. His face tight, he turned when she met his eyes and strode back toward his room. Alex didn't even know he'd been there. Gemma wasn't sure how the captain had gotten out.

" ... never do that," she finished, her heart hurting. "It ... it's part of my mission."

Alex gave her a radiant smile and slung an arm around Gemma's shoulders. "Come on. Let me give you a tour."

"I have some food for—"

"It?" Alex smirked. She wanted to punch him but kept her face neutral.

Alex took the tray and carried it down to the quarantine room, shoving it through the opening.

"Delivered. Let's go."

He walked her down the hall. There wasn't much traffic near the quarantine rooms, but soon the hallway opened into a massive, bright cavern with smooth walls, lined with levels of crowded walkways. Glass elevators whisked people from floor to floor, some wearing helmets, others in identifying uniforms. She looked down into the center of the cavern, a shopping center and a school a few stories below them.

"It's a shift change right now," Alex said, "so there's more people out than usual."

"It's a bigger operation than I imagined," Gemma said. Not surprising that Alex was in charge. He'd gone through a leadership program on Earth, designed to "groom future leaders." He had always commanded attention, and people had always listened to him. She would know better than most. "What do you mine here?"

"Osmium," he said. "It's an essential metal used in jump engines. And the tips of ballpoint pens. Among other things."

"Oh, wow."

"Want to see the mine?"

She straightened. She'd never seen a mine before. "Can I?"

He smiled. "Follow me."

Yeah, he had always been a show-off, too.

Alex led her to the nearest elevator and pushed the lowest level. The other people in the elevator stared at her and whispered behind their hands. *I guess they don't get many visitors here.* A few people glanced at her with hostile, narrowed eyes. *Or maybe it's because I'm with Captain Lee?*

"Our entire operation is underground," Alex said when they exited. "Residences, commercial, and mining operations. The surface isn't conducive to human living. Down here, we can create our own atmosphere and regulate the temperature."

They arrived at the center of the colony, and Gemma looked up at the big open space rimmed with high-railing glass balconies, the ceiling far above made of rock. Four glass elevators whisked people between floors.

"Wow," she murmured without meaning to. Pretty impressive for a dinky mining colony.

"We have our civil sector just above us at the bottom," he pointed to the first-level balcony above them, "with three floors of commercial businesses above that. The rest between there and the top floor are residential. We're currently expanding outward on all floors. And below everything is the mine—one layer down from us."

She took a moment to look Alex over. He looked good here, comfortable in his role in charge of the mining colony.

She wanted nothing more than to leave.

They arrived at an opening with warning signs posted around it. *"Danger: Active mine." "Warning! Mine site: authorized access only." "Site safety: Hard hat must be worn. Protective footwear must be worn. High visibility—"*

Alex grabbed a pair of helmets from a shelf and handed her one.

"Is it dangerous?" She looked toward the well-lit opening leading to steps with safety rails on each side. This had sounded like a good idea at first, but now doubt crept in.

"Not really," he said. "It's protocol."

She bit her lip, running the rim of the helmet between her hands. "But are there ever cave-ins?"

Alex shrugged. "Every workplace has its accidents. It's unlikely, but it happens." He took the helmet from her hands and placed it on her head. He beamed at her. She gave him a weak smile. *I'm not sure this is a good idea.* Now that she thought about it, she'd purposely chosen a career out in *space*, not a job *underground.*

The stairs led to a narrow, square tunnel, though not as narrow as the ship's corridors had been. Bright lights lit the gray mine shaft, exposing evenly spaced metal support beams bracing the ceiling. The smooth floor of the shaft made walking easy. She reached out to touch the rough, uneven rock walls on either side. Cold.

They passed other miners who nodded to Alex and stared at Gemma. Unflinching, she met their gazes, and they immediately looked away.

"We have state-of-the-art atmospheric generators and mining equipment," Alex said. She took a deep breath of the clear, cool air. "We refine the osmium here too, on a higher level." The tunnel sloped down. "The process is—"

The floor vibrated, as if the ship's engines had engaged.

But this wasn't a ship.

Gemma froze and Alex stopped talking.

"Um, Alex?" Gemma said, looking at the walls around them. She could have sworn a fine layer of dust suspended in the air where there hadn't been any before.

He frowned and clicked a comm attached to his lapel. "Jordan, what's going on in the mines?"

"I believe they're opening a new shaft today, Mr. Steele," his comm chirped. "Why?"

Another rumble, but this lasted longer. Gemma whimpered. Then the lights flickered.

"Something's wrong," Alex said, taking her hand.

At a crash, miners ran toward them from deeper in the mine, waving their arms and shouting. "Get out!"

A hard shake sent them to the ground.

TREVOR PACED THE QUARANTINE ROOM. AFTER WAITING FOR HOURS, he'd picked the lock and gone out looking for Gemma to try to plan. They still had a mission to carry out. That's when he saw her with Alex. He'd felt a hot flash of ... something, seeing them together. He'd gotten angry for no reason. Hearing what she said about him quickly doused the anger, leaving him cold.

Of course she would think that. He'd known since he was a kid how people felt about—about Tubies. Why was he so shocked?

And hurt. Why had it hurt him so much?

Because ... because when he was with her, he felt—she made him feel like ...

He resisted the urge to kick the bed across the room. He knew having a woman onboard was a bad idea.

It was her fault. She'd ... she'd taken over his mind. He couldn't go two steps without wondering where she was, how she was.

This was bad. Charlie and Dad always told him, don't get too close to people. He'd only get hurt. A Tubie could never have a real relationship. It was a wrong thing to do.

He stopped pacing. Why did it feel right?

No. It wasn't her fault. It was his.

A vibration under his feet. He stopped his pacing.

A second rumble, this time stronger and longer. Then the walls groaned as they swayed slightly.

He opened the door as a construction worker ran by. "What's going on?" Trevor demanded.

"Something's wrong in the tunnels!" the man shouted, before he turned a corner.

Trevor had a bad feeling, an itching on the back of his neck. He slapped his ship keys, still hanging around his neck. "Pilot, come in."

"Captain!" He could barely make out her words through the static. "Help!"

An instant rush of adrenaline tensed his muscles, and he slammed the door open all the way.

"Where are you?" He ran down the hall and turned at the same corner he'd seen the other man go, his soft shoes slapping against the tiles.

"We're—the tunnels—ceiling won't hold—"

"Pilot? Pilot!"

The hallway let him out into the center of the subterranean colony. The crowded walkways overwhelmed him momentarily, everyone lined up at the railing and looking down, their voices raised. He grabbed the nearest person, a woman.

"Where are the tunnels?" he demanded.

"It's on the lowest level. My husband is down there!" she said, her eyes wide.

Trevor released her and shoved his way over to the railing. Four elevators worked, crammed with people and moving too slowly for him. He looked down. It was only about five floors to the bottom, with railings on each level between here and there.

He vaulted over the edge amid screams.

At each level, he caught the railing to pause his momentum before dropping to the next one, until he ran out of railings and landed hard on the lowest level. He gasped at the pain in his ribs, but then he was up and following the stream of running people toward the tunnels.

"Pilot! Are you there?" He couldn't keep the panic out of his voice.

Static.

A crowd gathered around the tunnel entrance. "The ceiling caved in!" someone said.

Trevor pushed his way to the front. "Where is she?"

"Ten people clocked in," a man at the front said. "That means there are ten people down there who can't get out. We need volunteers to try to clear the rubble."

"I volunteer," Trevor said, shoving by him and jumping down the stairs.

He coughed in the dusty air and could make out three other people by the dim lighting.

"Here." Someone shoved a pair of gloves and a mask at him.

Trevor pulled them on, the filter on the mask whirring to life. "How can I help?"

"We've got to move these rocks." The shadowed man pointed. "We're waiting for machinery to get here, but that could take a while, and we don't know if they have any air on the other—"

"I'm on it," Trevor said. He grabbed the nearest large rock and swung it aside. "I'm coming, Gemma."

"Captain? Are you there?"

Nothing but static. And blackness.

Thick dust hung in the air as a near-dozen flashlights clicked on, illuminating the problem: the collapsed tunnel to the entrance.

Gemma only had a scrape on her knee from when she'd fallen to the floor. The other workers already scrambled to move the fallen rocks. Her heart hammered as she looked around.

"Alex, I thought you said—Alex!" Gemma knelt by him, letting him act as a distraction. "Are you okay?"

Alex's arm bent at a wrong angle, his face ashen, his breathing shallow.

"I'm okay," he said, but made no move to get up. "Everything's okay. They're working to get us out."

"What about air? Do we have air?" Gemma asked, her voice

higher than normal.

"It all depends if the machinery is damaged farther down the tunnel."

"Mr. Steele!" Another man knelt by his side. "We're all accounted for, sir, but we're boxed in on both sides."

"Any injuries?"

"It looks like yours is the worst, sir."

Alex tapped his lapel. "Jordan, you there?" Static.

"How are we on air?" Gemma asked, her voice getting even higher, her breathing faster.

The man shook his head. "We're cut off from the oxygen generator. We only have the air that's in here."

"Gemma." Alex took her hand, while the man went to work on digging them out. "I'm sorry I left you."

That snapped her out of the rising panic, though slowing her breathing took a lot of effort. "What? What are you talking about?"

She knew exactly what he was talking about.

Alex clutched her hand. "On Earth. When you got accepted to flight school ... I don't know, I felt like I needed to do something with my life. Something more. So, I went to the colonies. And I left." He blew out a breath. "Biggest regret of my life, leaving you."

"Alex ... " She smoothed a rogue, curly lock away from his face. The residual anger faded as she worked hard to focus on his face and not the rocks. It was true, he had needed to do something with his life. "You're talking like you're going to die."

"No, no, it's not that." He closed his eyes for a moment. "I wanted to tell you this. Over dinner, that is, not trapped in a mine shaft. I ... I want you to give me a second chance."

"Oh, Alex ... " She squeezed his hand, trying to ignore the

sounds of shifting rock around them. Would the ceiling above them collapse too?

"You don't have to answer now," he said. "Think about it?"

"I don't have to think about it," she said. "I—"

Loud scrapes came from the other side of the rock wall, and the working men moved back as rubble tumbled off it. A square of light opened, and the men cheered.

"How'd they get to us so quickly?" someone asked.

"It's impossible—but I'll take it!" said another.

"Pilot, you there?" a muffled voice called from the other side.

The heavy pressure lifted from Gemma's heart. "I'm here, Captain!" She knew he'd save her.

Us. He'd save *us.* Everybody, not just her.

The opening widened, then someone crawled through, followed by a second shadowy figure. It was hard to see their faces with the light behind them.

"Everyone alright in here?" asked the second person, his voice smothered by his mask.

"Everyone accounted for," said someone. "The supervisor is hurt."

"I'm fine—" Alex started, when the first person grabbed Gemma by the shoulders and pulled her to her feet. He yanked the mask down off his mouth.

"Pilot, are you alright?" Captain Lee demanded, his gaze intense.

"I'm okay," she said, patting his hand, trying to play it cool. "I knew you'd get me out." Inside, she quivered as if her knees might give, and she wanted to bury her face in his shoulder while he held her tight.

"Come on." He stepped toward her, and she put out a warning finger. She willed her knees to firm up. This would not only be embarrassing, but if Alex read into the captain's actions, it might put him in danger. "Don't you even think about picking me up. I'm fine. I don't need to be carried out of here. Help Alex."

Captain Lee hesitated, then took off his breathing mask, pulling it over Gemma's head and fitting it around her mouth.

"Captain!" she protested even as she took a deep breath of filtered air.

He ignored her objection as he offered a hand to Alex. They hauled Alex to his feet and supported him as he left the mine. Hands reached down and pulled them all out.

"Thank you," Alex said as he sat on the bed in the colony's infirmary. He'd had his broken arm wrapped and the nurse fussed with it, fitting his arm into a sling. "For helping us."

Gemma knew the captain was going to say he was just rescuing his pilot, so she elbowed him in the ribs. He winced, then said, "You're welcome."

"I've been working on a plan to get you guys home," Alex said. "I think I've figured it out. Meet at Gemma's room in an hour?"

"That's fine," the captain said. "Pilot, I'll walk you to your room."

"Gemma, stay with me," Alex said, holding out a hand.

Gemma hesitated, looking back and forth between the captain and Alex. She really wanted to go with Captain Lee. But she really needed to stay with Alex—and finish their conversation.

"I'll ... see you in an hour, Captain," she said. "Alex and I still have some catching up to do."

His face unreadable, the captain turned away and left the medical center.

"Alex," she said, turning to him. "I know what you're asking—"

"Don't decide now," he said, his voice desperate. "Think about it."

She shook her head. "I can't stay with you, Alex. I think Sandy was right: we were so young. Too young. We should never have had a serious relationship. And now I'm living a different life. I'm a different person."

Alex was quiet for a moment. "Are you choosing him over me?"

Gemma took a step back. "No! He—he has nothing to do with it. I'm choosing my life over you. I can't stay here."

Alex didn't say anything, but his expression spoke volumes. She had to get the captain out of this place as quickly as possible before Alex was tempted to turn on them.

Gemma left the medical center after that, alone and more than a little relieved to go. She was glad she found Alex, but things between them were definitely ... over. The sooner they could leave, the better. Away from this dinky little hole they called a colony.

ONCE ALONE, TREVOR DOUBLED OVER, HIS HANDS ON HIS KNEES AS HE took slow breaths, keeping the dark spots of his vision at bay. The residual rush of adrenaline and the relief at seeing her again made him clutch at his chest.

His chest was still tight when he stood again, and he forced himself to take a deep sigh of relief.

She was fine. She was okay, just a scratch on her knee, and maybe some emotional trauma—he'd felt the way she trembled in the tunnel—but overall, she was safe.

He had lost everything. He couldn't lose her, too.

After a shower and fresh clothes, Trevor made his way to Gemma's room using written directions. The few people in the halls avoided eye contact, and one or two even turned and walked the other way.

Trevor and Alex arrived at Gemma's room at the same time. Outwardly, Alex appeared fine, also showered and changed, his arm in a sling.

Inwardly? Trevor swallowed hard at the burning in Alex's narrowed eyes.

"Mr. Steele."

"Captain." Alex hesitated. Then he extended a hand. "Thank you, again, for saving us."

They shook hands, then Trevor knocked on the door.

He didn't look at Alex as his mind clicked with a jolt. *Hate.* The burning in his eyes was hate.

Gemma opened the door, her hair still wet from her own shower. "Please, come in."

Trevor lagged behind Alex as they entered and stayed next to Gemma as she keyed the door closed.

"Pilot, may I speak with you?" he whispered.

She glanced at Alex. "Now?"

He hesitated. "Probably not. But that's why I wanted to walk you to your room."

Her eyebrows went up, but he moved away.

Alex had already turned on her computer and sent the mirror image to hover in 3D above the table. He called up a star chart and circled two points, the coordinates written beneath each.

"This is where we are," he told them, pointing to one of the circles. "There's really only one safe port within a reasonable distance, here." He pointed to the other circle. "The flight usually takes three days. We have two options. The first is you can leave within a few days by taking a ship yourselves. We can only spare a small craft, but I can arrange to have enough food for a week stored aboard."

Perfect. Getting to Cerise should take about a week, and he could finish his mission.

"But I thought the flight was only three days?" Gemma asked.

"You never know what might come up," Trevor said.

"Exactly," Alex said. "It's better to be safe than sorry in space, especially way out here. If you get in trouble this close to the Terminus, it's unlikely that anyone but an Omni Authority ship will stop to help you."

"What kind of ship is it?" Gemma asked.

"It's ... it's my personal jetter," Alex said. "After you get to the port, you can trade it for another ship, or passage home."

Trevor turned to Gemma. "Will you be able to do that? Fly a jetter?"

She gave a smug smile that kicked his heart rate up. "If it's got an engine, I can drive it," Gemma told him. "Wings, and I can fly it."

Trevor looked away before she could see the color rising in his face. "What's option two?"

"If you wait a week or two, you can get passage to port on one of our delivery transports," Alex said. He hesitated. "It's not exactly safe here for you. First, you were shot down, so we don't know if someone's still after you. Second—people don't really want you around." He addressed this last part to Trevor.

Despite the hate in his eyes, Alex continued, "My decision to help you isn't exactly ... popular. I think the jetter is the best way to get you out of here safely."

"Even after he saved all those people?" Gemma demanded. "They still don't like him?"

"I understand," Trevor said, careful to keep the hurt off his face. "I'll keep to my room." For the first time in his life, his secret was out. He tightened his muscles to keep from flinching at the thought and fought the rising nausea. It wasn't as bad as he had always imagined—but this was only day one. No doubt that in time he would be in mortal danger. Gemma, too.

His heart nearly seized in his chest. Going with him on the jetter would put her in danger, too. He gritted his teeth with the realization: he had to get her to stay.

"When can we leave?" Gemma asked.

"Tomorrow morning," said Alex.

Trevor snapped back to the conversation. "How will we pay for the ship?"

"No payment is necessary," Alex told him, glancing at Gemma, who looked away. "I'll pay for it."

"Alex ... " She reached for his hand.

"Great!" Trevor clapped his hands together, relieved when she pulled her hand back. "Unless there's anything else, I think now would be a good time to eat."

"Of course. I can grab you something from the cafeteria," Alex said. "Any preferences?"

"No peanuts," Gemma said.

"Exactly, no peanuts. Or nuts in general," Trevor agreed. "I, uh ... don't like them."

"Not a problem," Alex said. "Gemma, did you want to come to the cafeteria with me, or eat in your room?"

"I'll come," Gemma told him. "Give me a minute and I'll catch up with you, okay?"

Alex hesitated, looking back and forth between them, but left.

The moment the door slid shut, she turned to Trevor. "Now talk. What is it you wanted?"

"I can't go back to Earth yet," he said.

Her jaw dropped. "What?! Why not?"

"I have to complete our mission," he said. "I don't expect you to come—"

"Complete our mission?" she repeated. "We nearly died! Our mission is over! Even if we did make it to our destination, we don't have any food or medical supplies to deliver. The mission is dead."

"That," he said, "was not the real mission. I don't expect—"

"What's the real mission?"

His blood pressure rising, he struggled to keep his voice even. "Pilot, I don't expect you—"

"What's the real mission?" she asked again, raising her chin.

"I don't expect you to come with me!" he shouted. She would hardly let him finish a sentence. He took a deep breath. "We can split up. I'll take the ship, and you take the delivery transport in a week. Your obligation has been fulfilled, you've completed your mission as far as you can, and no more is expected of you. You can go home."

She advanced on him, and he couldn't decide if her red face was adorable or if he should be afraid. As she drew closer, he backed up.

"My mission," she informed him, poking his chest and making him take another step back, "is to transport *you* so you can complete *your* part of the mission. You will never find a better pilot than me, and I don't have a lot of confidence in your flying. Now." She folded her arms. "What's the real mission?"

Trevor sighed even as his stomach tightened. She wanted to stay with him?

He shook his head. "No, you need to stay."

"Not going to happen."

His back now up against the wall with nowhere to go, he held up his hands as her eyes narrowed, inches away from him. He hoped she couldn't hear his heart thud.

"You need to be safe—" he started.

"No. What's the real mission?"

He looked away. "Fine," he said through gritted teeth, and she backed off.

Trevor pulled the pen from his pocket. "I have information. I have to deliver this flash drive safely to a man named Dr. Penn on our destination planet. It's ... medical data. I must get it there."

"Then I'm taking you," she said.

"It's dangerous—"

"End of discussion," she interrupted. "I don't care if you're the captain. You need me. I'm going with you. Got it?"

Trevor gave her a steady look. He knew he should argue. She needed to be safe at home. She needed to go back to Earth. He knew that.

So, why was he so happy she wasn't?

14

Alex burst back into Gemma's room.

"You have to leave," he said. "Now."

"What's happened?" Without waiting for an answer, Gemma grabbed her bag and stuffed an extra blanket and a change of clothes into it, her heart in her throat. Was there another cave-in? No, that wouldn't explain why they had to leave. A fire? A mutiny?

Had the ship that made them crash finally come for them?

Alex confirmed her worst fear. "A ship has landed. It's only a matter of time before they reach the colony, and someone is sure to sell you out." His glance at the captain told her why.

"Lead the way," Captain Lee said.

The three of them jogged down the hallway.

"Listen, I wasn't able to start loading," Alex said. "I had no idea you'd have to leave so soon."

"Loading? Loading what?" Gemma asked.

"The ship," he said. "You only have the three days' worth of food I keep in there, not five. The nearest food storage unit is a half mile away, but I don't think you have that kind of time."

Gemma kept silent. The trip to Cerise was four days, minimum.

"We'll be fine," the captain said.

Alex opened the door to a spacious hangar. The room had several ships housed in it. Alex must have cleared out all the people.

"Here're the keys." He handed her two tags. "Be careful, because they're not bio-keyed, and anyone can use them."

The captain walked up the ramp of the smallest ship there, pausing at the top.

She started to follow when Alex called her back. "Gemma."

She glanced back. "I told you; I can't stay."

"No, it's not that … "

The captain had turned back too, waiting for her.

Alex grabbed her hand, pulled her toward him, and kissed her long and hard. "Fly safe," he breathed.

It was a good kiss, but it didn't make her heart race like it used to.

She touched his cheek. "Take care, Alex." She ran up the ramp. "And call your mother!"

The door closed behind her, locking with a hiss.

"Pilot." The captain cleared his throat as she took the pilot's seat and flipped the switch to warm up the engine. "If you want to stay … "

"I don't," she snapped. "Now shut up until we're out of here."

Without a second chair, he stayed standing.

The little ship zipped out of the hangar, and she brought up the tactical display. The yellow dot in the center represented their ship, with a blinking red dot in the distance.

"One ship detected," Gemma said. "I think I can lose it."

"Then do it!"

She rolled her eyes. "Calm down, Captain. Could you not lean over me?"

"Sorry." He stepped back.

Gemma pulled up to break through to the upper atmosphere, then shot the ship around the other side of the planet. The captain gripped the back of her chair to keep from floating before she engaged the gravity.

"We have eight minutes before they can see us," she said

"Move over, I'll plot a course," the captain said.

"You know how to—"

He didn't even wait for her to move, just reached around her. Her heart hammered, pressed between his shoulder and the pilot chair, his fingers flying across the console. Within a minute, he backed up.

"Go, go!" he ordered.

She snapped upright in the chair, and they zoomed away at top speed. Soon, the display didn't see the ship anymore, out of range.

"Look, Pilot," the captain said. "Before we go too far ... I've been thinking more about this. You should go back."

Gemma sighed. "We already talked about this. I'm staying with you."

"I don't think you understand how dangerous this is." He loomed over her, looking intently into her eyes.

She arched an eyebrow. He really thought he could intimidate her? "I understand perfectly. You don't think I'm up to the task?" She stuck out her chin.

He jerked back. "I didn't say that! But—"

"No way. I'm not leaving you to fend for yourself in deep space." No matter that he'd lived in space his whole life, he'd probably never faced it alone before.

"Pilot," he said, his voice rising, "I order you to return and disembark—"

"Not going to happen."

"I will not lose another pilot!" he shouted.

Her eyes narrowed. "What do you mean, 'lose another pilot?' What happened to the last pilot?" She flicked on the autopilot and stood to face him.

His mouth snapped shut, wide eyes not meeting her gaze as he backed away. "I meant ... I've lost too many people to ..."

She leaned in close, resisting the urge to grab him and shake him. She probably couldn't budge him anyway. "What. Happened. They told me he died of a heart attack, but that's not the whole story, is it?"

He shook his head. "I can't. It'll hurt Charlie. He feels responsible."

"Charlie's dead!"

The captain flinched. Gemma slapped her hand over her mouth, eyes wide.

Silence stretched between them. He wouldn't look at her.

"I'm sorry, I'm so sorry," she said, teary-eyed. "I shouldn't have—"

"No, you're right." He ran a hand through his hair. "You should know the truth."

Gemma bit her lip and sat in the pilot's chair, quiet, waiting.

"On our last mission," he said, "we were out on foot when we came under heavy fire. It wasn't supposed to be dangerous, but they came out of nowhere. Chase and I were injured, but Jakob ... We didn't even know if he was alive. I had to drag him. We called for help. Charlie—" His voice strangled, and he cleared his throat. "Charlie was still on the ship. He thought he was off duty so he ... he'd been drinking. A lot. He used to do that, ever since his wife died.

"Charlie came to us, but he passed out, and I could only

carry one of them back to the ship. We thought Jakob was dead, so … I made the tough call. Hardest thing I've ever done."

He let out a shaky breath. "Charlie hasn't touched a drop since, but he never forgave himself."

Gemma had the feeling Captain Lee hadn't forgiven himself either.

"Captain … that wasn't *your* fault."

He didn't look at her. "I'm the captain. Everything is my fault."

"But—"

"Will you stop arguing with me?" He met her eyes with a sigh. He looked tired. "I can't make you go back, can I?"

"No, sir."

"Let's get on with it then. Out of the chair, I need to map our route beyond just escaping."

Gemma surrendered the chair, then leaned over his shoulder. "Are you sure you know what you're doing?"

The captain called up the maps and input coordinates. "I was a navigator before being given my own ship. I could plot a course in my sleep."

"But have you been to the Ruby District? What if the map isn't accurate?"

"I guess we'll find out." His weak smile reassured her, and he turned back to his button pushing.

After a few minutes, he spun the chair around to face her. "Good news is it should be an easy trip. Bad news, it'll take four days. We'll have to ration the food."

Gemma's stomach growled in response. In the rush to escape, they hadn't eaten.

The tiny ship, meant for only one person, could handle the trip, but it wouldn't be comfortable.

"We'll sleep in shifts," the captain said, surveying the

single bunk and the food supplies Alex had stashed. "I want one of us awake at all times to keep watch."

Gemma stayed in the chair fiddling with the controls, although they'd already set the autopilot. The captain paced the small room.

"We could play cards or something," Gemma suggested, to break the awkward silence. But they didn't have cards.

"Pilot." She swiveled around to find the captain looking at her, his face serious. "I never got to thank you. For sticking with me, even when you found out—"

"You earned it. It's not like being labeled a Tubie will change the person I've come to know. You're a good captain." She paused. "Well, usually. When you're not mad at me." She shrugged. "I mean ... as long as we're being honest ... I think you get hung up on the fact that I'm a woman and you think you need to 'protect' me and all. But when that doesn't get in the way, you're top-notch."

He hung his head. "I apologize."

She turned back to the controls, hiding her smug smile.

He cleared his throat. "Maybe you should know about this, too. I, uh ... "

She glanced back at him. He still looked at the ground, tapping the toe of his shoe on it.

"Something happened," he blurted.

"What?"

The look on his face made her pause. His skin pale, he squeezed his eyes shut, hissing through his teeth. As if in pain.

"Not you," he managed. He shook his head and took a breath. "She and I were doing maintenance in the engine core." He paused.

"Who's 'she'?" Gemma asked gently, leaning forward.

"Anne. Her name was Anne." He took another breath. "It was a freak accident. An electrical short engaged the engine.

The gears started turning. She ... her leg got caught in them, and it just kept—just kept pulling her in.”

Gemma's hands covered her mouth, her eyes wide.

He took another deep breath, tilting his head back to look at the ceiling. “I just stood there. I couldn't do anything as she screamed. They got her out. She lived, just barely. She would never be whole again. But ... Space is dangerous. None of us were able to protect her.”

His breathing shuddered. “She ... she was so nice. Kind, really. She should never have—”

He stiffened with a sharp intake of breath when Gemma threw her arms around him, holding him tightly. As tight as she could.

“How old were you?” she whispered into his chest.

His body still tensed, she braced herself to be pushed away. But then his arms wrapped around her too, his chin touching the top of her head.

“I was ten.”

Gemma pulled him even tighter, her heart breaking. “I'm so sorry.” She looked up at him. “I know you blame yourself. But you are not at fault.” She pressed her face against his shirt again.

He didn't say anything. They stayed that way for a moment, until he stopped trembling. His arms around her finally relaxed, but she held on.

He cleared his throat, patting her on the head. “I'm okay now.”

“Okay.” She hesitated but let go.

He immediately backed up a step. He coughed. “I was afraid ...”

“That something was going to happen to me, too,” Gemma finished.

He hung his head. “You seem... to be able to take care of

yourself. And of me, when the situation calls for it. You've been a good pilot." He smirked. "Mostly."

"Mostly?"

"You did try to kill me."

She gasped, her face heating up. "That was an accident!" Was he going to hold that against her forever?

"I know, I know!" He ran a hand through his hair. "I never did get to tell you ... dinner tasted really good."

"I—thank you," she said, surprised by how the compliment warmed her.

"Do you mind taking the first shift?" he asked her. "I'd like to get some sleep. Just for a couple hours."

"Sure, as long as you need," she said. She turned back to the console with a sigh. What was she going to do while he slept? This was going to be a looooong trip.

15

"It took me two years to get into the flight academy," Gemma said, stretched out on the bed. The captain sat in the chair, flicking through the screens. "Two. Years. To even be accepted. There were three women accepted that year, but I was the only one who stuck with it. I don't think it was the training that made them drop out. It was probably the critical attitude of the faculty. Or the hostility. The other students gave us a hard time. The pranks got pretty vicious. I thought us girls would support each other, but then they left.

"I mean, the guys weren't *all* bad. There was Phil. He was older, he'd left his office job for a new career. I think the younger guys gave him a hard time, too. Called him old, stupid stuff like that. But he made it through. I wonder what he's doing now. I think I'll look him up when I get back to Earth. How did you become a captain for Omni Authority?"

"Huh?" The captain looked up.

She propped herself up on her elbows, shooting narrowed eyes at him. "Were you even listening to me?"

"Of course I was listening," he muttered. "I can't help but listen. You give me no choice, but to listen."

"Then what did I say?" she asked.

"How did I become a captain."

A pause.

"And the answer?" she asked.

He shrugged. "I worked my way up. Been on cargo ships my whole life. Started as an engineer's assistant, spent my free time studying, eventually qualified as a navigator. Kept working till I earned my captain's commission."

He stopped talking and turned back to the screens, not even looking at her.

Gemma frowned at his back. "And that's it?"

"That's it."

"What do you do when you're not working?"

"I'm always working."

"I mean, when you're not in space." Was he taking this conversation seriously, or blowing her off?

"I'm always in space."

"You are not!" Gemma stuck her lip out in a pout. "I mean when you're on-planet."

"If I'm on-planet, then I'm getting ready to go into space."

She rolled her eyes. He was maddening. "What would you do if you didn't need to work? Like, if you had a million dollars, what would you buy?"

His grin reflected off the screens he swiped through. "A new ship."

Gemma groaned. "You're impossible! Okay, if you weren't working in space—you're grounded on Earth, and you have to do something else. What would you do?"

He paused, turning to her, his brow furrowed. "I have no idea. I guess I've never really thought about it. What would you do?"

She blinked. She hadn't expected him to turn it around on her. "I guess ... I could fly commercial airplanes."

He smirked. "Nope. You said, 'grounded.'"

Gemma gave a huff. "I don't know either, okay?"

"What were you doing before you got this job?"

"Heh, uh." She gave a sheepish smile. "Mostly ... playing video games all day." She thought for a moment. "Well, not only. I spent a lot of time in the mountains near where we lived. I love hiking and finding new places. And those were free pastimes." She sighed. "My family and I always loved exploring. We used to do it a lot."

"I think ..." He licked his lips and wouldn't look at her. "I'd like to learn to play the guitar. Not as a job or anything. Just—I don't know, as a hobby."

Her eyebrows rose. "You would?" That had to be the first normal thing she'd ever learned about him. She had no idea he liked music. "That's great! Why don't you now?"

"I'm pretty busy—"

"You should totally do it! I *love* music." Gemma smiled at him.

He smirked. "I know you do."

"So why don't you?" she pressed. "You don't need to be nervous; everyone starts out terrible. I think you'd be great. Maybe someday you can play for me."

His face reddened. "I don't have time for it," he snapped. He turned his back to her. "You should get some sleep."

Gemma hummed to herself during her watch

The navigation controls flickered, then went out. Her brows drew together. She flipped some switches to restart it, but the screen stayed dark.

"Um, Captain?"

He woke with a start, sitting straight up. "What?"

"Something's wrong with the navigation—Are you okay? Did you have a bad dream?"

He rubbed his face and got up. "I'm fine. What's wrong with it?" He leaned over her shoulder and tried the same switches she had. "Hmm. Move aside."

He crouched down and tried to pry the cover off the bottom of the control panel. "Need a screwdriver."

"I'll get it!" Gemma found the toolbox and gave him a multi-tool. With the screws out, the cover popped open. A tangled mess of wires crowded the space.

"Could really use Zane right about now," he muttered. A painful twinge made her flinch. Zane ...

Louder, he said, "Full stop. We don't want to wander too far off course."

Lying on his back, he scooted under the control panel. "Do we have a flashlight?"

Gemma dug through the supply cabinets. "Got one." She flicked it on. Nothing. "Uh, it needs batteries." She looked through the rest of the cabinets. "No batteries."

The captain slid out. "Then take them from something else."

Gemma found an emergency communicator, unscrewed the cover, and pulled the batteries out.

He disappeared again with the flashlight. After a few minutes, he came back out, a short length of wire in hand. "Does this look chewed to you?"

All the blood drained from her face.

"We've got a stowaway," he said, his face grim. "Check the food."

The food supplies were untouched, but the mystery animal had wreaked havoc on the navigation system.

"I think it was trying to build a nest here," the captain said. "I must have scared it off when I opened the panel."

Shaking, Gemma climbed onto the pilot's chair, pulling her feet off the ground as she curled into a ball. "Then where is it now?" she asked, her voice a hoarse whisper.

A scratching, scrabbling sound came from above her head. Gemma couldn't stop herself from screaming.

The captain jerked at the sound, banging his head on the underside of the console. "Calm down, Pilot!" He rubbed his head. "See if you can find a weapon."

She swallowed hard. "Where?"

"Check the cabinets." He ducked back under the control panel.

"But what if it's in there?" she asked, her grip tightening on the chair.

He sighed and crawled back out. "It's in the ceiling, not the cabinets."

Gemma shook her head and wouldn't budge.

"Fine, I'll look," the captain grumbled.

She watched him search, but he found nothing useful as a weapon.

He came back with the toolbox. "If I can't fix the navigation, we're dead in space."

"You can fix it," she said, hoping she sounded confident.

After a few minutes with no more sounds from their mystery guest, Gemma began to relax. "Can't you navigate by the stars?"

"Sure, if I was back on Earth." His voice echoed from under

the control panel. "Or had a star chart of the area. But I don't know any of these stars."

"Navigation is pretty important," she said. "Maybe I should learn how to do it."

"Never hurts to have another skillset."

"But I'd still need the nav system?"

"You'd still need the nav system."

"Is it hard to navigate?"

"I'd say, yes," he said. "It's physically easier than some jobs, but mentally harder than others."

"Can't you say all jobs are easier and harder than others?"

He paused. "Haven't thought about it."

"I'll stick with flying." She took a lazy turn in the chair. "I've always wanted to fly. For a long time, I had to settle for driving. Grandpa taught me to drive a tractor when I was eight. My sister hated that I always wanted to drive with the windows open. She said it messed up her hair. I loved the feeling of the wind, you know?"

"I don't," the captain grunted from his position lying under the computer console, stripping and connecting wires.

"What do you mean? You don't like the wind?"

"The wind's okay," he said. "I don't get out much, only at spaceports. I guess it feels nice on my face, but it always smells of exhaust."

"I'll take you on a ride sometime," Gemma said. "Somewhere nice. You can't imagine what it's like when the air is sweet."

"Whatever you say." He crawled out from under the console. "Let's try this." He pressed a button, and the screen flickered to life.

With a *pop*, it went dark again.

He grumbled and crawled back under.

"You might as well get some sleep," he called. "This could take a while."

She hesitated. "You don't need my help?"

"There's not much to do except connect wires. Get some rest."

Gemma lay down, but didn't go to sleep. Humming to herself didn't help. She imagined the thing crawling in the walls and shuddered.

After a while, the captain sighed and crawled out from under the control panel. The chair creaked as he sat down, and she looked over at him. He rubbed his eyes, then pulled out his little notebook and pencil.

"What's that?" Gemma sat up.

He snapped the book shut and tucked it away. "What's what? I thought you were asleep."

"What are you writing?" She leaned forward. "Is that the notebook you always carry around? Is it a captain's log? A journal? Am I in it?"

"It's nothing." He turned to the other screens and flicked through them.

Her eyes narrowed. "Liar."

He ignored her.

"Is the navigation fixed?"

"Not quite. I needed a break," he muttered. He sighed, rubbing his eyes. "My head is killing me. Why are you up? You need to sleep."

"I can't," she said. "Not while knowing that—thing—is loose on the ship somewhere." She shuddered.

He rolled his eyes. "It probably can't get out of the walls, otherwise it would have gotten into the food. It's probably starving."

"Food?" She snapped her fingers. "That's how we can get it out! With food!"

"We don't have any to spare," he said.

"We can't keep wasting time fixing everything this thing breaks either."

The captain hesitated. "That's true," he admitted. He rubbed his stomach. "Are you hungry?"

"I could eat." She was famished.

They sat on the floor across from each other, sharing a food pouch.

"What's your name?" she asked.

He hesitated.

"Come on," she prodded. "What are you afraid of?"

"It's just—it's personal," he said, not meeting her eyes.

"Maybe you can tell me later?" she asked. She wanted to know. *Needed* to know. What made the captain tick?

He laughed. "I'll think about it."

"Will you tell me about ... um ..." She took a deep breath. "I think I deserve to know. Since I stood up for you and all. And that I'm trapped in a very small ship with you."

His brow furrowed. "Tell you about what?"

"About being a Tubie?"

He grimaced. "That term is a little offensive."

"Sorry! I meant—a genetically engineered super soldier?" she said. "I thought they were all ... gone. How did you ..."

He was silent for a long time. Gemma tried not to fidget.

"The—project—was going on longer than most people think," he said. "Years and years. The experiments only became public knowledge when they'd perfected the process. Then, you know, once everyone found out they were making super soldiers that could wipe out any planet for the right price, Omni Authority swooped in and destroyed everything. Threw all the scientists in prison for life. Wiped out their research and —eliminated the experiments."

"So, you're all clones?" she asked.

"Yes, we're all clones, but not all the same clone. That'd be a pretty dead giveaway of infiltration if everyone looked the same." He shook his head. "I don't know where they got the genetic material, but there was only one clone grown of each person. I think."

He swallowed, not looking at her. "They—we were grown in stages. When everything was wiped out, the soldiers were aged anywhere between infants and eleven years. I was fifteen at the time."

"I don't understand," Gemma whispered. She felt chills. What if he really was a monster, like all the super soldiers were supposed to be? *don't be stupid. This is Captain Lee. He isn't a monster.*

"The oldest perfected soldiers were eleven," he explained. "I was an earlier trial. They … threw me out when I was four."

Her eyes widened. "Threw you out?"

"In the trash," he said. "I was 'defective.' I had allergies. I was too … 'nice' of a child. I was smart enough, fast enough, and strong enough. But I wasn't what they wanted, so they dumped me. All the early trials were thrown out, for one reason or another."

He shook his head. "Not that I want to be a killing machine, but I remember being rejected and trashed. I was a *child.*" His haunted eyes met hers, his voice rough. "Do you have any idea what it's like when the people who have always cared for you shove you down a trash chute? When they pretend they can't hear you crying? I was the only one that survived, and that's only because a scavenger ship found me before I froze to death."

He paused; his voice low as he broke eye contact. "I've never told anyone about this before."

"What happened next?" Gemma whispered.

"Charlie was on that ship," the captain said. "He was

younger then. The mechanic onboard adopted me. He ... he made me his son. Named me after his father." He looked away. "They saved my life."

"But if you're not the final version, then why did the medical alarm go off?"

"From the beginning, all the children grown there had genetic markers. It's something I can't get away from." He shrugged.

"But, basically, you're human?"

"That's what Charlie keeps telling me," he said.

"Do you have a belly button?"

"What?" The captain sat up straight. "What kind of question is that?"

"Well, I don't know. Since you were grown in a—"

"I have a belly button."

"Can I see it?"

He leaned away. "No! What's wrong with you?"

"Any other allergies?"

He raised an eyebrow at her, but said, "Dryer sheets, as far as I know."

"What happened to the mechanic who adopted you?" she asked.

The food packet empty, the captain stood and walked to the pilot's chair. "You should get some sleep," he said, his voice rough.

She sighed as she climbed to her feet and turned towards the bed, crumpling up the empty food packet. She didn't understand him. He had finally opened up and abruptly shut down again.

As she pulled the cover over her, she heard him say, ever so softly, "He died."

She stayed where she was, without moving, her back still to him. "What happened?"

"He was sick. Real sick, for a long time. He died a few days after I got my captain's commission." He cleared his throat. "He said it was the proudest day of his life. And I guess that's all he was waiting for, because … he fell asleep and didn't wake up."

She turned toward him, her head still on the pillow as she looked at him. "At least he didn't suffer long."

The captain barked a laugh. "Everyone says that. Doesn't change the fact that he's gone."

Gemma's heart ached for him. "Do you have any other family? Any siblings?"

He gave her a sharp look. "Besides the dozens of other children murdered in cold blood?"

She winced. "I meant, did your dad have any other kids?"

"Oh." The hostility dissolved. "No, he was never married, never had a family. It was just the two of us."

"Do you want kids someday?" Gemma asked, sitting up with her arms wrapped around her legs, her chin on her knees.

He flinched. "Me? That would be irresponsible."

"What do you mean?"

He looked away. "I'm an abomination, remember? They destroyed us for a reason. Many reasons. I shouldn't even be alive. My DNA would poison the human gene pool. If I can even father children, which I don't know if I can, I don't have the right. I have no rights, I'm not supposed to exist. I'm designed to kill."

"But you're different. You're not like that—"

He gave her a hard, sad look. "I was not designed to be a parent."

They were quiet for a long moment.

"Adoption?" Gemma said.

The captain laughed, a genuine laugh, and she smiled.

"You never quit, do you?" he said.

She shook her head with a grin. "Never."

He sighed, his smile slipping away. "Can we talk about something else?"

"Sure, let me think." She drummed her fingers on her knee, then smiled. "Tell me your most embarrassing moment."

He groaned. "Pass."

"Sports?"

"Not exactly a lot of running room on a ship. The only sport I know is *The Blue*."

"But you work out."

He shrugged. "We all do."

"But—" She snapped her mouth shut. She wasn't about to tell him what she thought about the muscles she could see through his shirt. "Have you ever had a pet?"

"On a ship?"

"It's not unheard of."

"No, I've never had a pet."

"That's too bad," she said. "I miss my cat. I think how a person treats an animal says a lot about them. What do you think?"

He shrugged. "Never seen an animal in person before."

Her jaw dropped. "What?"

"Well, I take that back. We transported some monkeys once." He shuddered. "Never again."

"Not all animals are like monkeys."

"I sure hope not."

"What was it like growing up in space?"

He shrugged. "I don't know. What was it like growing up on Earth?"

"You first."

He rubbed his chin. "We never stayed in any one place for long. We were always moving. Every few years, we'd change ships and crews. Kept things interesting, I guess. Dad was a good guy. But he, uh … he and Charlie were drinking buddies. Things would get a little rowdy. And he was stubborn." The captain ran a hand through his hair. "Man, was he stubborn." He flashed a grin. "A bit like you."

"Shut up. What else was he like?"

"He cheated at video games." He gave her a wink. "Also like you."

"I do not!"

The side-long smile he gave her made her heart thud.

"He was really proud of his work. A lot of people look down on the mechanic. Maybe because he has grease on his jump-suit. They seem to forget that the mechanic keeps the ship flying."

"Is that why you dress like a mechanic?"

The captain laughed. "It irritates them to no end."

"Who?"

"Omni Authority."

"Did you always want to be a captain?"

"Not at first. But Dad dreamed of it. I guess it caught on. He was never captain material, but he wanted it for me."

"Do you like being captain?"

She caught the soft smile on his face. She knew the answer before he even said, "Love it."

"There's something I've been wondering about," Gemma said. "Who's Michal?"

He gave her a startled look.

"Your ship? She was named Michal?"

"Oh! Oh, that." He shook his head. "No, my dad's name was Michael, but a ship is supposed to be a girl's name … so I sort of named it after him?"

"Aww, that's sweet."

"Well." The captain climbed to his feet. "Enough goofing off. I should get back to working on the navigation."

Gemma lay down on the bed, but didn't close her eyes. He opened the panel and crawled inside.

"Hey, I just fixed this wire!" His voice echoed from inside the console. "And this one. I think I see something mov—whoa!"

The captain backed out of the hole so fast, he slammed into the pilot's chair.

A large, gray, squeaking rodent darted out of the hole.

Gemma screamed. The thing ran under the bed. She screamed again, leaping off the bed, running across the room, and jumping up onto the chair.

"Get a hold of yourself, Pilot!" The captain steadied her as she tilted, but she stopped screaming. He offered her a hand down, but she shook her head and pointed at the bed, her voice still too loud.

"Get rid of it!"

"At least it's not in the nav system anymore."

Gemma groaned. "No, this is so much worse! It's going to eat our food!"

The captain rubbed his chin. "You know, your idea should work."

She stopped yelling. "What idea?"

"To lure it out with food."

"Oh!" Gemma snapped her fingers. "You're right. We should set a trap."

"With what?"

"What do we have?"

Gemma stayed standing on the chair, her eyes riveted on the bed, while the captain dumped out the contents of the supply cabinet.

"Ah ha!" He came up with a roll of duct tape.

"Seriously?" Gemma demanded. "Tell me you're not serious."

"No, we can make this work," he said. "I have an idea. But you've got to help me."

She eyed the bed but allowed him to help her down from the chair.

Following his directions, they weaved long strips of tape together to make a sticky mesh. Then they laid it on the floor in front of the bed.

"Now what?" Gemma whispered.

"You get back up on the chair," the captain said. "You're not going to like this part."

He ripped open a food pouch and dropped a small portion of jerky onto the center of the mesh. Then he stood back and waited.

And waited.

"What's taking this thing so long?" Gemma asked from atop the chair. "I thought you said it would be starving."

"You would think so. Do you think it knows it's a trap?"

"More likely it's afraid of being in the light," Gemma said.

"Then I'll shut off the lights."

"No, wait!"

Turning off the lights plummeted the little room into pitch black.

Tears wet her eyes as she fought the urge to scream. "I can't believe you did that," she said, her voice shaking. "Turn them back on. Right now."

"Shh, I can hear it moving."

She could hear it moving too. She screwed her eyes shut until …

The rodent squeaked, then screamed. Gemma screamed. The captain flicked the lights back on and she saw the thing struggling, wrapped up in the duct tape mesh. It kept scream-ing. So did she.

The captain stepped around it, hitting the button to open

the inner airlock doors. He grabbed the thing, threw it inside, and locked the doors again.

"Pilot, shut up!"

Gemma slapped her hand over her mouth.

The captain gave her a hard look. "Do. Not. Cry."

Her hand still over her mouth, she nodded repeatedly, a tear escaping and sliding down her cheek.

Captain Lee ran a hand through his hair. "I told you not to cry!"

"I'm not crying!" she said, her voice muffled by her hand over her mouth as more tears followed, her shoulders shaking.

He groaned, his shoulders drooping. "I have no idea what to do. How do I get you to stop?"

She pulled her shaking hand away from her mouth, her voice a squeak. "Can you hug me?"

He jumped back a step, his mouth open. "Uh ..."

Ouch.

She sniffled, not looking at him. *Do the same thing I did for you, dummy.* "A pillow. Hand me the pillow."

He did, and she clutched at it, sobbing into it.

"Pilot ..." His voice was tentative. "It's going to be okay."

"Shut up, that's not helping!" she yelled into the pillow.

She hated, hated, hated to admit it, but fear squeezed her heart. The rodent had been the last straw. Crash landing, fighting, mine cave in, fleeing for their lives, stuck on a tiny ship with no food, flying into a situation that will probably kill them ...

Gemma gasped as the captain's arms surrounded her. Dropping the soaked pillow, she clung to him, tearful and shaking.

His arms tightened. "It's okay," he said softly, his voice vibrating beneath her cheek. "It's going to be okay."

She nodded, her tears still coming.

After a while, they slowed. She gave a sigh when they stopped. He felt so safe.

The captain cleared his throat. "Um." He shifted his weight. "Are you done now? Can I let go?"

She looked up at him. "I'm okay. Thank you."

He hesitated, raising a hand as if to touch her cheek. She silently begged him to.

Instead, he let his hand fall, and eased her out of his grip, not looking at her. "Good."

He turned away; his fists clenched.

Gemma rubbed her wet cheeks. "What are you going to do now?"

He glanced back at her. "Uh, am I supposed to do something else?"

"With the rat."

"Oh." Relief washed over his face. "That. I don't know. But it can't hurt anything from inside the airlock. We'll leave it in there for now."

"But you said it was hungry," she said. "What if it starves?"

He hesitated. "We can't afford to give it any of our food. Hopefully, it'll be able to hold out until we get there, then we can release it."

"Okay."

He looked at her. "You look tired. You should get some sleep."

She stepped down from the chair. "Right, yeah. You're right." She hesitated beside the bed. "Thanks for taking care of that ... thing."

He gave her a nod as he sank down into the chair. "Part of my job, ma'am."

Trevor had fixed the nav system and set the autopilot as Gemma slept.

After a few hours of absolute boredom, Trevor paced the tiny room. He was used to small spaces, but this was ridiculous.

His eyes settled on Gemma's bag under the bed. What did she have in there? He should really ask her when she woke up.

Or he could find out now. He couldn't think of anything else to do.

As he checked to make sure she was *really* sleeping, he sighed. She was too adorable.

He pulled out the bag and opened it. Maybe there was something of Zane's that would be useful.

A leak finder, a camera, a music player ... "Yeah, like that'll be useful," he grumbled.

Trevor didn't recognize the other devices, and it would be foolish to play with them. He'd have to ask Gemma after all.

He pulled out the camera and flicked it on.

A picture of Zane and Gemma came up first, both beaming for the selfie. Trevor's throat tightened. Next were some pictures of the port where they refueled, a close-up of some weird plant.

One with Joe mock-choking Zane. Chase with a rare smile. She'd even sneaked one of Trevor when he wasn't looking, his profile outlined against the glowing ship's controls.

The last one was of Charlie reading, a cup of coffee in his hand, his glasses perched on his nose.

Trevor put the camera away and returned the bag. He

rubbed his chest where a pain had formed. What was he going to do without Charlie?

He leaned back against a wall, then sank to the floor, his head in his hands. What had he done?

"Captain?"

The captain sat on the floor, his elbows on his knees and his face in his hands. He didn't say anything.

She looked past him to the view screen. Still no one in sight. She got out of bed and knelt beside him.

"Something wrong?" she asked.

He took a deep, shuddering breath, and she knew something was.

"Captain ..."

"It's just—Charlie." He rubbed his face, and she saw his red-rimmed eyes. "It's like ... it's like my dad all over again." He coughed. "And Joe. And Chase and Dak. And Zane, oh man, Zane." His eyes squeezed shut. "Zane shouldn't have died. I never should have hired him on."

"You wouldn't have been able to stop him. He seems like the stowaway type to me. Seemed ..." She touched his shoulder. He flinched, but she rested her hand there.

"It's all my fault," he said.

"It's not your fault."

"I'm the captain. Everything is my fault." Another cough to cover up a sob as his voice cracked. "I can't do this right now. I can't afford to be emotional. We have a job to do."

"Now is perfect," Gemma said, her voice soft. "There's no danger, and ..." She sat next to him, their shoulders touching.

"You're safe. You're safe with me. There's no better time than now."

His head dropped, his cheek resting on the top of her head, and she felt a hot drop soak into her hair.

She closed her eyes, feeling him so close, her skin warm wherever they touched. *Please trust me.*

After a while, an alarm at the controls roused them.

The captain rubbed his eyes and stood, not meeting her eyes. "Sorry."

"Anytime, Captain," she said, with a smile and tilt of her head. "I'm here for you."

He glanced at her, then turned away to the controls.

"It's a life support system alarm," he said. "The humidity removal and water reclamation systems are offline."

"Can you fix it?"

He typed a command, and the alarm stopped. He pulled up the ship schematics. "Here." He pointed. "The rat must have gotten into it." Tapping the screen brought up a diagram of the system. "I'll have to see what the damage is. The ceiling doesn't seem to be leaking, so at least it wasn't a hose. We'd never be able to recover the spilled water."

No ladder onboard. They stacked two smooth-sided storage boxes below the ceiling panel housing the water systems. Tools in hand, the captain climbed up and unscrewed a panel.

Gemma sat in the pilot's chair, her chin in her hand, staring out at the stars without really seeing them.

He carried so much with him. So much guilt and responsibility and pressure and—loneliness. She wanted to reach out and take some of that burden away from him. Help him hold it up, but she didn't know how.

She sighed. *He probably wouldn't let me help anyway.*

Clanking and grumbling came from the ceiling.

"Pilot! I need your help," the captain called, his upper body hidden in the ceiling.

She hit the autopilot and launched out of the chair to his side. "What is it?"

"Come on up."

"Uh ..." She eyed the makeshift ladder of storage boxes. It wouldn't take much for the smooth sides to slide.

"Hurry up," he said, his voice impatient. He offered a hand and hauled her up to the top, as if she weighed nothing. The boxes shifted under her weight but held their positions.

She squeezed into the opening beside him, her chin barely clearing the ceiling.

"Hang on." The captain wound his arm around her waist and hoisted her higher. She swallowed; her face hot.

"Do you see that wire?" He pointed down a narrow space between the pipes.

"I see it. It's blue?"

"I can't get it," he said. "My hands are too big. Can you reach it?"

"I think so." She slid her arm into the opening, reaching as far as she could, cheek pressed against a panel as she groped for the wire. "Almost got it."

"Be careful not to touch the—"

"Ahhh!" She snatched her arm away from the electrical shock, her elbow colliding with the captain's hard chest.

The boxes below them shifted again, then shot out from under his feet. The captain landed hard on his back, Gemma on top of him.

"Stripped screws ..." he groaned.

"Ouch. Maybe next time *lead* with the warning?" She rubbed her hand where the shock had hit. She winced, but it didn't appear to be burnt. "Are you okay?"

He gasped. "I think I broke another rib. Are *you* okay?" His eyes met hers as he touched her hand.

With their faces so close together, she stared at him, unable to move from her position on top of him. Her breath caught in her throat. His heat radiated right through her clothes. Warmth and safety. She gazed up at his wide, beautiful eyes, then she couldn't help it; her gaze dropped to his mouth.

He swallowed as he stared back. "Um ... uh ..."

On impulse, she reached out, her palm grazing the side of his face, his stubble scratchy under her fingers.

The captain cleared his throat and looked away. He gripped her shoulders, his hands gentle, and pushed her off him.

"Let's try again," he said, his voice rough.

"Right ..."

They restacked the boxes and climbed up, Gemma hyperaware of him so close. This time he gave her a glove to wear that swallowed up her hand and wrist, her fingertips not even reaching the ends of the fingers, but it would work.

She reached inside again. She paused at a wobble, his arm around her waist tightening. It distracted her, but she found the wire and dragged it out.

"Thanks." He took the wire in one hand, then offered her the other. She put the gloves in it. He chuckled. "I was going to help you down."

"Oh." She took his hand and held on tight as she climbed down. Her grip lingered in his, but he pulled out of it.

She stood there for a minute as he tinkered in the ceiling. He wasn't going to say anything? She bit her lip. Should *she* say something?

As much as she wanted to reach out to him, she winced, her face hot, at the thought of him pulling away again. Or pushing away. Same thing. She had already embarrassed herself on his ship with the misread-kiss situation. She would rather avoid that burning humiliation again.

When it became clear he wasn't going to say anything else, she returned to the pilot's chair.

"Captain!" she called.

He climbed down, wiping sweat from his brow. "What is it?"

"We've reached the Terminus," she said.

The Terminus was marked on the navigation charts as a thick white line. In reality, they saw a gigantic space buoy with a blinking blue light on it. A giant grid of buoys marked the Terminus, but they could only see the one.

"Continue on," the captain said.

They passed the Terminus, and the captain went back to work on the ceiling.

Gemma stayed at the helm. Space debris littered this side of the Terminus. Small pieces of scrap bounced off the shield, and she had to maneuver around the larger chunks. Most of the junk had collected into groups, pockets of debris, but plenty still floated around.

She shivered. The ship graveyard left no doubt in her mind that she had done the right thing in coming. He would be toast out here without her. *But ... but Sandy—*

"All fixed," the captain said, replacing the ceiling tile and screwing it in place.

"My sister's getting married, you know," Gemma said, her legs pulled up and her chin on her knees, still sitting in the pilot's chair.

He stepped down, wiping his hands on a rag. "No, I didn't know that."

She didn't look at him. "No, I know you didn't. I meant ... anyway. It's a big deal. Getting married."

"So I've heard."

"I think she found a great guy too," Gemma said. "His name is David; he's a computer guy."

"Is your sister into computers too?"

Gemma chuckled, looking up at him. "Sandy? Oh, no. Nooooo." She smiled. "She designs greeting cards. Computers are how they met, actually. She spilled coffee on her laptop and had a deadline that night. She took it to the shop and David fixed it up for her in time for her deadline."

Gemma laughed. "The next time she drenched her laptop, she was so embarrassed that David would find out, she tried to dry it with a hairdryer."

The captain chuckled. "I bet that *really* fried it." He paused, then snorted, trying to hold back another laugh.

"What? What's so funny?" she demanded.

"Your last name." He managed to get it out with a straight face—the quirk in the corner of his mouth belying it. "You're Gemma Stone. And she's—" He cracked up. "Sandy Stone!"

"Her real name is Sandra!" Gemma objected.

"Your parents must have had a sense of humor," the captain said, a grin across his face.

Gemma scowled at him. Yeah, her parents had thought it was really cute. The other kids in school ... not so much. "It's not that funny."

"Right, right." He couldn't smother his smile.

"Besides, her last name is going to change anyway when she gets married," Gemma said, crossing her arms.

"I hadn't thought of that. Then she'll be free of being—"

She smacked him in the shoulder. "Shut up!"

He still chuckled. "What's the matter?"

"She'll be starting her own family and a new life with David," she said, her voice soft. "I'm going to come in second place to him. I have trouble finding that funny."

That shot down his smirk. "Oh."

A moment of gloomy silence stretched between them.

The captain rubbed the back of his neck and looked away from her. "Were you going to marry Alex?"

Gemma blinked. "We were a little young for that. Like, *really* young."

"Oh. Right."

"But … we'd talked about it. And—" She fidgeted. "I think there was a time when I wanted to."

The captain was silent for a moment. "You've told me everything about yourself," he said. "But you never talk about your parents."

She shrugged. "Yeah, well …" She let the sentence hang. Her heart already ached with the thought of losing Sandy. The old, deep hurt of all the people she'd lost in her life didn't need to be dug up right now.

He nodded, his eyes on her. "I understand."

16

Trevor opened his eyes to see Gemma kneeling at the airlock, the door open a few inches.

He sat up. "What are you doing?"

Gemma slammed the door shut and whirled around; guilt written all over her face. "Nothing."

He stared at her. *No, she wouldn't* ... "You saved some food? And you're *feeding* it? I thought you were terrified of the thing."

"I am, but that doesn't mean it should starve. I promise, it's out of my half."

He closed his eyes and pressed his hand against his forehead. "No, it's just—" He looked at her. "*I've* been feeding it."

They stared at each other, before bursting into laughter.

"That thing is eating better than we are!" Gemma managed to say.

They laughed so hard, Gemma doubled over, tears streaming down her face, while Trevor's shoulders shook, unable to stop.

"Oh, gosh." Gemma wiped her eyes. "That felt good."

Trevor chuckled, a grin on his face. "Yeah. It really did."

Their laughter trailed off, leaving a silence.

IN THE PILOT'S CHAIR, GEMMA HEAVED A SIGH AND LOOKED UP AT THE ceiling. Instead of sleeping, the captain paced behind her. They'd run out of food that morning and she felt weak, but he kept going like some fidgeting Energizer bunny.

He was supposed to be sleeping. If he wasn't going to sleep, then he should let her have a turn. She shifted in the seat, her clothing grungy against her skin from wearing them too long. Her eyes burned with exhaustion. Exhaustion from not sleeping well, exhaustion from hunger, exhausted of small spaces, exhausted of space.

"Will you stop it!" Gemma spun around in her chair. "It's like being trapped in a tin can with a nervous elephant! Give it a rest."

He stopped. "What are you talking about?"

"You! Stomping around all the time. Back and forth and back and forth."

"I don't stomp."

"You're loud," she insisted.

"I don't think I am—"

She rolled her eyes. "You're not exactly a ninja. Your pacing is driving me crazy."

"And you think *you're* not driving *me* crazy?" he snapped. "You never shut up! You talk and talk, and when you're not talking, you're humming."

Her face heated, and her fists tightened. She wouldn't let him turn this around on her. "That's nothing compared to your fidgeting, shuffling, pacing—you never hold still!"

"You have no sense of personal boundaries," he said, throwing up his hands and trying to walk away. He ended up pacing again. "You're always pushing and pushing. Asking questions, standing so close. Everything about you drives me crazy! How you talk, how you laugh, how your hair sticks up in the morning, how you smell—"

"Are you saying I stink? Because I can't help that I only have two sets of clothes—"

"No, it's the opposite! It's ... *you.* It's your hair, your clothes, your skin, it's on the pillow every time I try to fall asleep. I can't get away from it! I—"

She left the chair and closed the space between them. He turned to see her standing *right there*, her wide eyes boring into him, forcing him to stop pacing.

Her heart hammered. "You like how I smell?" she whispered.

He swallowed. "It's ... it's maddening."

She stepped closer. "Captain—"

"No!" He stepped away from her and ran smack into the wall. "Just ... just—"

With a growl of frustration, he slammed his fist into a metal panel.

"Hey, watch it!" Gemma ran over to examine the dent he'd left. "This thing has to get us where we're going!"

He turned away, taking a deep, shaky breath.

"Why don't you get some sleep?" he said, his back to her.

A pause.

"What's your name?" she asked.

"Not this again!"

Her fists went to her hips. "I'm trapped in a tiny hunk of junk with you. I'd like to know who I'm flying with."

"You already know more about me than anyone else. You

and your incessant questions." He stomped over to the pilot's chair and dropped into it, his back to her. "Get some sleep."

She lay in bed, eyes closed, not sleeping, when the captain asked in a quiet voice, "Do you really think I'm not human?"

She opened her eyes, and her breath caught in her throat. "Captain ..."

"Sorry, it's not my business," he said quickly. The light from the screens outlined his profile as he leaned back and stared at the ceiling.

"I'm so sorry I said that," she said. "I had to because—"

He shrugged. "Never mind. It doesn't matter."

"It *does* matter," she said. "Captain, you're more human than a lot of people I've met."

He spun the chair away from her, but not before she saw his smile. "Thanks."

GEMMA YAWNED AND STRETCHED, FEELING HUNGRY BUT OH-SO-MUCH better. "Good morning, Captain."

"It's Trevor," he said.

Gemma's gaze snapped to him. "What?"

He wouldn't meet her eyes. "My name. It's Trevor."

A deep warmth spread through her, and she smiled. "Trevor."

He got a shiver and tried to cover it up by rubbing the back of his neck. "But don't use it in front of anyone, okay? It's ... private."

She hugged herself, quiet as she studied him. She had never reached this depth of feeling with another person before. Even Sandy.

He trusted her. And she could trust him.

"My parents died in a plane crash." She looked down at her fidgeting fingers. "They were on a trip for their anniversary. Freak accident. Sandy hasn't been on a plane since."

"Flying." His gaze turned to her. "I should have known."

"Excuse me?"

The captain—Trevor—shook his head. "No, I mean *The Blue.* It all has to do with adventure and flying. Your dad made it for *you.* He knew what you loved."

Gemma looked down. "Yeah. He and I were close. Mom and Sandy had a lot in common, but I was definitely a daddy's girl."

He smiled. "I can believe that." He rubbed the back of his neck and took a deep breath. "I sometimes wondered what it would be like to have a mom."

She laughed. "Do you think you'd be a mama's boy?"

He chuckled. "I don't know about that. But I never got the chance to find out."

Gemma stopped laughing. It wasn't funny anymore.

"It was amazing," she said.

He sighed, staring up at the ceiling. "I'd imagine so."

TREVOR LEANED BACK IN THE PILOT'S SEAT, HIS FEET UP ON THE console. His finger silently tapped out the rhythm to the song Gemma hummed. He recognized the same tune she always hummed to lull herself to sleep. He glanced back. She smiled a little while she hummed, her eyes closed. He wished he could make out the song.

A blip on the scanners made Trevor sit up straight. "It's another ship."

Gemma scrambled out of bed. She leaned over his shoulder to see the screens.

An anxious minute passed as they scrolled through the sensor data.

Gemma released a sigh. "It's just a commercial transport."

"Best to steer clear of it anyway." Trevor's fingers tapped against the screens to alter their course.

The ship ignored them.

After that, the sensors picked up more and more ship activity. Trevor and Gemma took turns watching, the thick tension in the room making it impossible to relax, even off-duty.

At one point, they came across a pair of fighters, circling and shooting at each other. Gemma gave them a wide berth.

"It's unlikely we'll see any full-on space battles," Trevor assured her. "We're on the very fringes of the war, and we're not going much deeper."

Gemma nodded and kept a tight grip on the control column.

Later, a ship chased down a cargo vessel in the distance, shooting its engines to disable it.

"Pirates," Trevor growled. "We're too small to be of any interest to them. But, just in case …"

They altered their course again.

"We're never going to get there at this rate," Gemma said, rubbing her eyes.

"We'll get there," he said, touching her shoulder. *Stay positive.* He didn't want to admit the hunger that gnawed at him, so sharp he wanted to double over. Or how weak he felt.

She didn't even respond, hunched over in the pilot's chair, dark smudges under her eyes.

Trevor frowned, and knelt to eye-level with her. "You want some sleep?"

She shook her head, exhaustion lining her face. "I don't

think I'll sleep until we arrive. And even then, I won't get any. Why don't you get some?"

He gave her shoulder the slightest squeeze and tried to give an encouraging smile. "I'm not leaving. We'll get through this."

"I haven't seen any other one-man ships like ours," she said, staring at the screens but not seeing them. "I hope that's not a bad sign."

Trevor's lips compressed. "We'll get there," he said again.

17

On the sixth day, they got their first glimpse of their target planet, Cerise. It grew larger and larger on their screen at an agonizingly slow rate. Trevor had never been in this part of the galaxy before. He'd rarely gone beyond the Terminus. He'd been pursued, shot at, gone in and out of conflicts—but a full-out war was all new territory. Hopefully, their window of peace still held.

"Wow," Gemma said as they passed other planets. "Now I know why this universe is called the Ruby District."

All the planets stood out in contrast to black space, each an amazing shade of red. One striped red and white, with angry-red storm eyes on it, not unlike Jupiter's. The next had violet rings around it.

She looked at the navigation screen. "Claret, Carmine, Cardinal ... who named these planets?"

"Someone with a thesaurus," Trevor said.

She laughed. Trevor smiled; he liked making her laugh.

"What do we know about Cerise?" Gemma asked during their final approach to orbit.

Trevor rubbed his chin. "We're pretty sure the on-planet fighting's stopped, but they're under martial law now. And there's a temporary cease-fire with another faction off-planet."

"Pretty sure?" Gemma repeated. "And are you saying they're having two wars right now?"

He nodded. "A civil war and a trade route war."

Gemma whistled and sank back into her chair.

"As soon as we're within distance, hail them and request permission to land." Trevor resisted the urge to pace and instead let his nervous energy out by tapping the back of the chair in a soothing rhythm. As tricky as it seemed, landing was the easy part. Leaving was likely to be much, much harder.

Gemma turned to look at him. "Will you stop that?"

His hands stilled. "Sorry."

"Maybe they'll believe our story and it won't be an issue," Gemma said, turning back to the screens. "After all, even in times of war, families still visit each other."

It had been Gemma's idea to pretend they wanted to visit someone on-planet.

"I wouldn't know," Trevor said. "The biggest problem is we don't have a name to give them. With martial law, they'll definitely ask." He shook his head. "We had a better chance when we were delivering cargo. I don't really know if this will work." *This isn't going to work.*

"Don't worry, Captain," Gemma said. "I'll get us down there." She tapped her screen. "We're within range. Ready for me to give them a call?"

"Do it." He gripped the back of her chair hard. This wasn't going to work. The heavily monitored planet made it impossible to land without clearance. If the people in charge denied them permission, the mission would be over ... And they would probably be shot down.

He sighed. If they managed to avoid *that*, then they'd probably starve to death. They had run out of food, and travelling to the nearest safe port would take over a week.

"Unknown jetter, identify yourself," the communicator squawked.

Gemma depressed a button. "Ship 1902 of mining colony 3X-527 requesting—"

"Identify yourself, or you will be shot down."

"Hello? Hello! Can you hear me?" She pushed it again. And again. The communicator indicator light stayed dark. "Hello?"

"I repeat, identify yourself or you will be shot down."

Gemma's eyes widened as she turned to him. "They can't hear me!"

"The rat must have knocked out communications." Trevor ran back to the supply closet and pulled out the emergency communicator. "Here, use this."

She pressed the power button, but that light didn't come on either. Gemma looked at him in horror. "I took out the batteries for the flashlight."

"This is your final warning, identify yourself or—"

"Find the flashlight!" Trevor ordered.

Gemma tore through the supply closet while Trevor dumped out the toolbox.

"What if you left it in the ceiling?" Gemma said, her voice high and frantic.

"You will be fired on in ten, nine—"

Adrenaline pumping through him, Trevor kicked the bed under the access panel—breaking the bolts holding it to the floor—and jumped up. He scrabbled with the ceiling panel edges for a second, before punching the metal tile, bending it just enough that he could get his fingers under it. He ripped the panel off, the metal screws holding it in place pinging on the floor.

"Eight, seven—"

He tossed her the flashlight. She missed the catch, and the casing popped open when it hit the floor. Trevor dove for the scattered batteries. Gemma's fingers fumbled as she inserted them.

"Five, four, three—"

"WE'RE HERE, WE'RE HERE!" GEMMA SHOUTED INTO THE transponder. "Ship 1902 of mining colony 3X-527 requesting permission to land!"

"Identify yourself."

She clutched her heart and let out a long breath to steady herself, her limbs shaking. Trevor hung on to the back of her chair, breathing hard.

"Gemma Stone." Her voice shook as she gave her ID number. *Calm down.*

Trevor gave her shoulder a squeeze. "You're okay."

"Purpose of your visit?"

"Visiting relatives." Gemma's heartbeat slowed as she took another long breath.

The silence lasted so long she thought the batteries might have died.

"You say you're from a mining colony?"

"Yes, sir," she said. "I'm on vacation and I came to visit my cousin. I borrowed the ship."

"Name of relative?"

Trevor tensed, but she remained calm and smiling. She believed people could hear your smile.

"You know, it's stupid, but I can't remember," she said. "Her first name is Maria, but she got married and moved here.

Her maiden name is Smith. Her husband does something-or-other with mechanics, and I *can't* remember his last name. It's *so* hard to pronounce, and I couldn't make it to the wedding, so I—"

"Do you have an address?"

"*As I was saying*," Gemma continued in an obnoxious voice, "I wanted to *surprise* her, so, no, I don't know her address. I was planning on calling her to pick me up once I was—"

"So, you have a phone number."

Gemma stopped short. "Uh ..."

A murmur over the comm. "One moment," the voice said, then clicked off.

Their eyes wide, Gemma and Trevor shared a look. "We're so dead," she whispered.

"They haven't shot us down yet." Trevor cleared his throat, wiping away a bead of sweat sliding down the side of his face. "There's still hope."

As much as she wanted to believe the captain's words, his face told her the real story. "You're a terrible liar."

A burst of static as the communicator reengaged. "I need you to answer some standard questions before clearance is given."

Gemma swallowed hard, trying to let her mind relax. These would be hard questions, and she'd have to be creative.

"While visitors are not restricted from Cerise, you do understand that we are under martial law, and therefore have heightened security?"

She blinked. It was a standard question. *They believed her?*

Trevor nudged her arm.

Answer, dummy!

"Yes!" she almost shouted. She lowered her voice. "Um, yes."

"You are not to enter any forbidden areas, which are clearly marked," the voice on the communicator continued. "There is a curfew of 1900 every evening until 0600 the next morning. Those still outside at that time will be placed under arrest. Do you understand and agree to these terms?"

"Yes."

"Once you land, you will go through the security checkpoint and customs. Do you have any passengers?"

She hesitated. "Yes."

Typically, their names and numbers were entered into a database and then ignored, only given attention if the name raised a red flag. Her name wouldn't raise any, but she didn't know if Trevor's would. The panicked look on his face didn't give her much comfort. She needed a name and number.

"Name?"

"David Channing," she said, and gave his number. She muted the microphone and whispered to Trevor, "It's my sister's fiancé's name."

Trevor's eyebrows raised. "And you know his ID number?"

The corner of Gemma's mouth quirked up. "I looked him up when he started dating my sister, of course."

"The purpose of his visit?" the voice on the line said.

"Uh ..." She didn't have a quick answer for that one. Sweat trickled down her back.

"Say something!" Trevor hissed.

"He's my boyfriend," she blurted. "He's meeting my cousin Maria too."

"Are you transporting anything? Any vegetables or biological specimens?"

"No," Gemma said.

"You are cleared to land. Uploading coordinates."

Disconnecting, she collapsed back into her chair and heaved a sigh of relief. Trevor had to take a knee to get his own breathing under control, his hand on his chest.

"I cannot believe that worked," he said.

"Of course it worked." She dragged herself back into an upright position. "It was my idea."

"Yes. Of course. Great job." He straightened and blew out another breath. "We did it. Now land the ship."

"*We* did it?" she snapped. "I don't see *you* doing anything."

"Of course I am." A corner of his mouth quirked. "I'm captaining."

She laughed harder than the weak joke warranted, but it steadied her enough to pilot the ship.

18

As they neared the docks, a glimpse of the city blinked by them, leaving an impression of strict black roads weaving through wild terrain.

The docks consisted of a large group of platforms, surrounded by a very long, very high bar fence: you could see through, but even a child couldn't squeeze between the iron slats. Like the city, the burned and black ground inside the fence contrasted with the unkept, tall grass outside it.

Gemma landed and powered down the engines. She took a deep breath to calm herself. Once they landed, the tall grass and weeds hid the city from their view.

Trevor offered her a hand. "We've got this." He pulled her to her feet.

She squeezed his hand hard before letting it go. They had arrived safely—somewhat safely—on Cerise. Hopefully not for a long stay.

What were they supposed to do now?

A uniformed man with a tablet greeted them when the door slid open. "Good morning—what is that?"

Their rodent stowaway waddled out of the airlock, still covered in duct tape, and disappeared under the ship.

Trevor shrugged. "I really have no idea."

Gemma snorted, trying to keep a straight face.

"Uh huh." The man's eyes narrowed. "Follow me, please."

Gemma shouldered her pack and walked down the ramp behind Trevor. She started to close the airlock behind her when the man stopped her. "We'll need to search your ship."

"Uh." She glanced back at the disaster they'd made searching for those stupid batteries. Snapped bolts, the bed out of place, the floor strewn with tools and supplies, and a hole in the ceiling.

Trevor touched her arm, bringing her gaze back to him. He gave a nod.

"You can search our ship, but the keys stay with us," he said to the man.

A breeze ruffled her hair, and she took a deep breath that left her coughing. More than exhaust and fuel, the air reeked of charcoal and smoke.

Their greeter escorted them through the docks devoid of people. Gemma shifted her bag on her shoulder, glancing around. Where were the other people? No one leaving, no one arriving, no maintenance crews. She hadn't expected a bustling spaceport, but the quiet gave her goosebumps, despite the sunny day.

They wound their way around a few powered-down ships, and into a small, one-story building with the word "Customs" stenciled on the outside. Inside, four cubicles divided the main room, all beige walls and white informational posters. Their greeter ushered them into the closest cubicle and seated them in plastic chairs in front of a desk, the man behind it typing. He wore the same uniform as their greeter, but with red tabs on his shoulders. Probably a higher rank. The large poster behind him listed prohibited items.

"State your business," he said without glancing at them. "What brings you to Cerise?"

"We're here to visit my cousin," Gemma said. She smiled. *Be cool. Be calm.*

The man stopped typing and looked at her. "Cousin Maria, is it?"

Her smile stiffened a little, but she kept it in place. She had been too memorable. "Yes, exactly."

"So that was *you* on the line," he said, removing his hands from the keyboard and folding them in front of him on the desk. "I know all about you."

Gemma broke out in a sweat, struggling to keep the corners of her mouth turned up. "You do?"

"Oh yes. We did a background check on you." He glanced at his screen, angled out of her view. "What brings you all the way here from Earth? And in a vessel belonging to a mining colony?"

"We stopped by the colony on our way here," Trevor said, his voice calm, but his hands fidgeting. "Our ship broke down there, and they were kind enough to lend us one while they fixed it."

"I thought you said you were on vacation."

"Uh, we are." Trevor swallowed. "We're taking a vacation from ... Earth. And stopped by the mining colony."

"So, you must be Mr. Channing." The man clicked the screen. "Your report says you're good with computers."

Trevor shrugged. "I get by."

Gemma tried not to fidget, too. His tense jaw belied the nonchalance he was trying to project.

"Mine is doing the strangest thing," the man said. "Every time I go to print, I get an error message saying the printer is not connected, when I can see the printer is *right there* connected to it. Any idea how to fix that?"

A beat went by.

"Have you tried turning it off and then on again?" Trevor asked.

Gemma bit the inside of her cheek to keep from snorting. David always said exactly that.

The man pursed his lips and considered them.

"All right, I'll let you through," he said. "Don't get into any trouble."

"Absolutely, sir."

"We won't, sir."

Gemma and Trevor stepped through a scanner while customs checked out the inside of her pack. She had to show them how Zane's clock worked, and that, no, it wasn't a bomb.

Approved for entry, they stepped outside the fence surrounding the docks.

They stood there a moment, dumbfounded. "We made it?" Gemma breathed.

Trevor glanced behind them. "It was a little too easy, wasn't it?"

"Easy!" Gemma slapped a hand to her chest. "I thought I was going to have a heart attack." She paused. "Now what?"

"Well, the plan was to deliver our relief supplies and meet up with a contact at the drop-off point." He scratched his head. "I don't know where that would be now. Come on, we can't just stand here outside the customs building."

They picked a random direction and walked along one of the sidewalks.

Outside the docks was one of the saddest sights Trevor had ever seen. Despite it being labeled 'Main Street,' the road by the docks had only two lanes, with wide sidewalks along each side. A few vehicles went by on the new pavement, mostly work vans and trucks. Several bikes and scooters weaved through traffic, but it looked as if the majority of the population walked. Which was ... odd.

Gemma's thoughts aligned with his. "What, no public transportation?"

"I guess not," he murmured, studying the passing people. "At least they re-paved the roads after the conflict so the city wouldn't shut down."

People hurried by with their heads down, as if afraid to make eye contact. Many looked at their phones, but few talked on them. Their drab clothing matched the threadbare bags they carried. One passing man wore an expensive suit, but with a glance Trevor saw the fraying hem, the graying elbows.

All the boarded-up businesses still standing along the street had spray-painted words scrawled across the wood: "WE'RE OPEN," "CC'S FOOD MARKET," "FURNITURE FOR SALE HERE."

"What is with this place?" Gemma asked, a little warble in her voice. "What happened?"

Empty shells of other buildings gaped at them, some structures gone all together, just rubble in the gap between its neighbors. The smell of smoke lingered.

"War," Trevor said.

Off the newly paved street, laser fire had burned gouges in

a ground torn with trenches. Fallen barricades and trash littered the area. A broken-down tank lay on its side. No one walked in the no-man's land, sticking to the new sidewalks.

"We'll have to make discreet inquiries," Trevor whispered as they walked, trying not to speak over the muted city sounds of footsteps and the chiming of bicycle bells. A vehicle honked, and a few people jumped at the sound.

"Who do we ask?" Gemma whispered back. She glanced at the war-torn areas and shivered. "We don't know anything about this place. Will you slow down?"

He shortened his stride so Gemma could keep up with him. "It might be best to start at a refueling station. That's where I'd go." He hesitated, looking around. The waves of people in the street parted before him. He tried to hunch his shoulders, only now realizing how conspicuous his height made him.

Footsteps approached from behind, the snap of new shoes on the pavement standing out from the crowd. At least, it stood out to Trevor. He tapped Gemma's arm and turned as a man approached them, his navy pinstripe suit not at all worn out.

The man nodded at them, giving them a wide, toothy smile. "Are you looking for Dr. Penn?"

Trevor and Gemma glanced at each other. As he'd said: Definitely too easy.

"No, sir. You've got the wrong guy," Trevor said.

"What are your names?" the man pressed, taking a step closer, the smile pasted in place.

The back of Trevor's neck itched, and he could tell from how passersby hurried past and went out of their way to keep their distance from them—even stepping onto the busy street —that this guy was trouble.

Trevor took Gemma's hand to keep her close as they stepped back. He could carry her if they had to run, but not if they got separated. He stood straight and pitched his voice low to dissuade the man from advancing further. "That's not your business."

"Oh, isn't it?" The man took another, purposeful step closer. "Are you not David Channing and Gemma Stone?"

Gemma gave a quiet intake of breath.

"Who are you?" Trevor demanded.

The man gestured toward the street behind him, where a limo idled. "Right this way."

Trevor didn't move except to pull Gemma closer.

"Is this as bad as I think it is?" Gemma murmured to Trevor.

Dr. Penn couldn't operate out in the open like this. Otherwise, why disguise the flash drive as a pen?

What about the people who shot them down?

Trevor's grip on Gemma's hand tightened. He tensed to turn and run—just as two men materialized out of the crowd, one on each side of them. They made no effort to hide their weapons.

Trevor could take them ... but not without someone getting hurt. He could protect Gemma, but what about the crowd around them?

He glanced at her. Going with this man not only jeopardized the mission, but worse, it put Gemma in danger.

They needed sleep. They needed to eat. And he had to protect her.

"Get in," the man ordered, his smile gone.

Gemma's hand trembled.

Trevor relented. They didn't have a choice.

After checking inside the empty back seat of the limo, Trevor let Gemma in first before he folded himself in. Though he had to hunch over, the limo gave him more legroom than he'd expected.

The door slammed shut, and the car began to move, Trevor and Gemma alone in the backseat.

Already knowing the answer, Trevor did a discreet test of the door handle. Locked.

"Captain—"

He put a finger to his lips, glancing at the opaque window separating them from the driver. Dark tint also obscured the back windows, too.

Trevor's mind churned during the tense half-hour ride. They were in trouble. He had to keep Gemma safe.

Trevor glanced at her out of the corner of his eye, her hand trembling slightly in his.

With a jolt, he realized they still held hands. It felt so natural, but now that he realized it, his hand grew hot and sweaty.

Trevor swallowed hard. She didn't seem to notice as she stared out the blacked-out window at nothing, her face expressionless.

When the car stopped, her grip tightened on his, her pulse pounding against his skin.

The door opened to a construction site of a huge, four-story building, big enough to hold at least two of Trevor's ship. Their two guards ignored a large sign declaring it a hard-hat area, and herded them past stacks of lumber, giant dumpsters, and several vehicles, some parked and others on the move.

People stood working on the roof of the building they approached, calling to each other over the *thunk-thunk* of a nail gun and the beeping of a truck backing up.

Trevor narrowed his eyes at the building. He counted two exits on this side, doors. The high, slit windows with stickers on the glass wouldn't help in an escape.

The armed men led them through an unpainted door surrounded by scaffolding, and into a tunnel of plastic sheeting that smelled of glue and paint. Vague shapes of people moved on the other side of the plastic.

Up an elevator and into a room with a window wall covered in plastic sheeting. Light filtered in, but Trevor couldn't see through it.

The room had new carpet and paint, a projection system already mounted and a computer set into the wall. A man in a lab coat waited for them, the two guards taking positions on either side of the door.

Trevor kept Gemma's hand in his. He wanted to be ready to move the second they had an opening.

"Mr. Channing," the man in the lab coat greeted them. "Ms. Stone."

That's how they got through customs. This guy had them in his pocket.

"Dr. Penn?" Trevor said, trying to appear as if he didn't suspect anything. Trevor's eye twitched as he attempted to keep a neutral face. Gemma called it; he had always been a terrible liar.

"Yes, of course." Sweat beaded on the forehead of 'Dr. Penn', his eyes dilated. He wasn't a very good liar either. He extended his hand to shake, but Trevor kept his in Gemma's.

"Right." The 'doctor' lowered his hand. "Please, have a seat."

Trevor didn't move, his grip on her hand keeping Gemma in place, too. The only way out was the way they came in. As soon as it opened, they would make a break for it.

The 'doctor' swallowed hard. "I believe you have something for me?"

"Of course," said Trevor, keeping his voice level. "Pilot, the bag."

Gemma handed her pack to him, eyebrows raised. He groped around in it for a minute, before coming up with a small square. He had no idea what it was but handed it to the Dr. Penn impersonator.

The man snatched it out of Trevor's hand and ran over to the computer.

"Run," Trevor whispered.

"What?" Gemma said.

One of the guards stepped close, his hand encircling Gemma's arm. "Ma'am, I'll need you to come with us."

Trevor saw red. "Don't touch her!" He dropped Gemma's hand and launched himself at the guard with such speed that Trevor had already pulled the man's stunner and zapped him by the time his partner pulled his weapon. Trevor zapped him too, sending him twitching to the ground.

"No! No, no!" said the 'doctor.' "Stop! Stop him, we need him!"

"Wait, what just—?" Gemma blinked at the downed guards as Trevor pulled her out of the room. He slammed open the heavy door next to the elevator, their footsteps echoing as they raced down the stairs.

"What are we doing?" Gemma asked, breathless.

"He's a fake," Trevor said. "We have to get off this planet."

"I figured *that*," she said. "But do you have a plan?"

"Working on it."

With a rush of static, a voice from a hidden speaker system announced, "We have two intruders loose in the facility. This is not a drill. All personnel on alert. Detain them. I repeat—"

They reached the ground floor and burst back into the plastic-sheeted hallway.

"Psst! Captain!"

They stopped short. A woman in a lab coat, her dark hair pulled back into a bun, leaned out of an opening in a dark section of the hallway and gestured to them. "This way!"

"Who are you?" Trevor demanded.

"I'm a friend," she said, raising her voice to be heard over the intruder alert. "Hurry, there's no time!"

Trevor hesitated. He couldn't tell if she was telling the truth.

Then he glanced at Gemma, panting next to him with a white-knuckle grip on his hand. *Can't risk it.*

He turned away from the mystery woman, grabbing the nearest sheet and tearing it down, revealing an unfinished wall and a doorway with a glimpse of sky beyond it. "This way."

"But what about—" Gemma said.

"We don't know her." Trevor glanced back at the woman; her brow creased. "I don't trust anyone right now." He pulled Gemma through the doorway.

The empty room's window let them out into the construction site. No one noticed them running out of the back of the building. They sprinted across the road and into a debris field.

They kept running, the debris field resembling an upturned and flattened city. Blaster fire blackened the mounds of rubble, and they had to edge around huge craters from shelling, the footing treacherous.

Every step crackled as broken glass and rubble crunched underfoot. Trevor kept her hand in his as their steps thudded against the roof of a vehicle half-buried in a pile of bricks. Their route zig-zagged through half-crumbled walls and buckled streets.

Trevor saw the trench ahead, dug deep to hide in from an attacking enemy. He could make the jump with ease.

He glanced back at Gemma, who hung onto his hand for dear life as he half-dragged her behind him. She wouldn't make it over.

For an instant, Trevor stopped, letting Gemma take a step past, before he caught her in his arms, under her knees and around her shoulders. She yelped as he lifted her, planting a foot against a splintered park bench, then kicking off hard to sail over the trench.

He slid to a stop, ducking around the side of an overturned dumpster, rust flaking off as his sleeve brushed against it. He knelt, keeping them low to the ground. With a quick glance around the side, he noted five teams of two fanning out to search for them.

"What did I give him?" Trevor asked.

When she didn't answer right away, he looked down at her still in his arms, her eyes wide as she looked up at him, her breathing fast. He could feel her heart pounding at every point they touched.

"Are you okay?" He leaned closer, inspecting her for injury. "Are you hurt?"

"N-no." She pushed against him gently, and he set her on her feet, both of them kneeling in the dust. "No, I'm fine."

Trevor eyed her, not sure if he believed her. He'd thought that her sun and acid burns had healed already, but her neck had reddened. "What did I give him?"

"A voice changer," she whispered over her belabored breathing, her eyes wide as she gasped for air through the lingering acrid smoke that settled over the field. "What now?"

"We have to get some distance between us and them," he said.

"So, we run for it?"

"Yes." He turned his back to her. "Climb on my back, I'm faster than you."

"You're not going to carry me."

He dropped his head with an irritated sigh at that all-too-familiar attitude in her voice. Stubborn woman. "Pilot, you're too slow, they'll easily catch us. But I'm fast—"

"I can't ask you to do that," she insisted.

He gritted his teeth and glanced around the dumpster

again. The people hunting them chose each careful step as they scanned the debris field. Even at their slow pace, they had grown closer. "For once, do as I say."

"You should go," she said. "You'll be faster without me. Besides, they won't kill me."

Trevor took her shoulders. "They killed five innocent people when they shot down my ship. I don't think one more will bother them. Get on. *Now*."

She hesitated, then wrapped her arms around his neck and leaned onto his back.

He hadn't expected the jolt that ran through him, even more so as he stood and she pressed tighter against him. He shook his head to clear it.

Grabbing her behind the knees, he took off at a run, keeping low.

"Holy cow, you're fast," Gemma murmured, her grip tightening.

No one shouted an alarm, and they'd run for about ten minutes when he stopped beside a stack of tires, the smell of burnt rubber assaulting his sinuses.

"What's wrong?" Gemma asked, slipping off his back.

He gasped for air, hands on his knees. "Not used ... to gravity... I weigh ... a ton." He was smart enough not to mention how much she weighed, too. His cracked ribs didn't help the situation.

"I think we got a good head start though." She looked back, but dropped to the ground, pulling Trevor down with her. "I can still see them!"

He blew out a breath. "We've got to get back to the ship."

"But—but how can we make it home with no food?"

"We'll worry about that when we get to it," Trevor said.

Gemma looked around. She pointed. "Think that bike works?"

A grime-covered motorcycle lay on its side under the shell of a car. Trevor lifted the car remains and chunks of plastic off and threw them aside. "I don't know how to drive a motorcycle."

"Hey, *I'm* the pilot." She grinned. "If it has a motor, I can drive it."

Trevor righted it and she climbed on. Pushing the START button did nothing.

"Hang on—" Trevor knelt on the ground beside her, pulling apart the front casing for the bike. He pulled out some wires, sorted through them, and tapped two together.

The bike produced a cough.

"Get off, let me look at it," he said.

She glanced back in the direction of the searchers. "We don't have time."

"Give me a minute." This had to work. Without food or sleep and with the extra weight—he couldn't keep running.

It took five minutes of tinkering and muttering, Gemma hovering over his shoulder the whole time. They could hear the searchers call back and forth between each other now, an occasional blast of static as someone used a communicator.

The bike had all its fluids, but he had to strain to straighten out one of the bent valves. He cleaned a nest out of the air intake. Then he tightened all the bolts and screws he could with oil-slicked hands.

This would be a lot easier with tools.

"They're coming," she whispered.

"Try it now."

She hopped on. With the wires he'd rigged up, it screeched to life as soon as she touched START.

Shouts from behind them.

Trevor swung a leg over and Gemma revved the engine. "Hang on to me."

He tried to hold on to the seat, but when she took off, he grabbed her waist.

Gemma smirked as she glanced over her shoulder. "Don't be squeamish, Captain. We're gonna go fast."

His grip on her tight, he had to close his eyes as she weaved through the wreckage. Fast. Bricks and splintered wood and charred machines sped by in his peripheral vision as they bumped along.

When they reached the street, she revved it up to top speed.

"Don't we need helmets?" he yelled, glad he wasn't prone to motion sickness.

"Not with me you don't."

Someone took a shot at them, the ground next to them exploding. The people around them ran for cover, probably screaming, but he couldn't hear them over the guttural, shrieking engine.

The bike wobbled, but then she hunkered down and sped away.

Usually bikes ran silent, but theirs made a high-pitched whine. On the plus side, people heard them coming and got out of the way.

Trevor looked back. No signs of pursuit. "I think we lost them!" he yelled over the racket. "Which way back to the docks?"

"How am I supposed to know?" she shouted back. She slowed to a more reasonable speed, and Trevor's grip on her waist loosened. "We'll have to ask someone."

She slowed the bike, navigating traffic to stop by the sidewalk. The whine quieted but had picked up a pinging sound as well.

"Excuse me, could you point me in the direction of the docks?" she asked to a passing man in gray. "Excuse me?"

No one slowed or even looked at her.

"They can tell we're in trouble," Trevor said in her ear. "They're probably afraid of the local law."

He swung a leg off the bike and offered her a hand. "Come on, let's go."

"What? But the bike's faster."

"Great, we can go the wrong way really fast," he said. She flinched. He hadn't meant to sound so sarcastic. "The bike is a dead giveaway now. Better to blend in with the crowd."

"Blend in? You're the tallest one here."

He gave a long-suffering sigh. "Get off the bike, Pilot."

Gemma grumbled as she powered down and dismounted the bike, ignoring his hand. "I really liked the bike."

They had only walked a few steps away when the high-pitched whine made them turn.

"Someone stole our bike!" Gemma said.

"Good. Maybe it will lead them away," Trevor said, nodding at the perfect turn of events. Certainly, they'll chase down the bike. He and Gemma still needed to get out of here before then. "Come on, we'll ask directions from someone inside a store."

They entered a crumbling building with second-floor windows devoid of glass, the spray paint outside declaring it a general store. On one side stood empty crates where fruits and vegetables should have been. A few people roamed the aisles of sparsely filled shelves of food packets.

Trevor's stomach hurt from hunger. It had been aching for days. He wished they had some money.

They approached the woman at the counter. "Could you give us directions to the docks?" he asked.

The pinch-faced woman with a bandana over her hair looked them up and down. "You have to buy something first."

They shared a glance.

"We don't have any money," Gemma said.

"Then leave my store."

Trevor looked at Gemma. She looked ragged, tired, and hungry like him. Her lip quivered.

He placed both hands on the countertop and spoke in a low voice. "We're not going *anywhere* unless we know where we're going."

"I'll call the police." But the woman trembled.

He gave her a hard look. "Do it."

"Fine." She pulled out a leaflet and took a few minutes to scrawl a crude map on the back of it. She threw it at him. "Now get out of my store."

"Thank you," Gemma said. The woman scowled at her.

Outside the store, they huddled around the map.

"That's a long way," Gemma said.

The city had originally been laid out in a grid system, but now the woman had crossed out huge areas of it, presumably the debris fields. The marked route snaked around these spots. What should have been a mile now looked like eight.

They could make it. "Then we'd better get started."

After a few blocks of keeping his head down and walking slowly enough for Gemma, Trevor risked a glance up. He caught sight of a police officer scanning the crowd.

Trevor immediately looked down, but not before the officer made eye contact.

They must have circulated their pictures. And no matter how hard he tried, Trevor still stood head and shoulders above the other pedestrians.

"Hey! Hey, you!" the officer said.

Gemma's shoulders tightened. "Does he mean us?"

Trevor grabbed her arm. "Run."

They ran off the sidewalk and into another debris field, this one not within sight of the construction. For some reason, the devastation in this one had left fewer things identifiable.

They dove behind a slab of concrete, leaning against it, breathing hard. The acrid, smoky air hadn't changed, but now oil tinged it. Not motor oil, exactly …

Why weren't they being chased? He glanced around the corner. The officer had stopped at the edge of the debris. The back of Trevor's neck itched. What did he know that they didn't?

"Something's not right," Trevor said.

Gemma turned to him. "What?"

Trevor rubbed his chin. "Something is dangerous out here, but I'm not sure what it is. Look around, see if anything—"

"Trevor."

His eyes snapped to her, shaking and staring at the ground.

Unexploded artillery littered the terrain. Trevor's stomach sank.

"Is this what I think is it?" she whispered, her voice hoarse.

He kept his voice low and calm. "We don't know if those are all live." She didn't look comforted. "As long as we're very, very careful and don't touch *anything*, we can make it out of here. Any touch or trip or bump could set one off."

Gemma swallowed and nodded. "Right."

Trevor risked a glance over the concrete barrier. The police officer spoke into his radio but hadn't budged an inch.

"Whoever is after us will no doubt be here soon," Trevor said. "If—"

"We should separate," Gemma interrupted.

"What? No!" That was the worst plan possible. He couldn't let her out of his sight. He had to protect her. She—he couldn't lose her, too.

"Captain. Listen to me." She grabbed his shoulders, their faces close together. "This makes sense. You're faster, and I'm smaller. I can hide or blend in with the crowd, and you can run." She hesitated. "Run very, very carefully."

He hesitated. "But I—"

"Trevor," she said, her voice soft. His heart skipped a beat. "This makes sense."

He ran a hand through his hair, anxiety kicking his heart into overdrive. Bad, bad plan. "But—"

"Trevor."

He gritted his teeth. It did make sense. "Fine. You go to the ship, and I'll draw them away and meet you there."

"Here, use this to distract them." She pulled the music player out of the bag.

He frowned. "What good is this going to do?"

"It's *really* loud. To use the delay function, press—"

"I know how to use a player," he snapped. Why was he letting her do this? Such a bad plan. "Here, take the map." Trevor shoved it into her hands. "Now get moving."

She caught his hand and squeezed it. "What about you? How will you find your way?"

"I memorized it. Now go! I'll call you." He tapped the ship keys around his neck.

She clutched her own. "Be careful." Then she picked her way through the debris field. Soon, she rounded a pile of charred wood slabs.

He didn't like this. He couldn't see her, and he hated it.

Trevor waited, his fingers tapping against the concrete barrier, and soon he saw a vehicle pull up. Seven people exited and fanned out, making their way toward him.

Time to go.

He jammed the player into a hole in the concrete, cranked the volume, and set it to give him a two-minute head start. With one last look in the direction Gemma had gone, he started the timer.

Trevor picked his way through the debris as fast as he could. The voices of his pursuers drew nearer to where he'd left the music player.

After two minutes, the screeching of an electric guitar riff tore through the air, stabbing through his skull as if he stood in front of a speaker at a rock concert. She hadn't been kidding. No doubt Zane's doing.

The people looking for him ran toward the source of the sound but had trouble getting close because of the sheer volume.

An explosion—a series of explosions—rocked the ground, and Trevor dove for cover. The vibration of the music had triggered something.

Trevor picked himself up and kept running.

Gemma left the debris field, trying to ignore the explosions in the background.

With shaky hands she looked at the map. This didn't look right. She turned it upside down. That didn't look right either.

She was already lost. *Definitely not navigator material.*

If only she could see the fence of the dock.

She climbed a rusty fire escape hanging off the back of a building. It shifted and swayed under her weight, and for a second, she froze.

Keep going.

Gemma pulled herself onto the roof, the view of the city even more depressing than on the ground. War had taken great bites out of it, the black path of the new streets snaking around them.

Far in the distance to her right, the building they escaped from towered above those around it, the only new construction work she could see in the entire city, besides the streets. Not even a re-build, but entirely new.

She spotted the tall, tall fence of the docks to her left and breathed a sigh of relief. It was closer than she thought, and now she knew what direction to go in.

Fewer people hurried through the streets as she made her way through the city. Her stomach hurt with hunger. She didn't know what they would do about food once they were back in the jetter.

She reached the fence, the sun uncomfortably close to the horizon. She crept along in the tall grass beside the metal bars, trying to find a way in. The ship was *right there*, but she couldn't get to it.

Hang on. She squinted. A crew of three people worked below the ship, attaching something to the hull.

They moved slowly and carefully. One held it in place, while another screwed it down. The third followed a schematic in his hands and attached wires. When they backed up, a little red light blinked on the object. The third man held a remote—also with a little red light.

Her stomach dropped out. What was that? A tracker? A signal scrambler? No, those were small things.

Explosives?

She walked farther down the street, trying to blend in with the thinning crowd. No one looked at her. She flicked on her comm. "Captain! Don't go to the ship! I repeat, don't go to the ship! It's rigged to explode. Do you copy?"

Static.

Trevor's comm sputtered to life. "—go to—ship! —repeat—go—" Then the connection dissolved into static.

"Pilot, can you repeat? I didn't get that."

Nothing. He looked at the communicator, its casing cracked.

He kept to the shadows the best he could, the sun a sliver of light when he reached the fence. Keeping low, he circled half the compound. No way in. They would spot him and shoot him down if he climbed it. No other entrance besides the customs building.

Crouching in its shadow, he gave the bars of the fence a shake, testing them. This could work.

After a last check for any witnesses, Trevor grabbed a bar in each hand and pulled. Hard. His teeth clenched, his eyes squeezing shut. After a moment, he paused, panting. It didn't look any different, but as he tried again, slowly, the metal gave. His arms shaking from the effort and his body screaming at him to stop, he got his shoulder between the bars and *pushed*.

He stopped with a gasp, took a few seconds for his breathing to slow, then slipped through the opening, not an inch to spare on either side.

Trevor paused on the ground inside the fence, weakness shivering through him from exertion and hunger. *Keep going.* If nothing else, he had to find Gemma and make sure she was okay.

He stayed low. No one in sight. From Gemma's message, he knew she had already reached the ship. No one was around. It was almost too easy, the outer airlock door wide open, the lights on.

Almost there.

Trevor jogged toward the ship but slowed at the edge of the landing pad.

Why would she leave the door open?

The force of the ship's explosion knocked him back a few feet, the heat washing over him as he shielded his face with his arms.

Gemma had been on that ship!

"Pilot? Pilot!"

Smoke overtook him and he coughed. He tried to get closer, but the heat kept him back as the remains burned white-hot. "Pilot!" His chest hurt and his eyes stung. "Gemma!"

This couldn't be happening. He couldn't lose her too. "Gemma!"

"Captain?"

He whirled. Gemma stood at the edge of the landing pad, squinting against the heat of the flames.

His hand went to his heart. *Gemma.* He ran to her, grabbing her in a tight hug. "Gemma!"

She tensed for a moment, then wrapped her arms around him, burying her face in his shoulder. "It's okay, Trevor. I'm okay."

Her saying his name snapped him out of it. He stepped back so fast that Gemma stumbled against him. He grabbed her arms to steady her, then his hands dropped away.

"Right." He cleared his throat, looking up and not at her. *Don't get emotional? This is way, way beyond emotional.* He wouldn't have greeted Dak or Joe like that. Just her.

Trevor gasped for breath as relief washed over him, a tidal wave of emotion. He pressed his hands into his eyes as he doubled over. *She's okay. She's okay.*

"Trevor!" She knelt and pulled his hands off his eyes. "What's wrong? Did you not get my message? I saw them attaching explosives. I couldn't even get in until I found the hole you made in the fence—how did you do that, anyway?"

"I'm glad you're ... you're not ..." He gestured to the burning ship. "In there."

Gemma stood, her fists planted on her hips. "Is that all you have to say to me?"

He swallowed, coughing as he tried to breathe the smoky air, and straightened, his hands still shaky. "I don't know what you mean." What did she want him to say?

She closed her eyes, took a deep breath—coughed—then waved a hand. "I'm glad you're alive, too. Come on, let's get out of here before whoever is trying to kill us comes back."

"I'm—I'm glad you're alive, Gemma." He was guessing, hoping he used the right words to tell her—

Tell her what?

Apparently, that still wasn't what she wanted to hear. "At least it got you to use my name," she grumbled.

They slid back out the gap he made in the fence as darkness fell, before fire crews arrived.

A drone buzzed overhead, and they took shelter in an alley behind a huge pile of sagging cardboard boxes. They sat side-by-side, backs against the mound of soggy cardboard.

Gemma shivered, and he put his arm around her. Her head rested against his shoulder.

"I'm hungry," she said in a small voice.

"I know." He held her tighter. "I am too."

She eventually dozed off. Every so often she would give a jerk, every muscle in her body tightening. She cried out at one point. He rubbed her back to soothe her, but she never woke up.

He took stock of their hiding place. The cardboard they hid

behind, a dumpster, a collapsed fire escape, a pile of bricks, and a blank wall at the back.

Dead end.

The buzz of drones grew lower. He shook her awake. "We need to go. Now."

They peeked out of the alley. Flashlights moved back and forth across the street. Searching.

They rose to a crouch but had nowhere to go.

"The dumpster, climb in." He pushed her toward it.

"No way," Gemma said. The buzz of a drone grew louder. "Aw, man!"

Trevor tried to hold his breath, but the stench that accosted him when he opened the lid made him retch. Gemma made a small sound of distress before disappearing into the pitch-black container. He followed her, but hit an uneven surface on the bottom, his hand touching slimy walls as he tried to keep his balance. His shoes splashed in an inch of what he hoped was water at the bottom, his ankle giving a sharp pain as he put his weight on it. That wasn't a good sign.

"At least it's empty," she whispered. He moved toward her voice, and she let out a yelp when his fingers grazed her arm.

"Shh, it's just me."

Then she was there, clinging to him, shivering. Neither slept the rest of the night.

19

When the light of dawn seeped through a rusted-out spot on the side of the dumpster, they climbed out.

After looking around the corner for the authorities, they wandered out into the crowd and followed the flow to an outdoor market. Trevor hunched over, head down as they walked.

He kept his voice low. "We have to eat."

"How? We don't have any money," she whispered back.

The only person Trevor knew who had lived on the streets was Zane—and he knew exactly what Zane would do in this situation. "We're going to have to steal something."

"But I've never stolen anything in my life," Gemma said. "I don't even know how."

"We'll figure it out," he said. "I can outrun anyone here." His ankle twinged. Could he?

"But won't it bring unwanted attention to ourselves?"

They might be getting unwanted attention already. People

gave them a wide birth, making an empty space around them. Their night in the dumpster wasn't working in their favor.

"We can't keep going like this," he said. Gemma looked like she could collapse at any second.

They weaved their way through the busy streets. People bumped into them despite their smell, and Trevor thought he felt fingers in one of his pockets. He had nothing to steal anyway. Except the pen, which was in Gemma's pack.

"Watch your bag," he muttered to her.

Off the main roadway, people lined the sidewalk begging for money or food. Some of them were curled up in doorways, not begging but looking just as needy.

Someone shoved Gemma hard, and she collided with Trevor.

"My bag!" she said.

Trevor saw a head duck into the crowd, a familiar duffle across his back. He took off after it.

"Wait, Trevor—!"

The duffle bobbed and weaved through the crowd, the carrier nimble and fast, but Trevor was faster. Even with his ankle screaming and having to push people out of the way, the distance between them swiftly shrank.

Almost an arm's-length away, the thief dropped the bag and kept running, disappearing into the crowd.

Hands on his knees, Trevor gasped for air before grabbing the bag off the ground.

He turned—but he couldn't see Gemma.

His chest tightened as his eyes darted between people in the crowd, his heart hammering. He'd left her! "Gemma!"

"Shh!" She shoved her way to him, tripping forward as she broke through the line of people.

Then his arms wrapped around her again. That had been

stupid. He should never have left her behind. He couldn't have her out of his sight.

"Knock it off." She pushed away from him, taking her bag. "I'm fine."

"Psst."

They froze, before slowly turning towards the voice.

"Hey," said a woman. She dug through her bag, by all appearances not paying any attention to them.

Trevor pushed Gemma behind him.

"You looking for Penn?" the woman asked.

Gemma shoved Trevor aside and stepped forward. "What if we are?"

He rolled his eyes. "Can't you just—"

"Follow me, Captain Lee." The woman hobbled off.

She knew his name. He wasn't sure if that was a good sign or not, but they had to follow. They had run out of options.

After a block, she ducked into a battered building, the bricks worn down and blackened at the edges. The cracked and peeling plywood over the front window said, FRESH ROLLS DAILY. A bakery, he realized, by the smell of fresh bread. His stomach growled. It hurt. He'd never been so long without food.

In the surprisingly bright interior, Trevor inhaled the rich scent of bread and pastry and warmth. Lightheaded, black spots danced around the edges of his vision.

"Are you okay?" Gemma asked, poking him. "You look like you're going to pass out. And that you might start drooling."

He took a calming breath and shook his head to clear it. Not now. "I'm fine."

The woman led them past the waiting line of sorry-looking citizens. The man behind a counter—glass, with a small crack in it—ignored them. They entered an "Employees Only" storage room, empty of people. The baking done for the day, the steel counters and pans gleamed shiny and clean. He could still smell the flour.

Their mysterious guide opened and gestured to an empty supply closet, numbered among several closed supply closets against the wall. "In."

"Gemma, I don't know about this," he whispered.

"At this point, I don't think we have any choice," she whispered back. "Either we accept help, or we're going to keel over."

He hesitated. She was right, they needed help.

They crammed inside the small closet. Trevor's head tilted to try to enter the short space, but no matter how he positioned himself, he couldn't fit until he crouched. Gemma's hip pressed against the side of his head, her hand on his shoulder. With all three of them inside, the woman shut the door.

"How do you know who we are?" he asked, his voice echoing slightly, light seeping in around the edges of the door.

"Either you are who we're all looking for," she said, "or you're the tallest, sorriest refugees I've ever seen." She wrinkled her nose. "You smell bad."

"You're the lady from the fake doctor's building," Gemma said. "The one who told us to come with you."

"Yes. I work undercover at the factory," the woman said.

"What kind of factory is it?" Gemma asked.

"Is that really what's important right now?" Trevor asked. There were so many more pressing matters. Who was this woman? Who did she work for? *What are we doing in a closet?*

"Oh, it's very important," said the woman.

By some unseen cue, the back wall swung open, revealing a flight of dark stairs going down.

"Well? Go on," the woman urged.

Trevor hesitated, but Gemma had already disappeared from his side as she descended the stairs.

"Gemma, wait—" He straightened and took a step, smacking his head on the angled ceiling.

"Be careful!" Gemma said.

He grumbled but followed her down. The door closed behind him, the woman still in the closet.

At the bottom, they stepped through a door into a bright room with computers lining the walls and a large table in the center. The three men leaning over the table looked up. Trevor recognized ship components hovering on the holographic screens in front of them.

"Ah, good, you're here."

The mustached man who spoke came forward, hand outstretched. He shook both their hands. "I'm so glad you're alive."

"Yeah, us too," Gemma said.

The man did a double-take at Gemma. "Are you the captain?"

Trevor snorted. "No, that would be me."

"I'm Dr. Penn," the man said. He held out a hand, palm up. "The drive, please."

Trevor hesitated. "How do I know you're the real Dr. Penn?"

He smiled. "Because I know it's a pen."

Trevor breathed a sigh, then fumbled with the pockets of Gemma's bag before handing over the disguised flash drive, amazingly undamaged.

"Are you sure no one has tried to open it?" the doctor asked, examining it.

"I'm sure," Trevor said.

"He gave *them* the wrong one," Gemma said. She paused. "Who are they?"

"Who are *you*?" Dr. Penn asked, eyeing her.

Gemma's fists clenched and her jaw tightened, her voice

rising. "I'm one of two survivors of a crashed cargo ship, who's been chased all across the galaxy by a group of people with advanced weaponry and extensive resources, just to bring you a stupid *pen*."

Dr. Penn wouldn't meet her eyes. "Fair enough. Come this way."

"Take it down a notch," Trevor whispered.

She looked him dead in the eye. "No."

Trevor raised his hands in surrender. *Pick your battles, Trevor.* "As you like."

Dr. Penn led them to the table and punched a few buttons. A menu popped up in the air above it. The doctor unscrewed the pen and held the point up to his eye. A tiny beam of light swept across his iris, scanning it. Then he pulled the pen apart and inserted the drive into a slot in the table.

"Ah, yes, it's all here." He scanned through the information displayed above the table, flicking files aside. "Right, very good."

He closed the files and opened a new one. A star chart outlined the territory of Omni Authority in blue. A red line outlined a large part of the map, meeting a blue edge at the Terminus.

"The people chasing you are a radical group of terrorists calling themselves the Conglomerate. They work against Omni Authority. As you can see, the Ruby District is in their territory. Before the civil war, this area all belonged to Omni Authority. The Conglomerate operates under the radar, using local wars as cover and funding. They profit from selling weapons and tech to both sides.

"They have a massive R&D community. Weapons developers, upgraded ships, shield improvements, increased scanning capabilities, the list goes on. Our operative on the inside—whom you've met—smuggles out information on their latest developments. The ship that blew you out of the sky? One of theirs."

Before Trevor could open his mouth, Gemma jumped in. "Why? What could they possibly hope to accomplish?"

"We don't know that," Dr. Penn said. "I just know they work against us."

Gemma arched an eyebrow. "Who's us?"

Dr. Penn blinked at her. "Omni Authority."

"What's on the flash drive?" Gemma demanded, again before Trevor could say anything.

"Will you let me ask the questions?" Trevor muttered under his breath.

"Schematics for a very special bomb," Dr. Penn said.

She shot a look at Trevor. "I thought you said it was medical data," she whispered to him.

He squirmed. "Yeah, about that ..."

Trevor's stomach growled.

Dr. Penn frowned. "How long has it been since you've eaten?"

"A few days," Gemma said.

"I'll call for some sandwiches."

That lightheaded feeling threatened to overwhelm him again. Sandwiches never sounded so good. "Lots of sandwiches."

"So, what's the bomb for?" Gemma asked. "What's so special about it?"

The doctor leaned forward. "Our information says the Conglomerate is trying to resurrect the super soldier program—to grow Tubies again."

Trevor gave an involuntary twitch, and Gemma gasped.

"This bomb, once we build it," Dr. Penn continued, "will not only destroy their operation, but will poison every genetically marked super soldier, without hurting any humans."

The world tilted, and Trevor grabbed the edge of the table. There were more? Like—like him?

Gemma's fingers brushed Trevor's, but he clenched his hand into a fist.

"I'll do it," he heard himself say.

She grabbed his arm. "No!"

Dr. Penn blinked. "Do what?"

"I'll plant the bomb."

Now Gemma tugged on his arm with both hands. "May I speak with you?"

"It's very dangerous." Dr. Penn's forehead wrinkled in a frown. "You've already done far more than was asked of you."

"I want to," Trevor said. He had to. He needed to be the one to do it.

"It will take some time for us to assemble the bomb," Dr. Penn said slowly. "At least a few hours to program it. Let's discuss this again after you've rested."

"You can't do this, Trevor," Gemma hissed after the doctor turned away. "You'll get hurt and probably die. I won't let that happen."

"You don't get a say," Trevor said, then winced. He hadn't meant to sound so harsh.

She looked hurt, then her expression hardened. She stepped closer. "Listen—"

The tray of sandwiches arrived. Trevor grabbed the first sandwich on top. He opened his mouth for a bite when Gemma snatched it from his hand.

"Hey!" He growled at her, hungry enough to bite her hand if it meant getting his food back.

"Pay attention. It's peanut butter and jelly," she said, just as annoyed with him. She shoved another sandwich into his hand. "Here, take the ham and cheese."

That doused his anger. "Oh. Thanks." He took a bite and closed his eyes. Best sandwich he'd ever had.

"Can I talk to you for a second?" Gemma said, tugging on his sleeve

"Can't I eat first?" he said around a full mouth.

"No, now."

Trevor glanced over at the other people in the room, talking in low voices and indicating various components displayed in the diagram.

"Don't say anything you wouldn't mind someone over-hearing," he murmured.

"What are you thinking? Are you out of your mind?" she whispered. "You can't do this mission."

"I have to."

"Why?"

"It's ..." He struggled to find the right words. "It's my responsibility."

"It is *not*—"

"I have to make sure it's done," he said. "And done right. I can't ... let this happen to anyone else."

"But—it could kill you." Her voice cracked. She rested her hand on his arm. "If it works, it likely will. Please don't do this."

"I'm willing to take that risk. To save others, I'll do it. You don't have to come."

She rolled her eyes. "Do I really need to say anything at this point? You can't get rid of me."

He felt a little weight lift from his shoulders. He wouldn't have to do it alone.

Dr. Penn returned to them to collect the empty sandwich tray. He wrinkled his nose. "Would you two like a shower?"

"Yes," they said in unison.

DR. PENN LED THEM TO A LOCKER ROOM THAT HAD SEEN BETTER DAYS. Dark grout surrounded the chipped tiles. Lockers lined the walls, some of them dented, rubble dusting the tops of them. It smelled strongly of bleach.

"Being underground, we were fairly well protected during the war," the doctor said. "But we still sustained some damage. We've tried to repair as best we could."

He opened an intact locker full of soaps, shampoos, razors and towels. "We bring various refugees through here. Leave your clothes on the floor. I'll have replacements brought."

Gemma dropped her bag onto the bench and stepped into the shower stall, pulling the plastic privacy curtain. Undressing, she threw her filthy clothing over the top of the curtain.

When the hot spray hit her, she hummed in delight.

A hiss of the shower in the next stall over reminded her that Trevor was there, and she stopped humming.

"Don't stop on my account," he said, his voice echoing against the tiles.

She didn't say anything, suddenly self-conscious. Her humming had annoyed him so much on the ship.

Although, it's true that now *he* didn't irritate her as much as he had at one point on their trip. Maybe he felt the same way about her.

Gemma smiled to herself. Maybe he liked her humming now. Not that she planned to test that theory.

The shampoo opened with a pop, and she rubbed it into her hair. With a wince, she felt the sting of every cut and scrape on her body.

The door to the locker room opened, and Gemma froze. That would be their new clothes. She peeked around the edge of the shower curtain and watched a young girl set a stack of folded clothing on the bench. To Gemma's relief, the girl didn't touch her bag.

After her muscles relaxed and every speck of grime washed away, she turned off the glorious hot water. She wrapped a towel around herself and stepped out of the shower.

She did a double-take at her reflection in the cracked mirror. She hardly recognized herself. Even after a wash, her face looked gray, with dark bags under her eyes, and purple splotches of bruises across her skin. The scrape along the side of her face from the crash had scabbed over, still a raw red.

She was trying to do something with her hair when Trevor's water turned off, and he stepped out, a towel around his waist.

They both froze.

"Hi," Gemma blurted, wishing her towel were longer.

And yes, he had a belly button.

His eyes widened, his face red. Then he ducked back into the shower.

He cleared his throat from behind the curtain. "Could you pass me my clothes?"

"Clothes. Right." Gemma handed them over the shower curtain, her face on fire.

She dressed in the clothes left for her as fast as she could. Gemma's T-shirt swallowed her up, the sleeves reaching her elbows. She rolled up her pant legs and cinched the belt as tight as it would go, but the waist still hung low on her hips. She guessed it would be too much to ask for new underwear.

She hurried to brush her hair.

"Gemma. Are you ... decent?"

"Yes."

She turned. Trevor stepped out from behind the curtain, fully clothed. The pants weren't quite long enough for him, and his belt also tightened. He'd shaved his week's worth of beard. She liked him better clean-shaven.

He stepped toward her. His mouth opened, then closed again. "I'm sorry about earlier."

She didn't want to talk about it. "I look ridiculous," she said instead, holding up her arms.

"No, you don't." His voice was low and raspy. "You look … cute."

Her heart thudded. She inched closer to him. "Do you like cute?" Less than a foot separated them.

Very slowly, he reached out and took her hand. "On you I do," he whispered.

She stepped closer and tilted her face toward him, and he leaned down—

The locker room door opened, and Trevor sprang back.

"Feeling better?" Dr. Penn asked. "You both look better."

"Yes." Trevor's voice strangled. He cleared his throat. "Yes, much better." He wouldn't look at Gemma.

"Excellent. Follow me then."

Gemma reached out a hand to Trevor, but he stepped away. She sighed and picked up her bag. *So* close.

Dr. Penn led them back to the projection table, where there was a map of the city and a picture of the factory on display. And more sandwiches.

"That's where they brought us," Gemma said. "Where the fake Dr. Penn was."

"No doubt you met with their head researcher, Dr. Sims," Dr. Penn said. He tapped his chin. "Somehow, they knew you were coming. Did you tell anyone about your mission here?"

"No one," Gemma said. "Our destination was a secret."

"What about Alex?" Trevor murmured around a mouthful.

"We didn't tell him we were still going to Cerise," she whispered back. Even if they had, Alex would never betray them. "Maybe the room was bugged."

"Tell us more about this factory," Trevor said, louder.

"It's a brand-new facility they began construction on after the fighting stopped," Dr. Penn said. "Building is almost complete. We must stop them *now*. We don't know at what stage their research is, or how many soldiers they've grown. Our guess is the experiments are not out of the gestation stage, yet."

"What's the plan?" Trevor asked.

"Tonight, after dark, our informant will smuggle you onto the site in a work truck. She'll stay there as long as possible, but if someone becomes suspicious and she must leave, you'll be on your own. We can't compromise her identity."

"Understood," Trevor said.

"The bomb has a timer. You need to place it somewhere on the factory floor, then get out. I'll have a ship ready for you at the docks to take you off-planet."

Gemma had trouble following the conversation. "Get in on a truck, set off the bomb, take the ship home," she said, to check if she'd understood right. She yawned, her eyelids heavy.

"You should get some sleep before you go. We'll wake you in a few hours," Penn said.

Penn took them down a hallway. A partially open supply door caught her eye. She slowed to peek inside. *I'll be back to check that out.*

He led them to a room empty of people, as it was midday, with two rows of neatly made beds, and left them.

Trevor chose a bed close to the door, and Gemma took the one next to it.

"Gemma ..."

"Hmm?" Her eyes were already closed.

"Would you—would you hum something for me? I ... kind of got used to it on the ship."

Gemma smiled and hummed a few bars of her favorite song. When she looked over at him, he was asleep.

Soon, she was too.

20

The woman—whose name they still didn't know, for her protection—drove through the night. Trevor and Gemma lay flat in the truck bed. Trevor glanced at Gemma, though he couldn't see her face in the dark. He focused on her even breathing. If she was calm, then he could be, too. Still, he had to resist the urge to put his arm around her. *Focus, Trevor.*

The truck stopped, and the woman said something under her breath.

"You have to get out," she said.

"Are we there?" Gemma asked.

"No, but there's a roadblock up ahead," the woman said. "They'll search the truck for sure. I'm sorry, I can't help you anymore. If you go straight that way," she pointed, "it should only be about half a mile."

Trevor already had the tailgate lowered.

"Thank you," Gemma said. The woman nodded. Once the door was shut again, the truck moved on, leaving them behind.

They trudged off the road through the no-man's land,

taking careful steps in the dark as they navigated around the abandoned warzone. Dr. Penn had given them a night scanner just in case, to help spot unexploded ordinances. It allowed them to see the ground without casting a light and giving away their position—especially helpful as the overcast sky blocked all light from the moons or stars. Gemma had insisted on carrying the bomb—which looked a lot like a heavy, black Rubik's cube—in her bag.

"It's kind of a nurture versus nature debate, isn't it?" Gemma said.

Trevor snapped out of his brooding. "What is?"

"Tubies," she said. "They're not inherently evil. Just because they exist doesn't mean they need to be destroyed. I mean, you're just a person. A strong, fast person."

"But people can be designed to—"

"Look at dog breeding. Just because a dog is bred for hunting or attacking, or whatever, doesn't make it a killer. With a good home and some love ... get what I'm saying? And people have a lot more autonomy than a dog does."

"I get it." Would he have turned out differently if he hadn't been rejected from the program? Was it possible to genetically modify compassion out of a person? "Still can't let it happen again. Whether it's nurture or nature or both, those kids don't stand a chance."

She hesitated. "Agreed."

They continued. Trevor's ankle twinged as it had when they'd hidden in the dumpster, but it could still bear his weight, so he forced himself to keep moving.

There's no other way. He couldn't take them with him. They *had* to be destroyed. It was the humane thing to do. He was saving his brothers from—

Trevor stumbled, pain shooting through his ankle so sharp he had to hide a wince.

The night scanner shook. It took him a moment to realize it was his hands shaking. *I'm saving them. This is the right thing to do.*

Soon they reached the facility chain-link fence. They stopped.

"Why's the gate open?" Gemma whispered.

Trevor looked around. No one in sight, a row of work vehicles parked inside the fence. A single, white light illuminated a steel door to the building.

"It's too easy," he said. "It's obviously a trap."

"Should we go back?"

"No, we—I have to do this." Trevor took a deep breath. "I have to see this through." Even if it killed him. He turned to her. "Please. Please will you go back?"

She gave him a soft smile. "Never."

He'd never met such a stubborn person in his life. It was aggravating and admirable all at the same time.

"What?" she asked.

Without realizing it, Trevor had stopped, gazing at her. If the bomb worked, these might be their last moments together. He studied her face, but he already had it memorized.

He shook himself. "Nothing. Let's go." His senses on high alert, they crept up to the door.

Gemma tried the knob, and the door opened an inch.

"Not locked," she said, eyes wide. "Do you think they're expecting us?"

His stomach clenched. He *knew* they were expecting them.

"You have to stay behind," he whispered to her. "Please."

"Shut up," she whispered back.

They entered the plastic sheet tunnel, the lights on full. He felt completely exposed.

Trevor grabbed the edge of the nearest sheet. "Ready?"

Gemma nodded. He yanked down hard.

The sheet fell away, revealing a massive space with rows and rows of tables. It was a giant lab. Every workstation had a computer built into the end of it, with unplugged wires hanging to the ground. Stacks of Petri dishes, beakers, and microscopes everywhere.

And the tubes. Each table had a tube on it, large enough to hold a baby.

Trevor froze. He remembered the tubes. But these were ... these were—

Gemma touched one of them. "Empty. They're all empty."

"What?" He stepped closer.

"Nothing's been grown here yet. They're not even done setting up the lab." Gemma kicked at a cardboard box, and it tipped over, empty.

Trevor sagged against a table, his hand on his heart, only now realizing why he had to come. His voice cracked. "I wouldn't have been able to do it."

Gemma laid a hand on his shoulder. "I know."

"I—I couldn't." He blinked back tears. "They're my brothers. I had to try and save them."

She took his hands. "They're not here. They don't even exist. You don't have to choose. You don't have to do anything. Just get out of here. I'll set the bomb and catch up to you."

"No." His grip tightened on hers. "I have to be the one to set the bomb. I must stop it from ever happening. You need to leave, and I'll catch up."

"But—but if you're not out of range in time—"

"Same for you if you're not out of the blast radius." The thought made his chest hurt again. "I can't put you at risk."

Her eyes were wet. "You could die."

"Gemma." He pulled her into him and embraced her. "I have to see this through."

She took a shuddering breath. "I know." She pulled away and looked at him. "We'll see it through together."

He was trying to figure out how to convince her to leave when a voice behind them said, "Welcome, Captain."

They both whirled around to face an intercom on the wall. Trevor recognized that voice. It was the fake Dr. Penn—Dr. Sims.

"Welcome back to our facility," the voice continued. "As you can see, we're not quite up and running yet. In fact, we've hit a little snag. Thankfully, you've provided us with a solution."

Two guards with weapons raised stepped out of the dark corners and closed in on them.

"Get down," Trevor said, pulling the stunner he carried. He squeezed the trigger but only had time to take down one of them. The return fire from the other man hit him square in the chest, and he went down twitching. At least at half power, he didn't lose consciousness.

"Trevor!" Gemma knelt next to him and fumbled with the weapon he had dropped, but the remaining guard kicked it away.

"Stand up," the guard ordered. Gemma raised her hands and stood. Trevor struggled to his knees as the guard pressed his stunner against the back of Gemma's head.

"Cooperate," he said. "Or ..." He thumbed the power dial to max.

"Alright, alright!" Trevor put up his hands.

They marched back to an unfamiliar room on the first floor. The vials on the counter and exam table in the center of the room made Trevor shudder.

"Lay down," Dr. Sims ordered, gesturing to the table with a gloved hand. Trevor stiffened, but Dr. Sims held up a finger. "You don't want her hurt, do you?"

At that, the guard holding the stunner to Gemma's head grabbed her arm and twisted it behind her back.

"Ow!"

Heat flashed through him, his whole body tensed as he took a step toward her, his fists clenched. "Don't hurt her!"

"Then I suggest you get on the table."

"Don't, Captain," Gemma said. Her shallow breathing and the way she gritted her teeth told him she was in a lot of pain.

Trevor took a deep, shaky breath. There wasn't time. She would be hurt before he'd even reached her. To make it worse, the first guard he'd stunned when they'd entered shuffled into the room. Although he looked pale and shaky, that didn't make his stunner any less dangerous.

With another glance at Gemma, Trevor lay down on the cold, metal table, and the doctor strapped him down. *Patience. There will be an opening to save Gemma. It will come. Just wait— then take it.*

"You see," said the doctor, preparing a needle, "our information on the super soldier program is incomplete. For years we've been tracking down the data, but a few key files are still missing. We had intended to use the brute-force trial-and-error method in this factory, starting very soon. But, now that you're here, you've put us years ahead." Dr. Sims came toward him with the needle, and Trevor flexed against the restraints.

"Ah ah." The doctor waved a finger. He gestured to Gemma's captor, who tightened his grip. Gemma flinched.

Sweat sliding down his sides, Trevor forced himself to relax as the doctor proceeded to draw blood from his arm.

"No!" Gemma shouted.

"Take her out," Dr. Sims said, removing the needle and holding up the vial, as if admiring a nugget of gold.

She fought as she was dragged from the room.

"Stop! Bring her back!" Trevor heaved against the straps on

his wrists. "Gemma!" He thrashed, and the bolts holding the straps down began to bend.

The doctor backed up a step, the vial of blood clutched in his hand. "Extraordinary," he said in wonder.

Trevor strained, the thought of Gemma in danger sending adrenaline coursing through him.

"Hey! Stop moving!" said the second guard, leveling his stunner at Trevor.

Too late. Trevor shot his freed foot against the guard's head, knocking him to the ground.

With a twist and a violent jerk, the rest of the bolts snapped free. Trevor rolled off the table but landed wrong and the twinge in his ankle became a spike.

He grabbed the doctor's collar, lifting him into the air. "Where is she? Where are they taking her?"

"Extraordinary," the doctor said again. "You're even stronger than I imagined."

"Where is she?" Trevor demanded. He wrapped his other hand around the doctor's throat. The doctor finally looked sufficiently afraid.

His eyes bugged, the doctor shook his head. "She won't be harmed. We had an agreement with our source."

"What agreement?"

"A trade." Dr. Sim's voice rose higher. "Information about you in exchange for her safety."

"With who?" Trevor shook him. Hard.

The doctor grabbed at Trevor's wrist as Trevor's grip tightened. "I—I don't know!"

Trevor dropped him in a heap, then snatched the vial of his blood off the table and smashed it on the floor.

"No!" The doctor crawled over to it as Trevor ran out of the room.

He entered the lab and collided with Gemma. She bounced

off him and went down hard, the stunner in her hand going off. The beam shot harmlessly into the wall.

"Gemma!" He helped her to her feet. She winced. "Are you alright? How did you get away?"

She grinned. "You think you're the only one who can work a stunner? Come on, let's get out of here." She took his hand and pulled him, but he didn't budge.

"I can't go," he said.

"What are you talking about? Are you hurt?"

"Not that, but I have to stay and set off the bomb." He held out a hand. "Give it to me."

She pulled the bomb out of the bag and handed it to him. "Set the timer. That way we can both get out."

He shook his head. "This never should have happened. See how dangerous I am? Using me could resurrect the program. I shouldn't be alive."

Her eyes shimmered with tears, and she held onto his arm. "Trevor, please don't talk like that."

"I'm serious, Gemma. I must destroy all trace of the super soldier program. I won't let you spend the rest—" he stuttered. "Any more time with me puts you in constant danger."

Her face hardened. "No, Trevor. I'm not leaving you here to die." She snatched the bomb from him and hit the button.

"Give that ba—"

She tossed it to him, and he bobbled it before getting a firm grip. "What is wrong with you, throwing a bomb like that!" Then he stared. "Five minutes? You set the timer for five minutes!"

"I'll never clear the blast radius in time," she said, chin up. "But you can."

"Gemma, I can't—"

She pulled a canister out of her bag and threw it at his

head, and he nearly dropped the bomb catching it. A mask dangled at the end of a tube attached to it—an oxygen mask.

"Put that on so you won't get poisoned," she said.

"Where did you get this? And when?" Trevor asked, aware of the ticking clock as his mind scrambled to catch up and formulate a plan to get her out of here.

"I liberated it from one of Dr. Penn's supply closets. The poison in the bomb won't hurt me, just you, so I brought it for you." She held out her arms. "You'll never be able to save me if you die. Pick me up and let's get out of here."

"I can't run," Trevor said, the realization sinking into his heart. He would never be able to move fast with her added weight.

"What? Why?"

"I hurt my ankle."

Gemma's eyes bugged. "What?!"

He looked around, trapped between destroying himself—the only right way—and saving Gemma.

The choice was obvious.

He looked at the bomb—impossible to disable—and set it gently on a table.

"Come on." He took her hand and pulled her deeper into the building. "We have to find somewhere to shelter."

They ran together—even with the limp, he still outran her—through the large space filled with empty tubes on tables, the clock ticking down in the back of Trevor's head.

They batted away another plastic sheet, and Trevor froze, his muscles locking up. Gemma's hand still in his, she kept going and nearly dislocated her arm at the sudden stop.

"Ow! What in the world?" She rubbed her shoulder with a wince.

That snapped him out of it, all his attention on her. "I'm

sorry, I'm sorry. I ... just—" He glanced up, then focused again on her face.

Gemma now looked around the room they'd entered and shuddered. "I'm okay. I can understand why."

The fluorescent lights cast harsh light on the fully outfitted laboratory, the smell of disinfectant sharp. It took Trevor only a moment to take it all in. Chemicals in stopped-up flasks, microscopes, petri dishes and small test tubes filled the glass-fronted cabinets, labeled drawers tucked under the long counter tops. None of the equipment was plugged in, all the vials and glass beakers empty. An eye wash station and emergency shower were installed next to the sink, a fire extinguisher beside them, and then a variety of labeled disposal cans. He glanced over at the gas valves, a potentially fatal hazard.

Trevor swallowed, his arms shaking as he forced himself to look at what stood in the center of the room. The largest tube of all, a cylinder with a flat bottom, stood upright, tall and wide enough to fit Trevor in. Completely clear, the thick glass was six inches of polycarbonate. He shuddered, involuntarily falling back a step. If he was ever put in one of those, he wouldn't be able to break out. A metal lid with screws sat on the floor next to it.

"There's no other exit here," he said, unable to keep his voice from shaking. "We have to hurry—"

When he turned away, Gemma tugged him back. Her pale face looked up at him, and he knew what she was going to say.

"This might be—"

"I know," he cut her off, his voice sharp. He looked up at the ceiling and ran a hand through his hair. The clocked ticked. "I know."

I can't. I can't do it. He remembered being in the tube. It hadn't bothered him as an infant, but the thought of it now—

"That tube is nearly indestructible, isn't it?" she asked, her voice soft.

He groaned. "Yes."

"Maybe we should—"

"I know." His gaze dropped to the ground, his shoulders slumped. "It's our best chance."

Without another word, they unclamped it and let it fall to its side with a soul-crushing thud against the linoleum floor.

Tick, tick, tick.

"Hurry, get in," he said, offering his hand.

Gemma slipped inside, feet-first, her eyes wide. "Your turn."

He froze, his breathing coming too fast, his thoughts spinning. He bent over, trying to breathe instead of gasping, light-headed. *I'm going to throw up.*

"Trevor."

When he looked up, Gemma had climbed back out, her face in front of him, her hand on his. "There's no time. Get in."

"What are you doing out here?" he demanded. "Get—"

"You go first," she insisted, her eyes as hard as the grip she had on his hand. "Now."

He grimaced, then forced his hands to grip the edge of the tube. Screwing his eyes shut, he slipped in.

It was as bad as he feared. His breathing echoed back at him, and he struggled not to thrash and fight against it.

Then Gemma was there. She slipped in beside him, and his arms clenched around her, a comforting warmth as he buried his face in her hair.

She gave a squeak and fought against him until his grip eased. His arms spasmed, trying to hold onto her without crushing her.

"It's not too much smaller than a life pod," she said, her

voice muffled against his chest. She patted his back. "You're okay."

As long as the lid isn't on, I'm fine. I'm fine.

He gasped. Only seconds left on the clock.

"Brace yourself," he said, bracing himself against the walls while keeping Gemma tight against him. She pressed the oxygen mask against his face, clutching the canister to her chest.

The flash hit before the deafening roar, all the glass in the room instantly shattering, smaller explosions going off at the release of the chemicals in the cabinets. The force of the explosions, and the subsequent explosion of the gas line, hurled the tube against, then through, the back wall. The air getting sucked out of their tube cut Gemma's scream short as they bounced and rolled and smashed against unseen obstacles, hidden in the black smoke.

After an eternity, they rolled to a stop, air returning in a hot flash as fire and smoke surrounded them.

Gemma coughed, as if she'd been drowning. He pushed her out of the cylinder before climbing out himself.

The tube had cracked but held.

Gemma coughed again as he held her, then they stumbled away from the tube as he tried to get his bearings. His oxygen mask had survived their violent escape and allowed him to breathe.

Trevor couldn't hear anything over the ringing in his ears, but continued to trudge away from the wreckage until they could see something beyond the smoke. Gemma may have been talking to him, but he just kept a tight grip on her shoulders and walked.

21

Once they'd gotten their bearings, Gemma clung to Trevor's arm as he turned them toward the docks.

It took them most of the night before they again entered the fence at the docks, lying in a muddy ditch, looking for the ship Dr. Penn promised them.

"This can't be the right dock," Gemma whispered. She'd never been so exhausted in her life, every limb heavy and her head cloudy as she concentrated to make sense of what she saw. "It's surrounded by guards. Unless they work with Dr. Penn?"

Trevor said something, his words garbled by the gas mask he wore.

"What?"

He shook his head and pointed. Each guard had a shoulder patch of Omni Authority's symbol—with a slash across it.

"But Dr. Penn said the ship would be—"

Trevor talked while he looked around. She sighed. Yes, it saved his life from the poison, but she had no idea what he said.

"Trevor, I can't understand you."

He pointed, and she followed him, crawling on her stomach across dirt burned by a thousand takeoffs. They crept along in the dark. He indicated the other ships resting on platforms, five in all, unguarded. With them all so far apart, they would get one shot to run across the open space between them without being spotted.

"How can we steal another ship without a key?" Gemma asked.

He hesitated, then pulled the mask off his face.

"Put that back on!" she ordered.

"But you can't understand me."

"But you'll be alive!"

"I think we should break in, then steal the key from the next person who walks in."

She shoved the mask back onto his face. "Your plans consistently involve mugging people, you know that?"

They crawled a few platforms over, farther from the guards.

"How about this one?" Gemma asked. She'd practiced flying on these older duo models before, but this one was nicer than any she'd ever seen. The platform lights gleamed off its shiny, dark red outer hull. They could see into the bright interior through the windows, and it appeared empty.

Trevor nodded and led the way. They ran through the open space between their hiding spot and the ship's door.

No one raised an alarm.

Trevor pulled out a multi-tool from Gemma's bag and popped off the door key panel.

He talked again, possibly muttering to himself.

The door slid open.

"Huh," he grunted.

"You did it!"

They stepped inside and sealed the airlock behind them. He removed his mask. "I didn't do anything. It was unlocked."

They stepped warily into the ship, the interior warmer than it had been outside. Bigger than the jetter, this duo model had a kitchenette and another room at the back. Gemma leaned into the back room with a bunk bed bolted to the ground. An open access panel in the floor worried her. What if they'd left the ship here mid-repair? She hoped the critical systems were all online.

Trevor scratched his head. "No one here."

Gemma slid into the pilot's seat. "Then let's leave before they come back."

"But we still don't have a key—"

The control panel came to life beneath Gemma's hands. She looked at him in surprise. "Maybe it doesn't need a key?" But that didn't make sense. She'd never been on a spaceship that didn't require a key.

The communicator sputtered to life. "Transport vessel 88-CR, you have not been cleared for takeoff. Power down now."

Trevor leaned over her shoulder. "We need to go. Now." Outside the window, a man pointed at their craft, his mouth moving. The security detail turned toward them. "Go now, Gemma!"

"Shut up!" she ordered, flipping switches and checking the numbers. The whine of the engines starting up was soon drowned out as the thrusters came online and engaged.

"Sit down and hold on!" she shouted over the roar. Their ship rose, laboring against the planet's gravity. The men outside scattered from the heat of the thrusters, many of them ducking for cover while a handful scrambled into nearby ships.

Trevor strapped himself in as they tilted, angling away from the port as they continued to gain altitude.

"They're following! They're ..." Trevor trailed off, his voice unnecessarily loud. The engines had quieted to a hum in the thin upper atmosphere.

"Seriously, Captain, you need to stop talking," she said, tapping the screen to check the readouts. It looked like all systems were functioning at optimal levels. "There aren't any decisions for you to make right now, so you need to be quiet and let me work."

He opened his mouth again, but she shot him a glare and he snapped it shut.

Two ships followed, newer but not necessarily faster than Gemma's. She pulled a lever, gunning the engines and forcing them back into their seats.

"How's it looking?" Trevor asked.

"We might get away with this, if there are no more surprises," she said. She pointed to the fuel gauge. "I don't like the looks of these numbers, but if—"

Laser fire flashed across their bow, and she flinched.

"Hey! Who are you? What are you doing in here?"

Gemma gasped at the unfamiliar voice and glanced behind her to see Trevor leap from his seat and tackle a man in a red uniform.

Her eyes snapped back to the view screen as an alarm beeped. Weapons locked on. She couldn't afford to be distracted right now and had to ignore the sounds of a fight behind her.

She gritted her teeth, her knuckles white from her tight grip on the control column as she banked sharply to avoid fire.

The planet's gravity still pulling at them, the two men crashed into the wall.

"Search him for the key!" she shouted. "We need his key or we're dead in space!" She pulled up, sending them shooting into orbit. There was a crash as the struggling men were thrown off their feet before artificial gravity engaged.

"Will you stop that?!" Trevor shouted.

"You'd rather die in a fiery wreck?" she snapped back. Two ships were on an interception course with them. She twisted the ship to avoid them.

A mechanical rattle revved up behind her, then a panel to her left exploded, and she screamed. She looked behind her to see a weapon flash in the hand of the stranger. Trevor grabbed at it, but not before the man got off another shot.

"Captain!" she shouted. More beeping on the control panel turned her back to the viewer.

A door banged shut in the back of the ship, then a hiss.

"Captain?" she said, afraid to take her eyes off the ships altering course to chase her. "What's going on back there?"

There was a clank, then one of the life pods launched. "Trevor!"

The two following ships veered off course to converge on it.

"Relax, Gemma. I'm right here." The ship's key flashed in her peripheral vision, and she snatched it from him.

"I thought you'd launched yourself," she snapped.

He clapped a hand on her shoulder. "Can't get rid of me that easily. I sent him on a little ride."

Her grip on the control column eased. Those ships couldn't catch up now. "But now we only have one life pod."

"Hopefully, we won't need it."

"Where did he even come from?"

"Looks like he was doing maintenance in the engine room." Trevor rubbed his arm and grimaced.

"You okay?" she asked.

He flashed her a smile. "I'm fine, just hit the bunk bed. What's our status?"

THEY'D LEFT THEIR PURSUERS BEHIND, FLYING AT TOP SPEED, THEIR solar sails extended. Trevor rubbed his eyes, trying to input a flight plan. But his vision kept blurring.

"Gemma, I'm not sure—" He cocked his head to the side. "Do you hear something?"

Gemma suppressed a sudden yawn. "No."

"It's like a hissing sound ..."

"Captain." She unclipped her harness and stood, wobbling, then took a step toward him. "I've got something to say to you," she said, her words slurred. She poked a finger at his chest. "And you're gonna listen."

He blinked, his thoughts sluggish. Something wasn't right. She wasn't talking right. He wasn't ... wasn't navigating right.

A warning flashed on the ship's screen. "Atmosphere compromised."

"My head hurts ... Trevor—" Gemma stumbled and fell to the floor.

"Gemma!" He knelt next to her. Breathing, but unconscious.

In his brain fog, he wanted to do nothing more than lay down beside her and go to sleep.

Trevor shook his head. *Snap out of it.* There was that hissing. That had to be it. Something hissed that wasn't supposed to.

A leak.

He fumbled with Gemma's bag and pulled out Zane's leak finder. He flicked it on, and the lights and dials went crazy with readings.

They were being poisoned.

He followed the indicator on the leak finder to one of the holes left by the weapon's fire. Trevor ripped off a length of electrical tape with his teeth and wrapped it around the exposed hose with shaking hands.

The hissing stopped.

His body immensely heavy, Trevor sat on the floor, breathing hard, sweat trickling down the side of his head. It took every ounce of willpower not to fall asleep. Even with the leak patched, it would still take some time for the air to clear. He fought against the dizziness and concentrated on the screen above him. One hour until the atmosphere normalized.

He glanced at where Gemma lay still on the floor. He didn't have the strength to move her yet. She lay on her side, facing him, eyes closed.

He looked away, but her sleeping face drew his gaze again.

With a groan, he tried to stand but ended up dragging himself over to her. A lock of hair had fallen over her eyes. He reached out to brush it away but stopped.

He couldn't touch her. He had no right. In fact, it would be wrong.

"You're a freak," he muttered. "You don't deserve her."

His shaking hand hovered an inch from her. He wanted to, but he shouldn't. Couldn't.

Wouldn't.

He pulled his hand back and crawled away again. He propped himself against the wall, staring at the ceiling. Even without looking at her, he could see her.

Don't be emotional.

He sat there for a long time, looking at nothing, drifting in and out of awareness, until a noise roused him. A red light on the control panel flashed in time to the beeping. He stumbled to his feet and fell into the pilot's chair.

"Proximity alert," he muttered, the dense fog in his mind beginning to clear. No ships detected in the area. He switched screens, and his stomach clenched.

"Gemma!" Trevor fell to his knees beside her, taking her by the shoulders and shaking her. "Wake up! You have to wake up. There's an asteroid field ahead."

Her head flopped to the side, and for the most terrifying second of his life, he thought she was dead. His fingers fumbled on her neck, and he breathed a sigh of relief when he felt the steady throb of a pulse. She just wouldn't wake up.

He ran back to the chair and slid in.

"I can do this," he said, switching to manual. "I can do this."

Somewhere in the back of his mind, he wondered where the asteroid field had come from. They hadn't passed one on the way to Cerise.

Small asteroids bounced off the shield. A few larger ones got past and dinged against the hull. He slowed the ship and turned the shield up to full power.

Slowing didn't help. The asteroids hurdled toward him at high speeds.

Trevor's head pounded as he struggled to focus. A huge rock three times their size barreled toward them.

He pushed down on the control column, and they dived.

The ship shook, then gave a violent jerk. Trevor had avoided a direct collision between the asteroid and the ship, but the solar sail had gotten caught, the asteroid pulling them along with it.

"Gemma!" he shouted, but she didn't stir.

Lights flashed, a soft alarm beeping. With the view through the view screen partially blocked, Trevor brought up the sensor screen. The ship's blue outline had attached to a large red shape and sped toward an even larger red asteroid.

Trevor tried to retract the sails, but the ship just shuddered. With the shift he could see the other asteroid grow larger in the view screen.

He turned the engines up to full power and heaved on the control column. With a jolt, the ship wrenched away from the asteroid as it smashed into the next one, cracking in two with the impact.

When Trevor let up, the slightly bent control column made the steering wonky. Warning lights flashed on the screens, half the solar sails flashing red on the diagram of the ship. He punched the control to retract what was left of them.

He gritted his teeth as they bounced and scraped their way through the asteroid field. The shield held.

Almost there.

He could see clear space ahead when the shield flickered. At that instant, a small rock hit, smashing a hole in the hull.

More alarms went off, and tremendous suction pulled at him as they vented atmosphere. A section of wall at the back of the ship flashed red on the screen.

Trevor unclipped his harness and stumbled over to the golf ball-sized hole in the wall. He grabbed a blanket and stuffed it in, but it instantly shot into space. He searched around for anything to plug the hole.

Gemma lay on the floor in the control room. He had to do something quick. He had to save her.

A panel. An interior wall panel welded in place would work.

His strength back, he punched one to dent it, just enough to get a grip on the edges. He ripped it off the wall and covered the hole.

It stayed. The leak slowed, but they still vented precious oxygen.

Trevor searched the back room with the open panel in the

floor. He dropped through it into the engine room. A welder sat right there, out in the open. *Finally, a break.*

It took a few minutes to weld the panel into place. The alarms silenced, and he breathed a sigh of relief.

Now he had to figure out where they were and how to get back. *And* how to do it at half power.

He pulled up a map. They had gone in the opposite direction of the Terminus, far from a jump-point. If they could get into jump-space, he could get them back on course.

Think, Trevor. Think.

They flew close to a solar system. No M-class planets, but the sun was …

The sun, a yellow giant.

As a navigator he had taken remote-learning courses on jump-space travel theory. Something about gravity and punching a way into jump-space. Theoretically.

Desperation made the decision for him. *It's not like we have a better option.*

Unfurling the shredded solar sails, the ship limped toward the sun. It was going to get hot.

He wiped the sweat off his forehead with the hem of his shirt. The poison should have been neutralized in her system by now, but Gemma still slept. He picked her up off the floor and laid her on the bed in the back room.

"Gem, please wake up," he said, his voice soft. He smoothed her hair away from her face. "Wake up. I need you."

She jerked. "Hmm? Captain?"

He leaned closer. "Pilot, wake up."

She coughed, her eyes still closed. "Oh, my head. I think I'm dying." She rolled away from him.

He smirked and rolled her back. "Nope, you're very much alive."

"But I'm so hot. Why's it so hot?" Her fingers fumbled with the hem of her shirt.

Trevor grabbed her hand before she could lift it, a pulse of heat that had nothing to do with the sun washing through him. "No, no! Don't do that."

"But I'm so hot!" she whined, cracking open an eye. She opened both eyes. He was so relieved to see her eyes again. Then they narrowed. "Why's it so hot?"

"Uh, well ... we may be close to a sun."

She sat up with a wince. "Why? What's happened? Are we adrift?"

"No, not adrift." He tensed. "But we're running on half power. And ... going the wrong way."

"Half power? Going the wrong way? What happened? And why are we so close to a sun?" She lurched to her feet and stumbled to the window.

He followed her, concerned. "Hey, don't go too fast, you might—"

She gasped. "What happened to the solar sails?"

"We hit an asteroid field," he said. "We barely got out of there with—"

"Why didn't you wake me?" She whirled on him, pressing a hand against the wall to steady herself. "You thought you could do it on your own? What a stupid—"

His brows lowered. "I *couldn't* wake you. What was I supposed to do?"

"How about a full stop until I woke up?" She wobbled, and he reached out to steady her, but she knocked his hand away.

"Did you forget we're being chased? I couldn't risk it." His voice rose, and he struggled to lower it.

She turned away from him and screamed at the window. "Now we're going to die because of your ego!"

"Hey, my thinking was pretty muddy at that point," he

said, defensive. "But if I were put in that position again with a clear head, I probably would have done something similar. You're being overdramatic."

"No, I'm not!" she shouted.

"Gemma, calm down."

"Don't tell me to calm down! And why are we headed *towards a sun?*"

"Gemma." He took her by the shoulders and looked into her wide eyes. He didn't see anger there, but panic. "Look at me. It's going to be fine. Trust me."

Her breathing fast, tears welled up in her eyes. "I can't, I can't—"

He pulled her close and hugged her, rubbing her back and murmuring, "We'll get through this, we can do it."

Her breathing slowed, and he held her tighter. "Do you trust me?"

She nodded against his chest and pulled away. He reluctantly let go. She nodded again. "Okay." A pause. A deep breath. "Okay." She looked up, her expression hardening, eyes dry. "I'm ready."

He let out a sigh of relief. "Good. Let me show you why we're going towards the sun." He led her over to the navigation screen. "You know that space-jumping travels from one depression of exotic matter to another, right?"

"Right."

"There's a theory that a distortion in space could be used in the same way."

"A *theory?*"

"And gravity," he continued, "creates a distortion in space. The greater the gravity, the greater the distortion. So, since I didn't have a black hole available, I plotted a course into the nearest sun—"

"*Into the sun?*"

"We won't get there." He tapped the screen. "We'll space-jump long before then."

"Before or after we burn up? And it's just a theory?"

He gripped her hand. "*Trust me.* This will work."

She took another deep breath. "Okay."

GEMMA TOOK THE PILOT'S SEAT AND GASPED. "WHAT HAPPENED TO the control column?"

"Uh ..."

"Never mind." She'd never seen a bent control column before—and they definitely never taught her how to use one in flight school—but she moved it around to get a feel for it with the bend. Warning lights and diagrams blinked at her. Trevor must have turned off the audio alarms. "How long do we have before we jump?"

"The stronger the gravity, the better chance we have of this working," Trevor said. "We have to get as close to the sun as we can stand."

"It's already like an oven in here." She tried to fan herself, but it didn't help. "How will we know?"

"When the shield is at critical." He pointed to a gauge, the needle already in the red, and still moving. "As soon as the alarm sounds, we've got to jump. Fast."

"What happens if we can't enter jump-space?" Though she had a feeling she already knew.

He hesitated. "This will work." He pushed a few buttons. "Our course is already laid in. Shift us into jump-space and we'll be set."

"I heard you hesitate," she said, trying to sound angry so

her voice wouldn't shake. "I did *not* come here for a hands-on lesson in spaghettification."

"No lessons, honest. Just a very—uh, *hot*—entrance into jump-space."

The air grew hotter. Gemma wiped the sweat from her eyes, her clothes soaked.

"Almost there," he said, leaning over her shoulder.

She flipped up the red cover and her thumb hovered over the switch. She took a steadying breath of the hot, thick air.

They waited.

The alarm sounded, the line around the ship flashing in the diagram.

"Now!"

Gemma flipped the switch and gunned the engines.

The ship shook violently, jerking from side to side. Gemma struggled to maintain control as they were snapped up and down.

Trevor hadn't buckled himself in and flew back with a crash.

"Trevor!"

The ship jolted along, like a small boat speeding against high waves. She strained on the control column to keep them on course. Bumping the side of the wormhole would shred their ship like grass in a lawnmower.

Then the ride smoothed out, only white visible through the windows.

"We made it," she whispered, then smiled as it sunk in. "We made it!" She turned in her seat. "Trevor, we—Trevor?"

He lay still at the back of the ship, crumpled against the foot of the bed.

"No!" Her fingers fumbled trying to unbuckle her harness. She ran to his side and knelt, calling his name.

Unconscious, blood seeped from a deep cut on the back of his head.

She grabbed his collar to shake him awake but let go. What if he had a neck injury?

Where was the emergency medical kit?

She searched the cupboards, dumping everything onto the floor until she found it. The medical scanner gave a soft beep as she waved it over him. His neck was fine, but he had a slight concussion, and his ribs were broken.

Pulling out handfuls of gauze, she bandaged his head, making a huge mess. The sloppy dressing finally slowed the bleeding. She cleaned Trevor up as best she could, but the blood had completely ruined their clothes.

"Trevor, wake up," she said, touching his cheek.

The medical scanner said to check his pupils. She raised an eyelid, and he gasped.

"Trevor!" She threw herself at him in a hug, and he yelped. "Sorry! Sorry. I forgot about your ribs."

He struggled to sit up. "What happened?"

"Well, your pupils look normal," she said. "The scanner says to ask you questions to test your—"

"What happened?!" Trevor grabbed her blood-covered arms. "Are you alright? Where are you hurt?"

"I'm fine," she said, pulling herself out of his grip and taking his hand. "It's your blood, not mine."

He touched the bulky bandage on his head.

"The transition was rough," she said, "and you weren't strapped down. But we made it! Are you woozy? You have a concussion."

"No, not woozy." He climbed to his feet and swayed. Gemma jumped up to support him. "Maybe a little."

"What's your name?" she asked.

He gave her a look like she was crazy. "Who has the concussion here?"

She almost smacked him upside the head. "I'm testing your memory, stupid!"

"Trevor."

"What's my name?"

He smiled. "Gemma."

The way he said it gave her a shiver, and the way he looked at her— "Okay, I think you're fine. How long do we need to stay in jump-space?"

"Uh ..."

"Don't tell me you forgot *that!*"

"No, no, let me think." He clutched his head and winced. "Twenty-two hours."

She punched a few buttons, setting an alarm to alert them when it was time to jump.

"Can I get some sleep?" he asked.

"Sorry, you have to stay awake for a while because of the head injury." She patted his hand. "Let me see if there's any entertainment on this rig. It's got to have more than the jetter."

He shook his head. "I don't feel like it. Could you just—just stay by me for a few minutes? Please."

The concussion really did a doozy on his thinking. She looked down, feeling warmth spread into her cheeks. Not that she was complaining.

She nodded, and they sat on the floor with their backs against the wall. He rested his head on her hair with a deep sigh.

GEMMA SAT ON THE BED, STARING AT THE WHITE BEYOND THE window. Trevor sat in the pilot's chair, fooling with a tablet he had found, trying to unlock it. The ship had finally cooled down, and her sweat-drenched clothes made her shiver.

Their shield functioned at minimal efficiency. Hopefully, it was enough to get them through the Terminus scrapyard. At least the hull was still intact.

She glanced at the patch on the back wall. Mostly.

Her fists clenched. They *had* to make it home. She missed Sandy. They had never gone so long without seeing each other. Even during flight school, they visited every weekend.

"What's wrong?" Trevor asked.

Gemma snapped out of her reverie. "Wrong? What makes you think something's wrong?"

"You're quiet," he said. "You're *never* quiet."

"Oh, I'm just hungry." Not a lie.

He crossed his arms and raised an eyebrow.

She fiddled with the hem of her shirt. "Have you ever been homesick?"

"No," he said without pause.

"Never? You didn't even think about it."

He rubbed his chin. "I guess ... I miss my dad. Sometimes it's worse than others. Is that the same thing?"

"I miss Sandy," she said. "And I miss the house I grew up in. And my parents. But it's mostly Sandy." She pressed a hand against her heart. "So much it hurts. And I don't know if I'll ever see her again."

He looked at the ceiling and scrubbed at his face.

She knew that look. "Did I say something wrong?"

"No, no. It's just, it's my fault that we're here—"

"Shut up!" She crossed her arms, glaring at him. Not this again. "I signed up for this mission, knowing the risks. It is not your fault."

He still wouldn't look at her. "I hate to see you hurt," he said, so soft she almost didn't hear it.

Gemma knew he cared. How many times had he risked his life for hers? But when he said it like that … She wanted nothing more than to throw her arms around him and never let go.

She stood and took a step toward him, but he turned away to the instrument panel.

"Why do you do that?" she demanded.

"Do what?" He flicked through the screens, and she knew he wasn't even looking at them.

He was impossible. "Forget it." She sat down with a huff, arms crossed, looking out the window—not missing his glance back at her.

TREVOR JERKED AWAKE, FALLING OUT OF THE CHAIR.

On the bed, Gemma sat up straight, her eyes barely open. "Huh? Are you okay?"

He groaned from the floor, his whole body feeling like one giant bruise, and his head pounding. "Stripped screws."

She rubbed her eyes and yawned. "You're not woozy, are you?"

"No, not woozy. Honest. I just … fell." He didn't want to admit he fell asleep. He shouldn't have. A glance at the clock. And he'd been out for almost ten hours.

"*Suuuuuuuure.*" She got up, throwing the blanket she'd kicked to the floor onto the bed. "Do you want a nap?"

"No, I'm good."

Gemma paused. "You're just going to lie there on the floor?"

Everything hurt. "Yep."

She shrugged, tossed the pillow to the floor next to him, then lay down on it.

They were quiet, staring up at the ceiling.

"For a minute there, I thought you were giving me the pillow," he said.

She hugged the pillow. "I don't like you enough to give it up."

Trevor chuckled. "You know what you like."

"Yup." She counted with her fingers. "First, food. Second, pillow. Third, Trevor."

"I'm surprised I made the list." Third wasn't bad.

The corner of her mouth quirked. "Barely. What's on your list?"

He thought for a minute. "Usually, I'd say my ship is first, but ..."

Gemma winced. "Will you be able to get a new one?"

"I think so. I hope so."

"Am I on it?"

Trevor propped himself up on his elbows so he could see her face. "On my ship?"

"On your list."

"Oh, right. Um. Yes, you're on my list." He wasn't going to tell her how high up on the list she was.

She smiled, and his heart beat a little harder.

He looked away, then back at her. "Do you want to be on my ship though? The new one, I mean?"

She sat up straight. "Yes! Absolutely!" Her smile spread into a grin.

"All right, then. Great."

Neither looked at the other for a long moment.

"Did you really say, 'stripped screws' earlier?" she asked.

He tried not to laugh as he lay down again; it hurt too much. "A habit I picked up from my dad. It's what he'd say when he was trying not to swear in front of me."

Gemma chuckled. "I guess a lot of things changed for him when he found you." She gave him a nudge. "He must have been so happy."

The thought warmed him. He'd always worried about being a burden to his dad. It reassured him that Dad hadn't been the sort to keep people around he didn't want. The two of them had a lot of fun.

"Do you know the real reason Chase went into space?" she asked.

Trevor smiled.

"What?" she said.

"Nothing. I think I'm getting used to your sudden subject changes."

She rolled her eyes. "What's the answer?"

He shrugged. "Nope."

"You don't? Weren't you curious?"

"Not really," he said. "If you haven't noticed, I appreciate privacy. He passed the background check, and the *why* of it all is none of my business."

"It just occurred to me. Is Chase his first name, or his last name?"

He smiled. "I'm not about to tell on someone's name."

"You suffer from a severe lack of curiosity," Gemma said, punching his arm. He tried not to groan. It hurt.

"I have a confession to make," she said, her fingers twisting together.

He swallowed and tried to sound casual. "What is it?"

She rolled onto her side to face him. "I have your notebook."

He blinked. "I thought I'd lost it."

"I saved it. It's in the front pocket of the bag."

"Have you—" He licked his dry lips. "Have you read it?"

"Yeah."

He cringed.

"It was amazing," she said, her voice soft.

His eyes snapped to hers. She had read them. He'd never even let Dad or Charlie read them.

"I had no idea you wrote poetry," she said. "I mean, it's a little dark, but still really good."

"It's not poetry," he corrected. "They're songs."

"Wow." She smiled at him. "Color me impressed. I've only read a couple of pages. Do you mind if I keep reading?"

"Uh, sure. I guess." He gave a one-shoulder shrug, as if he didn't care. But he did care. He desperately wanted her to like them. "If you really like them."

"I do."

His heart thudded.

"Do you read poetry too?" she asked. "Was that what you were trying to hide from me that time on the bridge?"

He looked up at the ceiling. "Are you going to make fun of me for it?"

"What? No!"

"I'll answer," he said, meeting her gaze, "if you will."

She narrowed her eyes. "What's the question?"

A sly smile slid across his face. He knew the answer, but he wanted to hear her say it. "Did you steal my tablet that day?"

"Oh, man!" She slapped her hand against her forehead. "Yes. Yes, I did. I was trying to break into it to see what you were reading, and I locked it."

He smiled. "Then, yes, I read poetry. But I write *songs*."

"Sure you do." She sat up. "I'm hungry. Are you?"

"Starving." His stomach felt like it was going to cave in on itself.

She scoured the kitchen area and came up with an insta-soup cup.

"Not much nutritional value, but better than nothing." She sat back down on the floor next to him. Trevor sat up, his back leaning against the wall.

After snapping the heating element to activate it and waiting a few minutes, they lifted the lid to a cloud of steam.

Gemma got the first bite. "Mmm."

"Save some for me."

They could only find one spoon, so they took turns with it. Gemma looked like she was enjoying it, but to him, it was just hot.

"I can't taste anything," Trevor said. "Is that bad?"

The ship's alarm went off.

He groaned. "What now?"

"It's the timer I set," Gemma said. "It's time to leave jump-space. Strap down this time."

They both buckled in, and she grabbed the bent control column.

"This one should be smoother," he said.

Gemma eased out of jump-space and the familiar star-studded black popped into existence around them. The light of the Terminus buoy blinked in the distance.

He sagged in relief.

"We're almost there!" she said, gripping his arm.

The blaring proximity alarm went off. They'd come out of jump-space between the Terminus and a large ship.

"Oh no," Gemma moaned.

He looked at the readouts. It was the same ship that shot them down over 3X-527.

"How did they find us?" she asked, her eyes wide, her fingers twisting together.

"They knew where we were going. They were waiting." Trevor put his hand on her shoulder to reassure her. She looked like she was on the verge of panic. "We can make it."

The ship was still far away, well out of firing range.

Gemma took a deep breath to steady herself. She took hold of the control column.

They used every trick they knew to get the ship to go faster, but the dot in the viewer grew closer.

"They're too fast," she said, her voice calm now. "We're at top speed, and they're still gaining. We're in no condition to outrun anything. They'll catch us in … three hours."

Trevor tried not to say anything while she punched a few buttons.

"There aren't any asteroid fields to lose them in … but there are a few pockets of bad space debris nearby. Dead ships from battles … There's a moon with a *lot* around it—"

"No good," Trevor said. "Do you think we can make it over the border before they get within firing distance?"

"Maybe," she told him. "We can get darn close. But I don't think it will make a difference, I think they'll follow us right into friendly space. We might get there, but they'll shoot us down before we can get any farther."

"That's okay," he told her, searching the closets for anything they could use. "I have an idea. I want you to find the biggest pocket of space junk you can, close to the border, preferably on the other side of it. Got it?"

"Aye-aye, Captain," she said, punching in coordinates.

They said little during the tense two-and-a-half-hour ride, the whole ship vibrating as the engines pushed to max power.

"We're almost there," Gemma said. "But we'll be within firing distance soon."

"How soon?"

"Twenty minutes."

"In nineteen minutes, steer toward a debris field." *Please let this work.*

"Whatever you say."

The ship was almost in firing range when she switched the controls to manual and steered toward the closest space junk graveyard.

"I don't know if this is a good idea," she said. "Even I'll be hard-pressed to get through that, especially at top speed. And they can just go around and catch up again. It won't buy us any time."

"It's not time I'm looking for," he said. "It's camouflage. Come on, let's get to the back." He reached over her shoulder and punched the autopilot.

"But on autopilot we don't stand a chance!"

He grabbed her hand and pulled her to her feet. "Trust me, Gemma."

She hesitated, then nodded once. "Let's go."

THEIR SHIP REACHED THE DEBRIS FIELD. THE AUTOPILOT MADE A valiant twist and a turn, thrusters firing and the strain of the engine shaking it. Small pieces of metal shot through the minimal shield, bombarding the hull and punching holes in it. The ship wavered but kept course until it collided with a gutted transporter. Cartwheeling through the air, larger shards of metal shredded it, and the ship flared before the vacuum instantly doused the flames.

Soon the old duo ship slowed and joined the drifting

debris, crushed and unrecognizable, only the smallest glint of red paint visible around the ripped metal.

The pursuing ship stopped before reaching the junk yard. A smaller scout ship deployed from its underbelly, approaching the space junk at a slow and steady speed. It spent an hour combing the wreckage before returning to the larger ship.

As Trevor had planned.

"They're leaving!" Gemma cried in relief. She and Trevor floated close together, sharing the one life pod the ship had. Had he been alone, he'd have enough room to have his back against one side and fully extend one arm to the other side. Okay, maybe not even that much room. Having her there considerably shrank his space. At least it accommodated his height. The life pod wasn't similar enough to the tube to bother him more than a general uncomfortable feeling.

Having ejected early within the debris field, the chasing ship hadn't detected them, dismissing the life pod as one more scrap of metal.

They planned to broadcast the distress signal after the ship left; they'd disconnected the beacon so it wouldn't engage too early. The controls in the life pod could make small course corrections to their drift in space, but not much else. Only the distress signal could save them.

"Omni Authority patrols the border," Trevor said. "I figure they'll be along eventually."

"I can't believe we're still alive," Gemma said. "Do we have enough air?"

"Well, that's an issue," he admitted. He hadn't wanted to bring that up. "This life pod was only designed to support one person. The CO2 scrubbers won't be able to keep up. We have maybe twelve hours."

Gemma stared past him and out the little window. "Will they find us in time?"

"I don't know. Our signal can't go very far, so there's a low likelihood it'll reach a passing ship. If only there were a way to boost the signal."

"Signal ..." she repeated, rubbing her chin. "Signal!"

He winced. "It's an awfully small space; you don't need to yell."

"We *can* boost the signal," she said, grabbing his shoulders. "We might live after all!"

"But how will we boost the signal? We've got nothing in here," he said gently.

"I need to get to my pack ..."

She tried to reach down, but her face rammed into his shoulder. "Ow."

"Hang on, I'll get it." He pinched the bag between his feet and kicked it upward. It floated toward them until Gemma caught it out of the air.

"There must be something in here," she muttered, digging around. "Zane talked about a boosted signal. Anything look useful and signal-y to you?"

"I don't even know what half this stuff is," Trevor said.

She pulled out a sphere. "This is the clock Zane made me."

"Not useful."

"Right. Camera, signal scrambler ..."

"Probably could have used that at some point on Cerise."

"And—a scanner! Ta da!" She beamed at him. "This will help us boost the signal."

He tried not to look doubtful. "What kind of scanner?"

"A lifeform scanner." She flicked it on. "No one within fifty miles of us."

"Fifty miles?" Trevor took it from her hand, checking the readout. There was no way. "That's quite the range."

Gemma grinned. "It's got a booster in it that triples the range!"

"Are you sure it's not broken?" Trevor asked.

She arched an eyebrow. "Zane designed it himself."

Trevor examined the lifeform scanner, the digital readout giving him a small sliver of hope. If Zane made it, then it probably worked. *Probably.*

The contents of her bag floated around them as he found his multi-tool and opened the casing.

"Uh, do you know what you're looking at?" she asked. "Because I don't."

"Let me think." His brow furrowed. Then he tapped a small yellow chip at the bottom. "This I don't recognize. It must be the booster."

He very carefully disconnected the chip and pulled it out. He held it up. *Zane, you mad genius.*

"You'll have to help me install it," Trevor said.

"What do I have to do?"

"Hold it in place."

They crammed themselves into one end of the life pod, and Trevor removed the control panel of the distress signal.

"Your hands are shaking," Gemma said.

"I have no idea what I'm doing." He tried to keep his voice even. "Cut me some slack."

It took a while, but Trevor finally screwed the booster in place. "Well, that does it. We'll see if it works."

"Holy cow, we're going to live!" She grinned. "I could kiss you!"

He jerked, smacking the back of his head against the wall, stifling a groan. His face burned at the thought, the memory of her lips brushing his cheek that first time ...

"Can I turn it on now?" Gemma asked, her eager smile lighting a warmth in his chest.

He cleared his throat. She was so close, he really could lean forward a few inches to press his mouth to hers— "No, better wait a bit."

"But won't we run low on air?"

"Better than the Conglomerate returning," he said. "But with the booster, we have a much better chance of being found." *If it worked.*

They waited, back-to-back, looking out the small windows. Time passed slowly.

Trevor hung on to a handle to keep himself against the wall. The narrowness of the pod made it impossible to keep from bumping into her. He bit his lip, hyperaware of every touch.

"Maybe you should strap yourself down," he suggested. The life pod had one set of belts to strap in. "So you're not—So you're safer."

"No, I'm okay." She tapped his shoulder. "Can you turn around? If we're going to die together, I at least want to be talking to your face."

He tensed but spun in zero gravity. Only inches separated them.

"Something wrong?" she asked. "You should be relieved, we're almost home free."

"I am relieved." But it wasn't only the unlikelihood of them being saved that cast a shadow across his face. Every accidental brush against her was so hot it was painful.

Her eyes narrowed, her face so close he could see the flecks of amber in her eyes. "No, you're not. You're shaking even worse than earlier, Trevor."

Goosebumps raced up his arms at his name. His hands tightened on the wall handles. "I'm fine," he said, a little sharper than he meant to, and he spun back around to face the window.

"Okay then." She spun around herself.

Their backs touched, and he closed his eyes, savoring the warmth of her pressed against him.

Gemma hummed to herself. Trevor glanced over his shoulder and chuckled.

"What?" she asked.

"No, nothing." He hadn't wanted her to stop.

She spun around again, grabbed his shoulder, and forced him to face her. "What?" she demanded.

"You, you just—" He chuckled again. "You're a terrible singer."

She gasped. "I thought you liked my humming!"

"I do! It's just ... it's terrible. Really, you're awful." He couldn't help himself.

She glowered. "And you think you can do any better?"

"Yes, actually."

"Let's hear it, then."

He hesitated. Not where he'd wanted that to go. "You mean, right now?"

"Right now." She lifted her chin. "Sing me one of your songs."

He cleared his throat. Her face was so close to his. Her lips looked so soft.

"Maybe later," he said, his voice strangled.

She frowned. "You okay? Your voice does sound a little weird. Is your head hurting? Maybe—"

Gemma raised a hand to his face, but he caught her wrist.

"I'm fine," he said.

He released her and pushed himself as far away from her as he could. Which wasn't much. They stared at each other for a long moment, Gemma's eyes questioning as she studied his face for answers.

She knew more about him than anyone else in the galaxy. There were no more questions to ask.

"We've probably waited long enough," he said after a while. "You can send out the distress signal now."

"Aye-aye, Captain." She reached upward and bumped into him. He flinched.

"Hang on," she said, "almost got it."

He watched her hands reconnect the emergency beacon to its power source, trying to ignore her body touching his.

"Done." She pushed the button.

He breathed a sigh of relief. "Well, the lights didn't go out. No explosions, no fires. I think we might have done it."

Gemma opened her mouth in shock. "There was a chance of that?"

"Er—yes. A chance." In his opinion, they'd defied the odds.

"Captain ..." she said, her eyes meeting his.

He looked away. "What is it?"

She hesitated. "Nothing."

His fingers drummed against the handles, and he looked everywhere but at her.

She stared at him, then reached out and touched his shoulder. "Trevor ..."

He shifted away.

"Do you not like being touched?" she asked.

"It's not like that," he said.

"Then what's it like?"

He wanted her to touch him again, so bad. "Forget it, alright?"

"No, I won't." She crossed her arms. "You tell me right now why I make you flinch, why you can't stand to look at me right now. Why?"

"Gemma—"

"Tell me, Trevor." Her voice was soft.

She waited.

"It's nothing."

She grabbed his shoulder and shoved him against the wall, holding him there with her hand against his chest. He blinked in surprise.

"You are such a liar!" she shouted, deafening in the small space. "Stop lying to me!"

"Lying about what? Why are you so angry?"

"You keep saying it's 'nothing.' Nothing means anything to you! You've said," her voice dropped, " ... nice things to me. But then you shove me away. Do you hate me?"

He looked away again. "I don't hate you."

She grabbed his chin and forced him to face her. "Then what is it?"

"Nothing!"

"Liar!"

"I love you," he blurted. He winced and shut his eyes.

"What?" She released him. "Then why won't you ... respond to me? You act like you don't even want me around."

He took a deep breath, opening his eyes. But he still couldn't meet her gaze. "It hurts when you touch me."

She drew back. "What do you mean?"

He rubbed his chest where her hand had been. "It's ... electricity."

"Like, static?"

"I mean—I mean ..." He cleared his throat, his voice tight. "I can't stand for you to touch me because—I can't have you."

She frowned. "What does that even mean?"

"I can't ... I can't *have* you," he repeated.

"Why not?"

"Because—because ..." He took a shaky breath. He wasn't even human. He knew that; he'd always known that. The shame of it had never been so intense than it was now. His voice instinctively dropped lower. "I'm a Tubie."

A smile crept across Gemma's face. "That's why? This

whole time? We have only hours to live, and you're still hung up on that?"

He wouldn't look at her, his whole body aching for her.

"Trevor," she said. She reached out and placed a hand on the back of his neck. "Haven't I told you? You're the most human guy I know."

Their eyes met, then she drew his face toward hers. His eyes widened as their lips touched.

The kiss was clumsy, and he didn't know what to do with his hands, at first.

Then he wrapped his arms around her and pulled her tighter against him as the kiss deepened. He was never going to let go. They were probably going to die like this, and he'd never been so happy.

The communicator crackled to life.

"Come in life pod. Is anybody in there?"

They jumped, Trevor banging his head again with a groan.

Gemma gasped. "Is that—is that Chase?"

Trevor depressed the communicator button. "Life pod to ship, we're alive." He hesitated. "Is that you, Chase?"

A pause. "*Captain?*"

"What? You found the captain?" At the sound of Zane's far-away voice, Gemma clapped her hand over her mouth, her wet eyes meeting his. They were alive.

"What about Gemma?" Zane asked.

"Captain, where's Gemma?"

"She's here," Trevor said.

Another pause. "You're *both* in there?"

Trevor could feel his face flush. "We're both here. If you wouldn't mind picking us up?"

"Right away, Captain. We'll be there in a moment."

22

With a *clank* and a *hiss*, the life pod was secured in the cargo airlock. Chase reached in and pulled Gemma out.

"Gemma!" Zane said with glee. He ran toward her, then stopped with a gasp. "Gemma?" This time he sounded horrified.

"Zane!" She gave him a smile, then he hugged her so hard she winced.

"What happened to you?" Zane asked, releasing her.

"It's a long story," Trevor said, climbing out of the life pod.

"Huh. You *were* both in there." Zane craned his neck to look inside, but Trevor blocked his way. "Captain! You look terrible!"

Trevor grimaced. "Thanks."

"Sorry, I mean—"

"You should both probably see Charlie," Chase said. "I've already called him."

Gemma shared a glance with Trevor. He really did look awful—his head bandaged, stance off-center as he nursed his ankle, his wrists and hands scraped and raw, clutching his side and clearly in pain, his clothes stiff with blood—and she couldn't be much better.

A man stepped forward from behind Chase and extended a hand to Trevor. "Captain Steve Brant," he said. "Welcome to my ship."

Captain Brant commanded attention when he walked into a room. Mid-fifties, gray hair, neatly trimmed beard, straight-back, he somehow managed to keep his uniform crisp after even months in space.

Trevor shook his hand. "Thanks for the rescue. How did my crew come to be on your ship?"

"Same way you did. We fished their life pods out of space."

That's when Charlie ran in. When he saw them, he sucked his breath in through his teeth.

"Captain." He touched Trevor's shoulder, then gave Gemma a gentle hug, as if she would break. "Both of you, sick-bay. Now."

Captain Brant nodded. "We'll talk later."

The sickbay on this ship was larger than the one on Trevor's. They each sat on an examination table, Trevor's legs dangling almost to the floor and Gemma's cross-legged.

Charlie had Trevor take his shirt off to examine him, and Gemma tried hard not to stare. Trevor caught her looking and raised his eyebrows, but she flicked her gaze away, face hot.

"What happened?" Charlie asked, peeling the bandages off Trevor's head.

"We went into jump-space using the gravity of a sun, and he wasn't strapped down," Gemma said.

Charlie shook his head. "Not just this—wait, you what? Never mind. You're both ... you look ... Have you been eating? Sleeping? How did you get all these injuries?"

"It's a long story," Trevor said. "We'll—we'll tell everyone at once. It was a ... wild ride."

"Is that what you'd call it?" Gemma shuddered. "I'd have said a nightmare."

"Gemma, will you wait outside while I finish examining the captain?" Charlie asked. "You're both a little more banged up than I initially thought."

She slid open the sickbay door and ran right into the rest of the crew. Joe, Dak, Chase, and Zane stood outside.

"Gemma girl!" Joe hugged her.

Dak took a turn hugging her. "What happened?"

She shook her head. "We'll tell you all about it. Later."

Someone brought a chair, and they made her sit down, plying her with questions. She couldn't answer any of them, just closed her eyes and touched her forehead.

"Guys, give her some space," Zane said. "Can't you see she's exhausted?"

The sickbay door slid opened. "Someone feed him, have him take a shower, then put him to bed," Charlie said, sending Trevor out. "Gemma, your turn."

Gemma had the most thorough exam of her life, then was sent to eat too. Zane escorted her. He kept glancing at her, his forehead furrowed.

"Zane, what is it?" she asked. "Please tell me why everyone's acting so weird."

He shook his head. "You look half-dead."

She winced. "Oh." Zane wasn't wrong.

Dak made her a sandwich, and she'd only take a few bites before she began to sway, her eyes heavy. Zane and Joe stood on either side, holding her steady.

"Let's get her to bed," Joe said.

They led her to a bunk, and she fell asleep before they'd even left the room.

She awoke to a murmur of voices and opened the door to see Zane and Trevor standing in the hallway outside her door.

She rubbed her eyes. "How long have I been asleep?"

"Thirteen hours," Zane said. "How are you feeling?"

"Like I crash-landed." She winced. "Which I did, at one point."

"You should take a shower. It will help," Trevor said. "Afterwards, everyone's waiting in the common room for us." Trevor reached out toward her, then let his hand drop. "Captain Brant has sent over some clean clothes for you."

The shower perked her up, and the clothes she'd been given almost fit. The white doctor's shirt fit perfectly. She could just barely pull the khaki pants over her hips, but the wide legs covered the rest of her well.

She paused. Where did the women's clothing come from? Was there a female doctor on board?

When she stepped out, Zane offered her his arm. She clung to him, her body still heavy. "I'm hungry."

"We'll get you something to eat," Zane said, patting her hand.

Gemma joined Trevor at the common room table, and someone got her a plate. Between bites, they gave the abridged version of the events following the crash—leaving out the parts about the super soldier program.

"You survived the *crash*?" Zane said.

Having gotten some sleep and filled her belly, Gemma turned her attention to the rest of the crew. "What happened to you guys? How are you alive?"

"We all made it to the life pods," Dak said.

"But you and Chase were on the bridge when the gravity went out," Trevor said.

Dak shook his head. "After the first shot, we knew the ship

couldn't take many more like that, and we scrambled for the life pods."

"Then Brant picked us up," Zane said. "We headed down to the planet to check out the crash. We tried to find you—"

"But by the time we got to the colony, you were already gone," Joe said.

"We thought the ship that shot us down was after us," Gemma said, her hand going to her mouth. "But it was you. We were running away from you." Her eyes welled up. If only they had stayed.

Charlie's hand touched her shoulder. "We've been patrolling the Terminus ever since, hoping to find you. We have you back, now."

Gemma squeezed his hand. "It's been horrible."

"Before we left the planet, Captain Brant arrested someone who sent messages to an organization called the Conglomerate," Chase said. "We weren't able to decode the messages, but we know he told them you were coming."

"So that's how they knew—" Gemma breathed. Trevor gave her a warning glance and she shut her mouth.

"It's lucky Brant came along when he did," Trevor said. "What's he doing way out here?"

"He was on his way back from a science exploratory mission, when he stopped by to pick up a supply of whatever they mine on that planet," Chase explained. "He didn't have to go back to Earth right away. Under the circumstances, Omni Authority asked him to stay out here longer to look for you. We knew you'd come back this way, if at all."

Zane sat up straight. "Don't talk like that!"

Chase shrugged. "The argument is moot now. We've got them back."

After a day of meetings and explanations, Gemma finally got to a computer and opened her account. She sucked in her breath. Twenty-seven messages, all from Sandy. They hadn't spoken in over a week, maybe two. Gemma had lost count. Sandy must be worried sick. Gemma opened the first one.

"*WHAT DO YOU MEAN, 'CRASHED?'*" Sandy screamed at her.

AFTER SENDING WHAT SHE HOPED WAS A REASSURING MESSAGE TO Sandy, Gemma looked out into the hallway. For the first time since they'd been rescued, she was alone. Her stomach groaned, so she slid her door shut and made her way to the common room.

This ship was bigger than the *Michal* had been, and so was the common room. No one else was in there, which was a little surprising. She looked at the posted duty roster—her name wasn't on it—when Trevor stopped in the doorway.

She smothered a smile. The only uniform that remotely fit him was a mechanic's jumpsuit. Where did they dig up a clean one? He looked a little goofy, the pants a few inches too short. Now that they weren't running for their lives, she could appreciate it. The top fit his shoulders well—but again, too-short sleeves.

"Gemma, I've been looking for you," he said, his voice urgent. "I need to talk to you."

She felt a little thrill. He'd been looking for her. "Okay." She turned to him, unable to help a smile. "What's up?"

"I need to talk to you about, uh ... about—" He looked around, stepping into the room and lowering his voice. "The, uh—the kiss."

She cocked her head to the side, trying to look serious. "Okay."

"It's just that we can't ..." He took a deep breath. "We can't tell anyone about—"

Oh. Her heart sank. "We have to keep it professional," she finished.

He looked relieved. "Yes, exactly."

"Of course, Captain," she said. She looked down at the floor so he wouldn't see her disappointment. They'd come so far together. She'd never been closer to another person than she was to him.

"Yes. Right." He hesitated, looking around the room, empty but for them.

With two steps he closed the space between them, taking her face in his hands and kissing her.

Gemma's eyes closed, her arms sliding around his neck.

He broke it off, but his eyes begged for more. "No, we can't—"

She answered him by pulling his face back to hers into another kiss.

"Gemma—"

She kissed him harder, and he finally shut up.

Once they'd come up for air, Trevor had dragged Gemma into the galley. Now she sat on the counter-top, eating leftover potato salad out of a bowl, swinging her feet as Trevor paced the room. It was between meals, so no one was likely to interrupt them.

"What are we going to do?" he mumbled, rubbing his chin.

Gemma watched him. Back and forth and back and forth. He was going faster now, running his hand through his hair, which had grown considerably since they'd left Earth. "I don't know what to do."

"I like your hair this length," she said.

He stopped. "What?"

"Do you have a middle name?" she asked.

He stared at her, mentally trying to catch up. "Uh, yeah. It's Jordyn."

"Trevor Jordyn Lee, you need to calm down," she said, hopping off the counter, her bowl empty. "You're working yourself up."

"But what are we going to do?" he asked again. "My head's telling me we've got to stop. End it. Right here, right now."

"What do you *want* to do?" she asked, taking his hand and running her fingers across his knuckles.

"You're—you're distracting me," he said. "I'm trying to think." He lifted his other hand and tucked a loose strand of hair behind her ear.

"I can tell you right now, *I* don't want to end it," Gemma said. She stepped close on tiptoe, and he obligingly leaned down for her to kiss him.

"Now you're *really* being distracting," he murmured, his hands on her hips.

"Good."

He sighed. "We can't tell anyone. We … we just can't."

"Okay, okay." Gemma stole one more kiss and backed up a step, hands raised. "I won't tell."

"And no public displays of affection."

"Right. Just private ones."

He hesitated. "This is such a bad idea."

Gemma batted her eyelashes at him. "But it makes me so happy."

A slow smile spread across Trevor's face, and he pulled her closer. He decided right then and there that if she was happy, then that's all he needed out of life. He bent down for another kiss.

Gemma's happiness, her smile, was all he needed.

THE NEXT DAY, GEMMA WAS DOING THE WASHING UP FROM DINNER. The fact that the crew for this ship had grown by 50% meant the little dishwasher couldn't keep up, and the rest had to be washed by hand. It had been Zane's turn, but Gemma volunteered. She knew how much Zane hated doing dishes, and she wanted to feel useful.

Trevor poked his head in the door. "How are you doing?"

"Fine." She held up her hands. "My fingers are wrinkled. Whoever cooked used every pot and pan in the kitchen."

Trevor chuckled, coming into the room. He brushed her hip briefly as he squeezed by her, and she felt heat rush through her at his touch.

"What are you doing here?" she asked.

He picked up a towel and began to dry the dishes stacked precariously high on the rack. "Checking on you."

"You don't have to do that." She said that, but hoped he'd stay. "I'm fine. Don't worry about me."

"I know." He smiled at her. "I want to help."

"You're such a liar," she said, flinging soapy water at him. "No one wants to do dishes."

"Apparently, you do." He leaned down toward her and gave her a brief kiss. "And I do, if it means spending time with you."

That made her smile, and she dropped her gaze to the sink, face warm.

The door slid open, startling both of them. Dishes clattered in the sink as Gemma dropped one. Thankfully, it didn't break.

"Captain? What are you doing in here?" Dak asked, opening the fridge and pulling out a soda.

"Drying dishes," Trevor said.

Dak paused. "Does this mean you'll dry the dishes for me next time I'm assigned kitchen duty?"

Trevor snorted. "Not likely."

"Uh huh." Dak narrowed his eyes at them but left without saying anything else.

Gemma laughed. "You're making them suspicious, you know."

His smile fell. "Maybe I should go."

"Too late." Gemma grabbed his collar and pulled him toward her for a kiss. "You've already started, have to finish now."

He sighed. "Fine, but you owe me."

She grinned. "Whatever you say."

The door slid open again and he straightened fast enough to give her whiplash. Her heart hammered. This secrecy stuff was going to give her a heart attack.

One of the other crew entered without giving them a second look.

"Are the leftovers in the fridge?" he asked, opening it and pulling out a food container. "Never mind, I found it."

"Late snack?" Gemma asked.

"The prisoner is hungry," he said, scooping food onto a plate and putting it in the microwave.

They shared a look. "The one who works for the Conglomerate?" Trevor asked.

"That's the one."

"Who is it?" Gemma asked, not expecting to recognize the name.

"An Alexander Steele," the man said.

"What?" This time the dish Gemma dropped on the floor did break, making the men jump. Before anyone could stop her, she shot out the door.

TREVOR CAUGHT UP TO HER OUTSIDE THE BRIG. GEMMA TOOK DEEP breaths, rubbing her palms on her pant-legs. She turned toward him when he approached.

"It's Alex," she said, her eyes wet.

"I know." Trevor took her hand, ignoring the bored-looking guard sitting outside the door, playing with a tablet.

"I have to see him."

"I know." He gritted his teeth. He would give anything for Gemma *not* to see him. But he knew she would never stop until she got her way, so he looked at the guard. "Can we speak to him?"

The guard shrugged. "Fine with me. Don't give him anything or let him out." He pulled out a key card and opened the door for them.

The brig looked basically the same as the sleeping quarters, but larger, with a small table and chairs bolted to the center of the room. Trevor frowned. It looked like being sent to the brig was an upgrade. The security was laughable, the prisoner not even cuffed.

"Alex!" Gemma stopped just inside the door. "What happened?"

"Gemma! I'd heard they picked you up. I'm so glad you're

safe!" Alex came toward her with a smile, one of his arms still in a sling from its break in the mine, but his good arm outstretched. He stopped short when Trevor stepped in behind her. Alex's lip curled. "What's *it* doing here?"

"What did you do?" Gemma demanded. "You told the Conglomerate we were coming. And Dr. Sims said you told them ... about the captain."

"I swear, Gemma," Alex said, placing a hand over his heart, "they promised me they wouldn't hurt you."

She stiffened, her face pained. "It's—it's true?"

Trevor's hands tightened into fists, his nails digging into his palms. He wasn't sure if the adrenaline pumping into his system was because he was furious at being betrayed—or because Alex had hurt Gemma.

"Please, Gem—"

"I think you've said enough," Trevor said, a hand on Gemma's shoulder as he steered her toward the door. Her face pale, she numbly moved where he led her.

Alex's face contorted. "Get your hands off her."

Gemma went rigid, then ducked under Trevor's arm and whirled to face Alex.

"I can't believe you!" she shouted, her eyes wet, her hands fisted at her sides. "What kind of weak, slimy coward would do such a thing? You betrayed us! You betrayed Omni Authority. You betrayed my captain—who saved your *life*, by the way—and you betrayed—" Her voice cracked, then dropped to a whisper. "And you betrayed *me*."

"I was doing what I thought was best. That thing," Alex looked directly at Trevor, "Can't be allowed to live. They promised they wouldn't hurt you." He reached for her, but Trevor's steel grip caught his wrist.

"Don't. Touch. Her."

Gemma's eyes overflowed, and she ran from the room.

TREVOR KNOCKED ON GEMMA'S DOOR. "GEMMA? ARE YOU IN THERE?"

A sniffle, then a warbling, "Come in."

He slid open the door. "Are you alright?"

"Trevor—"

Then she was pressed against him, sobbing into his shirt. "I thought he was my friend."

"I know." He held her tight, careful not to crush her, because crushing someone to a pulp was exactly what he wanted to do to Alex.

They were still standing in the hallway, so he ushered her into her room, closing the door behind them. He sat her on the bed, kneeling in front of her.

"I mean, I felt betrayed when he left," she said between sniffles. "It hurt. But that was nothing compared to this. He's a good guy. Or he used to be. I thought he was."

"How good can he be if he left you?" Trevor said, taking her cold hand and rubbing it between his own warm ones. "What an idiot."

Two minutes. That's all he'd need; to be alone with Alex for two minutes to ensure that he never hurt Gemma again.

She leaned on Trevor's shoulder and choked back a sob. "He said leaving me was the biggest regret of his life."

"Well, now he'll have two regrets," Trevor said, his voice hard.

Gemma's lip quivered.

"I'm not helping, am I?" He raked a hand through his hair. "I'm sorry. I've only done this twice before, and I didn't do a very good job."

"It's fine," she said, leaning into him. "You being here is enough."

A knock on the door. Trevor jumped to his feet, his elbow thunking against the wall in the small space.

"Um, who is it?" Gemma called, her voice strangled.

"Gemma? You alright?" Zane asked through the door.

Trevor shot her a panicked look, shaking his head, but she closed her eyes and took a deep breath. "Come in."

Zane slid the door open. He took one look at Gemma's face and narrowed his eyes at Trevor. "What did you do?" he demanded.

"What? I—" Trevor backed up into the wall, hands raised. "I didn't do anything!"

"I went to see Alex," Gemma said, and the tears started up again.

"Aw, no." Zane sank down onto the bed next to her. "Don't cry. It's going to be alright."

Trevor looked between them and stepped toward the door.

"No." Gemma caught his hand. "Don't go. Stay."

Zane looked at their clasped hands.

"If you'd like," Trevor said, nervous under Zane's gaze.

Trevor was helpless; he couldn't say no to her.

Gemma gave them both a watery smile. "You are my two best friends," she said. "Besides Sandy, I mean."

Zane pointed at Trevor. "Him? Really? I didn't think he was anyone's friend."

Trevor arched an eyebrow. "Thanks for the endorsement, Zane."

"Heh, sorry." Zane gave him a sheepish smile.

"I'm glad you're both here for me," Gemma said, taking Zane's hand, her other hand still holding Trevor's.

"Come on." Zane pulled her to her feet as he stepped out the door. There was no room for all of them to stand. "Let's play a video game, huh? That might cheer you up. I finished the dishes already."

"Sounds great." Gemma dropped Zane's hand, but still held Trevor's. Zane's eyes narrowed again.

"After you." Zane let her go first. Gemma finally let go of Trevor.

The severe look Zane shot Trevor left no doubt that he suspected something. Trevor hoped he wasn't sweating through his shirt.

Zane booted up the console and passed out the controllers. Gemma sat between them on the couch.

"You know who was really worried about you guys?" Zane said. "You know, besides me. And everyone else."

"Who?" Gemma asked, rubbing away her tears.

"Chase."

Trevor raised an eyebrow. "Really?"

"Really. He took every watch-duty assignment Captain Brant would let him have, trying to find you."

"Aw, that's sweet," Gemma said.

"That's odd," Trevor said. "I didn't peg Chase for being the worrisome type. And he's hardly talked to us at all since we got back." He turned to Gemma. "Unless he's talked to you?"

She shook her head. "I've hardly seen him. Just ... usual Chase."

They chatted about unimportant things, trying to keep Gemma's mind off Alex. Trevor could tell when her thoughts wandered back to him again. Her eyes would become glassy, her lip quivering ever so slightly.

After sending a panicked look at Zane—who abruptly changed the topic—Trevor figured it out, and between him and Zane they soon had her chuckling. It felt good to see her smile.

Gemma still looked worn out, and it wasn't long before she yawned. Zane caught it too, and yawned.

"Gemma, you should get some sleep," Trevor said. He clapped Zane on the shoulder, handing him their controllers. "Why don't you turn in, Zane? I'll walk her back to her room."

Zane looked like he was about to argue, but said, "Will do."

"Thank you," Trevor murmured to him. "I didn't know what to do when she started crying."

Zane gave him a thumbs up. "No problemo, Captain. You'll have to tell me later who Alex is."

Trevor and Gemma left the room, and as soon as they were out of sight, she took his hand. "I really do feel better," she said.

"You sure?"

She shrugged. "Trying not to think about it, really. It's so— I'm sorry, I was so wrapped up in myself. How are you doing?"

Trevor smiled. "I'm fine."

They'd reached her room. He glanced around, then pulled her close and gave her a kiss. "Sweet dreams," he whispered.

"Holy cow!"

They turned to see Zane standing there, jaw hanging open. He pointed a finger at them. "I *knew* something was up."

"Stripped screws," Trevor said under his breath.

23

Gemma woke before the morning lights came on and went to find Zane. She and Trevor had sworn him to secrecy the night before, but she still wanted to talk to him, just the two of them.

He wasn't in his room, which was unusual for this time of day. She went to the common room.

Zane sat at the table, his tools and various parts spread out in front of him. The corners of his mouth turned down, he stared at nothing, his chin propped up between his hands.

She slid into the seat next to him. "What's the matter, Zane? Have you been up all night?"

"Huh?" At her touch on his shoulder, his gaze snapped up. "Oh, nothing—maybe something. Couldn't sleep."

"Well, what is it?"

"I ..." He rubbed the back of his neck. "I thought *I* was going to marry you," he blurted.

It took everything Gemma had to keep a straight face. "Aw, Zane, I'm sorry. But ... I am a little old for you."

"No, you're not," he said earnestly. "Give me a couple of years, and I'll be old enough to—"

She shook her head. "No, Zane. Maybe I'm not too old for you, but you're too young for me. I'm sorry, but I think of you more like a little brother. And ... well, I kinda have someone else now."

He blew out a breath. "Yeah, I know. Don't tell the captain, alright?"

Gemma smiled and hugged him. "It's our secret."

Zane looked down at the floor. "Gemma, I have a confession to make."

Besides the love confession you just made? She cocked her head to the side. "What is it?"

He took a deep breath. "I broke into your room last night."

She drew back. "What?"

"Don't be mad at me," Zane begged.

Her brows lowered, and she struggled to keep her voice even. She thought she could trust Zane. "Why?"

"You were screaming." His eyes were wide and frightened. "I heard you screaming, and then you wouldn't answer the door. But when I got inside, you were asleep.

Her anger evaporated. "Oh, Zane ..."

"You were thrashing around and talking nonsense," he said. "Are you sure you're fine?"

She patted his hand. "I'm sure I'll be okay. Thanks for your concern. And your honesty."

"Who's Trevor?"

She froze. "Uh—"

"You said it while you were sleeping. Was your nightmare about him?"

"Don't worry about it." She gave a small smile. "He's someone special to me who I worry about."

"Back on Earth?"

"I certainly hope to see him when I get back."

WHEN TREVOR ENTERED CAPTAIN BRANT'S ROOM, HE GAPED. YES, this ship was larger than his had been, but even so, Brant's living quarters were *huge* by ship standards. A queen bed, kitchenette, a pair of easy chairs in the corner, and a low table surrounded by cushions that could comfortably seat four. Trevor's room had been barely long enough to pace in.

The two of them sat on easy chairs. Trevor had briefed him on all that had happened, including the Conglomerate's attempt to revive the super soldier program.

Brant rubbed his chin. "Let me ask you a question."

Well, Trevor hadn't told him *all* of it. "Yes, sir?"

Brant leaned forward, elbows on his knees. "Our prisoner is making some pretty wild accusations about you. At first, I thought he was just trying to make trouble, but now that I know about the program resurrection, I'll be blunt. Are you a Tubie?"

Trevor raised his eyebrows, as if surprised, but sweat slid down his sides. He'd known it was coming. "That rumor was spread at the mining colony. It endangered my life, in fact."

"But are you?"

Trevor kept his face still, his gaze meeting Brant's. This tactic usually got him through a poker game. "It's impossible. I may be adopted and not know my parents, but I'm too old to be a Tubie."

Brant seemed to accept that and nodded, settling back into his chair. "And your mission at the factory was successful?"

"Yes, sir."

"I suppose if you had been a Tubie the bomb's poison would have killed you." Brant rubbed his chin again, and Trevor thought he might have gotten away with it. "Write up your report and send it directly to Director Hart. I'm sure he'll want to meet with you personally after we land. You've done good work."

"Thank you, sir."

The usual soft vibration of the engines intensified into a rumble that rattled the drinking glasses on Brant's shelves.

Both captains jumped to their feet.

"That felt like cargo release," Trevor said.

Brant tapped his communicator at the same time a channel opened.

"Bridge to captain! Our cargo just ejected."

"Full stop," Brant ordered as he and Trevor ran from the room, reaching the bridge in record time.

Sure enough, the giant cargo container floated free behind the ship. At least it hadn't broken open.

"What happened?" Brant demanded.

His security officer gave a helpless shrug. "I don't know. It was just me and Jim here, and neither one of us were active on a console at the time it ejected. The ship just—let go."

"Ships don't just let go," Brant said.

"I think it was a sensor error," said Jim, the ship's electrician. "But everything seems normal now."

This didn't feel right. Trevor had never heard of something like this happening while in space. There were too many safeguards for it to be automatic. He'd have to ask Zane about it.

"Hm." Brant considered this. "Do a full system diagnostic. How long will it take to retrieve the cargo?"

"Maybe an hour?" said the security officer. "I'll get Carl up here."

"Gemma can do it in ten minutes," Trevor interrupted. "Should I call her?"

The security officer scoffed, earning a hard look from Trevor, but Brant shook his head.

"No, thank you, we'll take care of it," Brant said.

"I could have Zane help with the diagnostic," Trevor offered.

"I don't need help from a *child*," Jim responded with a sneer.

Ooookay then. Trevor nodded to Brant and left the bridge.

He kept his voice low as he tapped the new communicator they'd issued him, which could connect him to his crew. "Captain to Zane."

"Here, Captain."

Trevor walked back toward his room. "Have you ever heard of cargo accidentally being dumped by a sensor error?"

"So that's what the rumbling was? No, I've never heard of that." Trevor could imagine Zane rubbing his chin. "I'm not sure how that would work. Want me to take a look?"

"Should I go to the bridge to help them reload the cargo?" Gemma asked over the link. They must be playing a game or watching a movie together.

"No, they want to keep the cleanup in-house," Trevor said. "But thank you both. Just—just keep your ears open." He terminated the connection.

Trevor woke up gasping.

"Gemma?" he called, but he was alone in his too-small room.

He stumbled out into the hallway, hitting his head on the top of the door frame and running into the wall.

A door slid open. "Captain?" Joe peered out at him. "What's the matter?"

"Where's Gemma? Is she okay?" he demanded, eyes bleary. He rubbed his head where he'd hit it and winced. That would leave a bruise.

"I'm sure she's asleep in her room, Captain." Joe took his shoulders as Trevor lurched toward her door. "Let her be. She needs the sleep."

"But how do I know she's alright?"

"Come on, let's get a cup of coffee." Joe steered him to the common room.

Joe pushed him into a chair, then made coffee. Trevor held the hot cup in his shaking hands.

"What happened?" Joe asked, sitting across from him.

"The ship," Trevor said. "The ship exploded, and she … she was on it." He covered his eyes.

"Captain?" Charlie entered the room. Joe must have called him. Charlie sat beside him, his hand on Trevor's shoulder. "Tell me about it."

"I was meeting Gemma on the ship, and it—it exploded. There was fire everywhere. I tried to run in to help her, but it was too hot." Trevor's voice cracked.

"What happened next?" Charlie's gentle voice guided him through his swirling thoughts. At some point, Joe had slipped out the door.

"Then … then she—" Trevor collapsed back into the chair with a gasp, nearly dropping his cup of coffee. He remembered. "She wasn't on the ship. She's alright. She's alright."

Charlie patted his back. "Trevor …"

Trevor choked down a sob of relief. She was fine. "Where is she? Can I see her?"

"You'll see her in the morning," Charlie assured him. "Let's get you back to bed."

Before the morning lights came on, Trevor paced the hall in front of Gemma's room. The second the bulbs illuminated, he knocked on the door.

It opened and she blinked up at him with sleepy eyes. "Huh? Trev—Captain?"

He wrapped his arms around her and breathed her in. "I'm so glad you're alright." He kissed the top of her head, then her cheek.

"Wha—"

His kisses reached her mouth, and she pulled him into her room.

"Trevor, what's wrong?" she asked when she'd slid the door closed.

"Nothing." He held her again and sighed, nuzzling her neck. "Nothing's wrong. You're alright and nothing's wrong."

"That tickles." She wrapped her arms around him. "Everything is fine. Don't worry, I'm here."

An alarm blared and they jumped. A flashing red light accompanied the steady beeping.

"Wow, I'm wrong already. Something is most definitely not fine," Gemma said.

"It's the proximity sensor." Trevor slammed open the door but stopped in the hall when a siren began to wail. Then another alarm that resembled a foghorn went off.

A recorded woman's voice broke through the noise. "All personnel, to the life pods. Evacuate the ship. I repeat, evacuate the ship."

Another voice began to play over it. "All personnel, to battle stations. All personnel, to battle stations."

The sheer wall of noise drove Trevor to his knees, hands over his ears. Gemma was yelling something, her hand gripping his shoulder. He screwed his eyes shut; his teeth clenched against the stabbing in his skull.

The noise stopped.

"Belay that order!" Brant's voice yelled over the intercom. "Do *not* eject life pods. False alarm!"

"More like *lots* of false alarms," Gemma muttered, tugging Trevor's arm until he climbed to his feet. He rubbed his temples, his ears still ringing.

He twitched as another alarm chirped once, then switched off again.

Two distinct pulses rattled the floor under Trevor's feet. Two life pods had been ejected.

"Stay here," he ordered Gemma, running to the bridge.

Gemma's footfalls tapped behind him. Was she ever going to listen to him?

The rumble of the engines silenced as the intercom clicked on. "Attention all crew," said Brant. "We've had a serious malfunction in our sensors. We have two life pods to retrieve, and it will take several hours to recalibrate the system. We are not, I repeat, *not* in danger."

They reached the ladder to the bridge as Brant slid down.

"What happened?" Trevor asked.

Brant sighed, his mouth a tight line. "We're not sure. Every sensor in the ship went off, and then offline."

"I'll get Zane up here to help," Trevor said.

"We have it under control," Brant assured him.

"Zane is the best there is!" Gemma's fist went to her hip. "You need to stop looking down on him and use him."

"Thank you, Ms. Stone—" Brant began.

"It wouldn't hurt to have a second pair of eyes," Trevor added, a little more diplomatic. Brant needed Zane and didn't know it.

Brant rubbed his chin. "Alright. Call him up here. In the meantime, Ms. Stone, will you help retrieve the life pods?"

"Yes, sir."

Trevor tapped his communicator. "Zane to the bridge."

Trevor slid open the sickbay door and leaned in. "You okay, Charlie?"

Charlie waved him in. "I'm fine, I'm fine. Not the first time I've been accidentally launched into space. I'm glad you're here. I've been meaning to speak with you."

The other doctor was absent, so Trevor leaned back on the exam table. "Everything okay? Is Gemma okay?"

Charlie's eyes narrowed. "So, you call her Gemma now?"

Trevor shrugged, not seeing the problem.

"Trevor ... to be honest—well, I'm concerned."

Trevor raised his eyebrows. "What's wrong?"

"I'm concerned with your actions and conduct involving Gemma," Charlie said.

Trevor crossed his arms, not looking at Charlie. Did Charlie know? "What exactly is concerning you?"

"I think you're becoming too close to her," Charlie said.

Trevor let out a controlled breath. Charlie didn't know. It would be best to keep it that way.

"You've been through a traumatic experience together, so it makes sense to feel an attachment to her," Charlie continued. "But if it goes too far and gets too serious, it will only cause you heartache later."

"How?" Trevor demanded. His calm exterior was cracking,

but he was so sick and tired of hearing this, he didn't care. "How, Charlie? You think she's going to break my heart if we ... if we ..." He searched for the word. " ... get ... romantically ... involved?"

Charlie sighed, but his voice sharpened. "You know it's wrong and inappropriate and irresponsible. You cannot—"

"Stop telling me what I can and can't do," Trevor snapped.

Charlie paused, his voice calmer. "Think about her needs. What does she want out of life? Her sister is getting married, right? Settling down? What would happen to you if she wanted that? What if she wants children?"

Trevor went very still, except for his heart, which thudded so loud he was sure Charlie could hear it.

Charlie laid a hand on his shoulder. "You can never have a family."

Trevor looked away. "I know."

"You can never—"

"I know!" Trevor rubbed his face, then, softer, said, "I know."

"Keep her at a distance," Charlie said, a warning tone in his voice. "Keep it professional. I know you care for her, but you can't let that get in the way of logical decision-making."

"Right." Logical. He was a captain. He had to be logical.

"Zane to Captain," his communicator chirped.

"Go ahead Zane."

"Uh, can I talk to you a minute?"

THEY MET AT ZANE'S ROOM.

"What's going on, Zane?" Trevor asked.

"Shh, in here." Zane dragged Trevor into his room, shutting

the door behind him. He turned to Trevor. "I think someone is sabotaging the ship."

Trevor frowned, arms crossed. "Did you tell Brant?"

"I tried, but his guys kept cutting me off." Zane gave a frustrated huff. "They said they couldn't explain it, just a malfunction of the router. But I traced an unknown login to a computer in an airlock. This happened before the cargo was ejected. I think someone uploaded something, then erased their tracks."

Hmm. This cast a new light on the sensor failures, too. "What did they upload?"

Zane shrugged. "It's hard to say. It could be a virus designed to attack different systems at different times. It could be a back door that would allow someone to access the system invisibly and change whatever they wanted, whenever they wanted. I'd need a day to run a full diagnostic. But I'm certain someone on this ship did this on purpose."

"That's a pretty serious accusation, Zane." But it made sense.

"But you believe me, right, Captain?" Zane's eyes pleaded. The poor kid was being pushed aside and discounted by Brant's 'experts.'

"Of course I do," Trevor assured him. How to explain it to Brant, though? "Do you have any solid proof?"

Zane shook his head. "Nothing. They wiped their tracks pretty good, but not perfectly. I could see the slightest indication that anything had been changed." He crossed his arms and looked at the floor, muttering, "Not that they'd listen to me, anyway."

Trevor laid a hand on Zane's shoulder. "Zane, you are far more qualified than they are. You've done good work."

Zane smiled, his confidence trickling back in. "I'll keep looking."

"Keep me posted."

KEEP IT PROFESSIONAL ... YOU CAN NEVER HAVE A FAMILY.

Trevor mulled over Charlie's words, hands shoved into his pockets, on his way to the common room. Her humming announced her even before she turned the corner.

"Gemma." He jogged over to her. "We should talk."

As she turned and looked up at him, her lips slightly parted, the corners of her mouth turning in a smile, he realized he didn't want to talk. Charlie was wrong. And—and even if he wasn't, it would never get that far.

And no one had to know about the two of them.

"What is it?" she asked, with a slight tilt of her head.

No one was around, and the common room was empty. He pulled her inside, then leaned down and kissed her.

"Hi, Gemma!" Zane called, leaning into the room from the hallway.

Trevor's voice lowered to its most dangerous. "Keep walking, Zane."

"Bye, Gemma!" Zane disappeared from the doorway.

Trevor grabbed her hands and pulled her into the galley.

"Captain, what—?"

He closed the door and turned to her. "We can't do this."

"Do what?"

He gestured between them. "*This.*"

She planted her fists on her hips. "Uh, *you* kissed *me.*"

"I know, I know! I'm sorry. I shouldn't have." He shook his head. "But this can't go on. We have to stop."

Gemma crossed her arms, hurt in her eyes. "Why?"

"I've been thinking a lot about this." He paced. "It's ... it's not appropriate, and—" He swallowed. "I can't give you what you want, what you need," he said in a rush. "I don't have a house; I can't have a family. I live in space; there's no stability in my life. I couldn't get a job on Earth if I wanted to—"

She reached out and touched his arm, stopping him. "I don't want those things."

He blinked. "You don't?"

"No."

"Oh." Trevor's brow furrowed. "But Charlie said ... and Sandy—"

"Sandy and I want different things," she said. "Why else would I leave Earth and go into space?"

He paused. "What kinds of things do you want?"

"What I want," she said, stepping closer to him, only inches away, her low voice raising a shiver through him, "is adventure. And you have adventure written all over you."

Then she looked up at him with those eyes, and he groaned. "Why can't I say no to you?"

She grinned. "Because you love me."

They kissed.

Trevor winced. "Charlie is going to kill me."

"Keeping this a secret is a stupid idea," Gemma said, her thumb tracing his jawline. "Like, a really, really stupid idea. You have to tell everyone."

He looked away. "I don't know ..."

She leveled her gaze at him. "Are you ashamed of me?"

He took a step back. "What? No!"

"Do you want to be with me?"

He took her hands and pulled her into a hug. "Yes," he said into her hair.

She pushed him a few inches away and looked up at him. "I'm not going to be someone's secret." Gemma raised her chin. "You have to tell them. No more sneaking around."

What would Charlie say? What would everyone say? Wouldn't keeping it a secret be easier?

He rubbed the back of his neck. It *was* unfair to her. "You're right," he said after a minute. "You're right, you're right."

She grinned. "Say what? I didn't hear you. What am I?"

Trevor laughed, his hands on her hips as she leaned into him. "You're right. I'll tell them. Later."

"Oh, no." She pushed him away. "You should tell them *now*."

He hesitated. "Right." He stole one more kiss before stepping out the door. "I'll call a crew meeting."

The crew of the *Michal* stayed in the common room after dinner was over and cleaned up. Trevor sat on the couch, his leg bouncing and his hands sweaty. When they were alone—just him and his crew—he stood.

Trevor took a deep breath, taking a moment to make eye contact with every single crew member. "It's been a rough couple of weeks for all of us. But I called you here because, as your captain—and your friend—I feel obligated to tell you something."

"Captain." Chase walked over and laid a hand on Trevor's shoulder. "We know."

"You … know." Trevor hesitated. "Know what, exactly?" He looked at Zane, who raised his eyebrows.

"I told them," Charlie said. "I couldn't exactly keep it a secret, not when the entire colony knew."

His stomach plummeted, and his body went cold. What they meant had nothing to do with Gemma.

They *knew*. About him. About … all of it.

Gemma gave a soft gasp behind him as she realized it, too.

"And you're still—" Mouth dry, he cleared his throat. "Are you going to turn me in?" he asked, his voice scratchy.

"No, sir," Chase said.

"You're our captain," Joe said.

They know. Trevor balled his hands into fists to keep them from shaking. It didn't help. *They know they know they know they know—*

"I should have figured it out sooner," Chase said.

"Yeah, right," Zane said, rolling his eyes.

"How could you suspect someone of that?" Joe said. "It's more far-out than aliens."

"All the signs were there." Chase shrugged. "I just didn't add them up."

Gemma stepped toward Trevor. "Captain, are you okay?"

He bolted out of the room as she called after him and made it to the toilet in time before he threw up. He kicked the door shut behind him. *They know they know they know …*

That secret, that weight he'd always carried around with him, afraid to bring it to light. All his life, he'd hidden it, and now it had been shoved into the spotlight—blinding him. Everyone knew. Everyone he cared about knew.

Trevor squeezed his eyes shut. He had to get off this ship. If he reached Earth, he would be executed.

A knock on the door. "Captain?" Charlie sounded concerned.

Trevor's stomach heaved again, but nothing came up this time. He sank to the floor, wiping a shaking hand across his forehead.

But they … they said they weren't going to turn him in. Their faces—Joe's had been concerned. Zane was openly curious. Chase's had been unreadable, which was normal, but so had Dak's, which wasn't normal. And Charlie …

Charlie had betrayed him.

"How could you tell them?" Trevor said, his voice breaking.

"Captain, I had to. The entire colony knew. It was better for them to hear it from me. They deserved to know anyway. They're your crew." A pause. "Gemma knows too, right?"

Trevor groaned. He couldn't have this conversation right now.

"How did she react when she found out?" Charlie asked.

"Her reaction was that she saved my life." Trevor's eyes welled up, and he rubbed it away. *They know. They know, but they ... they don't hate me.* Gemma didn't either.

Gemma.

Trevor lurched to his feet. "Gemma! Is she alright?" He'd promised to tell them, and he hadn't gone through with it. Would she be angry?

"Why wouldn't she be alright?" Charlie asked.

"Captain?" her voice called.

"I said I would handle this," Charlie's voice said, annoyed.

"Well, I'm helping," Gemma said outside the bathroom door. Trevor imagined her raising her chin. "Don't even think about trying to get rid of me."

Trevor rinsed out his mouth and checked himself in the mirror—a little pale, but she'd seen him worse—and opened the door.

"Gemma, I'm sorry I didn't—"

"No." She patted his arm. "This was more important."

Charlie looked back and forth between them, then at Gemma's hand on Trevor's arm. He shook his head.

He knows.

Now, everyone knew everything.

But, instead of Trevor's stomach tightening, his shoulders unclenched. He felt ... lighter. He took a deep breath.

Charlie didn't look lighter, though. Charlie had taken a step back, like Trevor had slapped him.

"Charlie, I was going to tell you—"

"But you didn't." Charlie's mouth was a tight line.

"Just now at the crew meeting—"

"You should have told me before the meeting. You should have told me when we … had that discussion. Earlier."

Trevor hung his head. "You're right. I'm sorry."

"For what?" Gemma demanded. She stepped between them. "Charlie, I love you, but you've got to back up. Trevor is a grown man, and he doesn't answer to you."

Charlie's eyebrows went up. "You told her your name?"

"She …" Trevor's hands settled on her shoulders. "She earned it."

"That doesn't change the upset this dynamic will cause," Charlie said. "You have to work together. You'll see her every day."

"I don't see a downside to that," Trevor said.

"What if you have a fight?" Charlie asked.

Gemma waved that away. "We were already having fights. It's something that happens to everyone in close quarters. We're professionals, we won't let that get in the way of our working relationship."

Charlie eyed them. "As I recall, a fight between you two contributed to the crash."

Gemma tensed under Trevor's hands.

"We've learned from our mistakes," Trevor said. "Nothing like that is ever going to happen again."

Charlie threw up his hands. "She's going to be a horrible distraction."

Trevor smirked. "She always has been."

She swatted his arm. "Hey!"

"I cannot condone this," Charlie warned.

Trevor had known Charlie his whole life. Charlie had helped raise him, protected him. Was a friend when he needed one. His opinion mattered to Trevor.

Charlie was wrong this time.

"I'm not asking you to," Trevor said.

Charlie's face contorted. Trevor had never seen the thunderous anger that crossed his face.

Charlie turned and stormed off down the hall, the opposite way of the common room.

Trevor swallowed hard. He wanted to call him back so he could apologize.

He looked at Gemma. *No.* He wasn't sorry. It was time for him to stop letting Charlie have a say in his life decisions.

"Let's go back in," Gemma said.

Trevor felt ill again. "Can't I tell them later? One announcement seems like enough for today."

Gemma pulled him down the hallway. "Get it over with. Do it quickly. Like a Band-Aid."

She gave him a shove, and Trevor stumbled back into the common room. The conversation withered, all eyes turning to him.

"Right," he said. He swallowed hard, choked with emotion. "Thank you for ... your support ... and—I'm not sure what to say—I'm ... honored. By your loyalty, I mean—that's not really the reason I called you here."

A pause.

"Then what is it?" Joe asked.

Trevor gave Gemma a nervous glance. She nodded for him to continue.

Trevor avoided looking at anyone. "Gemma and I—well, see, we went through a lot. Together. And—well ... um."

Gemma stepped close to him, slipping her hand into his. "We're in a relationship," she finished.

Silence.

Joe laughed. "Dak! You owe me twenty bucks!"

Dak frowned. "Wait, even knowing he's—"

Gemma silenced him with the force of her glare. "Yep."

Dak raised his hands. "As you say."

24

The next day, they landed on the port planet for refueling.

"—and I expect everyone to stay out of trouble while we're in port," Captain Brant said. "We leave in nineteen hours. Be back on board no later than 0900." He eyed them. "Those who are late will be left behind."

The way he said it, Gemma didn't doubt he was serious.

He dismissed them from the ship, and both crews clattered down the ramp to the landing platform—except Chase, who insisted he stay with the ship. Trevor lagged behind, talking to Brant.

Zane dawdled, waiting for Gemma. She grimaced as the thick, sticky outside air hit her in the face. It hadn't been this humid last time.

"Are you allowed off the ship?" he asked.

"I don't know yet," she said. She and Trevor hadn't discussed it. She had hoped they could go somewhere together. "The captain—"

At that moment, Trevor came up behind her and draped an arm over her shoulders. He gestured to the stairs. "Shall we?"

Gemma looked him up and down. "Where did you get a captain's shirt?"

"Captain?" Zane interrupted, shifting his weight. "Could I get a moment with you?"

"I'll meet you at the bottom of the stairs," Gemma offered.

"Actually, I think you should know, too," Trevor said. "Is that okay with you, Zane?"

"Know what?" she asked.

"Someone installed a backdoor into the ship's systems," Zane said in a rush.

Trevor nodded. "Explain what that means."

"It means someone can log into a computer and access all systems at any time without being detected," Zane said.

"So, you're sure it's a backdoor and not a virus?" Trevor asked.

"I'm positive."

"But how can we stop it?" Gemma asked.

"I'd have to monitor the system to catch them in the act," Zane said.

Trevor nodded. "I'll consult with Brant." He turned to Gemma. "Wait just a few more minutes?"

"No problem," Gemma said.

He strode back up the ramp.

"Are they listening to you any better?" Gemma asked Zane.

Zane scoffed. "Not much."

"I guess that's what happens when you're a young genius, right?" she said with a smile.

"It ticks me off," he said through his teeth. "It's going to get someone killed."

Gemma's smile dropped. "Sorry. You're right. I tried to make light of something serious. Forgive me?"

His brow smoothed as he met her eyes. "I can't ever be mad at you."

Gemma squeezed his shoulder. "You do brilliant work. They wouldn't know a capacitor from a resistor if they exploded in their faces."

Zane chuckled. "Those are the only two electrical components you know the names of, huh?"

"Um, yes." She let out a slow sigh of relief as a smile flickered across his face. Zane deserved to always smile.

Trevor joined them again.

"What did he say?" Zane asked.

"Uh." Trevor rubbed the back of his neck. "He said they'd look into it."

The storm cloud crossed Zane's face again, but this time Gemma wasn't sure how to bring back the sun.

They descended the stairs to the street. Zane peeled off when they reached the bottom. Brant's crew had already disappeared into the crowd. Trevor took Gemma's hand and pulled her after him. They walked down the sidewalk, the crowd parting before them. Usually, she'd have to shuffle around people, but a tall boyfriend had its advantages.

"Where are we going?" Gemma asked. He must have borrowed the captain's uniform shirt from Brant. The sleeves were short on him, the chest a little too tight.

He smiled. "Somewhere I think you'll like."

He must have been excited because he was walking even faster than usual.

"Could we slow down?" Gemma asked, winded from trying to keep up. "I'm not as fast as you."

"Sorry." He slowed his steps to match hers.

"Wait, wait." She stopped him and rolled up his sleeve. "We have to fix this. You look a little silly with three-quarter length sleeves."

He gave a rueful smile. "I've never had anyone care about how I looked before." He paused as she rolled up the other sleeve. "Maybe that's not true. *Everyone* seems to care when I don't dress my rank. I meant—"

"You meant what?" she asked, slipping her hand into his.

"I've never ... had someone I wanted to look nice for."

She smiled, a little heat rising in her cheeks.

They resumed walking. If she hadn't known they'd landed on an alien planet, she would have sworn the street looked and sounded like any bustling city on Earth. She inched closer to Trevor at a busy intersection, not really used to being surrounded by so many people as they waited for the light to change. His grip tightened; he, too, was out of his comfort zone.

They turned down a side street and the crowd thinned, and they descended the stairs to the subway.

The glaring lights in the jerky subway car made her squint, but after only a short ride, Trevor led her out. She looked around for the steps to the street level, but he instead brought her to a secluded doorway surrounded by brick, a sleek sign out front declaring it the 'Captain's Club.'

"What is this place?" she asked.

"It's a restaurant-slash-lounge-slash-hotel that caters to captains," he said, holding the door open for her.

"But I'm not a captain," she said. "Am I allowed in?"

Trevor smiled. "You're my guest."

They ascended a carpeted staircase before they reached the hostess, who asked if they had a reservation. Gemma took Trevor's arm as they were led to a table. Soft music played in the background, and it took her a moment to adjust to the soft lighting provided by overhead chandeliers, the gentle murmur of conversations of other diners, and *holy cow, what is that amazing smell?*

Gemma's stomach grumbled, but she forgot all about it when they turned the corner.

She stood still and gasped.

A view of the jungle filled the entire glass wall, their table directly in front of it. Golden light from the sunset filtered down through the canopy. Exotic wildflowers and blue-leafed plants stretched upward for a taste. A yellow feathered creature flitted past.

"It's beautiful," she whispered. And here she'd forgotten the camera.

"You like it?" Trevor asked as they took their seats. "I know how much you wanted to see the planet. What we're looking at is part of a nature preserve."

"It's fantastic." Gemma smiled, not taking her eyes off the view. She almost had tears. Humans hadn't bulldozed it all, but kept a portion of the planet natural. She stared a long time, etching every detail into her mind.

"The food's good too." He tapped the menu she forgot she held. She laughed and ordered.

Night fell, and soon glowing insects and flashing eyes lit the jungle.

Gemma turned to him. "This is the coolest thing I have ever seen." She touched his hand. "Thank you."

He caught her fingers in his. "My pleasure."

They ate their dinner in silence, content to be together and watch the activity outside.

After a leisurely dinner—including a chocolatey dessert to die for—they rode the jarring subway back and stepped out into the nighttime streets.

Their fingers interlaced; they walked along the sidewalk lit with streetlights. The traffic had lessened, as had the crowd.

They made it back to the ship, a smile still on Gemma's lips.

"Tired?" Trevor asked her, his own smile pleased.

"Mm hmm." She sighed, content and more relaxed than she'd been in weeks.

He walked her to her room and pulled her close. "Did you have a nice time?"

"This was the best date I've ever had," Gemma said.

He kissed her forehead, then her mouth. "Sweet dreams," he whispered against her lips, unable to keep from smiling.

"Good night."

She lingered, her hand in his, until they let go and she entered her room.

Gemma flopped onto her bed, still smiling, and closed her eyes.

TREVOR STOOD WITH BRANT OUTSIDE THE SHIP THE NEXT MORNING, shaking his head as teams in orange jumpsuits ran around the platform, plugging hoses into the ship. "How could this happen?"

Brant shrugged. "Sometime early this morning, an alarm for contaminated water flashed on all screens on the bridge. The maintenance team here tested and confirmed that our water is not good. It wasn't hard to find the leak and patch it ..."

Trevor ran a hand through his hair. "But now you have to flush and sanitize the entire system before we can put any water back in."

Brant nodded, squinting in the sunlight as he looked at the clouds. "I'm starting to think someone wants to stop us from getting back to Earth."

Trevor's mouth formed a grim line. "Or at least slow us down." The Conglomerate ship was still out there somewhere. He reminded Brant about what Zane had found running his own diagnostics.

"We'll sort this out," Brant promised. "As for another matter, would you meet me in my quarters? There's something we need to discuss."

"Uh, yes, sir." Trevor swallowed hard as Brant walked away. Was this another Tubie discussion? Trevor had been able to keep the secret hidden for years because of his dad and Charlie—and because no one else knew. But now—now ...

Trevor took a couple of extra minutes to touch base with everyone in his crew over the communicator. All were onboard and well.

He resisted the urge to check on Gemma personally. She sounded fine on the communicator ... and he had to get over to Brant's for the mystery discussion.

Trevor blew out a breath and wiped his hands against his thighs. Everything was fine. Nothing to worry about. He knocked on Captain Brant's door.

"Captain, thank you for meeting with me," Captain Brant said.

Trevor nodded, entering the room. "Anytime. What did you want to see me about?"

"Here, sit, sit."

Trevor wanted to shake him, *tell me why you called me.* Instead, he awkwardly sat on a cushion at the low table in Brant's room. His bent knees didn't fit below the tabletop, but when he straightened his legs, his feet stuck out the other side.

"Would you like something to drink?" Brant offered, not appearing to notice Trevor's discomfort.

"No, thanks, I'm fine."

"Coffee?" Brant poured himself a cup.

"No, thanks. What's this about?"

Brant smiled and sat at the table, his knees on the cushion. *That's* the trick to it. "It's about your relationship with Ms. Stone."

Trevor went cold, and he swallowed hard. He'd scoured Omni Authority's code of conduct but hadn't found anything forbidding ... relationships.

"What's wrong?" Trevor blurted.

Brant raised his eyebrows. "Nothing, as far as I know. But I am under the impression that this is new territory for you, so I wanted to lay down some rules."

Trevor nodded for him to continue.

"To keep things professional," Brant said, "I have a no-PDA policy. You are to treat each other as crewmen first, anything else second."

"PDA?" Trevor repeated.

"Public displays of affection. In public areas—on this ship—you need to keep your hands off each other. Do you understand?"

Trevor let out the breath he'd been holding. "Yes, sir. Absolutely. I agree with that."

"I understand how difficult it is," Brant said. "My wife and I follow the same policy."

"Your ... wife?"

"Yes. Didn't you know? My wife is the ship's doctor." Brant laughed at Trevor's confused expression. "No, no. Not Dr. Neilson. He's temporarily filling in. My wife is on Earth, taking care of her sick mother."

"Oh." Trevor processed that. "May I ask you something ... personal ... sir?"

"Certainly."

"How do you keep from fighting?" Trevor asked. "And seeing each other every day, is that a problem?"

Brant leaned toward him. "You know, I was asked exactly that when I hired her. We'd gotten married while she was still in med school, and when she finished her residency, I put her on my crew. The director asked me if I was sure I wanted to do that. 'You'll see her all day, every day. You won't be able to get away from her if you need a break,' he said."

Trevor's attention was riveted on Brant. "What did you say?"

Brant smiled. "I told him I *liked* my wife. And I have never regretted it. We love working together. And you're right, sometimes we fight, but we never let it get in the way of the mission."

Trevor rubbed his chin. Charlie had been wrong. It was possible. "Thank you, sir. You really ... put this in perspective for me."

"Wonderful." Brant stood and offered him a hand. Trevor struggled to get his legs out from under the table, and Brant pulled him upright. "Now, how about that cup of coffee?"

"Yes, sir."

GEMMA CROSSED HER ARMS AND POUTED WHEN TREVOR CAME TO HER room to tell her about the no PDA policy. It was probably for the best. They'd been getting weird looks from everyone, and she was uncomfortable being the center of—

She blinked as Trevor's hand cupped her cheek, and he pressed his mouth against hers in a kiss.

"Don't make that face," he murmured. "I can't resist that face."

"What? You mean this face?" She pushed her lower lip forward in a mock-pout.

He laughed and kissed her again. "Yes, that face."

She gave him a wicked grin. "I'll have to remember that."

The only place they could be alone was in their rooms, so they were in her room. They sat on the bed, Trevor leaning against the wall with his legs stretched out the mattress—the room wasn't long enough for him to fully stretch out in any direction—Gemma's head on his chest, her eyes sleepy. She'd been taking a lot of naps since they'd gotten back. Charlie had told her it would take a while for her body to heal.

"What are you doing?" she asked with a yawn.

"Nothing," Trevor said, his eyes traveling across the page of the tablet he held in his other hand. "Reading."

"What are you reading?"

"Proofreading my report before I send it," he said.

"Not poems?"

"Not this time."

"Have you written anything lately?" Gemma asked, tracing lazy circles on his shirt. "Any new songs?"

A pause. "Maybe."

She looked up at him, but his eyes were still on the screen. "Can I read them?"

"No."

"Why not?" Gemma pouted, but he wasn't looking at her. She gasped. "Are they about me?"

"No," he said too quickly, his face reddening. He put down the tablet.

Gemma squealed. "Aw! You wrote a song about me! Please let me read it? Where's your notebook?"

She patted his pockets, and he pushed her away.

"Get off me!" He laughed.

"So, am I your girlfriend?"

Trevor blinked. "I've never had a girlfriend before. I never thought I would."

Gemma laughed. "Well, you do now." She kissed him, then sighed. "I need a nap."

"Go ahead," he said. "I'll be right here when you wake up."

GEMMA AWOKE WITH HER HEAD ON TREVOR'S LAP. HE SLEPT STILL sitting up on her bed with his back against the wall. She watched him for a moment, a small smile playing around her mouth. After giving his cheek a gentle kiss, she got up and left the room. She had an errand to run on a lower level.

"Can I speak to the prisoner?" Gemma asked the guard. She wanted to talk to Alex alone. The guard shrugged and let her through.

"Gemma." Alex had heavy bags under his eyes, his skin pale, his hair limp. He sat on his bed, his back propped up against the wall, not unlike Trevor's position upstairs. No smile for her this time. "To what do I owe the pleasure?"

The sight of him constricted her throat, but she squared her shoulders. "I've come to ask you a favor."

He laughed, but it was hollow. "What could I possibly do for you? I'm stuck in here."

Gemma braced herself. "I wanted to ask you to keep the captain's secret."

Alex's lip curled. "No."

"But Alex!" She clasped her hands under her chin. "You'll ruin his life. Please."

"Like he ruined mine?" Alex demanded.

Gemma dropped her hands, her voice hardening. "You did that all on your own."

"Tell me something." Alex stood and pointed a finger at her. "Are you—are you *with* him?"

She held her chin up. "Yes."

He cringed. "That's disgusting. I can't believe you would—"

"Believe it," she snapped.

Alex met her gaze, his jaw tight. "Then the answer is, never."

Gemma swallowed, her fading hope sapping her of the strength she had a minute ago. "Please," she begged, her voice quiet. "Please don't tell anyone about him."

Alex spoke through gritted teeth. "As long as you're with *it*, I will tell every soul I ever meet that secret."

Hot fury raced through her, and her fists clenched.

Trevor woke to a chirp. "Zane to Captain."

He rubbed the sleep off his face. When had Gemma left? "What is it, Zane?"

"Finally, you answered," Zane said, out of breath, speaking a mile a minute. "You gotta get to sickbay. Now. I mean, right now. Charlie wants you there now and I don't know what happened or why there's so much blood—"

"Hey, slow down." Trevor said. "What's the matter?"

"It's Gemma," Zane said. "She's in sickbay."

Trevor was already out the door and climbing up the nearest ladder.

He reached the sickbay door just as Gemma stepped out.

"Gemma! What happened?" he demanded, zeroing in on her bandaged hand and sleeve soaked in blood pressed to her side. "Are you hurt?"

"She'll be fine," Charlie said from behind her.

"What happened?" Trevor said again. "What happened to your hand? Are you alright? Can you still fly? Are you—"

"Trevor," she said, "calm down. You're freaking out."

Trevor took a deep breath. Charlie watched him out of the corner of his eye, and Trevor knew his thoughts. Getting over-emotional again.

"What happened?" Trevor asked, his voice calm.

Zane stopped beside him, his shoes giving off a squeak. "Did I miss anything?"

"I punched Alex in the face," Gemma said, a little dazed.

"It was a good hit too," Charlie said. "Got blood everywhere."

"Whoo! Way to go, girl," Zane said, holding out a hand. Gemma bumped fists with him, smiling, but Trevor could see the hurt in her eyes.

Trevor gently took her bandaged hand in his. "Why?"

She sighed and looked away. "Alex's going to tell. He's going to tell everyone."

Trevor swallowed hard, fighting down the rising nausea. He had known it was coming. "I know."

"What are we going to do?" Zane asked.

"We have to stop him," Gemma said. "We're going to stop him. Maybe—"

"We can't." Trevor tucked a lock of hair behind her ear as she looked up at him with wide eyes. "We can't stop him."

Charlie shook his head. "There's nothing we can do."

Gemma's face fell. "But—"

"We'll have to see how it plays out," Trevor said, holding

both her hands. "Right now, it's my word against his. We'll get through this."

"But if they want a blood test—"

"Gemma." Trevor's calm voice cut her off. He didn't feel the self-disgust that had always crushed him before, nor the crippling fear. Instead ...

It was her. Her acceptance of him, genetically modified or not, made him feel whole. He smiled. "With you, I feel like I can face anything."

She gave his hands a squeeze, then winced at the new bruise. "I'm with you."

"We all are, Captain," Charlie said, his hand on Trevor's shoulder.

Zane grabbed the other shoulder and gave it a shake. "We've got your back."

"Captain." Brant strode down the hallway toward them. Trevor dropped Gemma's hand. "Ms. Stone. A word?"

After dismissing Zane and Charlie, Brant faced them both. His face was stern, but not angry like Trevor had expected.

"Ms. Stone. What happened?" Brant asked.

Trevor stepped in front of Gemma. "Sir—"

"I'm asking Ms. Stone."

Gemma touched Trevor's shoulder, and he reluctantly moved aside. "Sir, it was entirely my fault," she said. "I'm prepared for whatever punishment you deem appropriate."

Brant sighed and rubbed the bridge of his nose. "I understand you and Mr. Steele have a history."

"Yes, sir."

"Why did you assault him?"

Gemma stayed silent; her lips pressed together. Brant gave her a hard look, but she said nothing. She held Brant's gaze without looking away.

Trevor shifted his weight, wanting to say something but knowing he'd only make it worse.

He didn't deserve her. For the first time, he hadn't thought he was unworthy because he was a clone. Rather, it was because no man deserved her unwavering loyalty.

His heart swelled, and he almost gasped at the lightness of it. He'd do everything in his power to earn that love.

"Usually, I'd confine you to quarters for the remainder of the trip for such behavior," Brant said. "But ... I understand you've been through an ordeal. I have read Captain Lee's report, and I can sympathize with the immensity of the pressure you've been under. Mr. Steele isn't pressing charges. So, I'll let it slide—this time." He held up a finger. "But I don't want any more incidents on my ship. Not a single one."

"Yes, sir."

"And you are to stay away from the prisoner."

"Yes, sir."

Brant nodded and left the room.

25

While Gemma went to take a shower, Trevor sat on the common room couch, staring at the ceiling.

He didn't deserve her. No one did, but especially not him. Why was she even with him?

Something had to be done. He wanted to make her happy, but he hadn't figured out how yet. The Captain's Club had been a good start. What else did she like?

Hated cooking and coffee. Loved video games and movies. Hot chocolate and popcorn. Flying, of course. She liked a good challenge. From what she'd told him, she'd been pretty adventurous back on Earth.

She liked him, for some reason. The thought made him smile.

He gave a frustrated sound, leaning forward with his head in his hands. She was the person he knew best in the galaxy—and he felt like he didn't even know her.

How could he make her happy? She wanted adventure, but what did that even *mean?*

He looked up at the footsteps and did a double-take.

Gemma stood in the doorway, smiling at him, her fingers fidgeting with the sleeve of her shirt. She'd done her hair differently again, twisted from the roots into two long braids.

"Doing okay?" she asked.

He nodded numbly, staring. How could someone become even cuter with just a hairstyle?

She plucked at her braid. "Do you like it? You acted weird last time I wore my hair like this."

His eyebrows shot up. "No! I mean, yes! I mean—like it. That's not it." He ran a hand through his hair while she came around the couch and sat by him.

She tilted her head. "Then what is it?"

"Can I ..." He tentatively reached out and touched a braid, running it between his fingers.

Gemma grinned. "So? What do you think?" she asked in a whisper.

His voice dropped to a low rumble. "Seeing you look like this ... I just—" He swallowed hard. "I come undone."

Her breath caught, and he gave a gentle tug on the braid, drawing her toward him.

Their lips brushed—

"Ahem."

They sprang apart, Trevor's hand clutching the shirt over his heart as he whipped around. "Jeez, Chase! Are you *trying* to be sneaky? You're the only one whose footsteps I don't hear coming. You're like some kind of ninja."

Gemma gasped, eyes wide as she grabbed Trevor's arm, her voice a stage whisper. "*Chase is a space ninja.*"

Her braids framing her face, the light in her wide eyes, her mouth hung open in awe, the serious way she had said it ...

Trevor groaned, his hand over his eyes as he leaned back against the couch.

"What? What's wrong?" she asked, her grip tightening.

Chase chuckled. "I think he's experiencing cuteness overload." He reached out and patted Gemma's head.

The hand Trevor had over his face snaked out, snatching Chase's wrist before anyone could even blink. "Don't touch her."

Now Gemma's eyes had a different sort of light in them, the sparkler replaced with red-hot metal. She slapped Trevor's arm away. "Knock it off!"

Trevor flinched. "Uh, right. Sorry." He released Chase.

"No worries, Captain." Chase rubbed his wrist with a wince.

"No, really, I shouldn't have—Did you need something?" Trevor asked, noticing the grim lines around Chase's mouth.

"We've reached the storm we encountered on the way to the Terminus," he said.

Trevor frowned. "I was hoping that would have burned itself out by now."

"Do they need me to fly?" Gemma asked.

"Not likely," Chase said. "I came to let you know. I expect Brant to call you to discuss."

"Thanks, Chase. Did they—"

"Brant to Captain Lee," chirped Trevor's communicator.

"Lee here."

"Meet me on the bridge. We have something to discuss."

"On my way."

No matter what he said, Gemma followed him up the ladder and down the hall. At the base of the ladder to the bridge, Trevor groaned. "Listen to me, okay? You can't come."

Gemma crossed her arms. "I'll leave when Captain Brant tells me to."

With a frustrated growl, Trevor climbed onto the bridge.

The storm churned onscreen, as huge and deadly as ever.

Brant turned to him. "This storm cost us a week of time going around it. But Chase said you flew through it?"

His pilot—Carl—threw up his hands. "Captain, I told you, Chase was *lying.*"

Trevor calmly considered them, his hands behind his back, silently begging Gemma not to say anything.

"Yes, we flew through it," he said.

The entire bridge froze, turning to look at Trevor. At that moment, Gemma leaned out from behind him and gave a cheery wave.

Ugh, this woman.

"Why would you make that decision?" Brant asked, his face unreadable.

"We were under a very tight deadline," Trevor explained. "Had we delayed, lives might have been lost."

"Did you encounter any problems flying through it?"

Gemma said, "Well—"

Trevor stepped in front of her. "We were in the storm for an hour. It was very tense and required some deft maneuvering. Our mechanic—who had disregarded my order to strap down —was injured during the flight. Long before we'd entered the storm, our environmental controls had shorted out, so he was attempting to fix it. Other than that, no problems."

Brant's eyebrows rose. "It only took an hour?"

"First of all," Carl interrupted, "their ship was much smaller. Second, they're lying. She can't be that good. She's practically a kid."

Gemma pulled an indignant breath to say who-knows-what, when Trevor turned and gave her his best glare. It must have been enough, because her mouth snapped shut.

Now Trevor pulled himself up to his full height and turned his attention on Carl, who flinched. "Are you accusing a captain of Omni Authority of lying?"

Carl looked at his hands, properly meek. "No. No, sir."

"Hmm." Brant didn't seem bothered by this exchange as he considered the storm. "I can see flying through in an emergency situation. But I do not think we are currently in such a situation. What do you think, Captain Lee?"

Trevor nodded. "I agree. If we have no deadline and no imminent threat, going around would be the best choice. The safest choice."

Brant nodded, pulled in a breath—and was interrupted by his communicator.

"Engine room to Captain! Turn it off! Turn it all off! Now!" screamed the mechanic.

"Full stop!" Brant snapped, and the familiar rumble of the engines faded.

Too late. A shrill alarm clawed at Trevor's ears.

Trevor sank to his knees, hands over his ears. Gemma grabbed his arm, her mouth moving but the alarm drowned her out.

Trevor looked up at Brant. His mouth moved, too, shouted conversations with the crewmen, looking over their readouts.

It hurts.

Gemma still tugged on his arm, but he couldn't move, paralyzed by the sound.

After an eternity, the alarm stopped.

Trevor collapsed in relief. When he opened his eyes, Gemma hovered over him. Her lips moved, but the ringing blocked out all sound.

Did my brain just get fried? Are my ears bleeding?

He touched a finger to his ear, but it came away dry. When he looked around, the two of them still knelt on the bridge, surrounded by frantic activity.

She pointed to the ladder. She was right, he had to get out of the way.

He slid down to the next deck, rubbing his ears, the stabbing pain making him squint.

Gemma's lips moved, but no sounds came out.

"Am I deaf?" Trevor asked, his muffled words coming from far away. He knew he had spoken; he'd felt the vibration in his throat. His ears couldn't make out the words.

Gemma took his shoulders, her eyes wide. She spoke rapidly, but he shook his head.

"I can't hear you."

She very slowly moved her lips: *Charlie.*

"Let's go," he said.

Charlie looked him over, but when he spoke Trevor couldn't make out his words.

"I still can't hear."

Gemma popped up next to Charlie, holding an info tablet. 'Are you in pain?'

He had to keep from smiling; she had terrible handwriting. "Yes."

Charlie handed him a pill and Trevor swallowed it down. Gemma held up the info tablet. 'It's for pain.'

She wrote on it again and flipped it back so he could see it. 'Doc says you can hear again in about an hour.'

Trevor raised his eyebrows at Charlie, who looked at Gemma.

'Explain later,' she wrote.

"What happened?" he asked. "What was the alarm for?"

Charlie and Gemma had a brief conversation, and she pointed to the same message: 'explain later.'

He gave a deep sigh. Now he had to wait.

Another conversation between Charlie and Gemma, this one obvious with a clear winner and loser, and Trevor couldn't stop his smile.

Charlie pointed at the door. Gemma shook her head.

Charlie made the same motion. Her face hardened, her chin going up. Trevor had only a vague idea of what she said, but Charlie's face said it all. His face tight, he said one more thing, pointing at her, before he stormed out.

When Gemma turned to Trevor, she frowned. He read her lips say, *What's so funny?*

He wiped the smile off his face and shrugged. She was a force to reckon with.

AFTER AN HOUR, GEMMA WAITED PATIENTLY FOR CHARLIE TO DISCUSS Trevor's injury with him. She could have done it and taken a lot less time: damaged super hearing will come back eventually, but for now he can hear as good as a 'normal' human. Why did Charlie have to get all technical?

"So, what was the alarm for?" Trevor asked.

"It's bad," Gemma jumped in, trying to keep the anxiety from her face and failing. "Really, really bad. It wasn't just an alarm." She hesitated. "The engines overheated."

His eyes widened. "What?" He ran a hand through his hair, muttering to himself.

She knew what he must be thinking. Engines could explode, which may or may not kill everyone. The ones that do live would be dead in space without engines. The solar sails won't help because they feed the energy they gather directly into the engine.

An overheated engine could superheat the metal and possibly warp it. Again, dead in space. The engine supplied most of the on-board power, so they'd be fully relying on the backup generator to keep life-support going. All non-essential systems would be offline.

And—

"Gemma, you're thinking too much," Trevor said with a gentle smile. "I see the gears turning in your eyes."

"Uh." She glanced away.

He took her hand, bringing her eyes back to his face. "Listen, calm down. Don't think about all the things that *might* happen. Tell me about what's happening right now. What is Captain Brant doing about the problem? And how can I help?"

Trevor stood, giving a nod to Charlie, then pulled Gemma out the door.

"The machine room is so hot, no one can get in," she explained. "They have to wait until it cools down to even assess it properly."

Trevor rubbed his chin. "Take me to Joe."

"How long do you think it will take to cool down?" Trevor asked Joe.

Joe winced. "At least a couple days. Brant is about to address everyone on how this will affect us."

"Were any other systems damaged?"

Joe shook his head. "Not that we can tell. The heat surge was caught just in time."

"How much of the engine was compromised?"

Joe sighed, looking at the ground. Trevor tensed, waiting for the bad news. "That's the thing: all of it."

Trevor's eyes bugged. Yeah, that was bad news, alright.

"The whole thing? Both engines?" Trevor frowned, scratching his head. "This can't have happened on its own."

"Why not?" Gemma asked.

He and Joe looked at each other. Joe gestured. "Take it away."

"First, what's the likelihood of it happening to *both* engines at the same time?" Trevor said.

"Unlikely?" Gemma ventured.

"Exactly. Even with one, usually an overheat is contained to one area," Trevor explained. "There are too many safety protocols that would have to go down simultaneously for the entire engine to heat that much. We can't even look for the initial cause of the overheat until it cools down. But ..." He tapped his chin. "If we could get Zane—"

"Already on it," Joe said with a nod.

"All personnel, report to the common room," came over the intercom.

Trevor smiled at Gemma, trying to hide his anxiety. Sabotage, violent storm, dead in space with no engine, and now they were going to have to make hard choices about what to spend their limited power on. The backup generator could only do so much.

Things were about to get uncomfortable.

"Let's go," Trevor said, taking her hand.

PDA or no-PDA, Gemma wasn't about to let go of the death grip she had on Trevor's arm.

"Is everyone here?" Brant had his arms crossed over his

chest, his face grim. Brant's fifteen crew members plus their seven filled the common room.

This does not bode well.

"As you know, our engines are currently non-operational," he said. "This means we will need to make changes to decrease our electrical needs, as the backup generator has only limited power."

We know this. What's going to happen?!

Trevor reached over and patted her hand on his arm. She made a conscious effort to relax.

"Here are some changes: we will keep the water reclamation system on, but working at minimum capacity. Essentials only. That means no showers, no clothes washing, and no washing dishes."

Oooooh, this is already not looking fun.

"Food and drink will have to be rationed. We're not shutting down our freezer—but we can't eat from it either. Using any cooking elements would put a strain on the system. We will be eating emergency rations."

She glanced up at Trevor in pity. Poor guy was always hungry, and he had to go through this again.

"All entertainment systems will be disconnected from the power grid. Gravity will be a little weaker than normal, the fitness center included, to save every electron we can.

"Oxygenating system will function as normal, but we will have to significantly limit our heat use. It's time to bundle up.

"We are still assessing our lighting systems. After our assessment, some non-essential areas of the ship will remain dark.

"Any questions?" Brant asked. No one raised a hand. "Excellent. Those who can, go about your duties. All others ... scrounge around for cards or board games. It's going to be a long couple of days."

As the crew dispersed, Brant made eye contact with Gemma.

She froze in place. She had no idea what it meant.

"Uh, Gemma?" Trevor tapped her. "You okay?"

She pointed as Brant approached.

"I need to speak to both of you," he said quietly. "Urgently."

"No." Trevor crossed his arms. "Absolutely not. Out of the question."

"This isn't a request, Captain," Brant said. "I'm telling you this out of courtesy. We will no longer be able to use the brig in which Mr. Steele currently resides. Shutting it off completely from the power grid gives us a significant amount of power. He's going to be moved out."

"Where will you put Alex?"

They both turned at Gemma's small voice, her face drawn and pale, her hands shaking.

"In one of the standard quarters," Brant said. Trevor appreciated that he kept his voice low and soothing. "He'll be in the farthest room, with a guard posted outside his door at all times. He will never be permitted to leave the room."

"I know what can happen," Gemma said softly. "What if the heat gives out? Then everyone will have to be in one room, so we don't freeze to death. Or if the oxygenators begin to fail? We'll have to adjust our movements to each disaster that space throws at us. And that may mean him leaving his room—or even seeing him." Tears welled up in her eyes.

"We will do everything in our power to ensure the safety

and wellbeing of all personnel," Brant said. "If you have any further concerns, Ms. Stone, come find me and I will be happy to listen."

It was nice of him to say, but Trevor's jaw tightened. He didn't like Brant lying to Gemma. There was no way he'd have time for her during this crisis.

Trevor took her hand. He would have to step up and be enough for her.

Brant nodded to Trevor. "Please excuse me for the moment, so we can plan to make the wisest use of our lighting."

Once he was gone, Trevor's arms enveloped her, her body shaking against him.

"I'm going to protect you, alright?" Trevor promised into her hair. "We'll make it through, and we'll get you home for Sandy's wedding."

Gemma clung to him, her shoulders shaking, her breathing ragged.

I swear.

GEMMA LOVED BEING IN SPACE, BUT WHEN SHE GOT HOME, SHE wanted an Earth vacation.

Not all space trips were as exhausting and perilous as this one, she knew. This one would be especially ... memorable.

She needed time to decompress, spend time with Sandy, and—

Gemma smiled. Spend some quality not-narrowly-escaping-death time with Trevor.

Be patient, Gemma. The vacation will come. Just a little longer.

Captain Brant decided that the common room would

operate on half-light, as would the corridors. The living quarters would have no light at all—apart from the prisoner's. Brant's quarters were taken entirely off the grid, as well as the brig and the fitness center.

Everyone was issued a flashlight and a thick coat.

"Hang in there, Gemma," Joe was saying. "It should only be one more night until we can get in that engine room."

She nodded mutely, turning up her collar and shivering.

"Keep your hood on," Trevor said, tugging it into place, his arm around her. He wasn't wearing a hood. His coat wasn't even zipped.

Zane sighed dramatically. "I can't even investigate the sabotages because all the power is going toward running the bridge."

"Can't they turn the heat up a smidge?" Dak asked, his hands restless.

They all sat on the floor of the common room. Over a dozen of the crew slept in there, as it was warmer than the dark quarters. Every towel, blanket, and sheet they could find was spread across the cold metal floor, making it tolerable to sit on.

Charlie stayed in sickbay, which, as an essential room, had a little more light and warmth. Chase could be seen pacing the halls at any time, day or night.

Gemma rubbed her hands together. *Is Alex cold? How is he feeling? Alone? Regretful?*

She remembered the last thing she saw on his face before she punched him: *hateful.*

I don't care how he feels.

"Cheer up, Gemma." Zane tried to smile, although not knowing why she had tears in her eyes.

Trevor shifted beside her. He might know, but it didn't matter. It wouldn't change anything.

Gemma looked up and out the common room window, her

humming sputtering as she looked out at the glowing points of light dotting the blackness.

"Still looking at the stars?" Trevor murmured.

"Yeah." A ghost of a smile crossed her lips. "Maybe they're not very interesting, but they're still beautiful."

Trevor took her hands and held them in his large ones to keep them warm. The open sides of his coat wrapped around her, and she leaned her head on his shoulder, comforted. He was always so warm.

"My turn?" Zane asked.

"With the captain or with Gemma?" Dak asked, his voice snarky.

Gemma chuckled. She loved her crew.

"Maybe we can both fit in there ..." Zane ventured.

"Get away from me, Zane." Trevor's voice rumbled under her cheek.

Dak scowled. "This is sickening." He turned away, lying down under a blanket, his hood over his head.

"What's eating him?" Zane whispered.

"He's been like this ever since the crash," Joe said. "Real isolated."

"I can hear you," Dak said.

"Do you need—" Trevor started.

"I'm fine," Dak snapped.

Gemma closed her eyes, the vibration of Trevor speaking lulling her to sleep. *One more night ... just one more—*

She sat up with a gasp, elbowing Trevor in the gut where he slept beside her. He groaned.

"Sorry, sorry," she whispered. She didn't know what had awoken her. The room whispered with the soft breathing—and some not-soft snores—of the crew. The cold bit at her face. Nothing was amiss. Why was she awake, why was she gasping for air as if she'd realized something terrifying? What had shocked her into wakefulness?

The dim, quiet room was still. Was someone missing? Yes. That was it, but she couldn't figure out who.

"What time is it?" Trevor muttered, hardly conscious.

"Never mind. It's fine," she whispered, pressing her hand to the side of his face. "Go back to sleep."

He took her hand and tugged her down next to him. "It's okay," he murmured, already drifting off. "Go back to sleep."

She nodded, closing her eyes. "Okay."

26

The engine room was finally safe to enter. Sort of.

The mechanics had to wear special heat-protective clothing, and they rotated often to prevent heatstroke.

Trevor, of course, had volunteered to help.

That's a good thing. He's a great mechanic and will get it fixed faster.

At least, that's what Gemma kept saying as she hugged herself tightly.

But why did he have to leave me alone?

As if sensing her thoughts, Zane bumped her shoulder. "I got us a snack!"

She tried to smile. Zane was a great friend with a splash of sunshine. He would be so much fun at a party.

Or a wedding.

"Want to come to my sister's wedding?" Gemma asked him.

Zane choked, and she had to pound him on the back to dislodge whatever he had been trying to eat.

"Are you serious?" he croaked. "You're inviting me to a wedding? Your *sister's* wedding?"

"Yes." She eyed him, unsure if she had insulted him or bestowed an honor.

He grabbed her hands, jumping up and down. "I want to! I definitely do!"

"Shh!" Gemma couldn't help but chuckle at all the looks they were getting. "Calm down. I absolutely want you to come. I think it'd be fun." *And hilarious.*

"I've never been to a wedding before." He gasped, his hands going to his cheeks. "I won't know what to do! What can I bring for a present? What kind of food will be there? Will I get some cake? I'm pretty sure I can't dance, but I'm willing to give it a try. And I don't know how to tie the bows the men wear around their necks. Wait, I have no idea what to wear at all! Do I have to make a speech?"

Gemma had covered her face, trying to smother her laughter. *Oh yes. This will be fun.*

When he'd calmed down, Zane leaned in close, raising his eyebrows. "Will I get to dance with you?"

She ruffled his hair. "I'm sure that can be arranged."

"Knock it off!" He shoved her hand off, but he still smiled.

Something behind her caught Zane's eye, and she turned to look.

Trevor leaned in the doorway. He pointed to each of them and gestured for them to follow.

"What's the news?" Gemma asked once they were in the hallway.

"Not here." Trevor looked around. He took her hand, and she jumped. His skin was *hot!* He didn't have his coat or jacket and wore the top part of his jumpsuit uniform open, the sleeves tied around his waist. He mopped his forehead on the sleeve of his sweat-soaked t-shirt.

"I take it you just came from the engine room?" Zane said.

"Meeting on the bridge," Trevor said.

Gemma and Zane had to squeeze onto the bridge, with Trevor right behind them.

Captain Brant had his security, engineer, mechanics, and electrician crew members. Trevor had Joe, Chase, Zane and Gemma.

She looked around but didn't see the other pilot.

"It was sabotage," Brant announced without preamble, his scowl darkening his face in deep creases. He nodded to his engineer, Joe, and Trevor. "Someone shoved multiple tools into the cooling system. They didn't *fall* in; it wasn't an *accident*. They were put there on purpose. And then all the electrical safeties were turned off." He nodded to Zane. "I should have listened to you sooner."

Brant's engineer spoke up. "The good news is we can salvage it. But we'll have to scavenge some parts from the jump engines. That means we won't be able to enter jump-space anymore." He hesitated. "But if we don't disassemble the jump engines, then we can't fix the main engines, and we won't move anywhere at all."

"How long will it take?" Brant asked.

Joe and the engineer conferred for a few moments. "That's the tricky part. It should only take a day with a typical work-force, but we have a saboteur onboard, so we don't know who we can trust."

Brant pinched the bridge of his nose with a sigh. "I assume that disassembling the jump engines will require some of the team to be spacewalk certified?"

"Er, yes," said the engineer.

Brant sighed again. "Here's what we're going to do: Zane, take the power you need and find me that saboteur. He's been poking around in the system and must have left evidence somewhere. Find him."

Zane straightened. "Yes, sir."

"My electrician will assist you."

The electrician looked like he'd eaten bad broccoli. "Yes ... yes, sir."

"For the engines, I will hand-pick trustworthy members of my crew to assist. Prepare a plan and execute it."

"Yes, sir."

Brant turned to the security officers. "We need someone to guard the prisoner, someone to keep an eye on the crew, and someone to man the bridge." He rubbed his chin a moment. "I will choose someone to guard the enemy. You two can babysit the crew. And between me, Captain Lee, and Ms. Stone, we'll monitor the bridge."

Gemma blinked. She was glad to be included, but *why* was she included?

"Uh." Trevor glanced at her. "Did you want me working on the engines too? Or space walking? Or ...?"

"No. You will stay here. Engineering and electrical, dismissed."

The room emptied out quickly, until it was just five: two captains, two security men, and a pilot.

"It gets worse," Brant said to Trevor. He nodded toward the display. "Show him."

The long-range sensor display came up. It didn't take Gemma long to see what they were showing them.

At the very outer edge—there was a blip.

She gasped, her knees going weak. "No."

"How far?" Trevor demanded, grabbing her arm to hold her upright.

"Best guess is three days," said Chase.

They were all silent for a moment.

"Is there the smallest chance that they might not be ..." Gemma's voice faded, knowing the answer. *I can't. I'm too tired.*

Trevor's eyes narrowed, and he nodded. "I think I see where you're going with this."

"Where?" Gemma demanded, struggling not to cry. She was sick of it. Sick and tired. "I don't see it!"

"The engine will be repaired in a day. Two days, tops," Trevor explained. "Then we can get moving again. *They* won't get here for three days. So, we'll be long gone."

"But ..." So many things could go wrong. "What if they can't fix the engine?"

"They will," Trevor said. She looked into his eyes and believed him. He couldn't lie well anyway.

"What if we can't get to top speed?" she asked. "How will they not overtake us? And we won't have jump-space."

"That's where you come in." He gently turned her toward the display of churning violet clouds spitting lightning.

Oh.

Gemma's eyes dried up as she considered the display calmly. "Okay."

Brant blinked. "That's it?"

"Yes, sir," she said, turning to him. "Finally, something that I can do." She tapped her chin. "I'll need to prepare. Your ship is bigger than ours was, has a different configuration, and—"

"Anything you need," Brant said. "Say the word, and it's done. I am at your service."

She looked up at Trevor, not expecting to see his grin as he wrapped his arm around her shoulders. "That's my girl."

Gemma wasted no time. She took the pilot seat to familiarize herself with the controls, the layout, the locations of the buttons, gauges, and readout screens she'd need, even how she would need to move in the space. Can't have elbows bumping the control panel.

Once she thought she had it, she began adjustments. The sensitivity of the controls, what her screen displayed, and obviously the tilt and location of the chair so she could reach the thruster pedals on the floor.

Since she couldn't test the speed or handling until after the engines were repaired, she did a little math to best-guess how to maneuver a ship this size. Trevor's ship had been smaller, making it easier to make snap changes to their course. This one was larger and longer. She would have to engage and sync back thrusters, too, to keep the whole ship from spiraling off course from its own momentum. Turning and altering their direction would need more energy.

She'd have to navigate the clouds a little slower, and the sides of the ship may brush against the lightning. The mechanics and electricians would be busy keeping essential systems online throughout the ride. It was risky not having them strapped in, but they didn't have a choice. All other crew members would need to be strapped in, preferably near the center of the ship.

There would be time to practice a few maneuvers, to get the feel of the ship before they entered the storm. At least, she hoped they had time.

She had a long list of notes for the engineers. She explained each item to Trevor so he could correctly pass on the information. He knelt next to her, making supplemental notes on an info tablet.

"Speed, of course, will be necessary, but I'm going to need handling from the thrusters. As much as I can get." She tapped the consol. "I've set the sensitivity and response time to its highest setting. I'll need constant readings sent to my screen on how hard I can push the ship without the engine gauges going into the red. To keep the back thrusters in sync, I'll need—"

She stopped as a shadow loomed over them, blocking one of the overhead lights. The usual pilot of the ship stood, arms crossed, and she could swear steam came out of his ears.

"What are you doing?" he demanded.

Trevor started to rise, but Gemma stopped him with a hand on his arm.

"Preparing to enter the storm," she said, her voice even and calm.

His teeth ground together. "That is my seat."

"Would you like to try it then?" she asked, her voice still even.

The pilot scoffed. "It's suicide. If you do this, you're going to get us all killed."

Gemma didn't even bat an eye. "The captain asked me to be here. This is an emergency and our only course of action for survival."

"You did that." He pointed a finger in her face. She squeezed Trevor's arm to keep him in place. "You made him think that it's an emergency. You're maneuvering things to get your way. What are you even getting out of this? Are you some kamikaze pilot for the Conglomerate?"

"If you have concerns, I suggest discussing them with your captain," she said. "Right now, I am busy, and you are wasting my time."

He gritted his teeth. "Look here, *kid,* I will *not* let you do this. Get out of my chair!"

Gemma flinched as he reached for her arm, but Trevor's hand snapped out, catching the pilot's wrist. The pilot tried to pull his hand back, but Trevor's grip was as hard and unforgiving as iron.

Trevor finally stood, his full height towering over the pilot. The trapped man let out an involuntary whimper.

"If you have a problem with the orders, go see your captain. But you are not *ever* to bother Gemma."

The pilot nodded repeatedly. Trevor released him, and the pilot backpedaled, rubbing his wrist. Within seconds, he slid down the ladder.

"You didn't hurt him, did you?" Gemma asked.

His face softened as he looked down at her. "Nah. His wrist may be a little bruised, but it won't inhibit his movement."

She sighed. "Thanks for letting me take care of it. Mostly."

"Um, yeah." He rubbed the back of his neck. "That was hard. But when he reached for you, I couldn't stop myself."

She smiled. He was getting better. *And I can't be mad at him for protecting me like that. I had no idea what I would do if the conversation escalated, and Trevor* hadn't *been there.* "Okay, next item on the list," she said. "I promise, we're almost done."

He knelt beside her again, looking down at the info tablet in his hand, ready.

She gazed at him for a moment. He trusted her. Implicitly. How could she ever deserve such a guy? She looked forward to having many, many adventures in the future, and she had the best partner.

Trevor waited for her to say something. When he looked up from the tablet, a question on his face, she hooked a finger under his collar and pulled him in for a kiss.

"Hey, we have work to do," he said, but couldn't keep the smile off his face.

"Back to work." She looked back at her list. "If there's any way they could …"

THEY FIXED THE SHIP IN RECORD TIME—IN ONLY A DAY—BUT IT FELT like forever to Gemma. They made her take a nap, but she'd only slept an hour.

The rest of the crew spent their time preparing the ship for the storm. They removed all the panels that usually covered essential electrical systems, for easy repair access during flight. Everyone knew their place and their assignment.

Once they *finally* gave the go-ahead, she took the controls.

Despite its size, the ship responded better than she had feared. She did a few simple maneuvers—then punched it, hitting its highest speed, for a few seconds before slowing.

Her com sputtered to life. "Gemma, take it easy!" Joe shouted. "We just fixed it. She's not up for racing."

"Sorry, Joe. Had to test out its top speed, in case of an emergency," she said.

Joe grumbled, "It better be a short emergency. It can't take more than ten minutes at that speed before engine burnout."

Everyone took their positions. They emptied the quarters, most of the crew strapped down in the common room—including Alex. There was no safe way to guard him in the sleeping quarters, not with the changes in acceleration they expected.

Joe and Brant's engineer manned the engine room. Zane, the other electrician, and the two mechanics had divided the ship between them, each taking care of overloads and repairs in their zone. Trevor knelt behind her, standing by on the bridge to fix any short outs there. The rest of the crew tensed as they prepared to enter the storm, Brant in the captain's chair.

Gemma shifted in her seat, uneasy. What if Zane had to unstrap to fix something and she had to make a sharp course change?

"Don't worry, he's wearing a helmet," Trevor murmured behind her.

She smiled, shaking out her hands and relaxing. Trevor knew her way too well.

Gemma glanced at Brant, who made the final announcement and then nodded. "Take her in."

"Yes, sir." She worked the controls to propel them into the storm clouds.

Ordered to silence, nobody spoke as Gemma steered, avoiding the masses of hot plasma bubbling out toward them. She still brushed the edges of the clouds—which would fry their ship if their shield hadn't been fully operational. Unable to avoid all the lightning that shot across the nose of the ship, she kept it slow, despite the lights flickering, the occasional sizzle, and the soft beep of an alarm that Trevor quickly deactivated. The plasma clouds posed the real danger.

She felt more than she saw Trevor moving around the bridge at astounding speeds. Her focus narrowed to her readings, controls, and the screen displays.

It was all in her hands.

An hour passed. Then two. Brant's ship nimbly moved through the storm, guided by her gentle touch, although inevitable sudden corrections threw people against their harnesses.

Trevor never lost his footing, continuing his repairs.

Gemma dove under a ribbon of plasma, when her screen flickered—then went out.

She gasped, but Trevor was already there, cutting wires, throwing the burnt metal and plastic aside. He stripped off a section of wire casing with his teeth, before twisting the ends together.

Her screen came back on.

Elation turned to horror as violet streams of plasma completely blocked their course, spraying the ship with lightning.

Gemma flicked on full reverse, which sent even Trevor tumbling. The precious seconds it gave her revealed a gap higher up in the ribbon—a tiny gap, that their ship would *just* fit through.

A quick burst of the stabilizers changed their course with a jolt, and she powered forward.

The gap was closing.

Gemma kicked the ship up to top speed, all the readings diving into the red, an alarm going off.

Ten minutes. Joe said I had ten minutes.

Sweat dripped down her face, straining at the controls as if it would make the ship fly any faster.

At the last second before the gap, she tapped the stabilizers to flip the ship sideways.

They sailed through, the shields giving off a tiny flicker as they brushed by the plasma.

Gemma blinked. Stars filled the screens in front of them, the roiling storm behind them.

"I can't believe we're alive," Brant blurted, sinking back in his chair, his trembling hand brushing away a slick sheen of sweat.

The rest of the bridge cheered. Gemma sat back, exhausted. She rubbed her eyes, the intensity of her open-eyed concentration leaving them dry and scratchy.

Then Trevor knelt by her side with a proud smile. "I knew you could do it."

She smiled back and engaged the autopilot. "Did you get hurt?" she asked.

He shrugged. "Nah."

Gemma gave him a knowing smile. "Liar."

"It's just a couple of bruises." He rotated his shoulders. "Pretty sure I'll feel it later."

After checking in with the electricians and the engineers—who were all fine, including the engine—Brant turned to Gemma.

"That was some amazing flying," he said. He tapped the ship-wide comms. "All crew are released from their emergency positions. We're through the storm." He clicked off and raised his eyebrows at Trevor. "Captain Lee, a word?"

Brant clapped Trevor on the shoulder. "Your crew performed tremendously today. The best I've ever seen."

Trevor nodded. "Yes, sir, thank you."

"I'd like to offer you a position," Brant said. "You'll be—"

"Thank you, sir," Trevor interrupted, "but I'm happy where I am and who I work with."

"I think you should listen to my proposal before dismissing it," Brant said, arching a brow.

Trevor sighed inwardly. "Yes, sir."

"The director is putting together an elite squadron to combat the advances of the Conglomerate," Brant explained. "I want you and your crew on it. This team will have the latest in technology, access to—"

"Captain!" Zane said through the communicator.

"Hang on, Zane, I'm—"

"It's an emergency!" Zane shouted.

Trevor held out a hand to Brant to wait. "Go ahead, Zane."

"I traced an unauthorized sign-on to a computer. It happened five minutes ago. It's—it's in sickbay."

Trevor was already in motion, sliding down the ladder as he tried to connect with Charlie. "Charlie! Come in! Charlie!"

No answer.

Trevor felt like he'd been punched in the gut as he ran, bile rising in his throat. *If Charlie—*

Reaching sickbay, Trevor slammed the door open, cracking it.

Charlie sprawled across the floor; his eyes closed.

Trevor's hand slapped against Charlie's neck a little harder than he'd meant to, checking for a pulse.

Charlie's eyes snapped open, and he screamed.

Trevor clutched his own chest. "You're alive."

"No thanks to you!" Charlie rubbed his throat, dragging in a deep breath. "You almost crushed my windpipe."

"I'm sorry, I just—" Trevor shook his head, trying to clear it. His limbs shook from the high adrenaline coursing through him, and his hands clenched, ready for action. "What happened?"

"It was Dak," Charlie said. "He figured sickbay was warmer than the common room and had been hanging out here. I saw him logging onto the computer, but the screen he accessed was new to me. When he turned around, he shot me with a stunner." Charlie shoved Trevor. "Go get him before something worse happens!"

Trevor didn't have to be told twice.

Already in the hall and running, Trevor slapped his communicator. "Zane! Charlie's fine. Do you know what it is that he did?"

"It looks like he targeted the oxygenator," Zane said. "Specifically, in the common room. I'll get it back right away."

Why in the common room?

When Trevor reached the common room, the door was already open. Every single person lay limp on the floor.

More carefully this time, he felt the nearest crewmember for a pulse. They were alive, just unconscious.

Trevor evaluated the room, his eyes darting everywhere as he turned in a circle. Nothing was different—

Except Alex was missing, an unconscious guard on each side of where he should have been.

"It's Alex," Trevor growled, opening the communication line to everyone. "Find Dak and Alex!"

"What do you mean, Alex?" Gemma's high voice demanded.

"Dak? What's happened to Dak?" Joe asked.

"Just find him! He's armed and dangerous!"

Trevor stepped out into the hallway and stopped. He closed his eyes to hear better.

That way. He turned to his left and gave chase.

New footsteps approached, but they weren't as loud as they should have been, and there was only one set—

Trevor rounded the corner and smashed into Gemma.

"Gemma!" He grabbed her shoulders. "You can't be here! Go back to the bridge."

"Ow." She gingerly touched her nose. "Am I bleeding?"

"Go back!" he ordered. He slapped his communicator. "Everyone, call in your positions."

Everyone did. They were spread out throughout the ship, but there was no sign of Alex or Dak.

"Let's all converge on my location to organize our search," Trevor said.

Gemma crossed her arms. "Well? Go get him!"

"I am not leaving you alone," he said.

"I've got her ... Captain!" Charlie came puffing up beside them. He bent over, his hands on his knees. "Go on—"

"Stay right there," said a voice behind them.

Every muscle in Trevor's body tightened, and they slowly turned to see Alex pointing a rattler at them, their traitorous navigator Dak beside him with a stunner. Too close for Alex to miss his shot, but too far away for Trevor to reach him.

Trevor pushed Gemma behind him. "Stay there," he ordered.

"Alex, please—" she said.

Alex bared his teeth, a crooked smile on his face, his eyes too wide open.

"Oh, I'm going to enjoy this," he said, pointing the rattler square at Trevor's chest. It rattled as it warmed up. Rattlers only had one purpose—to kill.

"Stop!" Gemma leapt out in front of him, putting herself between Trevor and the stunner. "Alex! Please!"

Trevor could have pulled his hair out. *Woman*—

Trevor grabbed for her, but she jumped out of his reach, closer to Alex. "Gemma!"

Alex hesitated, his hand shaking, the rattler's whine waning. He glanced at Dak.

Without hesitation, Dak swung his arm toward Gemma and pulled the trigger on his stunner.

"No!"

Her body twitched wildly as the stun hit her, Trevor catching her before she hit the ground.

"No!" He eased her down, her head on his lap. She didn't move or open her eyes.

Trevor looked up at Alex and growled, "You're a dead man."

"I don't think so." Alex's rattler had charged back up, and

he aimed it at Trevor's head. His finger tightened to squeeze the trigger.

Something hard and fast flew over Trevor's head, barely missing him. It hit Alex square on the forehead, dropping him to the ground in a heap.

Alex didn't move from where he'd fallen. Trevor stared at the knife still spinning on the floor, when Chase stepped over him, retrieving the weapon.

"It was just the hilt, Captain. He's only unconscious," he said. He gave a half-smile. "Tell Gemma that knife throwing really does come in handy in space."

"We've got her, Captain," Charlie said as both he and Chase knelt beside her. "Now get going."

Trevor stared at them.

"Dak! He ran!" Chase pointed down the hall. "Go catch him!"

Staggering to his feet—still trying to figure out what just happened—Trevor took off at a run.

Chase's voice came through the communicator. "One down, just Dak to go. The captain is chasing him through the outermost level. Where are you?"

"We're on our way Captain!" Zane shouted through the communicator. "Are you sure it was Dak?"

"I'm sure," Charlie said.

"We'll catch him from the other side!" Joe wheezed.

Dak's shoes slapped against the floor as he ran, the shape of the ship making it impossible for Trevor to see him around the continuous curve of the outside level. Dak's breath came in ragged gasps, which grew louder as Trevor gained on him.

With a *whoosh*, a door opened, then clanked shut again.

Trevor almost slid past the airlock, which *whooshed* open again when he slapped the controls.

Trevor stood framed in the doorway, breathing hard and

surveying the inky blackness. No lights here, except what streamed in from the hall behind him.

His eyes adjusted to the large space; this airlock was used for junk storage.

"Dak?"

"Get away from me, freak," Dak said, disgust tinging his voice into more of a growl. He grunted.

Trevor took a step toward the sound at the far back.

"You can't go anywhere," Trevor said, taking another step.

"Oh yeah? Watch me." Another grunt.

"What happened, Dak?" Trevor took another step forward. He had *trusted* Dak. One shift of Dak's perception of Trevor had made them enemies?

Trevor flinched. He'd gotten his hopes up with the acceptance of the rest of his crew. But there would always be people who hated him for what he was.

"*You* happened." *Grunt.* "Lying test tube monster. You should have been destroyed."

The dark room came into focus, revealing Dak wrestling on an exosuit that would protect him outside the ship.

"Stop!" Trevor dove toward him, but Dak had snapped the helmet into place before Trevor knocked him over.

"What are you doing? You have nowhere to go!" Trevor tried to wrestle the helmet off the suit, but his fingers slid over the smooth visor.

Dak landed a lucky kick, and was on his feet before Trevor recovered. He backed up to the opposite wall, groping around in the darkness, until he found the covered, red button: the airlock release. Dak activated his speaker. "Omni Authority may have missed you in the cleanup, but I'm going to finish what they started."

Dak jerked the cap off the airlock release.

Trevor froze. "Don't do it."

"You Tubies killed my dad," Dak snarled.

Trevor took a step back. "What?"

"Yeah. I know what you're capable of."

"But that doesn't mean I—'"

"He and his unit were the first inside the compound when the experiments came to light," Dak continued. "Omni Authority hadn't planned to kill the clones. After all, they were just children, right? *Wrong.* Before my dad's unit even knew they were in danger, those 'innocent' children slaughtered them. Tubies. The world was right to destroy them then. Just like I'm right to destroy you now."

"Wait, Dak—"

Trevor couldn't see Dak's expression as Dak slapped the palm of his hand against the red button.

Trevor dove to the side as the airlock door slowly opened, sucking the atmosphere out of the room and blowing it into space.

With a flash of Dak's stunner, the outside airlock door controls lit up and smoked, before darkening. Releasing his hold, Dak shot out into space, but Trevor grabbed a thick mesh lining the wall, designed to hold down cargo, wrapping his arm through it to keep himself inside.

Atmosphere rushed through the open inner door, dragging at Trevor. He could barely breathe, but he needed to hurry to reach the inner doors before they automatically closed.

His muscles strained against the suction as he pulled himself toward the doors.

With a clank, the inner doors shut, plunging him into darkness.

The rushing air stopped, but he could no longer breathe at all.

He desperately searched the wall, anything to give him oxygen.

He looked up at the inner airlock doors. Zane banged on the window, panic clear in his eyes.

I'll get you out! He mouthed.

Trevor went back to searching. Zane couldn't do anything for him.

As black dots appeared in his vision, Trevor clung to the mesh. He couldn't breathe.

Gemma ... He wanted nothing more than to be with her, going on her adventures together.

Together, they had defied the odds. Flying a ship at top speed into a jump point. Using the sun to get back into jump-space. Flying through a plasma storm, *twice*. They'd been hungry, tired, chased by the Conglomerate, completed their mission, and gotten back to safety. Maybe they could beat this, too—

If he died now, she'd be sad. He never wanted to be the reason Gemma cried.

Trevor's eyes closed.

A great *whoosh* snapped him back, nearly dislocating his arm still woven into the mesh. The inner airlock door had opened a couple of feet, but he didn't have the strength to climb anymore.

A sandy-haired ball of knees and elbows flew through the gap and slammed into him, dislodging him and sending them into space.

They jerked to a stop at the end of a tether, and the ball unfolded into a grinning Zane. Zane pressed an oxygen mask against Trevor's face, and the captain gasped in relief, gulping in deep breaths.

"Hi, Captain!" Zane said, looping a section of line around Trevor. "Now reel us in!"

Trevor easily pulled them back in, Zane clinging to his back. Once inside, the inner airlock doors that Zane had hot-wired open slammed shut, the bulkhead doors still open because Dak disabled the controls.

The two of them collapsed on the floor, exhausted and shivering.

"Charlie is on his way," Joe said, leaning over them.

Charlie? Trevor's brain drifted in and out of consciousness. Charlie said he would take care of Gemma.

"Gem—" he started to say.

Joe actually laughed. "You've got it bad for this girl. She's fine! She's with Chase until she gets her legs under her again. I'm sure we'll see her soon."

Reassured, Trevor let himself slide into darkness.

"TREVOR, YOU HAVE TO WAKE UP," SAID A FARAWAY VOICE.

"Let him rest," said another, deeper one. "He's been through enough to kill a regular man. He needs to recover."

Trevor drifted off again.

A SQUEEZE ON HIS HAND JERKED HIM BACK TO WAKEFULNESS, involuntarily crying out because it hurt. *Everything* hurt. He couldn't even open his eyes.

Gemma squeaked in surprise but grabbed his hand again. "Trevor!"

He groaned. "Gem?"

She leaned toward him, but the pressure against him made him flinch. "Ow ... please don't touch me."

"Right." She dropped his hand. He could hear her tears. "I'm so glad you're alive."

"Is Zane okay?" he asked, his tongue thick.

"He's okay. He wasn't here nearly as long as you."

"How long have I been out?"

"At least a day," said Charlie's deep voice.

Trevor groaned again. "I can barely move."

"Don't worry, you'll recover soon enough," Charlie said.

Trevor cracked an eye open in time to see Charlie preparing an injection.

"Don't you dare stick me with that," Trevor warned, both eyes open now.

Charlie smirked. "What are you going to do about it?"

It was over in seconds. Trevor hardly felt it.

"Gemma, you can go eat now," Charlie said.

She shook her head. "I'm not going anywhere."

Trevor frowned. "How long has it been since she's eaten?"

"Too long," Charlie said.

Gemma bit her lip, trying not to cry anymore. Despite his neck screaming at him to hold still, Trevor turned his head to look at her. He wanted to reach out and stroke her cheek, but even flexing his fingers hurt.

"Gemma, you should go eat," he said gently. He frowned, seeing the dark marks under her eyes. "You haven't slept either, have you?"

She hesitated.

"I promise I'll still be here when you come back," Trevor said. "Go eat and rest. That's an order. And I'm sending Zane after you to make sure you do so."

She chuckled, rubbing her eyes. "Yes, Captain."

Gemma left, and Trevor sighed. "What's the situation?" he asked Charlie.

Charlie leaned against the other exam table. "Pretty good, actually." He ticked items on his fingers. "All systems are online; we're back on course. Alex is back in the brig. No other problems, so it seems you've taken care of ... the saboteur." He hesitated, his words faltering. "They dragged Dak's body back in before we left. His helmet had cracked on decompression. It's ..."

"It's okay, Charlie." Trevor met his eyes. "You don't have to talk about it. I get the idea."

Charlie took a deep breath. "There's no sign of the ship following us. We can't use jump-space, so the trip will be a bit longer than planned, but we should be back to Earth in a few weeks. No one was seriously hurt—except you, of course. Your crew is worried sick about you. Did I miss anything?"

Trevor was quiet for a moment. "Does anyone know?"

"Just your crew."

He gave Charlie a sidelong look. "Are you still angry with me?"

Charlie chuckled, shaking his head. "There isn't any point in staying mad. But ..." He hesitated. "I thought you and Gemma were a bad idea. The worst idea. The most awful decision you or anyone else has ever—"

"I get the point," Trevor interrupted. At least Charlie wasn't angry; but his disapproval hurt. There weren't many people he looked up to, but Charlie was one of them.

"*But.*" Charlie leaned forward to meet his eyes. "I've realized how much you two care for each other. And the way she threw herself between Alex's gun and you ..."

Trevor groaned, his fist tightening—a little. "She should never have done that. It was stupid—"

"And exactly what you would do for her, right?"

"I ... uh." Absolutely. He would have done it in a heartbeat.

"You're both the same flavor of crazy." Charlie shook his head. "She's smart, talented, confident, affectionate, kind, friendly, puts others ahead of herself, fearless—"

"—and stubborn, never listens, reckless," Trevor continued. "never shuts up, hums off-key, pushy, cheats at video games, and ..." He sighed. "For some reason, I can't say no to her."

Charlie grinned. "She's a catch."

Trevor stared at him. "So, you mean ...?"

Charlie patted his shoulder, which made him wince.

"You'll make each other happy."

Happy. Trevor had never thought his life could be happy. Maybe content, productive, and useful. He smiled. He could be *happy.*

"Get some rest, Captain," Charlie said.

Trevor closed his eyes with a sigh. *Happy. She makes me happy.*

When he woke again, Zane stood by his bed. Zane saluted. "I have carried out your orders, sir. She has eaten and is now asleep."

Trevor smiled. "Good work, Zane. And, uh ... thanks for saving my life."

Zane grinned. "Does that mean you owe me?"

"No," Trevor said flatly.

Zane shrugged. "It was worth a try."

Between naps, Trevor had a constant stream of visitors. Gemma was almost always there, but Joe, Chase, and Zane all stopped by regularly. Captain Brant came at one point.

After a day, Trevor managed to sit up.

"You lie back down right now, mister," Gemma ordered, hands on her hips and frowning.

"Nah, it's time to start moving again," he said, slowly—so

slowly—stretching his arms. They ached, but the pain wasn't sharp anymore.

"No! I don't think you should move yet!" Gemma's eyes widened, and she put a gentle hand on his arm.

He cocked his head to the side, looking at her with a soft smile.

"What?" she demanded.

"I love you," he said. "You make me happy."

She stared at him for a moment, then carefully leaned forward and gave his mouth a quick kiss. "I love you, too," she whispered. "And you make me happy."

27

Despite Gemma's protests, Trevor insisted on standing the next day. His legs shook a little, but after a few minutes and some stretching, he seemed firmer.

"Should we go down to the common room?" he suggested. "I need to exercise my thumbs, and you're the only real competition here."

Gemma hesitated. He did look a lot better, color in his cheeks and smiling.

What if he couldn't make it that far? What if he fell? She wouldn't be able to pull him up. What if he fell and injured himself more?

Charlie slid open the door.

"Ah, I see you're on your feet," he said. "Your pain?"

"Tolerable."

"He wants to go to the common room," Gemma blurted. "Don't you think it's too soon for that?"

Charlie shook his head. "Let him do as he wants, as long as

he doesn't push himself too hard." Charlie looked at her. "You'll need to supervise him. I've heard that he can't say no to you."

She blinked.

"You're not supposed to tell her that!" Trevor rubbed his face. "Come on, Gem, before he does any other damage."

She didn't move, grinning. Was Charlie telling on Trevor's secrets? "Like what kind of damage?"

Charlie laughed. "There are so many things you still need to learn about each other. Enjoy it."

Her hand went to her mouth. *But I thought Charlie hated us*—She was afraid to say it out loud.

It seemed like Charlie heard her anyway. "I know when I'm beat," he said, laying a hand on Gemma's shoulder. "You're going to take care of him for me?"

Gemma grinned. "Absolutely."

Trevor held up a hand. "Wait, take care of me? What are you guys talking about?"

She hooked her arm in his. "Don't worry about it, Captain. You're in good hands."

He arched an eyebrow at her. "What happened to me being a grown man and not answering to anyone?"

"Trevor, *everyone* needs someone to look out for them," she said. She stood on tiptoe, and he leaned down so she could give him a kiss.

Charlie smirked and shook his head. "I'll *never* get used to that."

The weeks on Brant's ship traveling to Earth passed slowly, but also too fast for Gemma.

She groaned, leaning against the wall of the shower as the hot water eased her muscles. She hadn't realized how hard a workout could be until Trevor corrected her form and made her do the exercises correctly. He'd been exercising on ships his whole life, so he knew exactly how to work out. She hadn't really any idea, but doing it the way she was supposed to was torturous.

Besides workouts, they passed the time doing a few chores, playing lots of video games and even cards and board games. They even got Chase to play darts once, but it didn't last long once they realized how boring it was to play with him.

Joe slept a lot. Charlie said it helped Joe to process Dak's betrayal. Gemma and Zane checked on him often, and he put on a brave smile, but that smile never quite touched his eyes.

As chipper as ever, Zane scrounged for spare parts everywhere he could to work on gadgets—even parts that technically weren't "spares," but when had that ever stopped him?

Gemma and Trevor spent every spare moment together. Every night, while everyone else slept, they lay on the common room floor, feet propped up against the window and talked.

"Okay, when we get to Earth next week, what do you want to see?" Gemma asked him. They lay side-by-side, looking out at the stars. The dim lights in the common room didn't even reflect off the window. And, as it was midnight, they were alone.

"Huh?" He pushed himself up on his elbows. "Why would I stay on Earth?"

"Oh," she said. She kept her eyes on the stars so he couldn't see her disappointment. "Well, isn't it going to take time to get a new ship?"

"Not really." He lay down again, oblivious to the war in her head.

She had wanted to ask him to come to her sister's wedding. And then show him how beautiful Earth was.

"Are ... are you sure?" she asked. "I mean ... There's so much you've never seen." *And I want to show you all of it.*

He shrugged. "I don't really need to. I'm fine as I am."

"Oh."

"Are you alright?" he asked, on his elbow again and looking at her.

"Yeah, I'm fine."

"You don't look fine."

"Well, I am," she snapped. *I will find a way to make him stay. For sure. He's missing—he's missing out on so much. He doesn't even know, but I'm going to fix that.*

"Have I done something wrong?" he asked.

She sighed. She'd have to be patient and find the right time.

"No," she said. "I'm sorry." She smiled at him and reached out and pulled him into a warm kiss.

She wanted adventure with him. Both in space and on Earth. *And I will have it.*

GEMMA SAT IN FRONT OF THE COMPUTER IN AN EMPTY LAB WHEN A knock interrupted her.

Right on time. Her grin turned wicked as she jumped up and pulled Trevor inside.

"What is it?" he asked.

"Sit," she ordered. She pushed him into the chair and pointed at the computer. "Say hi!"

"Say ... what now?" He stared at her. "Are you okay?"

She took his chin in her hands and pointed his face toward the computer, coming up behind him and leaning over his shoulder.

Gemma couldn't stop grinning. "Say hi, Sandy!"

"Wha—uh ..." All the color drained from his face as he looked from the red recording light down to the mirror image of himself at the bottom corner of the screen. He swallowed hard, his eyes wide with panic. "You're sending this message to Sandy?"

"Yup! I wanted to introduce you two!" She kissed his cheek. "Say something! Introduce yourself."

"Um, hi." His voice strangled, and he cleared his throat. "I'm Captain Lee ..." He looked over his shoulder at Gemma. "Did you already tell her my name?"

"Of course I did." She beamed at him.

He groaned, covering his face before running his hands through his hair. "Then what am I supposed to say?"

"Isn't he cute when he's embarrassed, Sandy?" Gemma said to the screen, watching as Trevor's face went from pale to bright red.

"Bye, Sandy," he said, touching the stop button. He turned to Gemma. "Do not send that."

She reached past him, planted a kiss on his mouth, and hit *Send*.

He stared at her with his mouth open. "You didn't—"

"Oh yes, I did." Her smile couldn't get any wider.

"That's *it*." He stood, grabbing Gemma around the waist and throwing her over his shoulder. She yelped but couldn't stop laughing.

"I'm going to make you pay for that," he said, careful not to knock her head on the doorframe as he carried her out into the hall, still laughing.

"Oh, yeah? What are you going to do?"

She couldn't see Trevor's face, but could hear his smirk as he said, "Kitchen duty."

Gemma gasped. "What? No!" She tried to grab at the walls to pull herself free, but her fingers slid off. She tried pushing against his unbreakable grip. "You'll be punishing everyone, not just me! Put me down!"

They had reached the common room, Trevor ducking through the door as they entered.

"Zane! Help!" she squealed.

Zane sat at the table, tinkering. He looked up, his eyes magnified by the goggles he wore. "What's up, Captain?"

"Our pilot needs a little cooking lesson." Trevor made a beeline for the galley.

"Zane!" She reached for him, but Zane grinned.

"You probably deserve it," he called after them.

When he put her down in the galley, Trevor gave her a recipe, and then stood between her and the door, arms crossed, a smile in the corner of his mouth. She stomped and yelled, but he shook his head.

"You're not getting out of here until you make it."

The recipe was complicated—overly so. Trying to juggle pots and pans and an oven simultaneously—while glaring daggers at Trevor—was impossible. If it didn't burn, it spilled, or exploded, or curdled. Anything she tried to pour or mix splashed all over her.

Trevor couldn't stop laughing.

"You know I'm never going to try to cook again after this, right?" she wailed, throwing all the cooking gear in the sink. "You've ruined it for me, forever!"

He chuckled, wiping a dab of whipped cream off the tip of

her nose. "Nah. Next time, I'll help. I promise. Have you learned your lesson?"

She heaved a sigh, looking at the mess around her, and nodded.

Trevor's arms wrapped around her, and he leaned down for a kiss.

She grabbed the nearest pot from the sink and dumped the goopy, curdled sauce on his head.

He laughed and kissed her anyway, pulling her closer so the stuff dripping off his head dripped on her, too.

"Truce?" he asked.

"Truce," she agreed.

After the kitchen clean-up, Gemma dragged herself to her room. This close to Earth, Gemma and Sandy only had to wait an hour between messages. Sandy might already have responded.

"Oh my gosh, he really is so cute!" Sandy giggled. *"He is just like you described him. And did you color correct his eyes? I can't believe they're so blue!"* Sandy stopped giggling and narrowed her eyes. *"But does he not like video calls? Or did you not tell him your plan?"*

Sandy smiled. *"I'm sending a second message after this one— for him. Make sure he watches it."*

Gemma started the recording and grinned. "Meeting you was a surprise for him! But ..." She shrugged her shoulders. "He was probably really nervous. He's never had to 'meet the family' before, and I don't think it went like he wanted it to."

Gemma raised her hand to her eyes and groaned. "Don't worry. He got me back. And I'm not going to talk about it."

She went to find Trevor and begged him—*pleaded* with him—to come watch Sandy's message. No tricks this time, she swore.

His footsteps dragged as Gemma pushed him into the room and he sat again in the chair. Gemma hit play.

"Hi Trevor!" Sandy waved. *"It is so nice to finally talk to you, and I can't wait to meet you in person. I've heard great things about you."* She smirked. *"Well, mostly good things."*

Trevor pointed to Gemma. "That expression looks just like you." Gemma batted his hand away.

"Thanks for taking care of my baby sister. And, really—her face lights up whenever she talks about you. You mean the world to her." Sandy now pointed at the screen. *"Now get her back here as quick as you can!"*

The recording stopped.

Gemma waited as Trevor crossed his arms and leaned back in the chair. "That wasn't so bad," he admitted.

She leaned in, her face close to his. "Do you regret making me suffer in the galley now?"

He grabbed her chin and gave her a long kiss.

When they parted, he smiled. "Not in the least bit."

"WATCH OUT," TREVOR WARNED.

The image on the video screen jumped and turned red. Trevor, Gemma, and Clarence—one of Brant's crew—all groaned from the couch.

"We're dead," Clarence said, hanging his head. "Again."

"One more try," Gemma said, resetting the level. She leaned toward the screen, hunched over the controller as she tapped, her bright eyes narrowed in concentration. A stray lock of hair escaping her ponytail fell across her face, and she huffed it away, her gaze never losing their focus. She licked her lips, her thumb slowly circling the toggle switch.

She was so darn cute.

On the screen, Gemma's helicopter rose into the air, the cargo container swinging from its underbelly. Trevor's thumb hovered over the button to fire the laser cannons, while Clarence circled them in his smaller copter, keeping an eye out for unfriendlies.

They came out from behind the clouds.

"Come on, Captain!" Gemma said, mashing buttons. She jerked her controller to the side, as if that would make her helicopter turn faster. "I thought you were supposed to be good at this game. Your aim sucks."

"Well, if you would learn how to fly, maybe I'd be able to aim better." Though he had to admit, sitting next to her distracted him.

Gemma laughed and elbowed him, knocking his controller sideways.

"Hey! We're on the same team." Trevor nudged her back, bumping her into Clarence, who sat on the other side of her.

Clarence rolled his eyes. "Ugh, you guys are nauseating." He tossed his controller onto the table and stood.

"Hey, where are you going?" Gemma asked, as their cargo exploded on the screen again.

"I'm gonna hide till the lovey-dovey stage is over," he said over his shoulder. "Get a room, why don't you?"

Trevor and Gemma looked at each other and laughed.

"At least now we're alone," Gemma said, scooting closer to

him. He put an arm around her shoulders, the game forgotten. He closed his eyes and took a deep breath, breathing her in.

"What are you doing?" she asked.

"Nothing," he said, opening his eyes. He toyed with Gemma's stray lock of hair, rubbing it between his fingers.

"Let me have a turn." She reached up and ran her fingers through his hair. Trevor startled as her fingertips grazed against his skin, but when she pressed harder and began to rub circles into his scalp, his eyes shut of their own accord and he had to stifle a groan as a shiver ran through him.

"What—what are you … doing?" *Please never stop.*

"You've never had a scalp massage before?" He could hear her grin, even with his eyes still closed.

"That feels … amazing," he murmured, leaning into her, his head bowed.

Gemma laughed and let her fingers trail down his neck.

He opened his eyes, blinking at her. "Hey! I didn't say stop."

"Mmm." She gave him a playful push. "Maybe later. If you're good."

"Fine." Trevor slumped back with a dramatic sigh, his arm around her.

She sighed too, her legs curling under her as she leaned into him, her head on his shoulder. Trevor held her hand, tracing a figure eight against her palm with his thumb.

"We land on Earth tomorrow," he said, his voice soft.

"I know, I can't wait." Gemma looked up at him and smiled. "I sent Sandy a message this morning. She'll be waiting for me."

"Oh." Trevor's thumb stilled. "That's great. But I was wondering …" He took a breath. "After we land. You and I— what should—I mean, could we—"

"What are we playing?" Zane plopped down on the other

side of Gemma, popcorn spilling out of the sides of his over-filled bowl. He slurped on a soda. "Can I join?"

Trevor dropped his arm from around Gemma. All he wanted to do was tell Zane to get lost. "Uh, the helicopter level."

"Great! I love that one."

Gemma touched Trevor's knee. "We'll talk later."

Later never came. Zane made all the difference in the game, and after they'd delivered their fictional cargo, it was time for dinner.

With Gemma sitting next to him, Trevor carefully kept his hands to himself, but she kept bumping his leg under the table with her knee. He couldn't suppress the smile that quirked the corner of his mouth. He'd get her back later.

After dinner was cleaned up, Trevor, Joe, Zane, Charlie, Gemma, and Chase gathered for a crew meeting.

"Alright." Trevor clapped his hands together. "We need to talk about the future of our crew. When we get back, I'm hoping I'll get another ship and—" He swallowed hard. "Another navigator. I already have an appointment to speak to the director about it. What I need to know is, who wants to stay on?"

All hands went up. Trevor smiled. Better than he had hoped.

"Great. I'll ask for our next assignment, maybe something a little less—Gemma?"

Gemma had kept her hand raised after the others had lowered. "I might have to sit the next mission out, if it's right away," she said. "I have a wedding to go to."

Trevor's face fell. But he thought ...

He recovered quickly. "Right. That. Does anyone else—Charlie?"

"Captain," Charlie said, "after what we've been through, I think we could all use a vacation. Especially you."

"Vacation?" Trevor repeated, but everyone nodded in agreement. Outnumbered, he considered this for a moment. He'd never had a vacation before and hadn't really spent much time on Earth. If it meant waiting for Gemma before they left again ... "Alright then. Vacation it is."

"Can I come home with you, Joe?" Zane whispered loudly.

Joe chuckled. "I wouldn't have it any other way, kid."

"Thanks!" Zane said, still whispering loudly. Only Trevor noticed Zane's fists unclenching. Other than being on his crew, Zane had nowhere else to go.

They finished up the meeting by going over docking procedures and tasks, then they raided the fridge for ice cream and celebrated the last night of the mission. Trevor still couldn't taste anything after his head injury on the way back to the Terminus.

They docked on Earth early the next morning. Gemma skipped breakfast, and Trevor couldn't find her out of all the people busy with their tasks.

Then there she was, waiting at the outer airlock, tapping her foot as docking procedures finalized.

As soon as the ramp lowered, Gemma hurried off the ship.

"Gemma, wait." Trevor caught her hand. "Where are you going?"

"I have to go," she said. "My sister's waiting for me."

"Oh. I thought—"

"Will you come with me?" she asked, her hand squeezing his.

"Yeah, but—I mean, I want to, but I can't right now. Docking procedures take a while. Maybe when they're complete—"

"Call me, okay?" She stood on tiptoe, pulling him down to give him a peck on the cheek before hurrying away.

Trevor touched his cheek where she had kissed him. He wanted to remember what it felt like.

He flinched. He didn't have any way to contact her; all his records were destroyed in the crash. And he had stupidly not backed up his account before they left for the mission.

He took a step to run after her, when Chase called to him. "Captain, we need you."

With one last look in the direction where she'd disappeared, he shoved his hands into his pockets and walked back into the ship.

28

irector Hart's secretary looked up at the elevator doors opened. *"Captain Lee?"*

Trevor stepped out and nodded to her. "Good morning. I have an appointment with the director."

She continued to stare. "It's just—you look so ... I wasn't even sure you *had* a captain's uniform." She grinned, giving him a thumbs up. "You look great."

"Um, thank you." Trevor tried not to squirm under her gaze. His jaw clean-shaven, his hair styled and much longer than his usual buzz-cut, and not a speck of grease on his tailored captain's uniform. Even his boots shined.

He tried not to sigh. It was over-the-top. Too much. He should never have listened to Brant when he introduced him to a barber.

But would Gemma like it?

Without another word, the secretary buzzed him in.

Director Hart looked up from the report he was writing when the office door swished open.

Hart stared at him too but quickly pulled himself together.

"Captain!" Hart rose with a smile, and they shook hands. "I hardly recognized you. Welcome back. Congratulations on a safe return."

"Thank you, Director Hart," Trevor said.

"Please, take a seat. You did an excellent job, above and beyond what was asked," Hart said. "Captain Brant apprised me of the journey home and had nothing but praise for you. I heard all about your adventures on Cerise from Dr. Penn through our underground channels. I'm recommending you for an award."

"Thank you, sir," Trevor said, sitting in the offered chair.

"There is, however, an important matter we need to discuss." Hart folded his hands in front of him. "You know that the Conglomerate project on Cerise had the goal of reviving the super-soldier program. You've certainly dealt them a great setback with your work there. But there are disturbing rumors of a living Tubie. Did you hear or see anything about that during your mission?"

Trevor looked Hart in the eye. "I heard the rumors, but didn't see anything to confirm them. My navigator was led to believe them to be true, and acted under those assumptions, which led to ... what happened."

Hart waited, but Trevor didn't volunteer any further information.

Trevor knew he'd be asked that question. He had practiced for an hour in the mirror, trying to control his face and keep it neutral.

"Alright then." Hart reached for an info tablet. "I did hear about your navigator. My deepest condolences that you had to suffer through that."

After a respectful moment, Hart continued, "Captain Brant told me he had invited you to our elite force, but that you turned him down. I would also want you and your crew included in those assignments. What seems to be the issue?"

Trevor sighed inwardly. "I'm just a cargo ship captain—"

"You've proved to be far more on this particular mission," the director said.

He did sigh this time. "I think my crew and I are going to need some low-key assignments for a little while. Give me time, and we can revisit this discussion."

Hart considered him for a moment before nodding. "Alright. Now, I'd offer you and your crew a little paid time off, but I assume you, as usual, would rather—"

"Thank you very much, sir, I'd appreciate that time off," Trevor interrupted. "I accept."

Hart stared for a moment, uncomprehending, his mouth opening and closing as he searched for the words.

"You've never taken time off before," he blurted. "*Ever.* Even when your father died, you left for a mission the next day. What happened to you out there?"

Director Hart's face was hilarious. Trevor smirked. Even the director could be taken by surprise.

"Are you sure?" Hart managed.

Trevor nodded. "Positive."

"Well. Uh." Hart dropped the tablet he'd picked up, searching around his desk for something that apparently wasn't there.

Finally, Hart folded his hands in front of him again. "Alright, come back when you're ready, and you'll be given a new ship. Take all the time you need." He pressed the button for his secretary. "Claire, please draw up the paperwork for Captain Lee and his crew's paid vacation time."

"The captain is taking a vacation?" Claire sounded as shocked as the director before the intercom clicked off.

Hart stood, Trevor following his lead, and they shook hands again.

"Goodbye and enjoy your vacation." Hart smiled. "You've earned it."

"Thank you, sir," Trevor said, turning to leave. He paused after a step. *Now or never. This might be my only chance.* He turned back. "One more thing ..."

"Yes?"

"Could you give me Gemma's number and address again?" he said in a rush. "My records were destroyed in the crash." He winced. "I mean ... I need to contact *all* my crew, of course. I'll need all that information again."

"Gemma?" Hart repeated, a rare, genuine smile spreading across his face.

Gemma wasn't even in the mood for music. Sandy was out with the wedding planner touring reception halls. There was a lot to catch up on. As soon as Gemma had stepped off the ship, Sandy and David set a date.

Now she stood in front of the mirror, trying to do her hair while wearing her Maid of Honor dress.

Sandy had called the smooth, shimmery fabric lilac, and she had chosen well. It hugged Gemma in all the right places, with a sweetheart neckline and off-the-shoulder— well, Gemma wouldn't call them *sleeves,* exactly. Maybe a sheer and lacey distant cousin to sleeves. The long skirt would reach exactly to the floor when she wore her heels, but the high slit didn't really hide as much as Gemma wished.

She glanced over at her phone on the edge of the sink. It had been a week, and Trevor still hadn't called.

Closing her eyes, she sighed, trying to concentrate on the braided updo Sandy wanted her to wear. They'd go to a salon the day of, but Sandy liked to see things for herself before she spent any money.

Gemma groaned. *I'm pathetic.* She probably hadn't heard from him because he was busy getting a new ship. That took time, right?

Maybe he changed his mind about them. He came to his senses and realized what a stupid idea it was to date someone on his crew.

What if they'd left without her? They might have. She hadn't heard from anyone on the crew.

This was ridiculous. Another lock of hair slipped out, and she bared her teeth at her reflection. *Get it together.*

Gemma choked back the rising wave of sadness. Why hadn't he called? She was sitting around waiting for him ... and he might be off on another adventure. Without her.

They'd been through so much together; was he leaving without saying goodbye?

Her bottom lip quivered in the mirror, but she'd gotten one side of the style pinned in place. Now for the other side.

She paused at a deep, distant banging—then the doorbell.

The doorbell again—and again. Then thudding on the door.

"Gosh, I'm coming," she grumbled, racing down the stairs, her skirt hitched up so she wouldn't trip.

The frenzied doorbell ringing and thumping stopped as she reached the first floor.

Now they stop? She narrowed her eyes at the door, wondering if she even wanted to open it. Being sociable was *not* on her to-do list today.

Although ... maybe it was urgent. What if something had happened? She wished she'd checked her phone before running down.

"Ugh." Worry won out over laziness, and she swung the door open.

Gemma sucked in a sharp breath, her heart thudding.

He stood down the steps on the sidewalk, his back to her. No uniform, jeans, and a leather jacket, but there was no mistaking his height.

"Trevor," she breathed.

He whipped around. It was him.

His hair was longer than when she'd first met him, his jaw clean-shaven ... and he looked *really* good in jeans.

Trevor's jaw dropped at the sight of her, red rising on his face faster than the time it took the ship to overheat. His mouth moved, but no words came out.

"Heh." She looked down at her dress, her own face warming, all-too-aware of the low neckline and high slit reaching her mid-thigh. "Sorry, I-I wasn't expecting you."

"No, I'm sorry." He blinked rapidly, his mouth still trying to catch up. "I hope I'm not out of line. I should have—that is, seeing you ..." He trailed off.

"Oh. Um." Gemma swallowed hard; all the things she'd wanted to tell him dried up.

He looked frozen to the spot, and they stared at each other. Her gaze dropped to her painted toenails as she chewed her lip.

She tried again. "Hi."

Trevor cleared his throat, the spell broken as he stepped forward. "Hi." He couldn't seem to look away from her. "Your hair looks nice," he blurted.

Gemma chuckled, tucking a lock of hair behind her ear, the pull of the braid on the other side of her head reminding her of her half-done updo. "Liar."

He smirked. "I've seen it worse."

Gemma rolled her eyes. "Thanks a lot."

"No, no, it's still pretty. And that *dress* ..."

"I'm the Maid of Honor," she said stupidly. She looked up at him through her lashes as he cleared his throat again. This was so awful. She did not want to seem like a wimpy woman in a dress. She didn't want him to get the wrong idea.

"Um." He shifted his weight. "How's your sister?"

"She's great. Getting married at the end of the month. Actually, I ..." Gemma rubbed her arms, though she wasn't cold. She had no idea what his unwavering, intense stare meant. "I wanted to invite you. But I couldn't find an address. Or a phone number."

He shook his head, his eyes never leaving her. "Yeah, I don't have a phone. Can't use it in space."

"Right." *Duh, Gemma.* She took a deep breath. "Please stop staring at me."

His gaze snapped to the sky. "I'm sorry! I didn't realize I was doing it. It's just—" He glanced at her, before looking away again.

Way to make it even more awkward, Gemma. This was not how she had imagined seeing him again would go. "How's your head?"

"Oh, it's fine. No permanent damage. I can taste, now." He met her eyes and smiled, that smile that lit up his face.

An errant breeze blew his hair, and he closed his eyes, breathing deeply. "You're right, the air does smell good away from the space port."

A pause.

"Gemma. Um ..." He took the first couple of steps up the stairs and held out his fist to her, and for the first time, she noticed the flowers clutched in it. Daisies. "These are for you." He looked down, his heel tapping. "The director suggested it."

She smiled, taking them. "They're beautiful."

He hesitated. "I wanted to call." He shoved his hands into his pockets and looked away. "But I didn't have your number, and once I did, I realized ... I realized I wanted to see you." He looked at her, an unnamed emotion in his eyes. "And seeing you was definitely worth the wait."

The knot of doubt in her stomach eased. He really did love her.

She opened the door wider. "Would you like to come in?"

"Yes," he said without hesitation. He coughed. "Um, yes."

"I'm sorry about the dress," she said, her face hot as she moved aside for him.

"No, it's great," he said, stepping over the threshold.

"But—but I'm not some princess!" she blurted. "I hate for you to see me like this. I'd rather you see me dressed ready to travel the galaxy or explore some uncharted corner of the Earth, not dressed up for a fancy wedding."

"Fancy wedding, huh?" He reached for her hand, lacing his fingers with hers and smiling as the door closed behind them. He kissed her fingers. "I'd love to do all of those things, if you'll take me with you."

EPILOGUE

"Director, your next appointment is here."

"Send him in. Ah, Mr. Chase. How is your mission going?"

"Excellent, sir." Chase smiled. "I have some interesting information for you about Captain Trevor Jordyn Lee."

ACKNOWLEDGMENTS

Thank you to my sanity, who has stepped back and allowed me to write this novel. For the past 23 years.

Shout out to my two stalwart beta readers, Terra and Sarah, who help me dig deep and scour out the cringe.

I appreciate all the cheerleaders in my life, your support means the world to me. And thank you to those friends who are ever vigilant for final proofreading. (I'm talking to you, Tanna. Who finds a word *I made up* spelled *wrong* in the latter half of the book? Who does that? Who's that sharp? Tanna, that's who.)

Thanks to my writer's group, Writers of the Ridge, who help and inspire me. We are a tiny but powerful group.

Thanks, Mom. Dad and David, too, of course.

My deepest gratitude to Darrell, Dawn, Max, and Kaylee. You're not going to read this book, so it will be my little secret love note. (Don't tell them!)

Thank you to my editors at my publisher, Stag Beetle Books. I appreciate how you refine my writing to bring out the best (and cut out the worst). My favorite part of the editing process with you was reading the cheerleader notes in the margins (I liked the improvement notes, too, but I live for reader reactions). An extra note to my publisher: thanks for finding exactly the right covers that speak to my characters. It's tricky to do, and I love my covers so much.

And last, thank you to that advertisement in a skateboarding magazine I read when I was fourteen that pictured a skater doing this huge airborne stunt, and said, "You can't defy gravity. You can, however, taunt it a little."

Jessica Kaye
    www.JessicaKaye.net

FROM THE PUBLISHER

Thank you so much for reading *Taunting Gravity*!

We hope you enjoyed the journey and characters as much as we loved bringing them to you. Please leave a review on Amazon and Goodreads while the story is fresh in your mind. Reviews are writing fuel for authors and help their books get into the hands of other eager readers.

If you're a big fan of speculative young adult and middle-grade fiction, we invite you to join our street team. Get copies of our books in advance, early access to covers, and other freebies!

Stag Beetle Books
www.stagbeetlebooks.com